THE BETTY NEELS COLLECTION

Betty Neels's novels are loved by millions of readers around the world, and this very special *2-in-1 collection* offers a unique opportunity to relive the magic of some of her most popular stories.

We are proud to present these classic romances by the woman who could weave an irresistible tale of love like no other.

So sit back in your comfiest chair with your favorite cup of tea and enjoy these best of Betty Neels stories!

Romance readers around the world were sad to note the passing of **Betty Neels** in June 2001. Her career spanned thirty years, and she continued to write into her ninetieth year. To her millions of fans, Betty epitomized the romance writer, and yet she began writing almost by accident. She had retired from nursing, but her inquiring mind still sought stimulation. Her new career was born when she heard a lady in her local library bemoaning the lack of good romance novels. Betty's first book, *Sister Peters in Amsterdam,* was published in 1969, and she eventually completed 134 books. Her novels offer a reassuring warmth that was very much a part of her own personality, and her spirit and genuine talent live on in all her stories.

BETTY NEELS

Stars Through the Mist

and

All Else Confusion

Recycling programs
for this product may
not exist in your area.

ISBN-13: 978-0-373-60595-8

STARS THROUGH THE MIST AND ALL ELSE CONFUSION
Copyright © 2014 by Harlequin Books S.A.

The publisher acknowledges the copyright holders
of the individual works as follows:

STARS THROUGH THE MIST
Copyright © 1973 by Betty Neels

ALL ELSE CONFUSION
Copyright © 1982 by Betty Neels

Printed in U.S.A.

CONTENTS

Stars Through the Mist

CHAPTER ONE

THE OPERATING THEATRE was a hive of industry, its usual hush giving way to sudden utterances of annoyance or impatience as the nurses went briskly to and fro about their business. Sister Deborah Culpeper, arranging her instruments with efficient speed on the trolley before her, found time to listen to the plaintive wail of her most junior nurse, who was unable to find the Langenbeck retractors she had been sent to fetch, while at the same time keeping an eye on Bob, the theatre technician, who was trying out the electrical equipment needed for the various drills which would presently be needed. She calmed the nurse, nodded approval of Bob's efforts, begged Staff Nurse Perkins to get the dressings laid out in their correct order and glanced at the clock.

One minute to nine o'clock, and as far as she could see, everything was ready. She swung the trolley round with an expert kick and then stood, relaxed and calm, behind it, knowing that in a few minutes the rest of the staff would follow suit; she never badgered them or urged them on, merely saw to it that each nurse had her fair share of the work and time enough in which to do it. She looked ahead of her now, apparently at the tiled wall opposite her, aware of every last move being made, nothing of her visible beneath the green gown which enveloped her, only her dark eyes showing above the mask. She looked the picture of calm self-assurance, and her nurses, aware of their own hurried breath and rapid pulses, envied her. A quite unwarranted feeling, as it happened, for despite her outward tranquillity, Deborah's heart had quickened its pace to an alarming rate, and her breath, despite her efforts to keep it firmly under her control, had run mad. She gave her head a tiny, vexed shake, for it annoyed her very much that she should behave so stupidly whenever Mr van Doorninck was operating; she had tried every means in her power to remain uncaring of his presence and had mastered her feelings so well that she could present a placid front to him when they met and subdue those same feelings so sternly that she could scarcely be faulted as a perfect Theatre Sister; only on his operating days did her feelings get a little out of hand, something which she thanked heaven she could conceal behind her mask. She looked up now as the patient was wheeled in, arranged with nicety upon the operating table and covered with a blanket, to be followed immediately by the opening of the swing doors at the further end of the theatre and the appearance of two men.

Deborah's lovely eyes swept over the shorter, younger man—the Registrar, Peter Jackson—and rested briefly upon Mr van Doorninck. He was a very tall man with broad shoulders shrouded, as was every one else, in green theatre garb. His eyes above the mask swept round the theatre now, missing nothing as he walked to the table. His good morning to Sister Culpeper was affable if somewhat reserved, and his glance from under heavy lids was brief. She returned his greeting in a quiet, detached voice and turned at once to her trolley, wondering for the hundredth time how it was possible for a sensible woman of twenty-seven to be so hope-lessly and foolishly in love with a consultant surgeon who had never uttered more than a few brief conventional phrases to her. But in love she was, and during the two years in which she had worked for him, it had strengthened into a depth of feeling which had caused her to refuse two proposals of marriage. She sighed soundlessly and began the familiar ritual of arranging the sterile sheets and towels over the unconscious form on the table.

She worked with speed and care, knowing exactly how the silent man on the other side of the table liked them arranged; in two years she had got to know quite a lot about him—that he was even-tempered but never easy-going, that when the occasion warranted it, he could display a cold anger, that he was kind and considerate and reticent about himself—almost taciturn. But of his life outside the theatre she knew very little; he was yearned over by the student nurses to whom he gave lectures, sought after by the more senior female staff, and openly laid siege to by the prettier, younger nurses. No one knew where he lived or what he did with his spare time; from time to time he let drop the information that he was either going to Holland or had just returned. The one fact which emerged from the wealth of rumour which surrounded him was that he was not married—an interesting detail which had increased the efforts of the young women who rather fancied themselves as his wife. And once or twice he had mentioned to Deborah that he had parents in Holland, as well as brothers and a sister who had been to England to visit him. Deborah had longed to ask questions and had re-

strained herself, knowing that if she did he would probably never tell her anything again.

She finished the preliminaries, glanced at him, and at
his 'Ready, Sister?' gave her usual placid 'Yes, sir,' and
handed him the towel clips which he liked to arrange
for himself. After that she kept her thoughts strictly
upon her job—scalpel, artery forceps, retractors, and
then as he reached the bone, the lion forceps, the Langenbeck retractors, the rugines, the bone levers—she
handed each in turn a second or so before he put out
his hand to receive them, admiring, as she always did,
his smooth technique and the sureness of his work. Not
for nothing had he won a place on the top rung of the
orthopaedic surgeon's ladder.

The patient was a young man with a malignant tumour of the femur; his only chance of recovery was
extensive excision, a proceeding which Mr van Doorninck was undertaking now. Beyond a muttered word
now and then to his registrar or a request for some special instrument, he spoke little; only when the operation was three parts completed and they were stitching
up did he remark: 'There's a good chance of complete
recovery here—as soon as he's fit we'll get him fitted
with a leg—remind me to talk to Sister Prosser about
him, Peter.'

He turned away from the table and took off his
gloves to fling them into one of the bowls and walked
out of the theatre, back into the scrubbing-up room,
leaving Peter to supervise the removal of the patient
and Deborah to organise the preparation of the theatre for the next case, reflecting as she did so that Sister Prosser, plain and plump and fifty if she was a day,
was the most envied member of the nursing staff, be-

cause she saw Mr van Doorninck every day, and not only that, he took coffee with her frequently, and was known to have a great respect for her opinion of his patients' conditions.

The morning wore on; a child next with a Ewing's tumour over which the surgeon frowned and muttered to Peter, knowing that his careful surgery offered little hope of a permanent cure, then an old lady whose broken thigh was to be pinned and plated. It was like a carpenter's shop, thought Deborah, expertly changing drills and listening to the high whine of the electric equipment Bob was obediently switching on and off; what with drills and saws and mallets, it was a noisy way to spend a morning, although after five years of it she should be used to it. She had always been interested in bones and when she had finished her training and had had an opportunity of taking the post of staff nurse in the orthopaedic theatre, she had jumped at the chance, and a year later, when the Theatre Sister had retired, she had taken over her job, content with her lot—there was time enough to think about getting married in a year or two, in the meantime she would make a success of her new post, something she had done in a very short time so that there still seemed no urgency to take the idea of marriage seriously.

She was twenty-five when Mr van Doorninck walked into the theatre unit one day, to be introduced as the new orthopaedic consultant, and from that moment she had felt no desire to marry anyone at all, only him. She had realised how hopeless her wish was within a short time, and being a girl with common sense, had told herself to stop being a fool, and had accepted numerous invitations from a number of the younger doctors in the hospital. She had taken trips in fast sports cars, attended classical concerts, and visited cinemas and theatres, according to her escorts' tastes, but it hadn't helped in the least; she was left with the feeling that she had wasted her time as well as that of all the young men who had taken her out, for Mr van Doorninck's image remained clearly imprinted inside her head and refused to be budged.

She had come to realise over the last few months that there was only one way of escape from his unconscious toils; she would have to leave Clare's and start all over again somewhere else. Indeed she had already put this plan into effect, searching the *Nursing Times* for a suitable post, preferably situated at the furthest possible point from London.

They had a break for coffee after the old lady's fragile bones had been reinforced by Mr van Doorninck's expert carpentry. The talk was of the patients, naturally enough, but with their second cups, the two men began a discussion on the merits of the Registrar's new car and Deborah slipped away to scrub and relieve Staff for her own elevenses. They were still discussing cars when the theatre party reassembled around the table again to tackle a nasty shattered elbow, which Mr van Doorninck patiently fitted together like a jigsaw puzzle with Peter's help, several lengths of wire, a screw or two, and the electric drill again. That done to his satisfaction, he turned his attention to the last case, added hastily to the list at the last minute, because the patient had only been admitted early that morning with a fractured pelvis after he had crashed on his motor bike. It took longer than Deborah had expected. Half way through the operation she signed to Staff and one of the nurses to go to lunch, which left her with Bob and a very junior nurse, who, though willing and eager to please, was inclined to blunder around. It was long past two o'clock when the case left the theatre, and Mr van Doorninck, with a politely worded apology for running so far over his usual time, went too. She wouldn't see him again until Thursday; he operated three times a week and today was Monday.

The afternoon was spent doing the washdown in the theatre, and Deborah, on duty until Staff should relieve her at five o'clock, retired to her office to attend to the paper work. She had discarded her theatre gown and mask and donned her muslin cap in order to go to the dining room for her late dinner; now she spent a few moments repairing the ravages of a busy morning—not that they showed overmuch; her very slightly tiptilted nose shone just a little, her hair, which she wore drawn back above a wide forehead, still retained the smooth wings above each cheek and the heavy coil in her neck was still firmly skewered. She applied lipstick to her large, well-shaped mouth, passed a wetted fingertip across her dark brows, put her cap back on, and stared at the result.

She had been told times out of number that she was a very pretty girl, indeed, one or two of her more ardent admirers had gone so far as to say that she was beautiful. She herself, while not conceited, found her face passably good-looking but nothing out of the ordinary, but she, of course, was unaware of the delight of her smile, or the way her eyes crinkled so nicely at their corners when she laughed, and those same eyes were unusually dark, the colour of pansies, fringed with long curling lashes which were the envy of her friends. She

pulled a face at her reflection and turned her back on
it to sit at the desk and apply herself to the miscellany
upon it, but after ten minutes or so she laid down her
pen and picked up the latest copy of the *Nursing Times*;
perhaps there would be a job in it which might suit her.

There was—miles away in Scotland. The hospital
was small, it was true, but busy, and they wanted an
energetic working Sister, able to organise and teach student nurses the secrets of orthopaedics. She marked it
with a cross and went back to her writing, telling herself that it was just exactly what she had been looking
for, but as she applied herself once more to the delicate
task of giving days off to her staff without disrupting
the even flow of work, several doubts crept into her
mind; not only was the hospital a satisfying distance
from Mr van Doorninck, it was also, unfortunately, an
unsatisfying distance from her own home. Holidays,
not to mention days off, would be an almost impossible
undertaking. She went home to Somerset several times
a year now, and once a month, when she had her long
weekend, she drove herself down in the Fiat 500 she had
bought cheap from one of the housemen. She frowned,
trying to remember her geography, wondering if Somerset was further away from the northern coasts of Scotland than was London. She could always spend a night
with her Aunt Mary who lived on the edge of a ham-
let rejoicing in the incredible name of Twice Brewed,
hard by Hadrian's Wall, but even then she would have
to spend another night on the road. And what was she
going to tell her friends when they found out that she
intended to leave? She had no good reason for doing
so, she had never been anything but happy until Mr
van Doorninck turned up and destroyed her peace of

mind, and even now she was happy in a way because she was sure of seeing him three times a week at least. She frowned. Put like that, it sounded ridiculous—she would have to find some really sensible reason for giving in her notice. She picked up her pen once more; she would puzzle it out later, when she was off duty.

But there was no opportunity; she had forgotten that it was Jenny Reed's birthday and that they were all going out together to the cinema, so she spent the rest of the evening with half a dozen of the younger Sisters and shelved her problems.

There wasn't much time to think next day either, for the three victims of a car crash were admitted in the early hours of the morning and she was summoned early to go on duty and open up the theatre. Staff was already there when she arrived and so was the junior nurse, her eyes round with excitement as she began the humbler routine tasks which fell to her lot.

'Oh, Sister,' she breathed, 'they're in an awful bad way! Lottie Jones—she's on nights in the Accident Room, she says they've broken every bone in their bodies.'

Deborah was putting out the sharps and needles and collecting the electrical equipment. 'In which case we're going to be here for a very long time,' she remarked cheerfully. 'Where's Nurse Patterson?'

That young lady, only half awake, crept through the door as she put the question, wished her superior a sleepy good morning and went on to say: 'They're mincemeat, Sister, so rumour has it, and where's the night staff? Couldn't they have at least started…?'

'It's not only our three,' Deborah pointed out crisply. 'They've had a busy night, the general theatre has been on the go since midnight. Get the plaster room ready, will you, Nurse, and then see to the bowls.'

She was on the point of scrubbing up, ready to start her trolleys, when Mr van Doorninck walked in. She looked at him twice, because she was accustomed to seeing him either in his theatre gown and trousers, or a selection of sober, beautifully cut grey suits, and now he was in slacks and a rather elderly sweater. It made him look younger and much more approachable and it seemed to have the same effect on him as well, for he said cheerfully, 'Hullo—sorry we had to get you up early, but I wanted you here. Do you suppose they could send up some coffee—I can tell you what I intend doing while we drink it.' He glanced around him. 'These three look as though they could do with a hot drink, too,' a remark which sent Patterson scurrying to the telephone to order coffee in the consultant's name, adding a gleeful rider that it was for five people and was to be sent up at once.

Deborah led the way to her office, offered Mr van Doorninck a chair, which he declined, and sat down herself behind her desk. She had taken off her cap and had her theatre cap and mask in her hand, but she put these down now and rather absent-mindedly began to thrust the pins more securely into the great bundle of hair she had twisted up in such a hurry. She did it with a lack of self-consciousness of which she was unaware and when she looked up and caught his eye, she said, 'Sorry about this—there wasn't much time, but I'm listening.'

'Three cases,' he began. 'The first is a young man—a boy, I should say, fractured pelvis, left and right fractured femurs, I'm afraid, and a fractured patella—fragmented, I shall have to remove the whole thing.

The other two aren't quite so bad—fractured neck of femur, compound tib and fib and a few ribs; the third one has got off comparatively lightly with a comminuted fracture of left femur and a Potts'. I think if we work the first case off, stop for a quick breakfast, and get the other two done afterwards—have you a list for Mr Squires this morning? Doesn't he usually start at eleven o'clock?'

Deborah nodded. 'But it's a short list and I'm sure he'll agree to start half an hour later if he were asked.'

'How are you placed for staff? Will you be able to cover both theatres? You'll be running late.'

It was Staff's half day before her days off, but he wouldn't know about that. Deborah said positively: 'I can manage very well; Bob will be on at eight o'clock and both part-time staff nurses come in.'

She made a show of consulting the off-duty book before her. She wouldn't be able to go off duty herself, for she was to be relieved by one of the part-time staff nurses; she would have to telephone her now, and get her to come in at one o'clock instead.

'When would you like to start?' she wanted to know calmly.

He glanced at his watch. 'Ten minutes, if you can.'

She got up from her chair. 'We'll be ready—you'll want the Smith-Petersen nails, and shall I put out the McLaughlin pin-plate as well? And will you want to do a bone graft on the tib and fib?'

'Very probably. Put out everything we've got, will you? I'll pick what I want, we can't really assess the damage until I can get the bone fragments away.'

He followed her out of the office and they walked together down the wide corridor to the scrubbing-up room, where Peter was already at one of the basins. Deborah wished him good morning and went to her own basin to scrub—ten minutes wasn't long and she had quite a lot to do still.

The operation lasted for hours, and unlike other jobs, there was no question of hurrying it up; the broken bones had to be exposed, tidied up, blood vessels tied, tissue cut away and then the pieces brought together before they were joined by means of pins or wires, and only then after they had been X-rayed.

Mr van Doorninck worked steadily and with the absorption of a man doing a difficult jigsaw puzzle, oblivious of time or anything else. Deborah, with an eye on the clock, sent a nurse down to breakfast with the whispered warning to look sharp about it; Staff went next and when Bob came on at eight o'clock and with him the other two student nurses, she breathed more freely. She still had to telephone Mrs Rudge, the part-time staff nurse, but she lived close by and with any luck she would be able to change her duty hours; she would worry about that later. She nodded to Bob to be ready with the drill, checked swabs with the junior nurse, and tidied her trolleys.

The case was wheeled away at long last, and as the patient disappeared through one door, Mr van Doorninck and Peter started off in the opposite direction. 'Twenty minutes?' said Mr van Doorninck over his shoulder as he went, not waiting for her reply.

'You must be joking,' Deborah muttered crossly, and picked up a handful of instruments, to freeze into immobility as he stopped abruptly. 'You're right, of course—is half an hour better?'

She said 'Yes, sir,' in a small meek voice and plunged

into the ordered maelstrom which was the theatre. Twenty minutes later she was in her office, her theatre cap pushed to the back of her head, drinking the tea Staff had whistled up for her and wolfing down buttered toast; heaven knew when she would get her next meal...

She certainly didn't get it at dinnertime, for although the second case proved plain sailing, even if slow, the third presented every small complication under the sun; the femur was in fragments, anyone less sure of himself than Mr van Doorninck might have felt justified in amputating below the knee, but he, having made up his mind that he could save the limb, set to work to do so, and a long and tedious business it was, necessitating Deborah sending Mrs Rudge to the second theatre to take care of Mr Squires who had obligingly agreed to take his list there, and she had taken two of the nurses with her, a circumstance which had caused Staff Nurse Perkins to hesitate about taking her half day, but it was impossible to argue about it in theatre; she went, reluctantly.

The operation lasted another hour. Deborah had contrived to send the nurses to their dinners, but Bob she didn't dare to send; he was far too useful and understood the electric drills and the diathermy machine even better than she did herself—besides, she was scrubbed, and at this stage of the operation there was no question of hampering Mr van Doorninck for a single second.

It was half past two when he finally straightened his back, thanked her politely for her services and walked away. She sent Bob to his belated dinner, and when Mrs Rudge arrived from the other theatre, went downstairs herself to cold beef and salad. There was certainly no hope of off-duty for her now. Mrs Rudge would go at

four o'clock and that would leave herself and two student nurses when Bob went at five. She sighed, eating
almost nothing, and presently went over to the Nurses'
Home and tidied herself in a perfunctory manner, a
little horrified at the untidiness of her appearance—
luckily it had all been hidden under her cap and mask.

It had just turned four o'clock when the Accident
Room telephoned to say that there was a small child
coming up within minutes with a nasty compound fracture of upper arm. Deborah raced round collecting instruments, scrubbing to lay the trolley while telling the
nurses, a little fearful at having to get on with it without
Staff to breathe reassuringly down their necks, what to
do next. All the same, they did so well that she was behind her trolley, scrubbed and threading needles when
the patient was wheeled in, followed by Mr van Doorninck and Peter.

'Oh,' said Deborah, taken delightfully by surprise,
'I didn't know that it would be you, sir.'

'I was in the building, Sister,' he informed her, and
accepted the towel clip she was holding out. 'You have
been off duty?'

She passed him a scalpel. 'No.'

'You will be going this evening?'

She took the forceps off the Mayo table and held
them ready for Peter to take. 'No,' then added hastily, in
case he should think she was vexed about it, 'It doesn't
matter in the least.'

He said 'Um' behind his mask and didn't speak again
during the operation, which went without a hitch. All
the same, it was almost six o'clock when they were finished and it would be another hour before the theatre
was restored to its pristine state. It was a great pity that

Peter had to put a plaster on a Pott's fracture—it was a simple one and he did it in the little plaster room, but he made a good deal of mess and Deborah, squeezing out plaster bandages in warm water for him to wind round the broken leg, found her temper wearing thin. It had been a long day, she was famished and tired and she must look a sight by now and there were still the books to write up. She glanced at the clock. In ten minutes the nurses were due off duty; she would have to stay and do her writing before she closed the theatre. She sighed and Peter cocked an eyebrow at her and asked: 'Worn out, Deb?'

'Not really, just hungry, and I haven't had time to do my hair properly or see to my face all day. I feel a fright.' She could hear her voice sounding cross, but he ignored it and agreed cheerfully:

'You look pretty awful—luckily you're so gorgeous, it doesn't matter, though the hair is a trifle wild.'

She giggled and slapped a wet bandage into his out-stretched hand.

'Well, it doesn't matter, there's no one to see me. I shall eat an enormous supper and fall into bed.'

'Lucky girl—I'm on until midnight.'

She was instantly sympathetic. 'Oh, Peter, how awful, but there's not much of a list for Mr Squires to-morrow afternoon and only a handful of replasters and walking irons—you might be able to get someone to give you a hand.'

He nodded. 'We're on call, aren't we?'

That was true; Clare's was on call until Thursday. 'I'll keep my fingers crossed,' she promised him. 'And now be off with you, I want to clear up.'

It was very quiet when the nurses had gone. Deborah

tugged her cap off her dreadfully untidy hair, kicked off
her shoes, and sat down at her desk. Another ten minutes or so and she would be free herself. She dragged
her thoughts away from the tantalising prospect of supper and a hot bath and set to on the operation book. She
was neatly penning in the last name when the unit doors
swung open and her tired mind registered the disturbing
fact that it was Mr van Doorninck's large feet coming
down the corridor, and she looking like something the
sea had washed up. She was still frantically searching
for her shoes when he came in the door. She rose to her
stockinged feet, feeling even worse than she looked because he was, by contrast, quite immaculate—no one,
looking at him now, would know that he had been bent
over the operating table for the entire day. He didn't
look tired either; his handsome face, with its straight
nose and firm mouth, looked as good-humoured and
relaxed as it usually did.

Deborah spoke her thoughts aloud and quite involuntarily. 'Oh, dear—I wasn't expecting anyone and I
simply...' She broke off because he was smiling nicely
at her. 'I must look quite awful,' she muttered, and when
he laughed softly: 'Is it another case?' He shook his
head. 'You want to borrow some instruments—half a
minute while I find my shoes...'

He laughed again. 'You won't need your shoes and
I don't want any instruments.' He came a little further
into the room and stood looking at her. She looked back
at him, bewildered, her mind noting that his Dutch accent seemed more pronounced than usual although his
English was faultless.

'How do you feel about marrying me?' he wanted
to know blandly.

CHAPTER TWO

SHE WAS SO amazed that she couldn't speak. Just for one blissful moment she savoured the delightful idea that he had fallen in love with her, and then common sense took over. Men in love, however awkward about the business, weren't likely to employ such a cool manner as his. He had sounded for all the world as though he wanted her to fit in an extra case on his next list or something equally prosaic. She found her voice at last and was surprised at its steadiness. 'Why do you ask me?' she wanted to know.

She watched his nod of approval. The light over the desk showed up the grey hair at his temples and served to highlight the extreme fairness of the rest. His voice was unhurried as he said pleasantly:

'What a sensible girl you are—most women would have been demanding to know if I were joking. I have noticed your calm manner when we have worked together, and I am delighted to see that it isn't only in the operating theatre that you are unflurried.'

He was silent for so long that Deborah, desperate for something, anything to do, sat down again and began to stack the various notebooks and papers neatly together. That there was no need to do this, and indeed it would merely give her more work in the morning sorting them all out again, escaped her notice. He might

think her sensible and calm; inside, happily concealed
by her dark blue uniform, she was bubbling like a caul-
dron on the boil.

Presently, in the same pleasant voice, he went on:
'I will explain. I am returning to Holland to live very
shortly; my father died recently and it is necessary for
me to live there—there are various obligations—' he
dismissed them with a wave of his hand and she wondered what they might be. 'I shall continue with my
work, naturally, but we are a large family and I have a
great many friends, so there will be entertaining and
social occasions, you understand. I have neither the
time nor the inclination to arrange such things, neither
do I have the slightest idea how to run a household. I
need a wife, someone who will do these things and welcome my friends.'

He paused, but she wasn't looking at him. There were
some retractors on the desk, put there for repair; she had
picked them up and was polishing their handles vigor-
ously with the cloth in which they were wrapped. He
leaned across the desk and took them from her without
a word and went on: 'I should tell you that I have been
married. My wife died eight years ago and I have had no
wish to become deeply involved with any woman since;
I do not want to become deeply involved with you, but
I see very little likelihood of this; we have worked together now for two years and I believe that I understand
you very well. I would wish for your companionship and
friendship and nothing more. I am aware that women
set great store by marrying for love and that they are
frequently unhappy as a consequence. Perhaps you do
not consider what I am offering enough, and yet it seems
to me that we are ideally suited, for you have plenty of

common sense, a delightful manner and, I think, similar tastes to my own. I can promise you that your life will be pleasant enough.' His blue eyes stared down at her from under half-closed lids. 'You're twenty-seven,' he told her, 'and pretty enough to have had several chances of marrying and settling down with a husband and children, but you have not wanted this—am I right?'

She nodded wordlessly, squashing a fleeting, nonsensical dream of little flaxen-haired van Doornincks as soon as it had been born. Because she simply had to know, she asked: 'Have you any children?'

'No,' his voice was so remote that she wished she hadn't spoken, 'I have two brothers and a sister, all married—there are children enough in the family.'

Deborah waited for him to ask her if she liked children, but he didn't, so after a minute or two's silence she said in a quiet little voice:

'May I have some time to think about it? You see, I've always imagined that I would marry someone I...' She stopped because she wasn't sure of her voice any more.

'Loved?' he finished for her in a depressingly matter-of-fact tone. 'I imagine most girls do, but I think that is not always the best way. A liking for each other, consideration for one's partner, shared interests—these things make a good marriage.'

She stared at him, her lovely eyes round. She hadn't supposed him to be a cold man, although he was talking like one now. Either he had been unhappy in his first marriage or he had loved his wife so dearly that the idea of loving any other woman was unthinkable to him. She found either possibility unsatisfactory. With a tremendous effort she made herself be as businesslike as he was. 'So you don't want children—or—or a wife?'

He smiled. 'Shall we discuss that later? Perhaps I haven't made myself quite plain; I admire and like you, but I'm not in love with you and I believe that we can be happy together. We are sensible, mature people and you are not, I believe, a romantic girl...'

She longed to tell him how wrong he was. Instead: 'You don't believe in falling in love, then?'

He smiled so charmingly that her outraged heart cracked a little.

'And nor, I think, do you, Deborah, otherwise you would have been married long ago—you must be single from choice.'

So that was what he thought; that she cared nothing for marriage and children and a home of her own. She kept her angry eyes on the desk and said nothing at all.

Presently he said, 'I have offended you. I'm sorry, but I find myself quite unable to be anything but honest with you.'

She looked up at that and encountered his blue stare. 'I've had chances to marry,' she told him, at the same time wondering what would happen if she told him just why she had given up those same chances. 'Did you love your wife?' The question had popped out before she had been able to stop it and she watched the bleak look on his face as it slowly chilled her.

He said with a bitter little sneer which hurt her, 'All women are curious...'

'Well, I'm not all women,' she assured him sharply, 'and I'm not in the least curious'—another lie—'but it's something I should have to know—you said you wanted to be honest.'

He looked at her thoughtfully. 'You're quite right. One day we will talk about her. Will it suffice for the moment if I tell you that our marriage was a mistake?' He became his usual slightly reserved self again. 'Now that I have told you so much about myself, I do not see that you can do anything else but marry me.'

She answered his smile and was tempted to say yes at once, but common sense still had a firm place inside her lovely head; she would have to think about it. She told him so and he agreed unconcernedly. 'I shall see you on Thursday,' he observed as he went to the door. 'I'll leave you to finish your writing. Good night, Deborah.'

She achieved a calm 'Good night, Mr van Doorninck,' and he paused on the way out to say: 'My name is Gerard, by the way, but perhaps I shouldn't have told you that until Thursday.'

Deborah did no more writing; she waited until she heard the swing doors close after him and then shovelled the books and papers into a drawer, pell-mell. They could wait until tomorrow—she had far too much on her mind to be bothered with stupid matters like off-duty and laundry and instruments which needed repairing. She pinned on her cap anyhow, found her shoes at last, locked the theatre, hung the keys on the hook above the door, and went down to supper. Several of her friends were as late as she was; they greeted her with tired good nature and broke into a babble of talk to which she didn't listen until the Accident Room Sister startled her by saying, 'Deb, whatever is the matter? I've asked you at least three times what van Doorninck did with those three cases we sent up, and you just sit there in a world of your own.'

'Sorry,' said Deborah, 'I was thinking,' a remark

which called forth a little ripple of weary laughter from everyone at the table. She smiled round at them all and plunged obligingly into the complexities of the three patients' operations.

'No off-duty?' someone asked when she had finished.

Deborah shook her head. 'No—I'll make it up some time.'

'He works you too hard,' said a pretty dark girl from the other side of the table. 'Cunning wretch, I suppose he turned on the charm and you fell for it.'

The Accident Room Sister said half-jokingly, 'And what wouldn't you give to have the chance of doing just that, my girl? The handsome Mr van Doorninck is a confirmed bachelor, to the sorrow of us all, and the only reason Deb has lasted so long in theatre is because she never shows the least interest in him, so he feels safe with her. Isn't that right, Deb?'

Deborah blushed seldom; by a great effort of will she prevented herself from doing so now. She agreed airily, her fingers crossed on her lap, and started on the nourishing rice pudding which had been set before her. She wouldn't have rice pudding, she promised herself. Perhaps the Dutch…she pulled her thoughts up sharply; she hadn't decided yet, had she? It would be ridiculous to accept his offer, for it wouldn't be the kind of marriage she would want in the first place, on the other hand there was the awful certainty that if she refused him she would never see him again, which meant that she would either remain single all her days or marry someone else without loving him. So wasn't it better to marry Mr van Doorninck even if he didn't love her? At least she would be with him for the rest of her life and he need never find out that she loved him; he hadn't discovered it so far, so why should he later on?

She spooned the last of the despised pudding, and decided to marry him, and if she had regrets in the years to come she would only have herself to blame. It was a relief to have made up her mind, although perhaps it had been already made up from the very moment when he had startled her with his proposal, for hadn't it been the fulfilment of her wildest dreams?

She retired to her room early on the plea of a hard day and the beginnings of a headache, determined to go to bed and think the whole preposterous idea over rationally. Instead of which she fell sound asleep within a few minutes of putting her head on the pillow, her thoughts an uncontrollable and delicious jumble.

She had time enough to think the next day, though. Wednesday was always a slack day in theatre even though they had to be prepared for emergencies. But there were no lists; Deborah spent the greater part of the day in the office, catching up on the administrative side, only sallying forth from time to time to make sure that the nurses knew what they were about. She went off duty at five o'clock, secretly disappointed that Mr van Doorninck hadn't put in an appearance—true, he hadn't said that he would, but surely he would feel some impatience? Upon reflection she decided that probably he wouldn't, or if he did, he would take care not to let it show. She spent the evening washing her hair and doing her nails, with the vague idea that she needed to look her best when he arrived at ten o'clock the next morning.

Only he didn't come at ten. She was in theatre, on her knees under the operating table because one of the nurses had reported a small fault in its mechanism. She had her back to the door and didn't hear him enter; it was the sight of his large well-polished shoes which caused her to start up, knocking her cap crooked as she did so. He put out a hand and helped her to her feet without effort, rather as though she had been some small slip of a girl, and Deborah exclaimed involuntarily, 'Oh—I'm quite heavy. I'm too tall, you must have noticed.' Her eyes were on his tie as she babbled on: 'I'm so big…!'

'Which should make us a well-suited couple,' he answered equably. 'At least, I hope you will agree with me, Deborah.'

She put a hand up to her cap to straighten it, not quite sure what she should answer, and he caught her puzzled look. 'Not quite romantic enough?' he quizzed her gently. 'Have dinner with me tonight and I'll try and make amends.'

She was standing before him now, her lovely eyes on a level with his chin. 'I don't know—that is, I haven't said…'

His heavy-lidded eyes searched hers. 'Then say it now,' he commanded her gently. It seemed absurd to accept a proposal of marriage in an operating theatre, but there seemed no help for it. She drew breath:

'Yes, I'll marry you, Mr van Doorninck.' She uttered the absurd remark in a quiet, sensible voice and he laughed gently.

'Gerard, don't you think? Can you manage seven o'clock?'

Her eyes left his chin reluctantly and met his. 'Yes, I think so.'

'Good. I'll fetch you—we'll go to the Empress if you would like that.'

Somewhere very super, she remembered vaguely. 'That will be nice.' An inadequate answer, she knew, but he didn't appear to find it amiss; he took her two hands lightly in his and said: 'We'll have a quiet talk together—it is essential that we should understand each other from the beginning, don't you agree?'

It sounded very businesslike and cool to her; perhaps she was making a terrible mistake, but was there a worse mistake than letting him go away for ever? She thought not. For want of anything better to say, she repeated, 'That will be nice,' and added, 'I must go and scrub, you have a list as long as your arm.'

It stretched longer than an arm, however, by the time they had finished. The second case held them up; the patient's unexpected cardiac arrest was a surprise which, while to be coped with, flung a decided spanner in the works. Not that Mr van Doorninck allowed it to impede his activities—he continued unhurriedly about his urgent business and Deborah, after despatching Staff to the other end of the table to help the anaesthetist in any way he wished, concentrated upon supplying her future husband's wants. The patient rallied, she heard Mr van Doorninck's satisfied grunt and relaxed herself; for a patient to die on the table was something to be avoided at all costs. The operation was concluded and the patient, still unconscious and happily unaware of his frustrated attempts to die, was borne away and it was decided that a break for coffee would do everyone some good. Deborah, crowding into her office with the three men and sharing the contents of the coffee pot with them, was less lucky with the biscuit tin, for it was emptied with a rapidity she wouldn't have prevented even if she could have done so; the sight of grown men

munching Rich Tea biscuits as though they had eaten
nothing for days touched her heart. She poured herself a second cup of coffee and made a mental note to
wheedle the stores into letting her have an extra supply.

The rest of the morning went well, although they finished more than an hour late. Mr van Doorninck was
meticulously drawing the muscle sheath together, oblivious of time. He lifted an eyebrow at Peter to remove
the clamps and swab the wound ready for him to stitch
and put out an outsize gloved hand for the needleholder
which Deborah was holding ready. He took it without a
glance and paused to straighten his back. 'Anything for
this afternoon, Sister?' he enquired conversationally.

'Not until three o'clock, sir.' She glanced at Peter,
who would be taking the cases. 'A baby for a gallows
frame and a couple of Colles.'

'So you will be free for our evening together?'

'Yes, sir.' Hadn't she already said so? she asked herself vexedly, and threaded another needle, aware of the
pricked ears and held breaths around her and Peter's
swift, astonished look.

Mr van Doorninck held out his needleholder for her
to insert the newly threaded needle. He said deliberately so that everyone could hear, 'Sister Culpeper and
I are engaged to be married, so we are—er—celebrat-
ing this evening.'

He put out a hand again and Deborah slapped the
stitch scissors into it with a certain amount of force,
her fine bosom swelling with annoyance—giving out
the news like that without so much as a word to her be-
forehand! Just wait until we're alone, she cautioned him
silently, her smouldering look quite lost upon his down-
bent, intent head. And even if she had wanted to speak

her mind, it would have been impossible in the little chorus of good wishes and congratulations. She made suitable murmurs in reply and scowled behind her mask.

But if she had hoped to have had a few words with him she was unlucky; the patient was no sooner stitched than he threw down his instruments, ripped off his gloves and made off with the long, leisurely stride which could only have been matched on her part by a frank run. She watched him go, fuming, and turned away to fob off the nurses' excited questions.

Her temper had improved very little by the time she went off duty. The news had spread, as such news always did; she was telephoned, stopped in the corridors and besieged by the other Sisters when she went down to tea. That they were envious was obvious, but they were pleased too, for she was well liked at Clare's, and each one of them marvelled at the way she had kept the exciting news such a close secret.

'He'll be a honey,' sighed Women's Surgical Sister. 'Just imagine living with him!' She stared at Deborah. 'Is he very rich, Deb?'

'I—I don't really know.' Deborah was by now quite peevish and struggling not to show it. It was a relief, on the pretext of dressing up for the evening, when she could escape. All the same, despite her ill-humour, she dressed with care in a pinafore dress of green ribbed silk, worn over a white lawn blouse with ballooning sleeves and a fetching choirboy frill under her chin, and she did her hair carefully too, its smooth wings on her cheeks and the complicated chignon at the back of her neck setting off the dress to its greatest advantage. Luckily it was late August and warm, for she had no suitable coat to cover this finery; she rummaged around in her cupboard and found a gossamer wool scarf which she flung over her arm—and if he didn't like it, she told her reflection crossly, he could lump it.

Still buoyed up by indignation, she swept down the Home stairs, looking queenly and still slightly peevish, but she stopped in full sail in the hall because Mr van Doorninck was there, standing by the door, watching her. He crossed the polished floor and when he reached her said the wrong thing. 'I had no idea,' he commented, 'that you were such a handsome young woman.'

His words conjured up an outsize, tightly corseted Titanic, when her heart's wish was to be frail and small and clinging. She lifted pansy eyes to his and said tartly, 'My theatre gowns are a good disguise...' and stopped because she could see that he was laughing silently.

'I beg your pardon, Deborah—you see how necessary it is for me to take a wife? I have become so inept at paying compliments. I like you exactly as you are and I hope that you will believe that. But tell me, why were you looking so put out as you came downstairs?'

She felt mollified and a little ashamed too. 'I was annoyed because you told everyone in theatre that we were engaged—I didn't know you were going to.'

He chose to misunderstand her. 'I had no idea that you wished it to remain a secret.' He smiled so nicely at her that her heart hurried its beat.

'Well—of course I didn't.'

'Then why were you annoyed?'

An impossible question to answer. She smiled reluctantly and said:

'Oh, I don't know—perhaps I haven't quite got used to the idea.'

His blue eyes searched hers calmly. 'You have had second thoughts, perhaps?'

'No—oh, no.'

He smiled again. 'Good. Shall we go?'

They went through the Home door together, and she was very conscious of the unseen eyes peering at them from the net-covered windows, but she forgot all about them when she saw the car drawn up waiting for them. She had wondered from time to time what sort of car he drove, and here it was—a BMW 3 OCSL, a sleek, powerful coupé which looked as though it could do an enormous speed if it were allowed to. She paused by its door and asked: 'Yours?'

'Yes. I could use a larger car really, but once I'm in it it's OK, and she goes like a bird. We'll change her, though, if you prefer something roomier.'

Deborah had settled herself in her seat. 'She's super, you mustn't dream of changing her.' She turned to look at him as he got in beside her. 'I always imagined that you would drive something stately.'

He laughed. 'I'm flattered that you spared even such thoughts as those upon me. I've a Citroën at home, an SM, plenty of room but not so fast as this one. I take it that you drive?'

He had eased the car into the evening traffic and was travelling westward. 'Well,' said Deborah, 'I drive, but I'm not what you would call a good driver, though I haven't had much opportunity…'

'Then we must find opportunity for you—you will need a car of your own.'

In Piccadilly, where the traffic was faster and thinner, he turned off into Berkeley Street and stopped outside the Empress Restaurant. A truly imposing place, she discovered, peeping discreetly about her as they went in—grandly Victorian with its red plush and its candelabra. When they were seated she said with disarming frankness: 'It rather takes my breath away.'

His mouth twitched. 'Worthy of the occasion, I hope.' He opened his eyes wide and she was surprised, as she always was, by their intense blue. 'For it is an occasion, is it not?'

She studied him; he was really extraordinarily handsome and very distinguished in his dinner jacket. After a moment he said softly:

'I hope I pass muster?'

She blinked and smiled rather shyly. 'I beg your pardon—I didn't mean to stare. It's just that—well, you never see a person properly in theatre, do you?'

He studied her in his turn. 'No—and I made a mistake just now. I called you handsome, and you're not, you're beautiful.'

She flushed delicately under his gaze and he went on blandly: 'But let us make no mistake, I'm not getting sentimental or falling in love with you, Deborah.' His voice had a faint edge which she was quick to hear.

She forced her own voice to normality. 'You explained about that, but supposing you should meet someone with whom you do fall in love? And you might, you're not old, are you?'

'I'm thirty-seven,' he informed her, still bland, 'and I have had a number of years in which to fall in and out of love since Sasja's death.' He saw her look and smiled slightly. 'And by that I mean exactly what I said; I must confess I've been attracted to a number of women, but I didn't like them—there is a difference. I like you, Deborah.'

She sipped the drink he had ordered and studied the menu card and tried not to mind too much that he was talking to her as though she were an old friend who had just applied for a job he had going. In a way she was. She put the idea out of her head and chose Suprême de Turbot Mogador and settled for caviare for starters, then applied herself to a lighthearted conversation which gave him no opportunity of turning the talk back to themselves. But that didn't last long; with the coming of the Vacherin Glacé he cut easily into her flow of small talk with:

'As to our marriage—have you any objection if it takes place soon? I want to return to Holland as quickly as possible and I have arranged to leave Clare's in ten days' time. I thought we might get married then.'

Deborah sat with her fork poised midway between plate and mouth. 'Ten days' time?' she uttered. 'But that's not possible! I have to give a month's notice.'

'Oh, don't concern yourself with that. I can arrange something. Is that your only objection?'

'You don't know my family.'

'You live in Somerset, don't you? We might go down there and see them before we go to Holland—unless you wish to be married from your home?'

It was like being swept along a fast-moving river with not even a twig in sight. 'I—I hadn't thought about it.'

'Then how would it be if we marry quietly here in London and then go to see your parents?'

'You mean surprise them?'

'I'll be guided by you,' he murmured.

She thought this rather unlikely; all the same it was a good idea.

'Father's an historian,' she explained, 'and rather wrapped up in his work, and Mother—Mother is never surprised about anything. They wouldn't mind. I'd like a quiet wedding, but in church.'

He looked surprised. 'Naturally. I am a Calvinist myself and you are presumably Church of England. If you care to choose your church I'll see about the licence and make the arrangements. Do you want any guests?'

She shook her head; it didn't seem quite right to invite people to a marriage which was, after all, a friendly arrangement between two people who were marrying for all the wrong reasons—although there was nothing wrong with her reason; surely loving someone was sufficiently strong grounds for marrying them? And as for Gerard, his reasons, though very different, held a strong element of practical common sense. Besides, he believed her to be in complete agreement with him over the suitability of a marriage between two persons who, presumably, had no intention of allowing their hearts to run away with their feelings. She wondered idly just what kind of a girl might steal his heart. Certainly not herself—had he not said that he liked her, and that, as far as she could see, was as far as it went.

She drank her coffee and agreed with every show of pleasure to his suggestion that they should go somewhere and dance.

He took her to the Savoy, where they danced for an hour or more between pleasant little interludes at the table he had secured well away from the dance floor. She was an excellent dancer and Gerard, she discovered, danced well too, if a trifle conservatively. Just for a space she forgot her problems and gave herself to the enjoyment of the evening, and presently, drinking champagne, her face prettily flushed, she found herself agreeing that a light supper would be delightful before he took her back to Clare's. It was almost three o'clock when he stopped the car outside the Home. He got out of the car with her and opened the heavy door with the latch key she gave him and then stood idly swinging it in his hand.

'Thank you for a delightful evening,' said Deborah, and tried to remember that she was going to marry this large, quiet man standing beside her, and in ten days, too. She felt sudden panic swamp the tenuous happiness inspired by the champagne and the dancing, and raised her eyes to his face, her mouth already open to give utterance to a variety of thoughts which, largely because of that same champagne, no longer made sense.

The eyes which met hers were very kind. 'Don't worry, Deborah,' he urged her in his deep, placid voice. 'It's only reaction; in the morning everything will be quite all right again. You must believe me.'

He bent and kissed her cheek, much as though he were comforting a child, and told her to go to bed. 'And I'll see you tomorrow before I go to Holland.'

And because she was bewildered and a little afraid and her head had begun to ache, she did as he bade her. With a whispered good night she went slowly up the stairs without looking back to see if he was watching her, undressed and got into bed, and fell at once into a dreamless sleep which was only ended by her alarm clock warning her to get up and dress, astonished to find that what Gerard had said was quite true; everything did seem all right. She went down to breakfast and in response to the urgent enquiries of her companions, gave a detailed account of her evening and then, fortified by several cups of strong tea, made her way to the theatre unit.

There wasn't much doing. Mr Squires had a couple of Smith-Petersen pins to insert, a bone graft to do, and there was a Carpal Tunnel—an easy enough list, for he kept strictly to straightforward bone work, leaving the bone tumours to Gerard van Doorninck. They were finished by one o'clock and Deborah had time to go down to dinner before sending Staff off duty. The theatre would have to be washed down that afternoon and she wanted to go through the sharps; some of the chisels needed attention, as did the grooved awl and one or two of the rugines. She would go down to the surgical stores and see what could be done. She had them neatly wrapped and was on the point of making her way through the labyrinth of semi-underground passages to the stores, when Gerard walked in. 'Hullo,' he said. 'Going somewhere?'

She explained about the sharps, and even as she was speaking he had taken them from her and put them on the desk. 'Later. I have to go again in a few minutes. I just wanted to make sure...' he paused and studied her with cool leisure. Apparently her calm demeanour pleased him, for he said: 'I told you that everything would be all right, didn't I?' and when she nodded, longing to tell him that indeed nothing was right at all, he went on: 'I've seen about the licence—there's a small church round the corner, St Joram's. Would you like to go and see it and tell me if you will marry me there?'

Her heart jumped because she still wasn't used to the idea of marrying him, although her face remained tranquil enough. 'I know St Joram's very well, I go there sometimes. I should like to be married there.'

He gave a small satisfied sound, like a man who had had a finicky job to do and had succeeded with it sooner than he had expected.

'I'll be back on Monday—there's a list at ten o'clock, isn't there? I'll see you before we start.'

He took her hand briefly, said goodbye even more briefly, and retraced his steps. Deborah stood in the empty corridor, listening to his unhurried stride melt into the distance and then merge into the multitude of hospital sounds. Presently she picked up the instruments and started on her way to the surgical stores.

CHAPTER THREE

THE WARMTH OF the early September morning had barely
penetrated the dim cool of the little church. Deborah,
standing in its porch, peered down its length; in a very
few minutes she was going to walk down the aisle with
Gerard beside her and become his wife. She wished suddenly that he hadn't left her there while he returned to
lock the car parked outside, because then she wouldn't
have time to think. Now her head seethed with the
events of the last ten days; the interview with Miss
Bright, the Principal Nursing Officer, and the astonishing ease with which she found herself free to leave
exactly when Gerard had wanted her to; the delight and
curiosity of her friends, who even at that very moment
had no idea that she was getting married this very morning; she had allowed them to think that she and Gerard
were going down to her parents in Somerset. She had
even allowed them to discuss her wedding dress, with
a good deal of friendly bickering as to which style and
material would suit her best, and had quietly gone out
and shopped around for a pale blue dress and jacket
and a wisp of a hat which she had only put on in the
car, in case someone in the hospital should have seen
it and guessed what it might be, for it was that sort of a
hat. But the hat was the only frivolous thing about her;
she looked completely composed, and when she heard

Gerard's step behind her, she turned a tranquil face to greet him, very much at variance with her heart's secret thudding.

He had flowers in his hand, a small spray of roses and orange blossom and green leaves. 'For you,' he said. 'I know that you should have a bouquet, but it might have been difficult to hide from your friends.' He spoke easily with no sign of discomposure and proceeded to fasten them on to her dress in a matter-of-fact manner. When he had done so, he stood back to look at her. 'Very nice,' was his verdict. 'How lucky that we have such a glorious morning.' He looked at his watch. 'We're a few minutes early, shall we stroll round the church?'

They wandered off, examining the memorials on the walls and the gravestones at their feet, for all the world, thought Deborah, slightly light-headed, as though they were a pair of tourists. It was when they reached the pulpit that she noticed the flowers beautifully arranged around the chancel. She stopped before one particularly fine mass of blooms and remarked: 'How beautiful these are, and so many of them. I shouldn't have thought that the parish was rich enough to afford anything like this.'

She turned to look at her companion as she spoke and exclaimed:

'Oh, you had them put here. How—how thoughtful!'

'I'm glad you like them. I found the church a little bare when I came the other day—the vicar's wife was only too glad to see to them for me.'

'Thank you,' said Deborah. She touched the flowers on her dress. 'And for these too.'

They had reached the chancel at exactly the right moment; the vicar was waiting for them with two people—his wife, apparently, and someone who might have been the daily help, pressed into the more romantic role of witness.

The service was short. Deborah listened to every word of it and heard nothing, and even when the plain gold ring had been put upon her finger she felt as though it was someone else standing there, being married. She signed the register in a composed manner, received her husband's kiss with the same calm, and shook hands with the vicar and the two ladies, then walked out of the little church with Gerard. He was holding her hand lightly, talking quietly as they went, and she said not a word, only noticed every small detail about him—his grey suit, the gold cuff links in his silk shirt, the perfection of his polished shoes—who polished them? she wondered stupidly—and his imperturbable face. He turned to smile at her as they reached the door and she smiled back while hope, reinforced by her love, flooded through her. She was young still and pretty, some said beautiful, men liked her, some enough to have wanted to marry her; surely there was a chance that Gerard might fall in love with her? She would be seeing much more of him now, take an interest in his life, make herself indispensable, wear pretty clothes...

'My dear girl,' said Gerard kindly, 'how distraite you have become—quite lost in thought—happy ones, I hope?'

They were standing by the car and he had unlocked the door as he spoke and was holding it open for her, his glance as kind as his voice. She got in, strangely vexed by his kindness, and said too brightly: 'It was a nice wedding. I—I was thinking about it.'

He nodded and swung the car into the street. 'Yes,

one hears the words during a simple ceremony—I have always thought that big social weddings are slightly unreal.'

It was on the tip of her tongue to ask him if his previous wedding had been just such a one, but it seemed hardly a fitting time to do so. She launched into a steady flow of small talk which lasted until they were clear of the centre of the city and heading west.

But presently she fell silent, staring out at the passing traffic as the car gathered speed, casting around in her mind for something to talk about. There was so much to say, and yet nothing. She was on the point of remarking—for the second time—about the weather when Gerard spoke. 'I think we'll lunch at Nately Scures—there's a good pub there, the Baredown. I don't know about you, Deborah, but getting married seems to have given me a good appetite.'

His manner was so completely at ease that she lost her awkwardness too. 'I'm hungry too,' she agreed, 'and I didn't realise that it was already one o'clock. We should be home by tea time.'

It was during lunch that one or two notions, not altogether pleasant, entered her head and quite unknown to her, reflected their disquiet in her face. They were sitting back at their ease, drinking their coffee in a companionable silence which Gerard broke. 'What's on your mind, Deborah?'

She put some more sugar into her cup although she didn't want it, and stirred it because it gave her something to do. She began uncertainly: 'I was just thinking—hoping that Mike, my elder brother, you know, will be home for a day or two with Helen—his wife.'

He smiled very faintly. 'Why?'

'Well, I was thinking about—about rooms. You see, the house is very old and there aren't...' She tried again. 'There is Mother and Father's room and a big guest room, all the other bedrooms are small. If Mike and Helen are there they'll be in the guest room, which makes it easy for us, because then we shall have our own rooms and there won't be any need for me to make an excuse—I mean for us not sharing a room.' She gave him a determinedly matter-of-fact look which he returned with an urbane one of his own. 'I don't suppose you had thought about it?'

'Indeed I had—I thought a migraine would fill the bill.'

'Do you have migraine?'

'Good God, girl, no! You.'

She said indignantly: 'I've never had migraine in my life, I don't even know what it feels like. I really don't think...'

He gave her an amused glance. 'Well, it seems the situation isn't likely to arise, doesn't it? We can hardly turn your brother and his wife out of their room just for one night.' He had spoken casually, now he changed the subject abruptly, as they got up to go.

'It was nice of you not to mind about going straight back to Holland. We'll go away for a holiday as soon as I can get everything sorted out at the Grotehof.'

She nodded. 'Oh, the hospital, yes. Have you many private patients too?'

He sent the car tearing past a lorry. 'Yes, and shall have many more, I think. I'm looking forward to meeting your family.'

She stirred in her seat. 'Father is a little absent-minded; he doesn't live in the present when he's busy on a book, and Mother—Mother's a darling. Neither of them notices much what's going on around them, but Mother never questions anything I do. Then there's Mike—and Helen, of course, and John and Billy, they're fourteen and sixteen, and Maureen who's eleven. There are great gaps between us, but it's never seemed to matter.'

They were almost at Salisbury when she ventured to remark: 'I don't know anything about your family and I'm terrified of meeting them.'

He slowed the car down and stopped on the grass verge and turned to look at her. 'My dear Deborah—you, terrified? Why? My mother is like any other mother, perhaps a little older than yours; she must be, let me see, almost sixty. My two brothers, Pieter and Willem, are younger than I, my sister Lia comes between us—she's married to an architect and they live near Hilversum. Pieter is a pathologist in Utrecht, Willem is a lawyer—he lives in den Haag.'

'And your mother, does she live with you?'

'No, she didn't wish to go on living in the house after my father died—I'm not sure of the reason. She has a flat close by. We see each other often.'

'So you live alone?'

'There is Wim, who sees to everything—I suppose you would call him a houseman, but he's more than that; he's been with us for so long, and there is Marijke who cooks and keeps house and Mevrouw Smit who comes in to clean. Mother took Leen, who has been with us ever since I can remember, with her when she moved to the flat.'

'Is your house large?'

'Large?' he considered her question. 'No—but it is

old and full of passages and small staircases; delightful to live in but the very devil to keep clean.' He gave her a quick, sidelong glance. 'Marijke and Mevrouw Smit see to that, of course. You will be busy enough in other ways.'

'What other ways?' asked Deborah with vague suspicion.

'I told you, did I not, that I need to entertain quite a lot—oh, not riotous parties night after night, but various colleagues who come to the hospital for one reason or the other—sometimes they bring their wives, sometimes they come on their own. And there is the occasional dinner party, and we shall be asked out ourselves.'

'Oh. How did you manage before?'

He shrugged. 'Marijke coped with the odd visitor well enough, my mother acted as hostess from time to time. Remember I have been away for two years; I spent only a short time in Amsterdam each month or so, but now I am going back to live I shall be expected to do my share of entertaining. You will be of the greatest help to me if you will deal with that side of our life.'

'I'll do my best, though it's rather different from handing instruments…'

He laughed. 'Very. But if you do it half as well you will be a great success and earn my undying gratitude.'

She didn't want his gratitude; she wanted his love, but nothing seemed further from his thoughts. Dinner parties, though, would give her the opportunity to wear pretty clothes and make the most of herself—he might at least notice her as a person. She began to plan a suitable wardrobe…

The road was surprisingly empty after they had left

Salisbury behind. At Warminster they turned off on to
the Frome road and then, at Deborah's direction, turned
off again into the byroads, through the small village
of Nunney and then the still smaller one of Chantry.
Her home lay a mile beyond, a Somerset farmhouse,
with its back tucked cosily into the hills behind it, and
beautifully restored and tended by Mr Culpeper and his
wife. It looked delightful now in the afternoon sun, its
windows open as was its front door, its garden a mass
of colour and nothing but the open country around it.
Deborah gave a small sigh of pleasure as she saw it.
'That's it,' she told Gerard.

'Charming,' he commented. 'I hope your parents will
ask us back for a visit. I can see that it is a most interesting house—those windows'—he nodded towards
the side of the house—'their pediments appear most
interesting.'

He brought the car to a halt before the door and as
he helped her out she said with something like relief:
'Father will be delighted that you noticed them, they're
very unusual. Probably he'll talk of nothing else and
quite forget that we're married.' They were walking to
the door. 'Do you really know something of sixteenth-
century building?'

'A little.' He smiled down at her and said unexpectedly: 'You look very pretty in that blue dress. Shall I
ring the bell?'

For answer she shook her head and let out a piercing
whistle, answered almost immediately by an equally
piercing reply followed by: 'Debby, is it really you?
I'm in the sitting room. Come in, darling. I can't leave
this...'

The hall was cool, flagstoned and bare of furniture

save for an old oak chest against one wall and a grand-father clock. Deborah went through one of the open doors leading out of it and walked across the faded, still beautiful carpet to where her mother was kneeling on the floor surrounded by quantities of manuscript.

'Your father dropped the lot,' she began, preparing to get up. 'I simply have to get them into some sort of order.'

She was a great deal smaller than her daughter, but they shared the same lovely face and pansy eyes. She leaned up to hug her daughter with a happy: 'This is a lovely surprise. Are you on holiday or is it just a couple of days?' Her eyes lighted upon Gerard. 'You've had a lift—who's this?' She added thoughtfully, just as though he wasn't there: 'He's very good-looking.' She smiled at him and he returned her smile with such charm that she got to her feet, holding out a hand.

'Mother,' said Deborah with the kind of cheerful res-ignation her children had acquired over the years, 'this is Gerard van Doorninck. We got married this morning.'

Her parent remained blissfully calm and shook hands. 'Well now,' she exclaimed, not in the least put out, 'isn't that nice? Debby always has known her own mind since she could handle a spoon. I should have loved to have been at the wedding, but since I wasn't we'll have a little celebration here.' She studied the tall quiet man before her. 'If I'm your mother-in-law, you're quite entitled to kiss me.'

And when he had: 'I hope Debby warned you about us. You see, my husband and I seldom go out, we're far too happy here and it's so quiet he can work undis-turbed—and as for me, the days are never long enough.

What do you do for a living?' she shot at him without pause.

'I'm an orthopaedic surgeon—I've been at Clare's for two years now. Deborah was my Theatre Sister.'

Mrs Culpeper nodded her slightly untidy head. 'Nasty places, operating theatres, but I suppose one can fall in love in one just as easily as anywhere else.' She spun round and addressed her daughter. 'Darling, how long are you staying, and when did you get married?'

'Just tonight, Mother, and we got married this morning.'

'In church, I hope?'

'Yes—that little one, St Joram's, just round the corner from Clare's.'

'Quite right too. Your brother's here with Helen— they're in the guest room, of course.' She handed Gerard the manuscript in an absentminded manner. 'Where am I to put you both?'

'Don't worry, Mother,' said Deborah in a hurry. 'I'll have my own room and Gerard can have Billy's—it's only for tonight—we couldn't think of turning Mike and Helen out.'

Her mother gave her a long, thoughtful look. 'Of course not, dear, and after all, you have the rest of your lives together.'

Deborah agreed with her calmly, not looking at Gerard.

'Good, that's settled—two such sensible people. Gerard, will you take these papers into the study across the hall and tell my husband that you're here? You may have to say it twice before he pays any attention; he found an interesting stone in the garden this morning—I believe it's called a shepherd's counting stone. You have a Dutch name.'

'I am Dutch, Mrs Culpeper.' And Deborah, stealing a look, was glad to see that Gerard wasn't in the least discomposed.

'I saw Queen Wilhelmina once,' Mrs Culpeper went on chattily, 'in London, during the war.' She turned to Deborah. 'Your father will be most interested, Debby. Come and put the kettle on for tea, dear.'

Deborah tucked her arm into her mother's. 'Yes, dearest, but wouldn't it be nicer if Gerard had me with him when he meets Father?'

'He looks perfectly able to introduce himself,' declared her volatile parent. 'I meant to have had tea hours ago. Come along, dear.'

Deborah looked across the room to where Gerard was standing, his arms full of papers. 'Do you mind?' she asked him.

'Not in the least. In fact it's an eminently sensible suggestion.' He smiled at her and she realised with astonishment that he was enjoying himself.

They all met again ten minutes later. She was standing at the table in the large, low-ceilinged kitchen, cutting sandwiches and listening to her mother's happy rambling talk while she arranged the best Spode tea service on a tray, when the door opened and the two men came in. Mr Culpeper was a tall man, almost as tall as his new son-in-law, with a thin upright body and a good-looking face which wore its usual abstracted expression. He was almost bald, but his moustache and neat Van Dyck beard were still brown and thick. He came across the room to where Deborah stood and flung an arm around her shoulders and kissed her with fondness. He said without preamble: 'I like your husband, Debby—no nonsense about him, and thank God I've at last found someone in the family who is interested in pediments.'

His eyes lighted upon the plate of sandwiches before her and he helped himself to one and bit into it with relish. 'Mike and Helen won't be back just yet, so let's have tea.' He took the tray from his wife and led the way to the sitting room.

Tea was a success, largely because Gerard joined in the conversation with an ease of manner which made him seem like an old friend of the family, and later, when they had been left together in her room—'for of course you will want to unpack for Gerard', her mother had said—Deborah asked him: 'You aren't bored? You see, we all love them very much and we don't in the least mind when they forget things and or start talking as though we weren't there...'

He took her hands in his. 'No, Deborah, I'm not bored, nor would I ever be here with your parents. They are charming people and they have found the secret of being happy, haven't they? I envy someone like your mother, who can cast down her teacup and dash into the garden because a thrush is singing particularly sweetly—and your father...they are a devoted couple, I believe.'

She was very conscious of his hands. 'Yes, they are. I suppose that's why they view the world with such kindness and tolerance and at the same time when they want to, the two of them just retire into a—a sort of shell together—they're very unworldly.' She looked at him a little anxiously. 'I'm not a bit like them,' she assured him.

'We're all very practical and sensible; we've looked after them all our lives.' She smiled. 'Even little Maureen!'

He bent his head to kiss her cheek gently. 'That's why you're such a nice person, I expect. You know, I had forgotten that people could live like this. Perhaps the rest of us have our values wrong, working too hard, making money we have to worry about, going on holidays we don't enjoy—just because everyone else does.'

'But you're not like that.' She was quite certain of it.

'Thank you for saying that. I hope I'm not, but I'm often discontented with my life, though perhaps now that I have you for a companion I shall find more pleasure in it.'

She was breathless, but it would never do to let him see that. She moved her hands ever so slightly and he let them go at once. She turned away, saying lightly: 'I shall do my best, only you must tell me what you like and what you don't like—but you must never think that I shall be bored or find life dull. There's always so much to see and do and I love walking and staring round at things.'

He laughed. 'How restful that sounds—I like that too. We'll walk and stare as often as we can spare the time. I have a small house in Friesland and several good friends living nearby. We must spend some weekends there.'

Deborah turned to face him again, once more quite composed. 'Another house? Gerard, I've never asked you because there hasn't been much time to talk and it didn't seem important, but now I want to know. You haven't a lot of money or anything like that, have you?'

The corners of his mouth twitched. 'As to that, Deborah, I must plead guilty, for I do have a good deal of

money and I own a fair amount of land besides.' He
studied her face. 'Would you have married me if you
had known?'

'I don't know. Yes, I do—I should have married you
just the same because you would have known that I
wasn't doing it for your money—at least, I hope you
would.'

She saw the bleak look erase all expression from his
face and wondered what she had said to cause it. 'Oh
dear, have I annoyed you?'

The look had gone; perhaps she had imagined it.
'No, Deborah, and I'm glad to hear that is how you feel
about it. Now supposing I take my case to Billy's room
and unpack what I need, and then do you suppose we
might have a stroll in your father's delightful garden?'

A suggestion to which she agreed happily enough.

It was good to see Mike and Helen again, and even
if they were surprised at her news, it was only to be expected. The evening was passed pleasantly, with some
of Mr Culpeper's prized Madeira brought out to drink
the bride's health and a buzz of family talk interrupted
by excited telephone conversations with Maureen and
her brothers. And as for Deborah, the evening had become a happy dream because when they had walked in
the garden, Gerard had given her a ring with the matter-
of-fact observation that she should have had it before
they were married; he had gone to Holland to fetch it
and had forgotten to give it to her. It was a beautiful
ring, a diamond, an enormous one, in a strange old-
fashioned setting of two pairs of hands supporting the
stone on either side. She had exclaimed over its beauty,
watching its rainbow colours as she turned her hand

from side to side in order to see it better, thanking him
nicely, trying to forget that he himself had forgotten.

He told her that it was the traditional betrothal ring
of his family. 'At least,' he had explained, 'there are
two, exactly alike. My grandmother left this one to me
as I was the eldest grandson, and—' he became silent
and she, anxious to help him out, said: 'What a sensible idea! The other ring will be left to—to whoever is
your heir—that means,' she hurried on, 'that the wives
don't have to give up their engagement rings. I wonder
how that all started?'

He replied casually, 'Oh, an ancestor of mine—he
had a very youthful wife, and when their son married
she was still a young woman and flatly refused to give
up her ring, so because he loved her to distraction he
had another made just like it.'

They had laughed about it together, although secretly
she thought it a charming story, and later the ring had
been admired and discussed and admired again. Only
when she was at last in her own room lying in her white-
painted bed amidst her small, familiar possessions, did
she allow herself to shed a few tears because the dream
would never come true, of course; she would have to be
sensible and make Gerard a good wife and be thankful that he at least liked her. But at the same time, she
promised herself fiercely through her tears, she would
never give up trying to make him love her.

She wakened early by reason of the early morning
sun shining in through the open window and was on
the point of getting up when there was a tap on the door
and Gerard came in. His good morning was friendly,
his manner as matter-of-fact as it had been the previous evening.

'I hoped you would be awake,' he said. 'I have been wondering if you would like to pay lightning visits to your brothers and sister before we leave for Holland? The boys are at Wells, aren't they? Twelve miles, no further, and Wells to Sherborne is under twenty-five and on our way, in any case, for we can pick up the Winchester road from there. The ferry doesn't sail until midnight, so as long as we don't linger over meals, we should have ample time.' He sat down on the end of her bed. 'Would you like that?'

Deborah smiled her pleasure. 'Oh, Gerard, how kind of you to think of it! I'd simply love it—you're sure there's time?'

'Positive.' He looked at his watch. 'It's half past six—a little early perhaps…?'

'Mother always gets up at seven. I'll go down and make the tea and tell her. We can have breakfast when we want, no one will mind. When do you want to leave?'

'Half past eight. I'll come down with you—better still,' he got off the bed, 'I'll go down and put the kettle on.'

By the time Deborah reached the kitchen he had the kettle boiling and a tray laid with cups and saucers and milk and sugar, which surprised her very much, for she hadn't supposed him to be the kind of man who would be handy about the house, indeed, even now, in need of a shave and in a dressing gown of great magnificence, he contrived to look more than elegant and the making of early morning tea seemed alien to his nature. There was, she guessed, a great deal to his character of which she knew nothing.

She took the tea upstairs, whispered their plans to her mother, who thought it a splendid idea and accepted

them without demur, and then went back to the kitchen
to drink her tea with Gerard, and because the morning
was such a beautiful one, they wandered through the
back door and strolled round the garden admiring the
flowers, their tea cups in their hands, stopping to take
an occasional sip.

'What a delightful way in which to start the day,'
commented Gerard, back in the kitchen.

Deborah agreed. 'And one can do it almost anywhere,' she pointed out, 'provided there's a strip of
grass and a few flowers, or a pleasant walk nearby...
have you a dog?'

'Yes, though he hasn't seen a great deal of me lately;
Wim stands proxy for me, though. And there are two
cats, but they belong to Marijke.'

'What do you call your dog?'

'Smith, he's a Jack Russell. He goes everywhere with
me when I'm home.'

'I hope he'll like me; I could take him for walks.'

'You shall.' He took her cup from her and put it tidily in the sink. 'Shall we get dressed? What do we do
about breakfast? Shall we get our own?'

'Everyone will be down—but we can always start
if they're not.'

They left exactly on time amidst a chorus of good
wishes and goodbyes and urgings to return as soon as
possible, coupled with a great many messages from Mrs
Culpeper for the boys and Maureen.

All of which Deborah faithfully passed on, although
her listeners were all far too excited to pay any attention to them; the boys, naturally enough, were much
more interested in the car than in their sister, and she
was agreeably surprised to find how well Gerard got

on with them. Her notions of him were sadly out, she admitted to herself as they took a boisterous leave of Billy and John and tore down the Fosse Way towards Sherborne and Maureen. She had always thought of him as being a perfect darling, of course, because she loved him, but also a little reserved as well as being a quiet man. He was still quiet, of course, but he obviously enjoyed the boys' company and she hadn't expected that.

It was mid-morning by now and Maureen came dancing out of her class to cast herself into her elder sister's embrace. 'Debby,' she shrilled, 'how lovely—tell me all about the wedding and what did you wear...?' She stopped to smile at Gerard and then throw herself with enthusiasm at him. 'Oh, you do look nice,' she assured him. 'Just wait till I tell the girls—can I come and stay with you soon?' She plucked impatiently at his arm. 'You're very good-looking, aren't you? which is a good thing because Debby's quite beautiful, isn't she, and thank heavens you're so tall because now she can wear high heels if she wants to.' She didn't wait for him to answer but turned her attention to Deborah again. 'You haven't told me what you wore.'

'This dress I'm wearing—it was a very quiet wedding, darling.'

Deborah smiled at her small sister; she and the boys were all so large, but Maureen took after her mother in her smallness, although at the moment she had no looks at all, only a great deal of charm.

'Shall I come and have lunch with you?' she wanted to know.

It was Gerard who answered her. 'Sorry, Maureen. We're on our way home to Holland, but how about paying us a visit in the holidays? We'll come over and fetch you.'

She flung her arms around him. 'Oh, will you? Will you really? Promise?'

'Promise.' He bent and kissed her small elfin face and looked at Deborah. 'We must go, my dear,' and he smiled half-humorously over the child's head.

They had time and to spare when they reached Dover, for the big car had eaten up the miles and they had stopped only briefly on the way. Gerard parked the car in the queue and invited Deborah to get out.

'There's an hotel just outside the dock gates,' he told her. 'We have ample time to have dinner before we go on board.'

When they reached the hotel it was long past the time that dinner was served, but Gerard seemed to have little difficulty in persuading the waiter that just this once he might stretch a point. They dined simply, watching the harbour below from their table in the window.

Deborah was surprised to find that there was a cabin booked for her when they got on board; the crossing was barely four hours and she wasn't in the least tired, but when she said so, Gerard merely smiled and told her that it would be a good idea if she were to get some sleep. 'It can be very noisy,' he explained. 'Even if you don't sleep, you can read—I'll get you some magazines. And my cabin is next to yours, so you have only to knock if you want anything.'

She thanked him, wishing that they could have spent the time together talking, for she suspected that once they got to his home he would be swallowed up in his work almost at once and she might see very little of him. He was going to take up the appointment which

had been waiting for him in the hospital where he had
been a consultant for some years; she felt sure that he
would want to start at once.

She lay down on her bunk and pulled a blanket over
her and opened the first of the magazines. Long before
the ferry sailed, she was asleep.

CHAPTER FOUR

DEBORAH WAS CALLED with a cup of tea and a polite request from the steward that she would join her husband in the lounge as soon as she was ready. Gerard was waiting for her, looking, at four-fifteen in the morning, quite immaculate, so that she was glad that she had taken trouble with her own appearance; her face nicely made up, her hair as neat as it always was, her blue outfit fresh and creaseless from its careful hanging while she slept.

It was still dark when they landed, but Gerard shot away as though he knew the road blindfold, which, she conceded, was probably the case. But although he drove fast he didn't allow it to interfere with the casual conversation which he carried on, explaining in which direction they were going, pointing out the towns as they passed through them and warning her when they approached the frontier between Belgium and Holland.

It was growing lighter now. They passed through the small town of Sluis with its narrow, twisting streets, still so quiet in the early morning and then out again on to the straight tree-lined road, making for the ferry at Breskens. 'There is another route,' he told her, 'through Antwerp and Breda, but it's usually loaded with traffic. Even with a possible delay on the ferry I find this way shorter now that the new bridges and roads are open to Rotterdam.'

It was light enough to see by now and Deborah, wide awake, asked endless questions and could barely wait to drink the coffee he fetched for her on board the ferry, because she wanted to see everything at once as they crossed the great river. She thought Flushing disappointingly dull, although the sea-front, which she could see in the distance, was probably delightful with its long line of hotels facing the beach. But she had little enough chance to do more than glimpse it, for Gerard skirted the town and took the motorway to Goes, past factories and shipyards and a great deal of dreary flat country. She would have liked to have commented upon this, for after Somerset she found it depressing, but she held her tongue, and presently, once they were past Goes, on the fine road crossing the islands, speeding towards Rotterdam, she cheered up, for here the country was green and pretty in the morning sunlight and the houses with their steep red roofs and the solid farms looked delightful enough. Even Rotterdam, even though there was little to see but towering flats and factories and docks, was interesting and bustling with early workers, and the more so because Gerard told her a great deal about it as he eased the car through the ever-increasing traffic with a patience and good humour she was sure she would never have had.

Once through the city and on the motorway once more, Gerard remarked: 'We could have crossed the river lower down and gone through Europoort on the new road to Delft, but you have already seen so many factories and blast furnaces—this way is more interest-

ing and we can stop in Delft and have breakfast. Reyn-
dorp's Prinsenhof will be open by now.'

Delft, Deborah discovered at once, was quite a different kettle of fish. Gerard parked the car in one of the
main streets of the picturesque little town and led her
across the road to the restaurant, where they obligingly
served them with an ample breakfast at a table in a window overlooking the street. There were already plenty
of people going to work on their bicycles, milk carts,
bread carts, carts loaded with vegetables and weaving
in and out of them, hordes of schoolchildren on their
motorised bikes.

'Everything seems to start very early,' Deborah exclaimed. 'Look, there's a shop open already.'

'A good many open at eight o'clock, sometimes earlier. I suppose we breakfast earlier than they do in England—we lunch at midday, and most people have an
evening meal about six o'clock.'

'That makes a very long evening.'

His blue eyes twinkled. 'Ah, yes—but the Dutchman
likes to sit at home reading his paper, drinking his glass
of gin and surrounded by his wife and children. Perhaps
you find that dull, but we don't think so.'

Deborah shook her head; it didn't sound dull at all.
She enjoyed for a fleeting moment a vivid picture of
Gerard and herself on either side of the hearth with
a clutch of small van Doornincks between them. She
brushed the dream aside briskly; he had told her that
he had a great many friends and entertained quite frequently and that they would go out fairly often, and
perhaps, as there were to be no little van Doornincks,
that was a very good thing.

They were less than forty miles from Amsterdam

now and once back on the motorway it seemed even less. They seemed to come upon the city suddenly, rising abruptly from the flat fields around it and Gerard had perforce to slow down, turning and twisting through narrow streets and along canals which looked so charming that she wished that they might stop so that she might take a better look. Presently he turned into a busy main street, only to cross it and turn down another narrow street bordering a canal.

'Where are we now?' she ventured to ask.

'The Keizersgracht. It's a canal which runs almost in a full circle round the city. There are other canals which follow its line exactly, rather like a spider's web. All of them contain beautiful old houses, most of which are embassies or warehouses or offices now.'

She peered around her; the houses were large, tall and built on noble lines with big square windows and great front doors, and despite this they contrived to look homelike. She said so and heard him laugh. 'I'm glad you like them, for here we are at my—our home.'

He had slowed the car and stopped outside a double-fronted, red brick house, its front door reached by a double row of steps, its windows, in orderly rows, large and square, its roof, Deborah could see, craning her pretty neck, ended in a rounded gable which leaned, very slightly, forward. She would have liked to have stood and stared, just as she would have paused by the canals, but Gerard was waiting for her. He took her hand as she got out of the car and drew it under his arm and mounted the steps to the door which opened as they reached it.

This would be Wim, she guessed, a short, thick-set man with grizzled hair and blue eyes set in a round,

cheerful face. He shook Gerard's proffered hand with
pleasure and when Gerard introduced him to Deborah,
took her hand too and said in heavily accented, difficult English:

'I am happy, Mevrouw. It is a moment to rejoice.
My felicitations.'

She thanked him, and without knowing it pleased
him mightily by remarking on his knowledge of English, adding the rider that she hoped that her Dutch
would be as good. Upon this small wave of mutual
friendliness they entered the hall, while Wim closed
the door behind them.

The hall was narrow, although it had two deep al-
coves, each with a wall table and a mirror hanging
above. Along one side, between them, was a double
door, carved and arched, and beyond them a carved
wooden staircase. On the other side of the hall there
were three doors and an arched opening reached by
several descending steps, coming up which now was
a tall, thin, middle-aged woman, with pale hair which
could have been flaxen or equally well grey. She wore a
rather old-fashioned black dress and a large print apron
and although her face seemed severe she was smiling
broadly now. She broke at once into speech and then
turned to Deborah, her hand held out, and began all over
again. When she finally stopped Deborah smiled and
nodded and asked Gerard urgently: 'Please will you tell
Marijke that I'll learn Dutch just as soon as I can, so
that we can have the pleasure of talking to each other?'

She watched him as he repeated what she had said in
his own language. It sounded like nonsense to her, but
she supposed that if she worked hard enough at it, she
would at least learn the bare bones of it in a few weeks,

and anyway, it seemed that she had said the right thing, for Marijke was smiling more broadly than ever. She shook Deborah's hand again, said something to Gerard in which the word coffee was easily recognisable, and went back down the steps while Wim opened the first of the doors in the hall for them to enter.

The room had a very high ceiling of ornamental plaster work and panelled walls ending in a shelf two thirds of the way up, upon which rested a collection of china which Deborah supposed was Delft. The furniture was comfortable, upholstered in a russet velvet which went well with the deep blues and greens and ambers of the vast carpet. The lampstands were delicate china figures holding aloft cream and russet shades. She found the room delightful, although it was a good deal more splendid than she had expected.

They had their coffee sitting side by side upon a small settee covered in exquisite needlework, and somehow the sight of the old, beautifully simple silver coffee service on its heavy tray flanked by cups which should by rights have been in some museum, so old and fragile were they, depressed her; she had expected comfort, certainly, but this was more than comfort, it was an ageless way of life which she would have to learn to live. She shivered a little, thinking of the dinner parties; possibly the guests would dislike her...

'It's all strange, isn't it?' Gerard was at his most placid. 'But it's home. All this'—he waved a large, square hand—'has been handed down from one son to the next, whether we have wanted it or not, though to be honest, I love every stick and stone of the place, and I hope that you will too.' He put down his coffee cup. 'You will be tired. Would you like to go to bed?'

She was quite taken aback. 'Oh, no, thank you, I'm not in the least tired. If I might just go to my room, I could unpack and change my clothes. I expect you have a great deal to do.'

She saw at once that she had said the right thing, for the relief on his face, quickly suppressed, was real enough. 'Yes, I have. Shall we meet again for lunch? I've asked Mother round.' He smiled nicely. 'You'll feel better once you have met her.'

She got to her feet and he walked with her to the door, opened it and called for Marijke. Even as Deborah started up the staircase in the wake of the older woman, she heard him cross the hall to the front door.

Her room was at the back of the house and her luggage was already in it. As soon as Marijke had left her she went to the window, to discover a small garden below, with a fountain in its centre and tubs of flowers grouped round it. There was grass too, only a very small circle of it, but it looked green and fresh, and brooding over the cheerful little plot was a copper beech, rustling faintly in the wind.

Deborah turned her back on the pleasant scene presently to survey the room; large and airy and furnished in the style of Chippendale, probably genuine pieces, she thought, caressing the delicate lines of the dressing table. There was a vast cupboard along one wall with a door beside it and on the opposite wall a tallboy. The bed was wide and covered with the same pastel pale chintz as the curtains, the carpet was a deep cream and the lamps and small armchair were covered in pink striped silk. A beautiful room. She sighed her content and hastened to open the first of its three doors. A bathroom with another door leading back on to the landing, she glanced quickly at its luxury and crossed the room. The second door opened on to a short corridor lined with cupboards and lighted by a window on its other side, there was a door at its end and she opened that too and went in. Gerard's luggage was there, so this was his room, smaller than her own and a little severe but just as comfortable. It, too, had a door leading on to the landing and a bathroom built into a deep alcove.

She went back the way she had come and had a bath and put on a plain cotton jersey dress the colour of apricots, then sat down at the dressing table and did her face with great care and arranged her hair in its smooth wings with the chignon at the back, put her engagement ring back on her finger and, after a long look at herself in the handsome mirror, made her way downstairs.

There were voices in the sitting room and she heard Gerard's laugh. His mother had arrived. She trod firmly down the staircase and had almost reached the bottom when he appeared in the sitting room doorway.

'I thought I heard you,' he greeted her smilingly, and whistled briefly. A small dog scampered past him and across the hall. 'Here's Smith, I've just fetched him from the vet.'

Smith had halted in front of her and she sat down on the stairs and put out a gentle hand. 'Hullo, Smith,' she said, 'I hope we're going to be friends.' The dog stared at her with bright black eyes, and after a moment wagged his tail and allowed her to stroke him, and when she got to her feet, walked quite soberly beside her to where Gerard was waiting.

He took her arm as they went into the sitting room and led her over to the window where his mother sat. She wasn't at all what Deborah had imagined she would be; small for a start, almost as small as her own mother, and her eyes were brown and kind. Her nose was an autocratic little beak, but the mouth below it was as kind as the eyes. She stood up as they reached her and said in excellent English:

'Deborah, my dear, welcome to the family. You do not know how happy I am to see Gerard married, and to such a lovely girl. I must say that he described you very well, but I have been longing to meet you. Gerard, bring a chair over here so that I can talk to Deborah— and pour us all a drink.'

And when Deborah was seated and he had gone to the other end of the room where the drinks were laid out on a Pembroke table: 'You must not think that I order him about, my dear. Indeed, I would not dream of doing any such thing, but just now and again I pretend to do so and he pretends to do as I wish. It works very well for us both. And now tell me, what do you think of this house?'

'I've only seen a very little of it; Gerard had things to do... What I have seen I find quite beautiful.'

The older lady nodded complacently. 'I knew you would like it—love it, I hope. I did, still do, but my husband and I were devoted and without him it doesn't seem the same—besides, I was determined to leave it the moment Gerard told me about you.' She smiled faintly. 'I think I guessed before that.' She gave Deborah a long, thoughtful look and Deborah looked back at her, her eyes quiet.

'Then he lived in a huge flat,' his mother explained, taking it for granted that Deborah knew what she was talking about. She shuddered delicately. 'He loathed it, although he never said so...' she broke off as Gerard came towards them.

'Champagne,' he announced, 'as befits an occasion,' and he lifted his glass to Deborah.

They lunched without haste, although the moment they had finished Gerard excused himself on the pretext of a visit to the hospital as well as his consulting rooms to see what his secretary had got for him. 'Mother will love to show you the house,' he told Deborah as he prepared to leave. 'Don't wait tea—I don't expect to be back much before six.'

She smiled and nodded because that was what she would have to learn to do cheerfully from now on; watch him go through the front door and then wonder where he had gone to and what he was doing and who he was with...it didn't bear thinking about. She turned to her mother-in-law with a too-bright smile and professed herself eager to explore the house.

Gerard had been right when he had described it as being full of narrow passages and old staircases, and some of the rooms were very small, although all were charmingly furnished. Deborah wandered up and down with Mevrouw van Doorninck, stopping to peer at family portraits or admire a mirror or one of the trifles of silver or china with which the house was filled. When they had finally completed their tour, she said: 'I feel as though I had turned you out, Mevrouw van Doorninck. How could you bear to leave?'

'It was a wrench, Deborah, but I have some of the furniture in the flat and all my personal treasures. I had made up my mind before Gerard's father died that I would leave, although Gerard didn't want it. You see, I wanted him to marry again, and if I had stayed here, he might never have done so. But living on his own, without a wife to greet his guests and arrange his dinner parties and run the house…that sounds all wrong, my dear, but I don't mean it to be. He talked about you several times when he came home from Clare's, you know. He told me what a quiet, sensible girl you were and how capable and charming, and I hoped that he would ask you to marry him, and you see that I have my wish.' She patted Deborah's hand. 'You must come and see me very soon—tomorrow if Gerard can spare the time, and then in a day or so I shall give a small dinner party for you so that you can meet the family. You will feel a little strange at first, but I'm sure that Gerard will arrange for you to have Dutch lessons and show you round Amsterdam and show you off to his friends. Very soon you will settle down quite nicely.'

And indeed, to all intents and purposes Deborah did settle down. To the world around her she presented a calm, unruffled face, charming manners and a smiling acceptance of her new way of life. True to her promise, Mevrouw van Doorninck had given her dinner party, where she had met Gerard's sister and brothers; three nice people anxious to make her feel at home. They were considerably younger than he and she liked them at once. She met the children too; Lia had two boys, and Pieter and Willem had a boy and a girl each, all rather alike with pale flaxen hair and blue eyes and just as willing as their parents to absorb her into the family, the older ones trying out their school English on her, the toddlers not caring what language she spoke.

And because Gerard had done nothing about it, she had asked Wim's advice and found herself an old dry-as-dust professor, long retired from his university chair at Leiden, and applied herself assiduously to her Dutch—a disheartening task, she soon discovered, what with the verbs coming at the end of a sentence instead of the middle and the terrible grammar, but at least she had learned a few dozen words, correctly pronounced— the old professor had seen to that. It was amazing the amount one could learn when one applied oneself and one had, sadly enough, time idle on one's hands.

But there was one person amongst the many whom she met whom she could not like—Claude van Trapp, a man younger than Gerard and a friend of the family since their boyhood days. He was good-looking, and what she would suppose could be described as good fun. He was certainly an intelligent man, and yet Deborah mistrusted him; she found his charm false, and the snide remarks he let fall from time to time seemed to her to be spiteful more than witty. It surprised her that Gerard tolerated him with a careless good humour which annoyed her, and when the opportunity occurred she had, in a roundabout way, tried to discover the reason for this. But he had only laughed and shrugged his great shoulders. 'A little sharp in the tongue, perhaps,' he conceded, 'but we have known each other since our pram days, you know.'

She hadn't pursued the subject, for it was apparent that Gerard was so tolerant of Claude's comings and goings to the house that he hardly noticed him and indeed probably believed him to be the boy he had known. She knew him to be incapable of pettiness or meanness himself, so he certainly wouldn't expect it or look for it in his friends. He was, in fact, blinded by familiarity and she could do nothing about it. But after the first few meetings, she contrived to slip away on some

pretext or other when Claude came to the house; easily
enough done, for she was taking her duties seriously
and there was always something to do around the house,
and when his company was unavoidable she behaved
with an impeccable politeness towards him, meeting
his malicious titbits of gossip and innuendoes with a
charming vagueness, ignoring his thinly veiled con-
tempt for her apparent dimness, just as she ignored his
admiring glances and sly looks.

It was after she had been in Holland a bare three
weeks that Claude called one afternoon. She was in
the little garden with Smith, sitting under the shade of
the copper beech while she learned the lesson Professor de Wit had set her. It was a beautiful day and she
felt a little drowsy, for the night before they had given
their first dinner party, quite a small one but nerve-
racking. All the same, it had been a success and she
had been elated by Gerard's pleased comments afterwards; she had even allowed herself the satisfaction of
knowing that he had admired her in the new dress she
had bought for the occasion, a pale green silk sheath.
She had worn the thick gold chain his mother had given
her and of course, her lovely ring. After the guests had
gone home, he had followed her into the drawing room
and leaned against the wall, watching her as she went
round plumping up cushions, restoring chairs to their
original places and moving the small tables carefully.
It was a room she already loved, its grandeur mitigated
by a pleasant homeliness, brought about, she was sure,
by the fact that it was lived in. She moved a priceless
Rockingham vase to a place of safety and said with satisfaction: 'There, now it looks like itself again—I think
your friends must love coming here, Gerard.'

'I daresay.' He sauntered across the pale Aubusson carpet towards her. 'A pleasant and successful evening, Deborah, and you were a perfect hostess. I knew that you would make me an excellent wife—you are also a very charming and beautiful one.' He bent and kissed her. 'Thank you, my dear.'

She had waited, hoping foolishly that he might say more; that he found her attractive, even that he was falling a little in love with her, but his bland: 'What a wise choice I have made,' gave her little consolation. She had said a little woodenly that she was pleased that she was living up to his good opinion of her and wished him a good night, to go to her room and lie very wide awake in her vast bed until the early hours of the morning. Three weeks, she had reminded herself, and that was only a fraction of the lifetime ahead of her, playing the hostess to Gerard's friends, helping him in every way she could, keeping his home just as he wanted it, taking an interest in his work on those all too rare occasions when he talked about it.

She remembered that she didn't even know where the hospital was, nor for that matter, his consulting rooms, and when she had asked him he had said kindly that he imagined she had enough to fill her days without bothering her head about such things, and then, sensing her hurt, had offered to take her to the hospital and show her round.

It was almost as though he were keeping her at arms' length…and yet he had been good to her and very kind; she had a more than generous allowance, and true to his promise, Maureen was to visit them in a week's time and when Deborah had admired a crocodile handbag he had bought it for her without hesitation. He had bought

her a car too—a Fiat 500—and opened accounts at all
the larger shops for her. He was generous to a fault,
and she repaid him in the only ways she knew how; by
breakfasting with him each morning even though he
was immersed in his post which she opened for him,
and after he had gone, sorted for his secretary to attend to when she came during the morning. And she
was always waiting for him when he got home in the
evenings, sitting with Smith in the garden or reading
in the sitting room. She wasn't sure if this was what he
wanted her to do, and it was difficult to tell because he
was unfailingly courteous to her, but at least she was
there if he should want to talk. In a week or two, when
she knew him a little better, she would ask him.

She applied herself to her Dutch grammar again and
twiddled Smith's ears gently. There was still an hour before Wim would bring the tea and Gerard had said that
he would be late that evening. She sighed and began to
worry her way through the past tense of the verb *to be*.

Her earnest efforts were interrupted by the appearance of Claude. She looked up in some surprise as he
lounged across the little plot of grass.

'Oh, hullo, Claude,' she forced her voice to politeness. 'I didn't hear the bell.'

'I walked in,' he told her coolly. 'A lovely afternoon
and nothing to do—I thought I might invite myself to
tea.'

She closed her book. 'Why, of course,' and felt irri-
tated when he sat down beside her and took it from her.

'What's this? Dutch grammar—my goodness, you
are trying hard, aren't you? Does Gerard know, or did
he fix it up for you?'

She became evasive. 'I have lessons from a dear old

professor—it's a difficult language, but I know quite a few words already, as well as one or two sentences.'

'"I love you," for instance, or should it be "do you love me?"' he asked, and added: 'Oh, I've annoyed you—I must apologise, but the idea of Gerard loving anyone is so amusing that I can't help wondering.'

Deborah turned to look at him, amazed at the fury of the rage she was bottling up. 'I know that you are a very old friend of Gerard's, but I don't care to discuss him with anyone. I hope you understand that.'

'Lord, yes,' he said easily. 'You have my fullest admiration, Debby—it must be hellishly difficult.'

'I prefer you not to call me Debby,' she told him austerely, and then, her curiosity getting the better of her good sense: 'What must be difficult?'

He grinned. 'Why, to be married to Gerard, of course. Everyone knows what a mess he made of his first marriage—no wonder the poor girl died...'

She had had enough; if he had intended to anger her, he had succeeded; her fury bubbled over as she got up, restraining herself with difficulty from slapping his smiling face. She said in a voice which shook with anger: 'I was told you were Gerard's friend, but you aren't behaving like a friend! I haven't the least idea what you're talking about, and I don't want to know. I think you should go—now!'

He didn't budge, but sat looking up at her, grinning still. 'If only I knew you better there would be a number of interesting questions I should like to ask, though I daresay you wouldn't answer them. I had no idea that you had such a nasty temper. Does Gerard know about it, I wonder?'

'Does Gerard know what?' asked Gerard from the

shadow of the door, and Deborah jumped at the sound of his quiet voice, hating herself for doing it, whereas Claude didn't move, merely said: 'Hullo, there—early home, aren't you? The newly married man and all that?'

Deborah suddenly didn't care if Claude was an old family friend or not; she said hotly: 'I was just asking Claude to leave the house, but now you're here, Gerard, I think he should tell you why.'

'No need, my dear.' Gerard sounded almost placid. 'I'm afraid I have been guilty of eavesdropping—it was such an interesting conversation and I couldn't bring myself to break it up.'

He strolled across the grass to join them. 'Get up,' he ordered Claude, and his voice was no longer placid, but cold and contemptuous. 'It is a strange thing,' he commented to no one in particular, 'how blind one becomes to one's friends, though perhaps friends isn't quite the operative word. Deborah is quite right; I think you should leave my house—this instant, Claude, and not come back.'

Claude had got to his feet. 'You're joking...'

'No.'

'Just because I was going to tell Debby'—he turned to look at her—'Deborah—about Sasja? Don't be ridiculous, Gerard, if I don't tell her someone else will.'

'Possibly, but they would tell the truth. What were you going to tell her, Claude?' The coldness of his voice was tinged with interest.

'I—? Only that...'

Deborah had had enough; she interrupted sharply: 'I'm going to my room.'

Her husband put out a hand and took her arm in a

gentle grip which kept her just where she was, but he didn't look at her.

'Get out,' he advised Claude softly, 'get out before I remember that you were once a friend of mine, and if you come here again, annoying my wife, I'll make mincemeat of you.'

Deborah watched Claude go, taking no notice of his derisive goodbye. She didn't look at Gerard either, only after the faint slam of the front door signalled the last of Claude van Trapp did she say once more: 'If you don't mind—I've a headache… I'll get Wim to bring you out some tea.'

'Wait, Deborah.' Gerard had turned her round to face him, his hands on her shoulders. 'I'm sorry about this—I had no idea that Claude…thank you for being loyal, and in such circumstances. You have every right to be angry, for I should have told you the whole sorry story before our marriage, but it is one I have tried to forget over the years, and very nearly succeeded—the idea of digging it all up again…'

'Then I don't want to hear it,' declared Deborah. 'What possible difference could it make anyway? It isn't as though we're—we're…'

'In love?' he finished for her. 'No, but we are friends, companions if you like, sharing our lives, and you have the right to know—and I should like to tell you.' He had pulled her close and his arms were very comforting—but that was all they were. She leaned her head against his shoulder and said steadily: 'I'm listening.'

'I married Sasja when I was twenty-eight. She was nineteen and gay and pretty and so young. I was studying for my fellowship and determined to be a success because I loved—still love—my work and nothing less than success would do. It was my fault, I suppose, work-ing night after night when we should have been out dancing, or going to parties or the theatre. Perhaps I loved her, but it wasn't the right kind of love, and I couldn't understand why she hadn't the patience to wait until I had got my feet on the bottom rung of the ladder, just as she couldn't understand why I should choose to spend hour after hour working when I could have been taking her out.' He sighed. 'You see, I had thought that she would be content looking after our home—we had a modern flat in Amsterdam—and having our chil-dren.' His even voice became tinged with bitterness. 'She didn't want or like children and she had no inter-est in my work. After a year she found someone else and I, God forgive me, didn't discover it until she was killed, with the other man, in a plane crash.'

Deborah said into the superfine cloth of his shoul-der: 'I'm sorry, Gerard, but I'm glad I know.' She lifted her face to meet his. 'I wanted to slap Claude—I wish I had!'

She was rewarded by his faint smile. 'He was right in a way, you know—I was really responsible for Sas-ja's death.'

'He was not! He made it sound underhand and beastly—quite horrible—and it wasn't like that, nor was it your fault.'

'Yes, it was, Deborah—I married the wrong girl just because I was, for a very short time, in love with her. Now you know why I don't want to become involved again—why I married you.'

'And if that's a compliment, it's a mighty odd one,' she told herself silently, and swallowed back the tears tearing at her throat.

Out loud, she said matter-of-factly: 'Well, now you've told me, we won't talk about Sasja again.' She took a heartening breath. 'You don't still love her?'

His voice was nicely reassuring. 'Quite sure. My love wore thin after a very few months—when she died I had none left.'

And Deborah's heart gave a guilty skip of joy; she was sorry about Sasja, but it was a long time ago, and she hadn't treated Gerard very well. She registered a mental resolve to find out more about her from her mother-in-law when the occasion was right, for it seemed to her that Gerard was very likely taking a blame which wasn't his. She drew away from him and said briskly: 'I'll get the tea, shall I? Would you like it out here?'

She was glad of the few minutes' respite to compose herself once more into the quiet companion he expected when he came home; she and Wim took the tea out between them and when she sat down again under the copper beech she saw that Gerard was leafing through her Dutch grammar.

She poured the tea and waited for him to speak. 'Something I forgot,' he said slowly. 'I should have arranged lessons for you.'

'As a matter of fact,' she began carefully, sugaring his tea and handing him the cup, 'I do have lessons. I asked around and I go to a dear old man called Professor de Wit four times a week. He's very good and fearfully stern. I've had eight lessons so far. He gives me a great deal of homework.'

Gerard put the book down. 'I have underestimated you, Deborah,' he observed wryly. 'Tell me, why are you going to all this trouble?'

She was taken aback. 'Trouble? It's no trouble, it's something to do. Besides, how can I be a good wife if I can't even understand my husband's language? Not all your friends speak English.'

He was staring at her, frowning a little. 'You regard our marriage as a job to be done well—is that how you think of it, Deborah?'

She took a sandwich with a hand which trembled very slightly; it would never do for him to get even an inkling. 'Yes,' she declared brightly. 'Isn't that what you wanted?' and when he didn't reply, went on: 'Maureen will be here next week. I know you won't have any time to spare, but will you suggest the best outings for her? I thought I'd take her to Volendam in the Fiat— all those costumes, you know—and then we can go to the Rijksmuseum and the shops and go round the canals in one of those boats. I'm longing to go—and the Palace, if it's open.'

'My poor Deborah, I've neglected you.'

'No. I knew that you were going to be busy, you told me so. Besides, I've had several weeks in which to find my own feet.'

He smiled. 'You're as efficient a wife and hostess as you were a Theatre Sister,' he told her. And because she thought he expected it of her, she laughed gaily and assured him that that had been her ambition.

Presently he got to his feet. 'I've a couple of patients to see at my consulting rooms,' he told her, 'but I'll be back within the hour. Are we doing anything this evening?'

She shook her head. Perhaps he would take her out— she would wear the new dress...

'Good. Could we dine a little earlier? I've a mass of

work to do; a couple of quiet hours in the study would be a godsend to me.'

Deborah even managed a smile. 'Of course—half past six? That will give you a lovely long evening.'

He hesitated. 'And you?'

She gave him a calm smiling look from her lovely eyes. 'I've simply masses of letters to write,' she lied.

CHAPTER FIVE

THEY FETCHED MAUREEN the following week, travelling overnight to arrive at Sherborne in the early morning, picking up an ecstatic child beside herself with excitement, and driving on to Deborah's home for lunch. The boys were home for the half-term holiday too and it was a noisy hilarious meal, with the whole family talking at once, although Mr Culpeper confined his conversation to Gerard, because, as he remarked a little severely to the rest of his family, he appeared to be the only calm person present. He had, it was true, greeted his various children with pleasure, but as he had just finished translating an Anglo-Saxon document of some rarity, and wished to discuss it with someone intelligent, he took little part in the rather excited talk. Deborah could hear various snatches of her learned parent's rambling dissertation from time to time and wondered if Gerard was enjoying it as much as he appeared to be. She decided that he was; he was even holding his own with her father, something not many people were able to do. They exchanged brief smiles and she turned back to Maureen's endless questions.

They left shortly afterwards, driving fast to catch the night ferry, and Maureen, who had sat in front with Gerard, had to be persuaded to go to the cabin with Deborah when they got on board; the idea of staying up all night, and on a boat, was an alluring one, only the pleasures in store in the morning, dangled before her sleepy eyes by Gerard, convinced her that a few hours of sleep was a small price to pay for the novelty of driving through a foreign country at half past four in the morning.

The weather was fine, although it was still dark when they landed. Maureen, refreshed by a splendid nap, sat beside Gerard once more, talking without pause. Deborah wondered if he minded, although it was hard to tell from his manner, which was one of amused tolerance towards his small sister-in-law. Once or twice he turned to speak to her and she thought that there was more warmth in his voice when he spoke, but that could be wishful thinking, for after the unpleasant business with Claude and all that he had told her about his marriage to Sasja, she had hoped that perhaps his feelings might have deepened from friendship to even the mildest of affection.

She was to think that on several occasions during the next few days, but never with certainty. Gerard, it seemed, could spare the time to take his small relative round and about where he had not found it possible with herself, and Deborah caught herself wondering if he was seizing the opportunity to get upon a closer footing with herself. He drove them to Volendam, obligingly helped Maureen purchase postcards and souvenirs, admired the costumed villagers, standing ready to have their photos taken by the tourists, and when Maureen wished that she had a camera so that she could take her own pictures, purchased one for her. And what was more, he showed nothing but pleasure when she flung her arms around him and thanked him extravagantly for it.

They lunched that day at Wieringerwerf, after the briefest of visits to Hoorn. The restaurant was on the main road, a large, bustling place, colourful with flags and brightly painted chairs and tables on its terraces; not at all the sort of place Gerard would choose to go to for himself, Deborah suspected, but Maureen, eyeing the coloured umbrellas and the comfortable restaurant, pronounced it super. She chose her lunch from an enormous menu card and told Gerard that he was super too, and when he laughed, said:

'But it's true, you are super. I'm not surprised that Debby married you. If you could have waited a year or two, I'd have married you myself. Perhaps you have some younger brothers?'

'Married, I'm afraid, my dear—but I have a number of cousins. I'll arrange for you to meet them next time you come and you can look them over.' Deborah saw no mockery in his face and loved him for it.

Maureen agreed to this. 'Though I don't suppose you'll want me again for a little while. I mean, there are so many of us, aren't there? You'll only want a few at a time.'

Gerard glanced at Deborah. 'Oh, I don't know,' he said easily. 'I think it would be rather fun if all of you were to come over and spend Christmas. There's plenty of room.'

She beamed at him. 'I say, you really are the greatest! I'll tell Mother, so's she can remind Father about it, then it won't come as a surprise to him—he forgets, you know.'

She polished off an enormous ice cream embellished with whipped cream, chocolate, nuts and fruit, and sighed blissfully. 'Where do we go next?' she wanted to know.

Gerard glanced at his watch. 'I'm afraid back home. I have a list this afternoon at four o'clock.'

'You won't be home for dinner?' asked Deborah, trying to sound casual.

'I very much doubt it. Can you amuse yourselves?'

'Of course.' Had she not been amusing herself times without number all these weeks? 'Shall I get you something cooked when you come in?'

'Would you? It could be any time.'

It was late when he got back, Marijke had gone to bed, leaving Wim to lay a tray for his master. So it was Deborah who went down to the kitchen and heated soup and made an omelette and a fresh fruit salad and carried them up to the dining room.

She arranged everything on the table and when Gerard was seated went to sit herself in one of the great armchairs against the wall.

'I hope it was successful,' she essayed, not knowing if he was too tired to talk or if he wanted to talk about it.

He spooned his soup. 'Entirely successful. You're referring to the case this afternoon—I had no idea that you knew about it.'

'I didn't. You always have a list on Thursday afternoons, but you have never been later than eight o'clock, so I guessed...'

He laughed. 'I keep forgetting that you've worked for me for two years. It was an important patient and he had come a long way in the hope that I could help him, but he refused utterly to allow me to begin the operation until his wife had arrived.'

'Was it a chondroma?'

'Yes.'

'Poor man, but I'm glad you could help him. His wife must be so thankful.'

Gerard began on the omelette. 'I imagine so,' and when he didn't say anything else she said presently: 'Thank you for spending so much time with us today. Maureen loved it.'

'And you?'

'I loved it too; it's all foreign to me, even though I live here now.'

He frowned. 'I keep forgetting that too. I shan't have a minute to spare tomorrow, but I'll manage an afternoon the day after—have you any plans?'

'Could we go somewhere for tea? Maureen loves going out to tea, especially if it's combined with sightseeing. I could take her on a round of the canals tomorrow.'

He speared the last of the omelette, complimented her upon her cooking and observed: 'I know I'm booked up for tomorrow, but how would it be if you both came to the hospital and had a look round? I'll get one of the housemen to take you round. Go to the—no, better still, I'll come home and pick you up, only you mustn't keep me waiting. Paul van Goor can look after you and see you into a taxi afterwards. Would you like that?'

She said very quietly: 'Enormously,' wondering if he was being kind to Maureen or if he was allowing her to share his life just a little at last. 'If you'll tell us what time you want us to be ready, we'll be waiting.' She got up. 'Would you like the brandy? I'm going to fetch the coffee.'

'Shall we go into the sitting room and share the pot between us?'

She loathed coffee so late at night, but she would gladly swallow pints of it if he wanted her to talk to. Perhaps the operation had been a bit of a strain—she had no idea who the important patient might be and she had too much sense to ask. All the same, when she had poured coffee for them both she asked him: 'I'd love to hear about the op if it wouldn't bore you—which method did you use?'

She had done the right thing, she could sense that. He told her, using terms he had no need to explain, describing techniques she understood and could comment upon with intelligence. It was very late when he had finished, and when he apologised for keeping her up she waved a careless hand and said in a carefully matter-of-fact voice: 'I enjoyed it.'

She took the tray back to the kitchen, wished him good night and went quickly upstairs, because she couldn't trust herself to preserve her careful, tranquil manner any longer.

She and Maureen were to be ready at half past one on the following afternoon, and at exactly that time Gerard came for them. He was preoccupied but, as always, courteous during the short drive. The Grotehof hospital was in the centre of the city, tucked away behind some of its oldest houses. The building was old too, but had been extended and modernised until it was difficult to see where the old ended and the new began. The entrance was in the old part, through a large, important door leading to a vast tiled hall. It was here that Gerard, with a muttered word of apology, handed them over with a hasty word of introduction to a young and cheerful houseman, Paul van Goor, who, obviously primed as to his task, led them through a labyrinth of corridors to the children's ward, talking all the time in excellent English.

From there they went to the surgical block, the medical block, the recreation rooms, the Accident Room, the dining room for the staff and lastly the theatre block, the newest addition to the hospital, he told them proudly. It consisted of six theatres, two for general surgery, one for ENT, one for cardio-thoracic work and two for orthopaedics. They couldn't go inside, of course, although Deborah longed to do so, and when she peered through the round window in the swing doors she felt a pang of regret that it was no longer her world; she amended that—the regret was because it was still Gerard's world and she no longer had a share in it, for at least at Clare's she worked with him. Now she was a figurehead in his house, running it smoothly and efficiently, dressing to do him credit, living with him and yet not sharing his life.

She sighed, and Paul asked her if she was tired and when she said no, suggested that they might like to go back through the hospital garden, very small but lovingly tended. They returned via lengthy staircases and roundabout passages, Deborah deep in thought, Maureen and Paul talking earnestly. They were passing a great arched doorway when a nurse flung it open and coming towards them from the other side was Gerard, a different Gerard, surrounded by a group of housemen and students, his registrar, the Ward Sister and a handful of nurses. If he saw them he took no notice; Deborah hadn't expected him to. She managed to snatch at Maureen's hand as she lifted it to wave to him.

'No, you can't, darling,' she said urgently. 'Not here, it wouldn't do. I'll explain later.'

She had done her best to do so on their way to Mevrouw van Doorninck's flat in the taxi Paul had got for them, but all Maureen said was: 'Oh, Debby, how stuffy you are—he's my brother-in-law, and you're married to him, of course he can wave to us if he wants to; important people do just what they like and no one minds.'

She was inclined to argue about it; fortunately she was kept too occupied for the rest of the afternoon, for Gerard's mother had gathered the family together to meet Maureen and the party was a merry one. 'Only,' as Mevrouw van Doorninck declared to Deborah, as they drank their tea and nibbled the thin sugary biscuits, 'it's such a pity that Gerard can't be here too. I had hoped now that he was married…it is as though he is afraid to be happy again.' She glanced at Deborah, who said nothing at all, and went on presently: 'He seems very fond of Maureen, such a sweet child. I look forward to meeting the rest of your family, my dear.'

'I'm sure they're just as eager to meet you, Mevrouw van Doorninck.' Deborah was relieved that they had left the subject of Gerard. 'They're all coming over to spend Christmas.'

'Christmas?' Her companion gave her another sharp look. 'A great deal could happen by then.'

Deborah would have liked to ask her mother-in-law what, in heaven's name, could happen in this well-ordered, well-organised world in which she now lived. A flaming row, she told herself vulgarly, would relieve the monotony, but Gerard was difficult to quarrel with— he became at once blandly courteous, placidly indifferent, a sign, she had decided forlornly, that he didn't consider her of sufficient importance in his life to warrant a loss of temper.

She and Maureen got up to go presently, walking back to the house in the Keizersgracht, to curl up in the comfortable chairs in the sitting room and discuss the delights of Christmas and the not so distant pleasures of the next day when Gerard had promised to take them out.

He telephoned just before dinner, to say that he was detained at the hospital and would dine with a colleague and she wasn't to wait for him. All the same she sat on, long after Maureen had gone to bed and Wim and Marijke had gone to their rooms. But when the clock struck midnight and there was no sign of him, she went to bed too, but not to sleep. She heard his quiet steps going through the quiet house in the early hours of the morning and lay awake until daylight, wondering where he had been and with whom.

He was at breakfast when she got down in the morning, looking, Deborah thought, a little tired but as impeccably dressed as he always was, and although she wanted very much to ask him why he had come home so very late the night before, she held her tongue, remarked on the pleasant morning and read her letters. She was rewarded for this circumspect behaviour by him saying presently:

'I promised to take you both out this afternoon. I'm sorry, but it won't be possible. Could you find something to do, do you suppose?'

She wouldn't let him see her disappointment. 'Of course—there are a hundred and one things on Maureen's list. She'll be disappointed, though.'

'And you.' His glance was thoughtful.

'Oh, I'll be disappointed too; I love sightseeing. As it's her last day, I'll take her to Schevingenen. She'll love it there, and your mother was telling me of a lovely tea-room near the sea.'

She smiled at him, a friendly, casual smile, to let him see that it was of no importance whatever that he had had to cry off, and picked up the rest of her post, only to put it down again as a thought struck her.

'Gerard, would you rather not take Maureen back tomorrow? I can easily take her in the Fiat. Rather a comedown for her after the BMW and the Citroën, I know, but I've been on the road several times now and you said yourself that my driving had improved…'

He frowned at her across the table. 'I don't like the idea of you going that distance, though I must confess that it would be awkward for me to leave.'

'That's settled, then,' she said briskly. 'Only if you don't mind, I think I'll spend a night at home; I don't think I'd be much good at turning round and coming straight back.'

'An excellent idea.' He was still frowning. 'I wonder if there's someone who could drive you—Wim's taking Mother up to Friesland or he could have gone; there may be someone at the hospital.'

'Don't bother,' said Deborah quickly, 'you've enough to do without that. I'll be quite all right, you know, you don't need to give it another thought.'

'Very well. I won't, though if it had been anyone else but you…'

She was left to decide for herself if he had intended that as a compliment or not.

They were on their way back from Schevingenen that afternoon when she found herself behind her husband's car. He was driving the Citroën, and seated beside him was a small, dark, and very attractive woman, a circum-

stance which made Deborah thankful that Maureen was
so taken up with a large street organ in the opposite direction that she saw nothing.

Presently the traffic allowed her to slip past him.
Without looking she was aware of his sudden stare as
she raced the little car ahead of the Citroën while Maureen chattered on, still craning her neck to see the last
of the organ. Deborah answered her small sister's questions mechanically while her thoughts were busy. So
Gerard couldn't spare the time to take them out, though
seemingly he had leisure enough to drive around with
a pretty woman during an afternoon which was to have
been so busy. She had, she told herself savagely, two
minds to stay home for a good deal longer than one
night. There were, if her memory served her right, several social engagements within the next week or so—let
him attend them alone, or better still, with his charming companion. She frowned so fiercely at the very idea
that Maureen, turning to speak to her, wanted to know
if she had a headache.

Gerard was home for dinner. Deborah greeted him
with her usual calm friendliness, hoped that his day
hadn't been too busy and plunged into an account of
their outing that afternoon, pausing at the end of it to
give him time to tell her that he had seen her, and explain his companion. But he said nothing about it at all,
only had a short and lively conversation with Maureen
and joined her in a game with Smith before shutting
himself up in his study.

Deborah exerted herself to be entertaining during
dinner, and if her manner was over-bright, her companions didn't seem to notice. After the meal, when Gerard
declared himself ready to take Maureen on a boat tour

of the lighted canals, even though it was almost dark and getting chilly, she pleaded a headache and stayed at home, working pettishly at a petit-point handbag intended for her mother-in-law's Christmas present.

She and Maureen left after breakfast the next morning to catch the midday ferry from Zeebrugge and Gerard had left the house even earlier; over breakfast he had had very little to say to her, save to advise her to take care and wish her a pleasant journey, but with Maureen he had laughed and joked and given her an enormous box of chocolates as a farewell present and responded suitably to her uninhibited hugs.

They made good time to the ferry, and once on board, repaired to the restaurant where, over her enormous lunch, Maureen talked so much that she didn't notice that Deborah was eating almost nothing.

The drive to Somerset was uneventful. By now the little girl was getting tired; she dozed from time to time, assuring Deborah that she did so only to ensure that she would be wide awake when they reached home. Which left Deborah with her thoughts, running round and round inside her head like mice in a wheel. None of them were happy and all of them were of Gerard.

They reached home at about midnight, to find her parents waiting for them with hot drinks and sandwiches and a host of questions.

Deborah was answering them rather sleepily when the telephone rang and Mr Culpeper, annoyed at the interruption, answered it testily. But his sharp voice shouting, 'Hullo, hullo' in peremptory tones changed to a more friendly accent. 'It's Gerard,' he announced, 'wants to speak to you, Deb.'

She had telephoned the house in Amsterdam on their

arrival at Dover, knowing very well that he wouldn't
be home and leaving nothing but a brief message with
Wim. She picked up the receiver now, schooling her
voice to its usual calm and said: 'Hullo, Gerard.'

His voice was quiet and distinct. 'Hullo, Deborah.
Wim gave me your message, but I wanted to hear for
myself that you had got home safely. I hope I haven't
got you out of bed.'

'No. You're up late yourself.'

His 'Yes' was terse. He went on quickly: 'I won't
keep you. Have a good night's sleep and drive carefully
tomorrow. Good night, Debby.'

She said good night and replaced the receiver. He had
never called her Debby before; she wondered about it,
but she was really too tired to think. Presently they all
went to bed and she slept without waking until she was
called in the morning.

She was to take Maureen back to school after breakfast and then continue on her return journey. It seemed
lonely after she had left her little sister, still talking
and quite revived by a good night's sleep. There hadn't
been much time to talk to her mother while she had
been home, and perhaps that was a good thing; she
might have let slip some small thing…all the same, it
had been a cheerful few hours. Her parents, naturally
enough, took it for granted that she was happy and beyond asking after Gerard and agreeing eagerly to the
Christmas visit they had said little more; there had been
no chance because Maureen had so much to talk about.
It would have been nice to have confided in someone,
thought Deborah, pushing the little car hard along the
road towards the Winchester bypass, but perhaps not
quite loyal to Gerard. The thought of seeing him again

made her happy, but the happiness slowly wilted as the day wore on. There had been brilliant sunshine to start with, but now clouds were piling up behind her and long before she reached Dover, it was raining, and out at sea the sky showed a uniform greyness which looked as though it might be there for ever.

She slept for most of the crossing, sitting in a chair in the half-filled ship; she was tired and had been nervous of getting the car on board. Somehow with Maureen she hadn't found it frightening, but going up the steep ramp to the upper car deck she had quaked with fright; it was a relief to sit down for a few hours and recover her cool. She fetched herself a cup of coffee, brought a paperback and settled back. They were within sight of land when she woke and feeling tired still, she tidied herself and after a hasty cup of tea, went to the car deck.

Going down the ramp wasn't too bad, although her engine stalled when she reached the bottom. Deborah found herself trembling as she followed the cars ahead of her towards the Customs booth in the middle of the docks road. Suddenly the drive to Amsterdam didn't seem the easy journey she had made it out to be when she had offered to take Maureen home. It stretched before her in her mind's eye, dark and wet, with the Breskens ferry to negotiate and the long-drawn-out, lonely road across the islands, and Rotterdam…she had forgotten what a long way it was; somehow she hadn't noticed that when she was with Gerard, or even when she had taken Maureen back, but then it had been broad daylight.

She came to a halt by the Customs, proffered her passport and shivered in the chilly night air as she wound down the window. The man smiled at her. 'You will go to the left, please, Mevrouw.' He waved an arm towards a road leading off from the main docks road.

Deborah was puzzled; all the cars in front of her were keeping straight on. She said slowly so that he would be sure to understand: 'I'm going to Holland—don't I keep straight on to the main road?'

He was still smiling but quite firm. 'To the left, Mevrouw, if you will be so good.'

She went to the left; possibly they were diverting the traffic; she would find out in good time, she supposed. She was going slowly because the arc lights hardly penetrated this smaller side road and she had no idea where it was leading her, nor was there a car in front of her. She was on the point of stopping and going back to make sure that she hadn't misunderstood the Customs man, when her headlights picked out the BMW parked at the side of the road and Gerard leaning against its boot. In the bad light he looked enormous and very reassuring too; she hadn't realised just how much she had wanted to be reassured until she saw him there, standing in the pouring rain, the collar of his Burberry turned up to his ears, a hat pulled down over his eyes. She pulled up then and he walked over to her and when she wound down the window, said: 'Hullo, my dear. I thought it might be a good idea to come and meet you and drive you back—the weather, you know...'

She was still getting over her surprise and joy at seeing him. Her 'hullo' was faint, as was her protesting: 'But I can't leave the Fiat here?'

She became aware that Wim was there too, standing discreetly in the background by his master's car. Gerard nodded towards him. 'I brought Wim with me, he'll take the Fiat back.' He opened the car door. 'Come along, Deborah, we shall be home in no time at all.'

She got out silently and allowed herself to be tucked up snugly beside him in the BMW, pausing only to greet Wim and hope that he didn't mind driving the Fiat home.

'A pleasure, Mevrouw,' grinned Wim cheerfully, 'but I think that you will be there first.' He put out a hand to take the car keys from her and raised it in salute as he walked back to her car.

As Gerard reversed his own car and swept back the way she had come Deborah asked: 'Oh, is that why he told me to come this way and not out of the main gate?'

'Yes—I was afraid that we might miss you once you got past the Customs. Did you have a good trip back?'

For a variety of reasons and to her great shame her voice was drowned in a sudden flood of tears. She swallowed them back frantically and they poured down her cheeks instead. She stared out of the window at the outskirts of the town—flat land, dotted here and there with houses, it looked untidy even in the dim light of the overhead street lamps—and willed herself to be calm. After a minute Gerard said 'Deborah?' and because she would have to say something sooner or later she managed a 'Yes, thank you,' and spoilt it with a dreary snivel.

He slid the car to the side of the road on to a patch of waste land and switched off the engine. He had tossed off his hat when he got into the car; now he turned his handsome head and looked down at her in the semi-dark. 'What happened?' he asked gently, and then: 'Debby, I've never seen you cry before.'

She sniffed, struggled to get herself under control and managed:

'I hardly ever do—n-nothing's the m-matter, it's just that I'm tired, I expect.' She added on a small wail: 'I was t-terrified—those ramps on the ferry, they were ghastly—I thought I'd never reach the top and I didn't notice with Maureen, but when I was by m-myself it was awful, and the engine stalled and it was raining and when I got off the ferry it s-seemed s-such a long way to get home.' She hiccoughed, blew her nose and mopped her wet cheeks.

'I should never have let you go alone, I must have been mad. My poor girl, what a thoughtless man I am! You see, you are—always have been—so calm and efficient and able to cope, and then last night when I telephoned you, you sounded so tired—I rearranged my work to come and meet you. I remembered this long dark road too, Deborah, and in the Fiat it would be even longer. Forgive me, Deborah.'

She sniffed. His arm, flung along the back of the seat and holding her shoulders lightly, was comforting, and she was rapidly regaining her self-control. Later, she knew, she would be furious with herself for breaking down in this stupid fashion. She said in a voice which was nearly normal: 'Thank you very much, Gerard. It was only because it was raining and so very dark.'

She felt his arm slide away. 'I've some coffee here— Marijke always regards any journey more than ten miles distant from Amsterdam as being fraught with danger and probable starvation and provides accordingly. Sandwiches, too.'

They ate and drank in a companionable silence and presently Gerard began to talk, soothing nothings about her parents and her home and Smith—perhaps he talked to his more nervous patients like that, she thought sleepily, before he told them that he would have to operate. He took her cup from her presently and said: 'Go to sleep, Deborah, there's nothing to look at at this time of night—I'll wake you when we reach Amsterdam.'

She started to tell him that she wasn't tired any more, and fell asleep saying it.

She wakened to the touch of his hand on her arm. 'A few minutes,' he told her, and she was astonished to see the still lighted, now familiar streets of the city all around them. But the Keizersgracht was only dimly lit, its water gleaming dimly through the bare trees lining the road. It was still raining, but softly now, and there were a few lights from the houses they passed. As they drew up before their own front door, she saw that the great chandelier in the hall was beaming its light through the glass transom over the door and the sitting room was lighted too so that the wet pavement glistened in its glow. Gerard helped her out of the car and took her arm and they crossed the cobbles together as the front door was flung open and Marijke, with a wildly barking Smith, stood framed within it.

Going through the door Deborah knew at that moment just how much she loved the old house; it welcomed her, just as Marijke and Smith were welcoming her, as though she had returned from a long and arduous journey. She smiled a little mistily at Marijke and bent to catch Smith up into her arms. They went into the sitting room and Gerard took her coat, then Marijke was there almost at once with more hot coffee and a plate of paper-thin sandwiches. She talked volubly to Gerard while she set them out on the silver tray and carried it over to put on the table by Deborah's chair. When she had gone, Deborah asked: 'What was all that about?'

He came to sit opposite her and now she could see the lines of fatigue on his face, so that before he could answer she asked: 'Have you had a hard day?'

He smiled faintly. 'Yes.'

'You've been busy—too busy, lately.'

'That is no excuse for letting you go all that way alone.'

She said firmly: 'It was splendid for my driving. I'll not mind again.'

'There won't be an again,' he told her briefly, 'and Marijke was talking about you.'

'Oh—I recognised one word—stomach.'

It was nice to see him laugh like that. 'She said that you look tired and that beautiful women should never look other than beautiful. She strongly advised nourishment for your—er—stomach so that you would sleep like a rose.'

Deborah said softly: 'What a charming thing to say, about the rose, I mean. Dear Marijke—she and Wim, they're like the house, aren't they?' And was sorry that she had said it, because he might not understand. But he did; the look he gave her was one of complete understanding. She smiled at him and then couldn't look away from his intent gaze. 'You saw me the other afternoon,' he stated the fact simply. 'You have been wondering why I couldn't find the time to take you and Maureen on a promised trip and yet have the leisure to drive around with a very attractive woman—she was attractive, did you not think so?'

'Yes.'

'I don't discuss my patients with you, you know that,

I think—although I must confess I have frequently wished to do so—but I do not wish you to misunderstand. The patient upon whom I operated the other evening was...' he named someone and Deborah sat up with a jerk, although she said nothing. 'Yes, you see why I have been so worried and—secretive. The lady with me was his wife. She had been to Schiphol to meet her daughter, who was breaking her journey on her way home to get news of her father. At the last moment his wife declared that she was unable to tell her and asked me to do it. We were on our way back to the hospital when you saw us. I should have told you sooner. I'm not sure why I didn't, perhaps I was piqued at the way you ignored the situation. Any other woman—wife— would have asked.'

'It was none of my business,' she said stiffly. 'I didn't know...'

'You mean that you suspected me of having a girl-friend?' He was smiling, but she sensed his controlled anger.

There was no point in being anything but honest with him. 'Yes, I think I did, but it still wouldn't be my business, and it shouldn't matter, should it?'

He hadn't taken his eyes off her. 'I believe you said that once before. You think that? But do you not know me well enough to know that I would have been quite honest with you before I married you?'

Her head had begun to ache. 'Oh, yes, indeed, but that wasn't what I meant. What I'm trying to say is that I've no right to mind, have I?'

Gerard got to his feet and pulled her gently to hers. 'You have every right in the world,' he assured her. 'I don't think our bargain included that kind of treatment of each other, Deborah. I don't cheat the people I like.'

She didn't look at him. 'No, I know that, truly I do. I'm sorry I was beastly. I think I'm tired.'

They walked together out of the room and in the hall he kissed her cheek. 'I'll wait for Wim, he shouldn't be much longer now. And by the way, I've taken some time off. In a couple of days I'll take you to the house in Friesland, and we might go and see some friends of mine who live close by—she's English, too.'

Deborah was half way up the stairs. 'That sounds lovely,' she told him and then turned round to say: 'Thank you for coming all that way, it must have been a bind after a hard day's work.'

He didn't answer her, but she was conscious of his eyes on her as she climbed the stairs.

CHAPTER SIX

BUT BEFORE THEY went to Friesland Deborah met some other friends of Gerard's. She had spent a quiet day after her return, arranging the menu for a dinner party they were to give during the following week, paying a morning visit to her mother-in-law, telephoning her own mother and writing a few letters before taking Smith for a walk. She was back home, waiting for Gerard's return from the Grotehof after tea, when the telephone rang.

It was a woman's voice, light and sweet, enquiring if Mijnheer van Doorninck was home. 'No,' said Deborah, and wondered who it was, 'I'm sorry—perhaps I could take a message?' She spoke in the careful Dutch the professor had taught her, and hoped that the conversation wasn't going to get too involved.

'Is that Gerard's wife?' asked the voice, in English now, and when Deborah said a little uncertainly: 'Why, yes—' went on: 'Oh, good. I'm Adelaide van Essen. My husband's a paediatrician at the Grotehof and a friend of Gerard. We got back from England last night and Coenraad telephoned me just now and told me about you. You don't mind me ringing you up?'

'I'm delighted—I don't know any English people here yet.'

'Well, come and meet me—us, for a start. Come this

evening. I know it's short notice, but I told Coenraad to ask Gerard to bring you to dinner—you will come?'

'I'd love to.' Deborah paused. 'I'm not sure about Gerard, he works late quite a lot and often works at home.'

She had the impression that the girl at the other end of the line was concealing surprise. Then: 'I'm sure he'll make time. We haven't seen each other for ages and the men are old friends. We live quite near you, in the Herengracht—is seven o'clock too early? Oh, and here's our number in case you want to ring back. Till seven, then. I'm so looking forward to meeting you.'

Deborah went back to her chair. The voice had sounded nice, soft and gentle and friendly. She spent the next ten minutes or so in deciding what she should wear and still hadn't made up her mind when Gerard came in.

His hullo was friendly and after he had enquired about her day, he took a chair near her. 'I met a friend of mine at the Grotehof this afternoon,' he told her. 'Coenraad van Essen—he's married to an English girl. They're just back from England and they want us to go round for dinner this evening. Would you like to go? It's short notice and I don't know if it will upset any arrangements you may have made?'

She chose a strand of silk and threaded her needle. 'His wife telephoned a few minutes ago. I'd like to go very much. She suggested seven o'clock, so I had better go and talk to Marijke.'

Marijke hadn't started the cutlets and the cheese soufflé; Deborah, in her laborious Dutch and helped by a few words here and there from Wim, suggested that they should have them the following day instead and apologised for the short notice. To which Marijke had a whole lot to say in reply, her face all smiles. Deborah turned to Wim. 'I don't quite understand…'

'Marijke is saying that it is good for you to see a lady of your own age and also English. She wishes you a merry evening.' He beamed at her. 'Me, I wish the same also, Mevrouw.'

She wore the pink silk jersey dress she had been unable to resist the last time she had visited Metz, the fashionable dress shop within walking distance of the house, and went downstairs to find Gerard waiting for her. 'I'm not late?' she asked anxiously as she crossed the hall.

'No—I wanted a few minutes with you. Shall we go into the sitting room?'

Deborah's heart dropped to her elegant shoes. What was he going to tell her? That he was going away on one of his teaching trips—that he wouldn't be able to take her to Friesland after all? She arranged her face into a suitable composure and turned to face him.

'Did you never wonder why I had not given you a wedding gift?' he asked her. 'Not because I had given no thought to it; there were certain alterations I wanted done, and only today are they finished.'

He took a small velvet case from his pocket and opened it. There were earrings inside on its thick satin lining; elaborate pearl drops in a diamond setting. She looked at them with something like awe. 'My goodness,' she uttered, 'they're—they're beautiful! I've never seen anything like them.'

He had taken them from their box. 'Try them on,' he invited her. 'They're very old, but the setting was clumsy; I've had them re-set to my own design. You are tall enough to take such a style, I think.'

She had gone to the mirror over the sofa table and

hooked them in and stood looking at them. They were exquisite, and he was right, they suited her admirably. She turned her lovely head and watched the diamonds take fire. 'I don't know how to thank you,' she began. 'They're magnificent!'

Thanking him didn't seem quite enough, so she went to him and rather hesitantly kissed his cheek. 'Do you suppose I might wear them this evening?' she asked.

'Why not?' He had gone over to the small secretaire by one of the windows and was opening one of its drawers. He returned with another, larger case in his hand. 'This has been in the family for quite some time too,' he observed as he gave it to her. 'I've had it re-strung and the clasp re-set to match the earrings.'

Deborah opened the case slowly. There were pearls in it, a double row with a diamond and pearl clasp which followed the exact pattern of the earrings. She stared at it and all she could manage was an ecstatic 'Oh!' Gerard took them from her and fastened them round her neck and she went back to the mirror and had another look; they were quite superb. 'I don't know how to thank you,' she repeated, quite at a loss for words. 'It's the most wonderful wedding present anyone could dream of having.'

He was standing behind her, staring at her reflection. After a moment he smiled faintly. 'You are my wife,' he pointed out. 'You are entitled to them.' He spoke lightly as he turned away.

He need not have said that, she thought unhappily, looking at her suddenly downcast face in the mirror. It took her a few moments to fix a smile on to it before she turned away and picked up her coat.

'Do we walk or go in the car?' she asked brightly.

He helped her into her coat and she could have been his sister, she thought bitterly, for all the impression she made upon him. 'The car,' he told her cheerfully. 'It's almost seven, perhaps we had better go at once.'

The house in the Herengracht was bigger than Gerard's but very similar in style. Its vast front door was opened as they reached it and an elderly man greeted them with a 'Good evening, Mevrouw—Mijnheer.'

Gerard slapped him on the shoulder. 'Tweedle, how are you? You haven't called me Mijnheer for many a long day.' He looked at Deborah, smiling. 'This is Tweedle, my dear, who has been with Coenraad since he was a toddler. I daresay you will meet Mrs Tweedle presently.'

'Indeed, she will be delighted,' Tweedle informed them gravely, adding: 'The Baron and Baroness are in the small sitting room, Mr Gerard.'

He led the way across the panelled hall and opened a door, announcing them as he did so, and Deborah, with Gerard's hand under her elbow urging her gently on, went in.

The room was hardly small and she saw at a glance that it was furnished with some magnificent pieces worthy of a museum, yet it was decidedly lived in; there was a mass of knitting cast down carelessly on a small drum table, a pile of magazines were tumbled on to the sofa table behind the big settee before the chimneypiece, and there was a pleasant scent of flowers, tobacco and—very faint—beeswax polish. There were two people in the room, a man as tall as Gerard but somewhat older, his dark hair greying at the temples, horn-rimmed glasses astride his handsome beaky nose. It was a kind face as well as a good-looking one, and

Deborah decided then and there that she was going to like Gerard's friend. The girl who got up with him was small, slim and very pretty, with huge dark eyes and a mass of bright red hair piled high. She was wearing a very simple dress of cream silk and some of the love-liest sapphires Deborah had ever set eyes on. She felt Gerard's hand on her arm again and went forward to receive the Baron's quiet welcome and the charming enthusiasm of his small wife, who, after kissing Gerard in a sisterly fashion, led her to a small sofa and sat down beside her.

'You really are a dear to come at a moment's notice,' she declared. 'You didn't mind?'

Deborah shook her head, smiling. She was going to like this small vivid creature. 'It was kind of you to ask us. I'm so glad to meet another English girl. Gerard has been so busy and—and we haven't been married very long. I've met a great many of his colleagues, though.'

Her companion glanced at her quickly. 'Duty dinners,' she murmured, 'and the rest of the time they're immersed in their work. Coenraad says you were Gerard's Theatre Sister.'

'Yes. I worked for him for two years while he was at Clare's.' She felt she should have been able to say more about it than that, but she could think of nothing. There was a pause before her hostess asked: 'Do you like Amsterdam? I love it. We've a house in Dorset and we go there whenever we can, and to my parents, of course. The children love it.'

She didn't look old enough to have children. 'How many have you?' Deborah asked.

'Two.' Adelaide turned to take the drink her husband

was offering her and he corrected her smilingly: 'Two and a half, my love.'

Deborah watched him exchange a loving glance, full of content and happiness, and swallowed envy as she heard her host say: 'Do you hear that, Gerard? You're going to be a godfather again—some time in the New Year.' And when Gerard joined them, he added: 'We'll do the same for you, of course.'

Everyone laughed; this was the sort of occasion, Deborah told herself bitterly, that she hadn't reckoned with. She made haste to ask the children's names and was at once invited to visit them in their beds.

'They won't be asleep,' their doting mother assured her, 'at least Champers won't. Lisa's only eighteen months old and drops off in seconds. Champers likes to lie and think.'

She led the way up the curving staircase and into the night nursery where an elderly woman was tidying away a pile of clothes. She was introduced as Nanny Best, the family treasure, before she trotted softly away with a bright nod. The two girls went to the cot first; the small girl in it was a miniature of her mother, the same fiery hair and preposterous lashes, the same small nose. She was asleep, her mother dropped a kiss on one fat pink cheek and crossed the room to the small bed against the opposite wall. There was no doubt at all that the small boy in it was the baron's son. Here was the dark hair, the beaky nose and the calm expression. He grinned widely at his mother, offered a hand to Deborah and after kissing them both good night, declared his intention of going to sleep.

They went back downstairs and were met in the hall by the Labrador dogs. 'Castor and Pollux,' Adelaide introduced them, and tucked an arm into Deborah's. 'Call me Adelaide,' she begged in her sweet voice. 'I'm going to call you Deborah.' She paused to look at her companion. 'You're quite beautiful, you know, no wonder Gerard married you.' Her eyes lingered on the earrings. 'I like these,' she said, touching them with a gentle finger, 'and the pearls, they suit you. How lucky you are to be tall and curvy, you can wear all the jewels Gerard will doubtless give you, but look at me—one pearl necklace and I'm smothered!'

They laughed together as they entered the room and the two men looked up. Coenraad said: 'There you are, darling—do you girls want another drink before dinner?'

The meal was a splendid one. Deborah, looking round the large, well appointed dining room, reflected how well the patrician families lived with their large old houses, their priceless antique furniture, their china and glass and silver and most important of all, their trusted servants who were devoted to them and looked after their possessions with as much pride as that of their owners.

She was recalled to her surroundings by Adelaide. 'So you're going to Friesland,' she commented. 'I expect Gerard will take you to see Dominic and Abigail—she's English, too—they live close by. They're both dears. They've a house in Amsterdam, of course, but they go to Friesland when they can. Abigail is expecting a baby in about six months.' She grinned happily. 'Won't it be fun, all of us living near enough to pop in and visit, and so nice for the children—they can all play together.'

Deborah agreed, aware that Gerard had stopped talking and was listening too. 'What are the schools like?' she heard herself ask in a voice which sounded as though she really wanted to know.

They stayed late; when they got back home the house was quiet, for Wim and Marijke had long since gone to bed, but the great chandelier in the hall still blazed and there were a couple of lamps invitingly lighting the sitting room. Deborah wandered in and perched on the side of a chair.

'You enjoyed the evening?' Gerard wanted to know, following her.

'Very much—what a nice person Adelaide is, and so is Coenraad. I hope I did the right thing, I asked them to join our dinner party next week.'

'Splendid. Coenraad and I have known each other for a very long time.' He went on: 'He and Addy are very devoted.'

'Yes.' Deborah didn't want to talk about that, it hurt too much. 'I'm looking forward to meeting Abigail too.'

'Ah, yes, on Saturday. We'll leave fairly early in the morning, shall we, go to the house first and then go on to Dominic's place in the afternoon. Probably they'll want us to stay for dinner, but as I'm not going in to the Grotehof in the morning, it won't matter if we're late back.'

She got up. 'It sounds delightful. I think I'll go to bed.' She put a hand up to the pearl necklace. 'Thank you again for my present, Gerard. I'll treasure it, and the earrings.'

He was switching off the lamps. 'But of course,' he told her blandly. 'They have been treasured for generations of van Doorninck brides, and I hope will continue to be treasured for a long time to come.'

She went upstairs wondering why he had to remind

her so constantly that married though they were, she was an—she hesitated for a word—outsider.

DEBORAH HALF EXPECTED that something would turn up to prevent them going to Friesland, but it didn't. They left soon after eight o'clock, travelling at a great pace through Hoorn and Den Oever and over the Afsluitdijk and so into Friesland. Once on the land again, Gerard turned the car away from the Leeuwarden road, to go through Bolsward and presently Sneek and into the open country beyond. Deborah was enchanted with what she saw; there seemed to be water everywhere.

'Do you sail at all?' she wanted to know of Gerard.

He slowed the car and turned into a narrow road running along the top of a dyke. He looked years younger that morning, perhaps because he was wearing slacks and a sweater with a gay scarf tucked in its neck, perhaps because he had a whole day in which to do as he liked.

'I've a small yacht, a van der Stadt design, around ten tons displacement—she sails like a dream.'

She wasn't sure what ten tons displacement meant. 'Where do you keep her?'

'Why, at Domwier—I can sail her down the canal to the lake. I've had no time this summer to do much sailing, though, and it's getting late in the year now, though with this lovely autumn we might have a chance— would you like to come with me?'

'Oh, please, if I wouldn't be a nuisance; I don't know a thing about boats, but I'm willing to learn.'

'Good—that's a dare, if the weather holds. We're almost at Domwier—it's a very small village; a church,

a shop and a handful of houses. The house is a mile
further on.'

The sun sparkled on the lake as they approached
it, the opposite shore looked green and pleasant with
its trees and thickets, even though there weren't many
leaves left. They drove through a thick curtain of birch
and pine and saw the lake, much nearer now, beyond
rough grass. She barely had time to look at it before Gerard turned into a short sandy lane and there was the
house before them. It looked like a farmhouse without
the barn behind it, built square and solid with no-nonsense windows and an outsize door surmounted by a
carving of two white swans. The sweep before the house
was bordered by flower beds, still colourful with dahl-
ias and chrysanthemums, and beyond them, grass and
a thick screen of trees and bushes through which she
glimpsed the water again. Smith tumbled out of the car
to tear round the garden, barking ecstatically, while
they made their way rather more soberly to the front
door. It stood open on to a tiled hall with a door on either side and another at its end through which came a
stout woman, almost as tall as Gerard. That she was
delighted to see them was obvious, although Deborah
could discover nothing of what she was saying. It was
only when Gerard said: 'Forgive us, we're speaking
Fries, because Sien dislikes speaking anything else,'
that she realised that they were speaking another language altogether. Her heart sank a little; now she would
have to learn this language too! As though he had read
her thoughts, Gerard added: 'Don't worry, you won't
be expected to speak it, though Sien would love you
for ever if you could learn to understand just a little of
what she says.'

'Then I'll do that, I promise. Do you come up here often?'

He corrected her gently: 'We shall, I hope, come up here often. Once things are exactly as I want them at the hospital, I shall have a good deal more time. I have been away for two years, remember, with only brief visits.'

'Yes, I know, but must you work so hard every day? I mean, you're not often home…' She wished she hadn't said it, for she sensed his withdrawal.

'I'm afraid you must accept that, Deborah.' He was smiling nicely, but his eyes were cool. He turned back to Sien and said something to her and she shook Deborah's hand and, still talking, went back to the kitchen.

Gerard flung an arm round Deborah's shoulders and led her to the sitting room. 'Coffee,' he invited her, 'and then we'll go round the place.' His manner was friendly, just as though he had forgotten their slight discord.

The room was simply furnished in the traditional Friesian style, with painted cupboards against the walls, rush-seated chairs, a stove with a tiled surround and a nicely balanced selection of large, comfortable chairs. There was a telephone too and a portable television tucked discreetly in a corner. 'It's simple'—Gerard had seen her glance—'but we have comfort and convenience.'

Most decidedly, she agreed silently, as Sien came in with a heavy silver tray with its accompanying silver pot and milk jug and delicate cups. The coffee was delicious and so was the spiced cake which accompanied it. They sat over it and Deborah, determined to keep the conversation on safe ground, asked questions about the house and the furniture and the small paintings hung each side of the stove. She found them enchanting, just as beautiful in their way as the priceless portraits in

the Amsterdam house; the ancestors who had sat for
Paulus Potter, the street scene by Hendrik Sorgh and
the two by Gerrit Berckheyde; she had admired them
greatly, almost nervous of the fact that she was now in
part responsible for them. But these delicate sketches
and paintings were much smaller and perfect to the
last hair and whisker—fieldmice mostly, small animals
of all kinds, depicted with a precise detail which she
found amazing.

'They're by Jacob de Gheyn,' Gerard told her. 'An
ancestress of mine loved small animals, so her husband
commissioned these for her, and they have been there
ever since. I agree with you, they're quite delightful.
Come and see the rest of the house.'

The dining room was on the other side of the hall,
with a great square bay window built out to take in the
view of the lake beyond, comfortably furnished with
enormous chairs covered in bright patterned damask.
There was a Dutch dresser against one wall, decked
with enormous covered tureens and rows of old Delft-
ware. There was a similar dresser in the kitchen too
which Deborah could see was as up-to-date as the latest model at the Ideal Home Exhibition, and upstairs the
two bathrooms, tiled and cosily carpeted, each with its
pile of brightly coloured towels and a galaxy of match-
ing soaps and powders, rivalled the luxury of the town
house. By contrast the bedrooms were simply furnished
while still offering every comfort, even the two small
attic rooms, reached by an almost perpendicular flight
of miniature stairs, were as thickly carpeted and as
delightfully furnished as the large rooms on the floor
below.

As they went downstairs again she said a little shyly:

'This is a lovely house, Gerard—how wonderful to come here when you want peace and quiet. I love the house in Amsterdam, but I could love this one as much.'

He gave her an approving glance. 'You feel that? I'm glad, I have a great fondness for it. Mother too, she comes here frequently. It's quiet in the winter, of course.'

'I think I should like it then—does the lake freeze over?'

They had strolled into the dining room and found Sien busy putting the finishing touches to the lunch table. 'Yes, though not always hard enough for skating. I can remember skating across to Dominic's house during some of the really cold winters, though.'

'But it's miles...'

He poured her a glass of sherry. 'Not quite. Round about a mile, I should suppose. We shall have to drive back to the road presently, of course, and go round the head of the lake. It's no distance.'

They set off after a lunch which Deborah had thoroughly enjoyed because Gerard had been amusing and gay and relaxed; and she had never felt so close, and she wondered if he felt it too. It was on the tip of her tongue to try and explain a little to him of how she felt—oh, not to tell him that she loved him; she had the good sense to see that such a statement would cook her goose for ever, but to let him see, if she could, that she was happy and contented and anxious to please him. But there was no chance to say any of these things; they left immediately after lunch and the journey was too short to start a serious talk.

Dominic's house, when they reached it, was a good deal larger than their own but furnished in a similar style. Dominic had come to meet them as they got out of the car, his arm around his wife's shoulders. He was another large man. Deborah found him attractive and almost as good-looking as Gerard, and as for his wife, she was a small girl who would have been plain if happiness hadn't turned her into a beauty. She shook hands now and said in a pretty voice:

'This is a lovely surprise—we heard that Gerard had married and we had planned to come and see you when we got back to Amsterdam. We were returning this week, but the weather's so marvellous, and once the winter starts it goes on and on.'

Inside they talked until tea came, and presently when Gerard suggested that they should go, there was no question of it. 'You'll stay to dinner,' said Abigail. 'Besides'—and now she was smiling—'I mustn't be thwarted, because of my condition.' There was a general laugh and she turned to Deborah. 'Well, I'm not the only one, I hear Adelaide van Essen is having another baby—isn't she a dear?'

Deborah agreed. 'It's wonderful to find some other English girls living so close by.' She added hastily, 'Not that I'm lonely, but I find Dutch rather difficult, though I am having lessons.'

'Professor de Wit?' asked Abigail. 'Adelaide went to him. I nursed his brother before I married Dominic.' The two girls plunged into an interesting chat which was only broken by Dominic suggesting mildly that perhaps Abigail should let Bollinger know that there would be two more for dinner.

Abigail got up. 'Oh, darling, I forgot. Deborah, come and meet Bolly—he came over from England with me, and he's part of the household now.'

She smiled at her husband as they left the room, and
Deborah, seeing it, felt a pang of sadness. It seemed
that everyone else but herself and Gerard was happily
married. Walking to the kitchen, half listening to Abigail's happy voice, she wondered if she had tried hard
enough, or perhaps she had tried too much. Perhaps she
annoyed him in some way, or worse, bored him. She
would have to know. She resolved to ask him.

She did so, buoyed up by a false courage induced by
Dominic's excellent wine. They were half way home,
tearing along the Afsluitdijk with no traffic problems
to occupy him.

'Do I bore you, Gerard?' she asked, and heard the
small sound he made. Annoyance? Impatience? Surprise, perhaps.

But when he answered her his voice was as cool and
casually friendly as usual. 'Not in the least. What put
such an idea into your head?'

'N-nothing. I just wondered if you were quite satisfied—I mean with our marriage; if I'm being the kind of
wife you wanted. You see, we're not much together and
I don't know a great deal about you—perhaps when you
get home in the evening and you're tired you'd rather
be left in peace with the paper and a drink. I wouldn't
mind a bit...'

They were almost at the end of the dyke, approach-
ing the great sluices at its end. Gerard slowed down and
gave her a quick look in the dark of the car.

He said on a laugh: 'I do believe you're trying to
turn me into a Dutchman with my gin and my paper
after a hard day's work!' His voice changed. 'I'm quite
satisfied, Deborah. You are the wife I wanted, you certainly don't bore me, I'm always glad to see you when I

get home, however tired I am.' His voice became kind. 'Surely that is enough to settle your doubts?'

Quite enough, she told him silently, and quite hopeless too. An irrational desire to drum her heels on the floorboards and scream loudly took possession of her. She overcame it firmly. 'Yes, thank you, Gerard,' and began at once to talk about the house in Friesland. The subject was threadbare by the time they reached Amsterdam, but at least she had managed not to mention themselves again.

It was late and she went straight to bed, leaving Gerard to take Smith for his last perambulation and lock up, and in the morning when she came down it was to hear from Wim that he had been called to the hospital in the very early morning and hadn't returned. It was almost lunchtime when he did, and as his mother had been invited for that meal, it was impossible to ask him about it; in any case, even if they had been alone, he would probably not have told her anything. She applied herself to her mother-in-law's comfort and after lunch sat in the drawing room with her, listening to tales of the family and making suitable comments from time to time, all the while wondering where Gerard had got to. He had gone to his study—she knew that, because he had said that he had a telephone call to make, but that was more than two hours ago. The two ladies had tea together and Deborah had just persuaded the older lady to stay to dinner when Gerard joined them with the hope that they had spent a pleasant afternoon and never a word about his own doings.

He told her the reason for his absence that evening after he had driven his mother back to her flat.

'Before you ask me any of the questions I feel sure

are seething inside your head, I'll apologise most humbly.'

'Apologise? Whatever for?' She put down the book she had been reading and stared at him in astonishment.

'Leaving you with Mother for the entire afternoon.'

'But you had some calls to make—some work to do, didn't you?'

He grinned suddenly and her heart thumped against her ribs because he looked as she knew he might look if he were happy and carefree and not chained to the hospital by chains of his own forging. 'I went to sleep.' And when she goggled at him: 'I know, I'm sorry, but the fact is, I had some work to do after we got home last night and I stayed up until two o'clock or thereabouts, and I had to go to the Grotehof for an emergency op at five.'

'Gerard, you must have been worn out! Why on earth didn't you tell me, why won't you let me help you…' That wouldn't do at all, so she went on briskly: 'And there was I telling your mother that you never had a minute to call your own, working at your desk even on a Sunday afternoon.'

He was staring hard at her. 'You're a loyal wife,' he said quietly, and she flushed faintly under his eyes.

'I expect all wives are,' she began, and saw the expression on his face. It had become remote again; he was remembering Sasja, she supposed, who hadn't been loyal at all. 'Shall we have dinner early tomorrow evening so that you can get your work done in good time? Have you a heavy list in the morning?'

'That was something I was going to tell you. I've changed the list to the afternoon—two o'clock, because I thought we might go for a run in the morning.'

A little colour crept into her cheeks again, but she

kept her voice as ordinary as possible. 'That sounds nice. Where shall we go?'

'Not too far. The river Vecht, perhaps—we could keep off the motorway and there won't be much traffic about this time of the year.'

Deborah agreed happily, and later, in bed, thinking about it, she dared to hope that perhaps Gerard's first rigid ideas about their marriage weren't as rigid as they had been. She slept peacefully on that happy thought.

They were out of Amsterdam by nine o'clock the next morning, driving through the crisp autumn air. Gerard took the road to Naarden and then turned off on to the narrow road following the Vecht, going slowly so that Deborah could inspect the houses on its banks, built by the merchant princes in the eighteenth century, and because she found them so fascinating he obligingly turned the car at the end of the road and drove back again the same way, patiently answering her questions about them. They had coffee in Loenen and because there was still plenty of time before they had to return to Amsterdam he didn't follow the road to Naarden again, but turned off into the byroads which would lead them eventually back to the city.

The road they were on stretched apparently unending between the flat fields, and save for a group of farm cottages half a mile away, and ahead of them the vague outline of a farmhouse, there was nothing moving except a farm tractor being driven across a ploughed field. Deborah watched the driver idly as they came level with him. 'He must be lonely,' she said idly, and then urgently: 'Gerard, that tractor's going to turn over!'

She was glad that he wasn't one of those men who asked needless questions; they weren't travelling fast, so he slid to a halt and had the door open as the tractor, some way off, reared itself up like an angry monster and crashed down on to its hapless driver.

Even in his hurry, it warmed Deborah's heart when Gerard leaned across her to undo her door and snap back her safety belt so that she could get out quickly. There was a narrow ditch between the road and the field; he bridged it easily with his long legs and then turned to give her a hand before they started to run as best they might across the newly turned earth.

The man had made no sound. When they reached him he was unconscious, trapped by the bonnet of the tractor, its edge biting across the lower half of his body.

It was like being back in theatre, thought Deborah wildly, working in a silent agreed pattern which needed no speech. She found a pulse and counted it with care while Gerard's hands began a careful search over the man's body.

'Nasty crack on his head on this side,' she offered, and peered at the eyes under their closed lids. 'Pupil reaction is equal.'

Gerard grunted, his fingers probing and feeling and probing again.

'I'm pretty sure his pelvis is fractured, God knows what's happened to his legs—how's his pulse?' She told him and he nodded. 'Not too bad,' and examined more closely the wound on the man's head. 'Can't feel a fracture, though I think there may be a crack. We've got to get this thing eased off him, even if it's only a centimetre.'

He slid a powerful arm as far as it would go and heaved with great caution and slowness. 'Half an inch would do it.' He was talking to himself. 'Your belt,

Debby—if we could budge this thing just a shade and stuff your belt in…'

She had her belt off while he was still speaking. 'How about trying to scoop the earth from under him and slip the belt in?'

He had understood her at once. He crouched beside the man, the belt in his hand, his arm ready to thrust it between the bonnet's rim and the man's body. Deborah dug with speedy calm; there was nothing to use but her hands. She felt the nails crack and tear and saw, in a detached way, the front of her expensive tweed two-piece gradually disappear under an encrustation of damp earth, but presently she was able to say: 'Try now, Gerard.'

It worked, albeit the pressure was eased fractionally and wouldn't last long. Gerard withdrew his arm with great care and said: 'We have to get help.' His voice was as calm as though he was commenting upon the weather. 'Take the keys and drive the car to that farm we saw ahead of us and ask…no, that'll take too long, I'll go. Stay here—there's nothing much you can do. Push the belt in further if you get the chance.' He got to his feet. 'Thank heaven you're a strapping girl with plenty of strength and common sense!'

He started to run back towards the car, leaving her smouldering; did he really regard her as strapping? He had made her sound like some muscly creature with no feminine attributes at all! Deborah chuckled and the chuckle changed to a sob which she sternly swallowed; now was no time to be feminine. She took the man's pulse once more and wondered how long she would have to wait before Gerard got back.

Not long—she saw the car racing down the road

and prayed silently that there would be nothing in the way. The next minutes seemed like eternity. Deborah turned her head at length to see Gerard with four or five men, coming towards her. They were carrying ropes and when he was near enough she said in the matter-of-fact voice he would expect of her: 'His pulse is going up, but it's steady. What are you going to do?'

'Get ropes round this infernal thing and try and drag it off.'

'You'll get double hernias,' she warned him seriously.

Gerard gave a crack of laughter. 'A risk we must all take. I fear, there's no other tractor for miles around.'

He turned away from her and became immersed in the task before him. They had the ropes in place and were heaving on them steadily when the first police car arrived, disgorging two men to join the team of sweating, swearing men. The tractor shuddered and rolled over with a thud, leaving the man free just as the second police car and an ambulance arrived.

Gerard scarcely heeded them; he was on his knees, examining the man's legs. 'By some miracle,' he said quietly to Deborah, 'they're not pulped. I may be able to do something about them provided we can get at him quickly enough. Get me some splints.'

She went to meet the ambulance men, making all the speed they could over the soft earth. She had no idea what the word splint was in Dutch, but luckily they were carrying an armful, so she took several from one rather astonished man, smiled at him and raced back to Gerard. He took them without a word and then said: 'Good lord, girl, what am I supposed to tie them with?'

She raced back again and this time the ambulance

man ran to meet her and kept beside her as she ran back with the calico slings. There was help enough now, she stood back and waited patiently. It took a long time to get the man on to the stretcher and carry him, with infinite caution, across the field to the waiting ambulance. She waited until the little procession had reached it before following it and when she reached the car there was no sign of Gerard, so she got in and sat waiting with the patience she had learned during her years of nursing. The ambulance drove off presently and one of the policemen leaned through the car window and proffered her a note—from Gerard, scribbled in his almost undecipherable scrawl. 'I must go with the ambulance to the Grotehof,' he had written on a sheet torn out of his pocket book. 'Drive the car back and wait in the hospital courtyard.' He had signed it 'G' and added a postscript: 'The BMW is just like the Fiat, only larger.'

All the same, reading these heartening words, Deborah felt a pang of nervousness; she had never driven the BMW; if she thought about it for too long she would be terrified of doing so. She thanked the policeman who saluted politely, and happily ignorant of the fact that she was almost sick with fright, drove away. It was quite five minutes before she could summon up the courage to press the self-starter.

She was still shaking when she stopped the car cautiously before the entrance to the hospital, wondering what she was supposed to do next. But Gerard had thought of that; Deborah was sitting back in her seat, taking a few calming breaths when the Medical Ward Sister, whom she had already met, popped her head through the window. 'Mevrouw van Doorninck, you will come with me, please.'

'Hullo,' said Deborah, and then: 'Why, Zuster?'

'It is the wish of Mijnheer van Doorninck.' Her tone
implied that there was sufficient reason there without
the need for any more questions.

'Where is he?' asked Deborah, sitting stubbornly
where she was.

'In theatre, already scrubbed. But he wishes most
earnestly that you will come with me.' She added plain-
tively: 'I am so busy, Mevrouw.'

Deborah got out of the car at once, locked it and put
the keys in her handbag. She would have to get them
to Gerard somehow; she had no intention of driving
through Amsterdam in the BMW—getting to the hospital had been bad enough. She shuddered and followed
the Sister to the lift.

They got out on the Medical floor and she was bustled through several corridors and finally through a
door. 'So—we are here,' murmured the Sister, said
something to whoever was in the room, gave Deborah
a smile and tore away. Deborah watched her go, knowing just how she felt; probably she was saying the Dutch
equivalent of 'I'll never get finished,' as she went; even
the simple task of escorting someone through the hospital could make a mockery of a tight and well-planned
schedule of work.

It was Doctor Schipper inside the room waiting for
her. Deborah had met him before; she and Gerard had
had dinner with him and his wife only the week before.
She wished him a good afternoon, a little puzzled, and
he came across the little room to shake her hand.

'You are surprised, Mevrouw van Doorninck, but
Gerard wishes most urgently that you should have a

check-up without delay. He fears that you may have strained yourself in some way—even a small cut...'

'I'm fine,' she declared, aware of sore hands. 'Well, I've broken a few fingernails and I was scared stiff!'

A young nurse had slid into the room, so Deborah, submitting to the inevitable, allowed herself to be helped out of her deplorable dress and examined with thoroughness by Doctor Schipper. He stood back at length. 'Quite OK,' he assured her. 'A rapid pulse, but I imagine you had an unpleasant shock—the accident was distressing...'

'Yes, but I think it was having to drive the car which scared me stiff. I only drive a Fiat 500, you know—there's quite a difference. Can I go home now?'

'Of course. Nurse will arrange for you to have a taxi, but first she will clean up your hands, and perhaps an injection of ATS to be on the safe side—all that earth...'

She submitted to the nurse's attentions and remembered the car keys just as she was ready to go. 'Shall I leave them at the front door?' she asked Doctor Schipper.

He held out a hand. 'Leave them with me—I'll get them to Gerard. He won't want them just yet, I imagine.'

Deborah thanked him, reminded him that he and his wife were dining with them in a few days' time and set off for the entrance with the nurse, where she climbed into a taxi and went home to find Wim and Marijke, worried about their non-appearance for lunch, waiting anxiously.

She was herself again by the evening, presenting a bandbox freshness to the world marred only by her deplorable nails and an odd bruise or two. She had deliberately put on a softly clinging dress and used her perfume with discreet lavishness; studying herself in the mirror, she decided that despite her height and curves, she looked almost fragile. She patted a stray wisp of hair into position, and much comforted by the thought, went downstairs to wait for Gerard.

He came just before dinner, gave her a brief greeting and went on: 'Well, we've saved the legs and I've done what I could with the pelvis—he's in a double hip spica.' He poured their drinks and handed her hers, at the same time looking her over with what she could only describe to herself as a professional eye. 'Schipper told me that you were none the worse—you've recovered very well. Thank heaven you were with me!'

'Yes,' she spoke lightly without looking at him. 'There's nothing like beef and brawn...'

His eyes strayed over her, slowly this time and to her satisfaction, not in the least professionally. 'Did I say that? I must have been mad! Anyone less like beef and brawn I have yet to see—you look charming.'

Deborah thanked him in a level voice while her heart bounced happily. When he asked to see her hands she came and stood before him, holding them out. There were some scratches and the bruises on her knuckles were beginning to show, and the nails made her shudder. He put his drink down and stood up and surprised her very much by picking up first one hand and then the other and kissing them, and then, as if that wasn't enough, he bent his head and kissed her cheek too.

CHAPTER SEVEN

DEBORAH HAD GONE to sleep that night in a state of mind very far removed from her usual matter-of-factness. She wakened after hours of dreaming, shreds and tatters with no beginning and no end and went downstairs with the remnants of those same dreams still in her eyes. Nothing could have brought her down to earth more quickly than Gerard's brief good morning before he plunged into a list of things he begged her, if she had time, to do for him during the day—small errands which she knew quite well he would have no time to see to for himself, but it made her feel like a secretary, and from his businesslike manner he must think of her as that, or was he letting her know that his behaviour on the previous evening was a momentary weakness, not to be taken as a precedent for the future?

She went round to see her mother-in-law in the afternoon. The morning had been nicely filled with Gerard's commissions and a lesson with the professor, and now, burdened with her homework, she made her way to Mevrouw van Doorninck's flat, walking briskly because the weather, although fine, was decidedly chilly. She paused to look at one or two shops as she went; the two-piece she had worn the day before was a write-off; the earth had been ground into its fine fabric and when she had shown it to Marijke that good soul had given her opinion, with the aid of Wim, that no dry-cleaner would touch it. She would have to buy another outfit to replace it, Deborah decided, and rang the bell.

Mevrouw van Doorninck was pleased to see her. They got on very well, for the older woman had accepted her as a member of the family although she had never invited Deborah's confidence. She was urged to sit down now and tell all that had happened on the previous day.

'I didn't know you knew about it,' observed Deborah as she accepted a cup of tea.

'Gerard telephoned me in the evening—he was so proud of you.'

Deborah managed to laugh. 'Was he? I only know that he thanked heaven that I was a strong young woman and not a—a delicate feminine creature.'

She turned her head away as she spoke; it was amazing how that still hurt. Her mother-in-law's reply was vigorous. 'You may not be delicate, my dear, but you are certainly very feminine. I can't imagine Gerard falling in love with any other type of woman.'

Deborah drank some tea. 'What about Sasja?' she asked boldly. 'Gerard told me a little about her, but what was she really like—he said that she was very pretty.'

'Very pretty—like a doll, she was also a heartless and immoral young woman and wildly extravagant. She made life for Gerard quite unbearable. And don't think, my dear,' she went on dryly, 'that I tried to interfere or influence Gerard in any way, although I longed to do so. I had to stand aside and watch Gerard make the terrible mistake of marrying her. Infatuation is far worse than love, Deborah, it blinds one to reality; it destroys...fortunately he had his work.' She sighed. 'It is a pity that work has become such a habit with him that he hardly knows how to enjoy life any more.' She looked at Deborah, who stared back with no expression at all. 'You have found that, perhaps?'

'I know he's very busy getting everything just as he wants it at the Grotehof—I daresay when he is satisfied he'll have more time to spare.'

'Yes, dear.' Mevrouw van Doorninck's voice had that same dryness again, and Deborah wondered uneasily if she had guessed about Gerard and herself. It would be unlikely, for he always behaved beautifully towards her when there were guests or family present—he always behaved beautifully, she amended, even when they were alone. Her mother-in-law nodded. 'I'm sure you are right, my dear. Tell me, who is coming to the dinner party tomorrow evening?'

Deborah recited the names. She had met most of the guests already, there were one or two, visiting specialists, whose acquaintance she had yet to make; one of them would be spending the night. She told her mother-in-law what she intended wearing and got up to go. When she bent to kiss the older lady's cheek she was surprised at the warmth of the kiss she received in return and still more surprised when she said: 'If ever you need help or advice, Deborah, and once or twice I have thought…no matter. If you do, come to me and I will try and help you.'

Deborah stammered her thanks and beat a hasty retreat, wondering just what Gerard's mother had meant.

She dressed early for the dinner party because she wanted to go downstairs and make sure that the table was just so, the flowers as they should be and the lamps lighted. It was to be rather a grand occasion this time because the Medical Director of the hospital was coming as well as the *Burgemeester* of the city, who, she was given to understand, was a very important person indeed. She was wearing a new dress for the occasion, a soft lavender chiffon with long full sleeves, tight cuffed with a plunging neckline discreetly veiled by pleated frills. There was a frill round the hem of the skirt too and a swathed belt which made the most of her waist. She had added the pearls and the earrings and hoped that she looked just as a successful consultant's wife should look.

'Neat but not gaudy,' she told herself aloud, inspecting her person in the big mirror on the landing, not because she hadn't seen it already in her room where there were mirrors enough, but because this particular mirror, with its elaborate gilded frame somehow enhanced her appearance.

'That's a decidedly misleading statement.' Gerard's voice came from the head of the stairs and she whirled round in a cloud of chiffon to face him.

'You're early, how nice! Everything's ready for you—I'm going down to see about the table.'

'This first.' He held out a large old-fashioned plush casket. 'You told me the colour of your dress and it seemed to me that Great-aunt Emmiline's garnets might be just the thing to go with it.'

Deborah sat down on the top tread of the staircase, her skirts billowing around her, and opened the box. Great-aunt Emmiline must have liked garnets very much; there were rings and brooches and two heavy gold bracelets set with large stones, earrings and a thick gold necklace with garnets set in it.

'They're lovely—may I really borrow them? I'll take great care…'

He had come to sit beside her. 'They're yours, Deborah. I've just given them to you. I imagine you can't wear the whole lot at once, but there must be something there you like?'

'Oh, yes—yes. Thank you, Gerard, you give me so much.' She smiled at him shyly and picked out one of the bracelets and fastened it round a wrist. It looked just right; she added the necklace, putting the precious pearls in her lap. She wasn't going to take off her engagement ring; she added two of the simpler rings to the other hand and found a pair of drop earrings. She added her pearl earrings to the necklace in her lap and hooked in the garnets instead and went to look in the mirror. Gerard was right, they were exactly right with the dress. 'Have I got too much on?' she asked anxiously.

'No—just right, I should say. That's a pretty dress. What happened to the one you spoilt?'

'It's ruined. I showed it to Marijke—the stain has gone right through.'

'I'm sorry. Buy yourself another one. I'll pay for it.'

Deborah was standing with the casket clasped to her breast. 'Oh, there's no need, I've got heaps of money from my allowance.'

'Nevertheless you will allow me to pay for another dress,' he insisted blandly.

'Well—all right, thank you. I'll just put these away.'

When she came out of her room he had gone. There was nothing to do downstairs, she had seen to everything during the day and she knew that Marijke and Wim needed no prompting from her. She went and sat by the log fire Wim had lighted in the drawing room and Smith, moving with a kind of slow-motion stealth, insinuated himself on to her silken lap. But he got down again as Gerard joined them, pattering across the room when his master went to fetch the drinks and then pattering back again to arrange himself on Gerard's shoes once he had sat down. A cosy family group, thought Deborah, eyeing Gerard covertly. He looked super in a black tie—he was a man who would never lose his good looks, even when he was old. She had seen photos of his father, who in his mid-seventies had been quite something—just like his son, sitting there, stroking Smith with the toe of his shoe and talking about nothing in particular. It was a relief when the doorbell signalled the arrival of the first of their guests, because she had discovered all at once that she could not bear to sit there looking at him and loving him so much.

The evening was a success, as it could hardly have failed to have been, for Deborah had planned it carefully; the food was delicious and the guests knew and liked each other. She had felt a little flustered when the *Burgemeester* had arrived, an imposing, youngish man with a small, plump wife with no looks to speak of but with a delightful smile and a charming voice. She greeted Deborah kindly, wished her happiness upon her recent marriage and in her rather schoolgirl English wanted to know if she spoke any Dutch. It was a chance to pay tribute to the professor's teaching; Deborah made a few halting remarks, shocking as to grammar but faultless as to accent. There was a good deal of kindly laughter and when the *Burgemeester* boomed: 'Your Dutch is a delight to my ear, dear lady,' her evening was made.

She had had no time to do more than say hullo to

Coenraad and Adelaide, but after dinner, with the company sitting around the drawing room, the two girls managed to get ten minutes together.

'Very nice,' said Adelaide at once, 'I can see that you're going to be a wonderful wife for Gerard—it's a great drawback to a successful man if he hasn't got a wife to see to the social side. When I first married I thought it all rather a waste of time, but I was wrong. They talk shop—oh, very discreetly, but they do—and arrange visits to seminars and who shall play host when so-and-so comes, and they ask each other's advice... I like your dress, and the garnets are just the thing for it—another van Doorninck heirloom, I expect? I've got some too, only I have to be careful—my hair, you know.' She grinned engagingly. 'Did you go to Friesland?'

Deborah nodded. 'Yes, I loved the house, we had lunch there and then we went to see Dominic and Abigail. It's lovely there by the lake.'

'And what's all this about an accident? The hospital was positively humming with it. Coenraad told me about it, but you know what men are.'

They spent five minutes more together before Deborah, with a promise to telephone Adelaide in a few days, moved across the room to engage her mother-in-law in conversation.

It was after everyone had gone, and Doctor de Joufferie, their guest for the night, had retired to his room, that Gerard, on his way to let Smith out into the garden, told her that Claude was back in Amsterdam after a visit to Nice. 'I hear he's sold his house here and intends to live in France permanently.'

'Oh.' She paused uncertainly on her way to bed. 'He won't come here?'

'Most unlikely—if he does, would you mind?'

Deborah shook her head. 'Not in the least,' she assured her husband stoutly, minding very much.

Her answer was what he had expected, for he remarked casually. 'No, you're far too sensible for that and I have no doubt that you would deal with him should he have the temerity to call.' He turned away. 'That's a pretty dress,' he told her for the second time that evening.

She thanked him nicely, wishing that he had thought her pretty enough to remark upon that too; apparently he was satisfied enough that she was sensible.

She ruminated so deeply upon this unsatisfactory state of affairs that she hardly heard his thanks for the success of the evening, but she heard him out, murmured something inaudible about being tired, and went to bed.

Doctor de Joufferie joined them for breakfast in the morning, speaking an English almost as perfect as Gerard's. The two men spent most of the time discussing the possibility of Gerard going to Paris for some conference or other: 'And I hope very much that you will accompany your husband,' their visitor interrupted himself to say. 'My wife would be delighted to show you a little of Paris while we are at the various sessions.'

Deborah gave him a vague, gracious answer; she didn't want to hurt the doctor's feelings, but on the other hand she wasn't sure whether Gerard would want her to go with him; he had never suggested, even remotely, such a possibility. She led the conversation carefully back to the safe ground of Paris and its delights, at the same time glancing at her husband to see how he was reacting. He wasn't, his expression was politely attentive and nothing more, but then it nearly always was; even if he had no wish to take her, he would never dream of saying so.

The two men left together and she accompanied them to the door, to be pleasantly surprised at the admiration in the Frenchman's eyes as he kissed her hand with the hope that they might meet again soon. She glowed pleasantly under his look, but the glow was damped immediately by Gerard's brief, cool kiss which just brushed her cheek.

She spent an hour or so pottering round the house, getting in Wim's way, and then went to sit with her Dutch lesson, but she was in no mood to learn. She flung the books pettishly from her and went out. Gerard had told her to buy a new dress—all right, so she would, and take good care not to look too closely at the price tag. She walked along the Keizersgracht until she came to that emporium of high fashion, Metz, and once inside, buoyed up by strong feelings which she didn't bother to define, she went straight to the couture department. She had in mind another tweed outfit, or perhaps one of the thicker jersey suits. She examined one or two, a little shocked at their prices, although even after so short a time married to Gerard, she found that her shock was lessening.

It was while she was prowling through the thickly carpeted alcove which held the cream of the Autumn collection that she saw the dress—a Gina Fratini model for the evening—white silk, high-necked and long-sleeved, pin-tucked and gathered and edged with antique lace. Deborah examined it more closely;

it wouldn't be her size, of course, and even if it were, when would she wear it, and what astronomical price would it be? She circled round it once more; it would do very well for the big ball Gerard had casually mentioned would take place at the hospital before Christmas, and what about the *Burgemeester's* reception? But the size? The saleswoman, who had been hovering discreetly, pounced delicately. She even remembered Deborah's name, so that she felt like an old and valued customer, and what was more, her English was good.

'A lovely gown, Mevrouw van Doorninck,' she said persuasively, 'and so right for you, and I fancy it is your size.' She had it over her arm now, yards and yards of soft silk. 'Would you care to try it on?'

'Well,' said Deborah weakly, 'I really came in for something in tweed or jersey.' She caught the woman's eye and smiled. 'Yes, I'll try it on.'

It was a perfect fit and utterly lovely. She didn't need the saleswoman's flattering remarks to know it. The dress did something for her, although she wasn't sure what. She said quickly, before she should change her mind: 'I'll take it—will you charge it to my husband, please?'

It was when she was dressed again, watching it being lovingly packed, that she asked the price. She had expected it to be expensive, but the figure the saleswoman mentioned so casually almost took her breath. Deborah waited for a feeling of guilt to creep over her, and felt nothing; Gerard had insisted on paying for a dress, hadn't he? Declining an offer to have it delivered, she carried her precious box home.

She would have tried it on then and there, but Wim met her in the hall with the news that Marijke had a delicious soufflé only waiting to be eaten within a few minutes. But eating lunch by herself was something quickly done with, so she flew upstairs to her room and unpacked the dress. It looked even more super than it had done in the shop. She put it on and went to turn and twist before the great mirror—she had put on the pearls and the earrings and a pair of satin slippers; excepting for the faint untidiness of the heavy chignon, she looked ready for a ball.

'Cinderella, and more beautiful than ever,' said Claude from the stairs.

Deborah turned round slowly, not quite believing that he was there, but he was, smiling and debonair, for all the world as though Gerard had never told him not to enter the house again.

'What are you doing here?' she asked, and tried to keep the angry shake from her voice.

'Why, come to pay you a farewell visit. I'm leaving this city, thank heaven, surely you've heard that? But I couldn't go until I had said goodbye to you, but don't worry, I telephoned the hospital and they told me that Gerard was busy, so I knew that it was safe to come, and very glad I am that I did. A ball so early in the day? Or is the boyfriend coming?'

Her hand itched to slap his smiling face. 'How silly you are,' she remarked scathingly. 'And you have no right to walk into the house as though it were your own. Why didn't you ring the bell?'

'Ah, I came in through the little door in the garden. You forget, my lovely Deborah, that I have known this house since many years; many a time I've used that door.' He was lounging against the wall, laughing at her, so that her carefully held patience deserted her.

'Well, you can go, and out of the front door this time. I've nothing to say to you, and I'm sure Gerard would be furious if he knew that you had come here.'

He snapped his fingers airily. 'My dear good girl, let us be honest, you have no idea whether Gerard would be annoyed or not; you have no idea about anything he does or thinks or plans, have you? I don't suppose he tells you anything. Shall I tell you what I think? Why, that you're a figurehead to adorn his table, a hostess for his guests and a competent housekeeper to look after his home while he's away—and where does he go, I wonder? Have you ever wondered? Hours in the Grotehof—little trips to Paris, Brussels, Vienna, operating here, lecturing there while you sit at home thinking what thoughts?'

He stopped speaking and stared at her pinched face. 'I'm right, aren't I? I have hit the nail on its English head, have I not? Poor beautiful Deborah.' He laughed softly and came closer. 'Leave him, my lovely, and come to Nice with me—why not? We could have a good time together.'

She wasn't prepared for his sudden swoop; she was a strong girl, but he had hold of her tightly, and besides, at the back of her stunned mind was the thought that if she struggled too much her beautiful dress would be ruined. She turned her face away as he bent to kiss her and brought up a hand to box him soundly on the ear. But he laughed the more as she strained away from him, her head drawn back. So that she didn't see or hear Gerard coming up the stairs, although Claude did. She felt his hold tighten as he spoke.

'Gerard—hullo, *jongen*, I knew you wouldn't mind

me calling in to say goodbye to Deborah, and bless her heart, she wouldn't let me go without one last kiss.'

She felt him plucked from her, heard, as in a dream, his apology, no doubt induced by the painful grip Gerard had upon him, and watched in a detached way as he was marched down the stairs across the hall to disappear in the direction of the front door, which presently shut with some force. Gerard wasn't even breathing rapidly when he rejoined her, only his eyes blazed in his set face.

'You knew he was coming?' His tone was conversational but icy.

'Of course not.' She was furious to find that she was trembling.

'How did he get in? Doesn't Wim open the door?'

'Of course he does—when the bell rings. He—he came in through the door in the garden. I had no idea that he was in the house until he spoke to me here.' She essayed a smile which wavered a little. 'I'm glad you came home.'

'Yes?' His eyebrows rose in faint mockery. 'You didn't appear to be resisting Claude with any great show of determination.'

She fired up at that. 'He took me by surprise. I slapped his cheek.'

'Did you call Wim?'

Deborah shook her head. Truth to tell, it hadn't entered her head.

Her husband stared at her thoughtfully. 'A great strapping girl like you,' he commented nastily. 'No kicking? No struggling?'

She hated him, mostly because he had called her a strapping girl. She wanted to cry too, but the tears were in a hard knot in her chest. She said sullenly: 'I was try-ing on this dress—it's new...' He laughed then and she said desperately: 'You don't believe me, do you? You actually think that I would encourage him.' Her voice rose with the strength of her feelings. 'Well, if that's what you want to believe, you may do so!'

She swept to her bedroom door and remembered something as she reached it. 'I bought this dress because you told me to and I've charged it to you—it's a model and it cost over a thousand gulden, and I'm glad!' She stamped her foot. 'I wish it had cost twice as much!'

She banged the door behind her and locked it, which was a silly action anyway, for when had he ever tried the door handle?

She took the dress off carefully and hung it away and put on a sober grey dress, then combed her hair and put on too much lipstick and went downstairs. She was crossing the hall when Gerard opened his study door and invited her to join him in a quiet voice which she felt would be wiser to obey. She went past him with her head in the air and didn't sit down when he asked her to.

'I came home to pack a bag,' he told her mildly, all trace of ill-humour vanished. 'There is an urgent case I have to see in Geneva and probably operate on. I intend to catch the five o'clock flight and I daresay I shall be away for two days. I'm sorry to spring it on you like this, but there's nothing important for a few days, is there?'

'Nothing.' Wild horses wouldn't have dragged from her the information that it was her birthday in two days' time. She had never mentioned it to him and he had never tried to find out.

He nodded. 'Good—' he broke off as Wim came

in with a sheaf of flowers which he gave to Deborah. 'Just delivered, Mevrouw,' he told her happily, and went away, leaving a heavy silence behind him.

Deborah started to open the envelope pinned to its elaborate wrapping and then stopped; supposing it was from Claude? It was the sort of diabolical joke he would dream up...

She looked up and found Gerard watching her with a speculative eye and picked up the flowers and walked to the door. 'I'll pack you a case,' she told him. 'Will you want a black tie, or is it to be strictly work?'

His eyes narrowed. 'Oh, strictly work,' he assured her in a silky voice, 'and even if it weren't, a black tie isn't always essential in order to—er—enjoy yourself.'

He gave her a look of such mockery that she winced under it; it was almost as if Claude's poisoned remarks held a grain of truth.

Outside she tore open the little envelope and read the card; the flowers were from Doctor de Joufferie. She suppressed her strong desire to run straight back to Gerard and show it to him, and went to pack his bag instead.

It was quiet in the house after he had gone. Deborah spent the long evening working at her Dutch, playing with Smith and leafing through magazines, and went to bed at last with a bad headache. She had expected Gerard to telephone, but he didn't, which made the headache worse. There was no call in the morning either; she hung around until lunchtime and then went out with Smith trotting beside her on his lead. She walked for a long time, and it was on her way back, close to the house, that she stopped to pick up a very small child who had fallen over, the last in a line of equally small uniformed children, walking ahead of her. She had seen them before, and supposed that they went to some nursery school or other in one of the narrow streets leading from the Keizersgracht. She comforted the little girl, mopped up a grazed knee and carried her towards the straggling line of her companions. She had almost reached it when a nun darted back towards them, breaking into voluble Dutch as she did so.

Deborah stood still. 'So sorry,' she managed, 'my Dutch is bad.'

The nun smiled. 'Then I will speak my bad English to you. Thank you for helping the little one—there are so many of them and my companion has gone on to the Weeshuis with a message.'

Deborah glanced across the road to where an old building stood under the shadow of the great Catholic church. 'Oh,' she said, and remembered that a Weeshuis was an orphanage. 'They're little orphans.'

The nun smiled again. 'Yes. We have many of them. The older ones go to school, but these are still too small. We go now to play and sing a little after their walk. Once we had a lady who came each week and told them stories and played games with them. They liked that.' She held out her arms for the child and said: 'I thank you again, Mevrouw,' and walked rapidly away to where the obedient line of children waited. Deborah watched them disappear inside the orphanage before she went home.

It was after her lonely tea that she had an idea. Without pausing to change her mind, she left the house and went back to the orphanage and rang the bell, and when an old nun came to peer at her through the grille, she asked to see the Mother Superior. Half an hour later she was back home again after an interview with that rather surprised lady; she might go once a week and play with the children until such time as a permanent helper could be found. She had pointed out hesitantly that she wasn't a Catholic herself, but the Mother Superior didn't seem to mind. Thursday evenings, she had suggested, and any time Deborah found the little orphans too much for her, she had only to say so.

The morning post brought a number of cards and parcels for her. She read them while she ate her breakfast and was just getting up from the table when Wim came in with a great bouquet of flowers and a gaily tied box.

'Mijnheer told me to give you these, Mevrouw,' he informed her in a fatherly fashion, 'and Marijke and I wish you a very happy birthday.' He produced a small parcel with the air of a magician and she opened it at once. Handkerchiefs, dainty, lace-trimmed ones. She thanked him nicely, promised that she would go to the kitchen within a few minutes so that she could thank Marijke, and was left to examine her flowers. They were exquisite; roses and carnations and sweet peas and lilies, out of season and delicate and fragrant. She sniffed at them with pleasure and read the card which accompanied them. It bore the austere message: With best wishes, G. So he had known all the time! She opened the box slowly; it contained a set of dressing table silver, elegantly plain with her initials on each piece surmounted by the family crest. There was another card too, less austere than its fellow. This one said: 'To Deborah, wishing you a happy birthday.'

She went upstairs and arranged the silver on her dressing table, and stood admiring it until she remembered that she had to see Marijke. She spent a long time arranging the flowers so that she was a little late for her lesson and Professor de Wit was a little put out, but she

had learnt her lesson well, which mollified him sufficiently for him to offer her a cup of coffee when they
had finished wrestling with the Dutch verbs for the day.
She went back home presently to push the food around
her plate and then go upstairs to her room. Her mother-
in-law was in Hilversum, she could hardly telephone
Adelaide and tell her that it was her birthday and she
was utterly miserable. Thank heaven it was Thursday; at
least she had her visit to the orphans to look forward to.

There was still no word from Gerard. Deborah told
Wim that she was going for a walk and would be back
for dinner at half past seven as usual, and set out. The
evenings were chilly now and the streets were crowded
with people on their way home or going out to enjoy
themselves, but the narrow street where the orphanage
was was quiet as she rang the bell.

The orphans assembled for their weekly junketings
in a large, empty room overlooking the street, reached
through a long narrow passage and a flight of steps, and
one of the dreariest rooms Deborah had ever seen, but
there was a piano and plenty of room for twenty-eight
small children. It was when she had thrown off her coat
and turned to survey them that she remembered that her
Dutch was, to say the least, very indifferent. But she
had reckoned without the children; within five minutes
they had discovered the delights of 'Hunt the Slipper'
and were screaming their heads off.

At the end of the hour they had mastered Grandmother's Steps too as well as Twos and Threes, and for
the last ten minutes or so, in order that they might calm
down a little, she began to tell them a story, mostly in
English of course, with a few Dutch words thrown in
here and there and a great deal of mime. It seemed to

go down very well, as did the toffees Deborah produced just before the nun came to fetch them away to their supper and bed. An hour had never gone so quickly. She kissed them good night, one by one, and when they had gone the empty room seemed emptier and drearier than ever. She tidied it up quickly and went home.

Indoors, it was to hear from Wim that Gerard had telephoned, but only to leave a message that he would be home the following evening. Deborah thanked him and went to eat her dinner, choking it down as best she could because Marijke had thought up a splendid one for her birthday. Afterwards, with Smith on her lap, she watched TV. It was a film she had already seen several times in England, but she watched it to its end before going to bed.

Gerard came home late the following afternoon. Deborah had spent the day wondering how to greet him. As though nothing had happened? With an apology? She ruled this one out, for she had nothing to apologise for—with a dignified statement pointing out how unfair he had been? She was still rehearsing a variety of opening speeches when she heard his key in the door.

There was no need for her to make a speech of any kind; it riled her to find that his manner was exactly as it always was, quiet, pleasant—he was even smiling. Taken aback, Deborah replied to his cheerful hullo with a rather uncertain one followed by the hope that he had had a good trip and that everything had been successful. And would he like something to eat?

He declined her offer on his way to the door. 'I've some telephoning to do,' he told her. 'The post is in the study, I suppose?'

She said that yes, it was and as he reached the door,

said in a rush: 'Thank you for the lovely flowers and your present—it's quite super—I didn't know that you knew...'

'Our marriage certificate,' he pointed out briefly. 'I'm sorry I was not here to celebrate it in the usual Dutch manner—another year, perhaps.'

'No, well—it didn't matter. It's a marvellous present.'

Gerard was almost through the door. He paused long enough to remark:

'I'm glad you like it. It seemed to me to be a suitable gift.' He didn't look at her and his voice sounded cold. He closed the door very quietly behind him.

Deborah threw a cushion at it. 'I hate him,' she raged, 'hate him! He's pompous and cold and he doesn't care a cent for me, not one cent—a suitable present indeed! And just what was he doing in Geneva?' she demanded of the room at large. She plucked a slightly outraged Smith from the floor and hugged him to her. 'None of that's true,' she assured him fiercely, and opened the door and let him into the hall. She heard him scratching on the study door and after a few moments it was opened for him.

They dined together later, apparently on the best of terms; Deborah told Gerard one or two items which she thought might interest him, but never a word about the orphans. The van Doornincks were Calvinists; several ancestors had been put to death rather nastily by the Spaniards during their occupation of the Netherlands. It was a very long time ago, but the Dutch had long memories for such things. She didn't think that Gerard would approve of her helping, even for an hour, in a convent. Her conscience pricked her a little because she was being disloyal to him; on the other hand, she wasn't a Catholic either, but that hadn't made any difference to her wish to help the children in some small way. She put the matter out of her mind and asked him as casually as possible about his trip to Geneva.

She might have saved her breath, for although he talked about Switzerland and Geneva in particular, not one crumb of information as to his activities while he was there did he offer her. She rose from the table feeling frustrated and ill-tempered and spent the rest of the evening sitting opposite him in the sitting room, doing her embroidery all wrong. Just the same, when she went to bed she said quite humbly: 'I'm really very sorry to have bought such an expensive dress, Gerard—I'll pay you back out of my next quarter's allowance.'

'I offered you a new dress,' he reminded her suavely. 'I don't remember telling you to buy the cheapest one you saw. Shall we say no more about it?'

Upon which unsatisfactory remark she went to bed.

It didn't seem possible that they could go on as before, with no mention of Claude, no coolness between them, no avoiding of each other's company, but it was. Deborah found that life went on exactly as before, with occasional dinner parties, drinks with friends, visits to her mother-in-law and Gerard's family and an occasional quiet evening at home with Gerard—and of course the weekly visit to the orphans.

It was getting colder now, although the autumn had stretched itself almost into winter with its warm days and blue skies. But now the trees by the canal were without leaves and the water looked lifeless; it was surprising what a week or so would do at that time of year, and that particular evening, coming home from the convent, there was an edge of winter in the air.

Deborah found Gerard at home. He was always late on Thursdays and when she walked into the sitting room and found him there she was surprised into saying so.

'I've been out,' she explained a little inadequately. 'It was such a nice evening,' and then could have bitten out her tongue, for there was a nasty wind blowing and the beginnings of a fine, cold rain. She put a guilty hand up to her hair and felt its dampness.

'I'll tell Marijke to serve dinner at once,' she told him, 'and change my dress.'

That had been a silly thing to say too, for the jersey suit she was wearing was decidedly crumpled from the many small hands which had clung to it. But Gerard said nothing and if his hooded eyes noticed anything, they gave nothing away. She joined him again presently and spent the evening waiting for him to ask her where she had been, and when he didn't, went to bed in a fine state of nervous tension.

Several days later he told her that he would be going away again for a day and possibly the night as well.

'Not Geneva?' asked Deborah, too quickly.

He was in the garden, brushing Smith. 'No—Arnhem.'

'But Arnhem is only a short distance away,' she pointed out, 'surely you could come home?'

He raised his eyes to hers. 'If I should come home, it would be after ten o'clock,' he told her suavely. 'That is a certainty, so that you can safely make any plans you wish for the evening.'

She stared at him, puzzled. 'But I haven't any plans—where should I want to go?'

He shrugged. 'Where do you go on Thursday evenings?' he asked blandly, and when she hesitated,

'That was unfair of me—I'm sorry. I only learned of it through overhearing something Wim said. Perhaps you would rather not tell me.'

'No—that is, no,' she answered miserably. 'I don't think so.'

Gerard flashed her a quizzical glance. 'Quid pro quo?' he asked softly.

She flushed and lifted her chin. 'When I married you, you made it very clear what you expected of me. Maybe I've fallen short of—of your expectations, but I have done my best, but I wouldn't stoop to paying you back in your own coin!'

She flounced out of the room before he could speak and went to her room and banged the door. They were going out that evening to dinner with a colleague of Gerard's. She came downstairs at exactly the moment when it was necessary to leave the house, looking quite magnificent in the pink silk jersey dress and the pearls and with such a haughty expression upon her lovely face that Gerard, after the briefest of glances, forbore from speaking. When she peeped at him his face was impassive, but she had the ridiculous feeling that he was laughing at her.

He had left the house when she got down in the morning. She had breakfast, did a few chores around the house and prepared to go out. She was actually at the front door when the telephone rang and when she answered it, it was to hear Sien's voice, a little agitated, asking for Gerard.

'Wim,' called Deborah urgently, and made placating noises to Sien, and when he came: 'It's Sien—I can't understand her very well, but I think there's something wrong.'

Sien had cut her hand, Wim translated, and it was the local doctor's day off and no one near enough to help; the season was over, the houses, and they were only a few, within reach were closed for the winter. She had tied her hand up, but it had bled a great deal. Perhaps she needed stitches? and would Mevrouw forgive her for telephoning, but she wasn't sure what she should do.

'Ask her where the cut is,' commanded Deborah, 'and if it's still bleeding.' And when Wim had told her, gave careful instructions: 'And tell her to sit down and try and keep her arm up, and that I'm on my way now—I'll be with her in less than two hours.'

She was already crossing the hall to Gerard's study where she knew there was a well-stocked cupboard of all she might require. She chose what she needed and went to the front door. 'I don't know how long I shall be, Wim,' she said. 'You'd better keep Smith here. I expect I may have to take Sien to hospital for some stitches and then try and find someone who would stay a day or two with her—she can't be alone.'

'Very good, Mevrouw,' said Wim in his fatherly fashion, 'and I beg you to be careful on the road.'

She smiled at him—he was such an old dear. 'Of course, Wim, I'll be home later.'

'And if the master should come home?'

Deborah didn't look at him. 'He said after ten this evening, or even tomorrow, Wim.'

She drove the Fiat fast and without any hold-ups, for the tourists had gone and the roads were fairly empty; as she slowed to turn into the little lane leading to the house she thought how lovely it looked against the pale sky and the wide country around it, but she didn't waste time looking around her; she parked the car and ran inside.

Sien had done exactly as she had been told. She looked a little pale and the rough bandage was heavily bloodstained, but she greeted Deborah cheerfully and submitted to having the cut examined.

'A stitch or two,' explained Deborah in her thread-bare Dutch, knowing that it would need far more than that, for the cut was deep and long, across the palm.

'Coffee,' she said hearteningly, and made it for both of them, then helped Sien to put on her coat and best hat—for was she not going to hospital to see a doctor, she wanted to know when Deborah brought the wrong one—locked the door and settled her companion in the little car. It wasn't far to Leeuwarden and Sien knew where the hospital was.

She hadn't known that Gerard was known there too. She only had to give her name and admit to being his wife for Sien to be given VIP treatment. She was stitched, given ATS, told when to come again and given another cup of coffee while Deborah had a little talk with the Casualty Officer.

'Can I help you at all?' he wanted to know as he handed her coffee too.

She explained thankfully about Sien being alone. 'If someone could find out if she has a friend or family nearby who would go back with her for a day or two, I could collect them on the way back. If not, I think I should take her back with me to Amsterdam or stay here myself.'

She waited patiently while Sien was questioned. 'There's a niece,' the young doctor told her, 'she lives at Warga, quite close to your house. Your housekeeper says that she will be pleased to stay with her for a few days.'

'You're very kind,' said Deborah gratefully. 'It's a great hindrance not being able to speak the language, you know. My husband will be very grateful when he hears how helpful you have been.'

The young man went a dusky red. 'Your husband is a great surgeon, Mevrouw. We would all wish to be like him.'

She shook hands. 'I expect you will be,' she assured him, and was rewarded by his delighted smile.

Sien's niece was a young edition of her aunt, just as tall and plump and just as sensible. Deborah drove the two of them back to the house, gave instructions that they were to telephone the house at Amsterdam if they were in doubt about anything, asked them if they had money enough, made sure that Sien understood about the pills she was to take if her hand got too painful, wished them goodbye, and got into the Fiat again. It was early afternoon, she would be home for tea.

CHAPTER EIGHT

BUT SHE WASN'T home for tea; it began to rain as she reached the outskirts of the city, picking her careful way through streets which became progressively narrower and busier as she neared the heart of the city. The cobbles glistened in the rain, their surface made treacherous; Deborah had no chance at all when a heavy lorry skidded across the street, sweeping her little car along with it. By some miracle the Fiat stayed upright despite the ominous crunching noises it was making. Indeed, its bonnet was a shapeless mass by the time the lorry came to a precarious halt with Deborah's car inextricably welded to it.

She climbed out at once, white and shaking but quite unhurt except for one or two sharp knocks. The driver of the lorry got out too to engage her immediately in earnest conversation, not one word of which did she understand. Dutch, she had discovered long since, wasn't too bad provided one had the time and the circumstances were favourable. They were, at the moment, very unfavourable. She looked round helplessly, not at all sure what to do—there were a dozen or more people milling about them, all seemingly proffering advice.

'Can't anyone speak English?' she asked her growing audience. Apparently not; there was a short pause before they all burst out again, even more eager to help. It

was a relief when Deborah glimpsed the top of a policeman's cap above the heads, forging its way with steady
authority towards her. Presently he came into full view,
a grizzled man with a harsh face. Her heart sank; awful
visions of spending the night in prison and no one any
the wiser were floating through her bemused brain.
When he spoke to her she asked, without any hope at
all: 'I suppose you don't speak English?'

He smiled and his face wasn't harsh any more. 'A
little,' he admitted. 'I will speak to this man first, Mevrouw.'

The discussion was lengthy with a good deal of ar-
gument. When at length the police officer turned to her
she hastened to tell him:

'It wasn't anyone's fault—the road was slippery—he
skidded, he wasn't driving fast at all.'

The man answered in a laboured English which was
more than adequate. 'He tells me that also, Mevrouw.
You have your papers?'

She managed to open the car's battered door and took
them out of her handbag. He examined her licence and
then looked at her. 'You are wife of Mijnheer Doorninck, *chirurg* at the Grotehof hospital.'

She nodded.

'You are not injured, Mevrouw?'

'I don't think so—I feel a little shaky.' She smiled.
'I was scared stiff!'

'Stiff?' He eyed her anxiously.

'Sorry—I was frightened.'

'I shall take you to the hospital in one moment.' He
was writing in his notebook. 'You will sit in your car,
please.'

Deborah did as she was told and he went back to talk

some more to the lorry driver, who presently got into his cab and drove away.

'It will be arranged that your car'—his eye swept over the poor remnant of it—'will be taken to a garage. Do not concern yourself about it, Mevrouw. Now you will come with me, please.'

'I'm quite all right,' she assured him, and then at his look, followed him obediently to the police car behind the crowd, glad to sit down now, for her legs were suddenly jelly and one arm was aching.

They were close to the hospital. She was whisked there, swept from the car and ushered into the Accident Room where Gerard's name acted like a magic wand; she barely had time to thank the policeman warmly before she was spirited away to be meticulously examined from head to foot. There was nothing wrong, the Casualty Officer decided, save for a few painful bruises on her arm and the nasty shock she had had.

'I will telephone and inform Mijnheer van Doorninck,' he told her, and she stifled a giggle, for Gerard's name had been uttered with such reverence. 'He's not home,' she told him, 'not until late this evening or tomorrow morning—he's in Arnhem. In any case, I'm perfectly all right.'

She should have suspected him when he agreed with her so readily, suggesting that she should drink a cup of tea and have a short rest, then he would come back and pronounce her fit to go home.

She drank the tea gratefully. There was no milk with it, but it was hot and sweet and it pulled her together and calmed her down. She lay back and closed her eyes and wondered what Gerard would say when he got back. She was asleep in five minutes.

She slept for just over an hour and when she wakened Gerard was there, staring down at her, his blue eyes blazing from a white face. She wondered, only half awake, why he looked so furiously angry, and then remembered where she was.

She exclaimed unhappily: 'Oh, dear—were you home after all? But I did tell them not to telephone the house...'

'I was telephoned at Arnhem. How do you feel?'

Deborah ignored that. 'The fools,' she said crossly, 'I told them you were busy, that there was no need to bother you.'

'They quite rightly ignored such a foolish remark. How do you feel?' he repeated.

She swung her legs off the couch to let him see just how normal she was. 'Perfectly all right, thank you—such a fuss about nothing.' She gulped suddenly. 'I'm so sorry, Gerard, I've made you angry, haven't I? You didn't have to give up the case or anything awful like that?'

His grim mouth relaxed into the faintest of smiles. 'No—I had intended returning home this evening, anyway. And I am not angry.'

She eyed him uncertainly. 'You look...' She wasn't sure how he looked; probably he was tired after a long-drawn-out operation. She forced her voice to calm. 'I'm perfectly able to go home now, Gerard, if that's convenient for you.'

He said slowly, studying his hands: 'Is that how you think of me? As someone whose wishes come before everything else? Who doesn't give a damn when his wife is almost killed—a heartless tyrant?'

She was sitting on the side of the couch, conscious

that her hair was an untidy mop halfway down her neck and that she had lost the heel of a shoe and her stockings were laddered. 'You're not a heartless tyrant,' she protested hotly. 'You're not—you're a kind and considerate husband. Can't you see that's why I hate to hinder you in any way? It's the least I can do—I'd rather die…'

She had said too much, she realised that too late.

'Just what do you mean by that?' he asked her sharply.

Deborah opened her mouth, not having any idea what to say and was saved from making matters worse by the entry of the Casualty Officer, eager to know if she felt up to going home and obviously pleased with himself because he had come under the notice of one of the most eminent consultants in the hospital and treated his wife to boot. He was a worthy young man, his thoughts were written clearly on his face, Deborah thanked him cordially and was pleased when Gerard added his own thanks with a warmth to make the young man flush with pleasure. She hadn't realised that Gerard was held in such veneration by the hospital staff; the things she didn't know about him were so many that it was a little frightening—certainly they were seen to the entrance by an imposing number of people.

The BMW was parked right in front of the steps; anyone else, she felt sure would have been ordered to move their car, for no one could get near the entrance, but no one seemed to find anything amiss. Gerard helped her in and she sat back with a sigh. As he drove through the hospital gateway she said apologetically: 'The police said they would take the Fiat away and they'd let you know about it. It—it's a bit battered.'

'It can be scrapped.' His voice was curt. 'I'll get you
a new car.'

That was all he said on the way home and she could
think of nothing suitable to talk about herself. Besides,
her head had begun to ache. Wim and Marijke were
both hovering in the hall when they got in. Gerard said
something to them in Dutch and Marijke came forward,
talking volubly.

'Marijke will help you to bed,' Gerard explained. 'I
suggest that you have something to eat there and then
get a good sleep—you'll feel quite the thing by the
morning.' His searching eyes rested for a brief, professional minute on her face. 'You have a headache, I
daresay, I'll give you something for that presently. Go
up to bed now.'

She would have liked to have disputed his order, but
when she considered it, bed was the one place where
she most wanted to be. She thanked him in a subdued
voice and went upstairs, Marijke in close attendance.

She wasn't hungry, she discovered, when she was
tucked up against her pillows and Marijke had brought
in a tray of soup and chicken. She took a few mouthfuls,
put the tray on the side table and lay back and closed
her eyes, to open them at once as Gerard came in after
the most perfunctory of knocks. He walked over to the
bed, took her pulse, studied the bruises beginning to
show on her arm, and then stood looking down at her
with the expression she imagined he must wear when he
was examining his patients—a kind of reserved kindli-
ness. 'You've not eaten anything,' he observed.

'I'm not very hungry.'

He nodded, shook some pills out of the box he held,
fetched water from the carafe on the table and said:

'Swallow these down—they'll take care of that head-ache and send you to sleep.'

She did as she was bid and lay back again against the pillows.

'Ten minutes?' she wanted to know. 'Pills always seem to take so long to work.'

'Then we might as well talk while we're waiting,' he said easily, and sat down on the end of the bed. 'Tell me, what is all this about Sien? Wim tells me that you went up to Domwier because she had cut her hand.'

'Yes—the doctor wasn't there and it sounded as though it might have needed a stitch or two—she had six, actually. I—I thought you would want me to look after her as you weren't home.'

He took her hand lying on the coverlet and his touch was gentle. 'Yes, of course that was exactly what I should have wanted you to do, Deborah. Was it a bad cut?'

She told him; she told him about their visit to the hospital at Leeuwarden too, adding: 'They knew you quite well there—I didn't know…' There was such a lot she didn't know, she thought wearily. 'I got the doctor there to find out if Sien had any friends or family—I fetched her niece, they seemed quite happy together.' She blinked huge, drowsy eyes. 'I forgot—I said I would telephone and make sure that Sien was all right. Could someone…?'

'I'll see to it. Thank you, my dear. What a competent girl you are, but you always were in theatre and you're just as reliable now.'

She was really very sleepy, but she had to answer that. 'No, I'm not. I bought that terribly expensive dress just to annoy you—and what about Claude? Have you forgotten him? You thought I was quite unreliable with him, didn't you?'

She was aware that her tongue was running away with her, but she seemed unable to help herself. 'Don't you know that I...?' She fell asleep, just in time.

She was perfectly all right in the morning except for a badly discoloured arm. All the same, Marijke brought her breakfast up on a tray with the injunction, given with motherly sternness, to eat it up, and she was closely followed by Gerard, who wished her a placid good morning and cast a quick eye over her. 'I've told Wim,' he said as he was leaving after the briefest of stays, 'that if anyone telephones about the Fiat that he is to refer them to me. And by the way, Sien is quite all right. I telephoned last night and again this morning. She sends her respects.'

Deborah smiled. 'How very old-fashioned that sounds, and how nice! But she's a nice person, isn't she? I can't wait to learn a little of her language so that we can really talk.'

He smiled. 'She would like that. But first your Dutch—it's coming along very nicely, Deborah—your grammar is a little wild, but your accent is impeccable.'

She flushed with pleasure. 'Oh, do you really mean that? Professor de Wit is so loath to praise. I sometimes feel that I'm making no headway at all.' She smiled at him. 'I'm glad you're pleased.'

He opened the door without answering her. 'I shouldn't do too much today,' was all he said as he went.

If he had been there for her to say it to, she would have told him that she didn't do too much anyway because there was nothing for her to do, but that would have sounded ungrateful; he had given her everything she could possibly want—a lovely home, clothes beyond her wildest dreams, a car, an allowance which she secretly felt was far too generous—all these, and none of them worth a cent without his love and interest. She had sometimes wondered idly what the term 'an empty life' had meant. Now she knew, although it wouldn't be empty if he loved her; then everything which they did would be shared—the dinner parties, the concerts, the visits to friends, just as he would share the burden of his work with her. Deborah sighed and got out of bed and went to look out of the window. It was a cold, clear morning. She got dressed and presently telephoned Adelaide van Essen and invited her round for coffee.

It was two days later that Deborah mentioned at breakfast that she had never seen Gerard's consulting rooms and, to her surprise, was invited to visit them that very day.

'I shan't be there,' he explained with his usual courtesy. 'I don't see patients there on a Thursday afternoon—it's my heavy afternoon list at the Grotehof, but go along by all means. Trudi, my secretary, will be there—her English is just about as good as your Dutch, so you should get on very well together.'

He had left soon afterwards, leaving her a prey to a variety of feelings, not the least of which was the sobering one that he had shown no visible regret at not being able to take her himself. Still, it would be something to do.

She went after lunch, in a new tweed suit because the sun was shining, albeit weakly. She was conscious that she looked rather dishy and consoled herself with the thought that at last she was being allowed to see another small, very small, facet of Gerard's life.

The consulting rooms were within walking distance, in a quiet square lined with tall brick houses, almost all of which had brass plates on their doors—a kind of Dutch Harley Street, she gathered, and found Gerard's name quickly enough. His rooms were on the first floor and Deborah was impressed by their unobtrusive luxury; pale grey carpet, solid, comfortable chairs, small tables with flowers, and in one corner a desk where Trudi sat.

Trudi was young and pretty and dressed discreetly in grey to match the carpet. She welcomed Deborah a little nervously in an English as bad as her Dutch and showed her round, leaving Gerard's own room till last. It too was luxurious, deliberately comfortable and relaxing so that the patient might feel at ease. She smiled and nodded as Trudi rattled on, not liking to ask too many questions because, as Gerard's wife, she should already know the answers. They had a cup of tea together presently and because Trudi kept looking anxiously at the clock, Deborah got up to go. Probably the poor girl had a great deal of work to do before she could leave. She was halfway across the sea of carpet when the door opened and Claude came in. She was so surprised that she came to a halt, her mouth open, but even in her surprise she saw that he was taken aback, annoyed too. He cast a lightning glance at Trudi and then back to Deborah. 'Hullo, my beauty,' he said.

She ignored that. 'What are you doing here?' she demanded, 'I'm quite sure that Gerard doesn't know. What do you want?'

He still looked shaken, although he replied airily enough. 'Oh, nothing much. Trudi has something for me, haven't you, darling?'

The girl looked so guilty that Deborah felt sorry for her. 'Yes—yes, I have. It's downstairs, I'll get it.'

She fled through the door leaving Deborah frowning at Claude's now smiling face. 'What are you up to?' she wanted to know.

'I?' he smiled even more widely. 'My dear girl, nothing. Surely I can come and see my friends without you playing the schoolmarm over me?'

'But this is Gerard's office…'

'We do meet in the oddest places, don't we?' He came a step nearer. 'Jealous, by any chance? Gerard would never dream of looking for us here…'

'You underestimate my powers,' said Gerard in a dangerously quiet voice. 'And really, this time, Claude, my patience is exhausted.'

He had been standing in the open doorway. Now he crossed the room without haste, knocked Claude down in a businesslike fashion, picked him up again and frogmarched him out of the room. Deborah, ice-cold with the unexpectedness of it all, listened to the muddle of feet going down the stairs. It sounded as though Claude was having difficulty in keeping his balance. The front door was shut with quiet finality and Gerard came back upstairs. He looked as placid as usual and yet quite murderous.

'Is this why you wanted to visit these rooms?' he asked silkily.

She had never seen him look like that before. 'No, you know that.'

'Why is Trudi not here?'

'Trudi?' She had forgotten the girl, she hadn't the least idea where she had gone. 'She went to fetch something for Claude—he didn't say what it was.'

'She is downstairs, very upset,' he informed her coldly. 'She told me that she hadn't been expecting anyone else—only you.'

Deborah gaped at him. 'She said that? But...' But what, she thought frantically—perhaps what Trudi had said was true, perhaps she hadn't expected Claude. But on the other hand he had told her that he had come to fetch something and that Trudi was an old friend.

'Oh, please, do let me try and explain,' she begged, and met with a decided: 'No, Deborah—there is really no need.'

She stared at him wordlessly. No, she supposed, of course there was no need: his very indifference made that plain enough. It just didn't matter; she didn't matter either. She closed her eyes on the bitter thought, all the more bitter because she had thought, just once or twice lately, that she was beginning to matter just a little to him.

She opened her eyes again and went past him and down the stairs. Trudi was in the hall. Deborah gave her a look empty of all expression and opened the door on to the square. It looked peaceful and quiet under the late afternoon sky, but she didn't notice that; she didn't notice anything.

Once in the house, she raced up to her room and dragged out a case and started to stuff it with clothes. There was money in her purse, enough to get her to England—she couldn't go home, not just yet at any rate, not until she had sorted her thoughts out. She would go to Aunt Mary; her remote house by Hadrian's Wall was exactly the sort of place she wanted—a long, long way from Amsterdam, and Gerard.

She was on her way downstairs with her case when

the front door opened and Gerard came in. He shut it carefully and stood with his back to it.

'I must talk to you, Deborah,' his voice was quiet and compelling. 'There's plenty of time if you're going for the night boat train. I'll drive you to the station—if you still want to go.'

Deborah swept across the hall, taking no notice, but at the door, of course, she was forced to stop; only then did she say: 'I'll get a taxi, thank you—perhaps you will let me pass.'

'No, I won't, my dear. You'll stay and hear what I have to say. Afterwards, if you still wish it, you shall go. But first I must explain.' He took the case from her and set it on the floor and then went back to lean against the door. 'Deborah, I have been very much at fault—I'm not sure what I thought when I saw Claude this afternoon. I only know that I was more angry than I have ever been before in my life, and my anger blinded me. After you had gone Trudi told me the truth—that Claude had come to see her. She is going to Nice with him, but they had planned it otherwise—I was to know nothing about it until I arrived in the morning and found a letter from her on my desk.' He smiled thinly. 'It seems that since Claude could not have my wife, he must make do with my secretary. None of this is an excuse for my treatment of you, Deborah, for which I am both ashamed and sorry. What would you like to do?'

'Go away,' said Deborah, her voice thick with tears she would rather have died than shed. 'I've an aunt—if I could go and stay with her, just for a little while, just to—to…I've not been much of a success—I'd do better to go back to my old job.'

He said urgently: 'No, that's not true. No man could

have had a more loyal and understanding wife. It is I who have failed you and I am only just beginning to see...perhaps we could start again. You really want to go?' He paused and went on briskly: 'Come then, I'll take you to the station.'

If only he would say that he would miss her— She thought of a dozen excuses for staying and came up with the silliest. 'What about your dinner, and Wim—and Sien?'

'I'll see to everything,' he told her comfortably. 'You're sure that you have enough clothes with you?'

Deborah looked at him in despair; he was relieved that she was going. She nodded without speaking, having not the least idea what she had packed and not caring, and followed him out to the car. At the station he bought her ticket, stuffed some money into her handbag and saw her on to the train. She thought her heart would break as it slid silently away from the platform, leaving him standing there.

By the time she reached Aunt Mary's she was tired out and so unhappy that nothing mattered at all any more. She greeted her surprised relation with a story in which fact and fiction were so hopelessly jumbled together that they made no sense at all, and then burst into tears. She felt better after that and Aunt Mary being a sensible woman not given to asking silly questions, she was led to the small bedroom at the back of the little house, told to unpack, given a nourishing meal and ordered with mild authority to go to bed and sleep the clock round. Which she did, to wake to the firm conviction that she had been an utter fool to leave Gerard—perhaps he wouldn't want her back; he'd positively encouraged her to go, hadn't he? Could he be in love with some girl at long last and wish to put an end to their marriage and she not there to stop, if she were able, such nonsense? The idea so terrified her that she jumped out of bed and dressed at a great speed as though that would help in some way, but when she got downstairs and Aunt Mary took one look at her strained face, she said: 'You can't rush things, my dear, nor must you imagine things. Now all you need is patience, for although I'm not clear exactly what the matter is, you can be certain that it will all come right in the end if only you will give it time. Now go for a good long walk and come back with an appetite.'

Aunt Mary was right, of course. After three days of long walks, gentle talk over simple meals and the dreamless sleep her tiredness induced, Deborah began to feel better; she was still dreadfully unhappy, but at least she could be calm about it now. It would have been nice to have given way to tears whenever she thought about Gerard, which was every minute of the day, but that would not do, she could see that without Aunt Mary telling her so. In a day or two she would write a letter to him, asking him—she didn't know what she would ask him; perhaps inspiration would come when she picked up her pen.

The weather changed on the fourth day; layers of low cloud covered the moors, the heather lost its colour, the empty countryside looked almost frightening. There was next to no traffic on the road any more and even the few cottages which could be seen from Aunt Mary's windows had somehow merged themselves into the moorland around them so that they were almost invisible. But none of these things were reasons to miss her walk. She set off after their midday meal, with strict instructions to be back for tea and on no account to go off the road in case the mist should come down.

Sound advice which Deborah forgot momentarily when she saw an old ruined cottage some way from the road. It looked interesting, and without thinking, she tramped across the heather towards it. It was disappointing enough when she reached it, being nothing but an empty shell, but there was a dip beyond it with a small dewpond. She walked on to have a closer look and then wandered on, quite forgetful of her aunt's words. She had gone quite a distance when she saw the mist rolling towards her. She thought at first that it must be low-lying clouds which would sweep away, but it was mist, creeping forward at a great rate, sneaking up on her, thickening with every yard. She had the good sense to turn towards the road before it enveloped her entirely, but by then it was too late to see where she was going.

Shivering a little in its sudden chill, she sat down; probably it would lift very shortly. If she stayed where she was she would be quite safe. It would be easy to get back to the road as soon as she could see her way. It got too cold to sit after a time, so she got to her feet, stamping them and clapping her hands and trying to keep in one spot. And it was growing dark too; a little thread of fear ran through her head—supposing the mist lasted all night? It was lonely country—a few sheep, no houses within shouting distance, and the road she guessed to be a good mile away. She called herself a fool and stamped her feet some more.

It was quite dark and the mist was at its densest when she heard voices. At first she told herself that she was imagining things, but they became louder as they drew closer—children's voices, all talking at once.

'Hullo there!' she shouted, and was greeted by silence. 'Don't be frightened, I'm by myself and lost too. Shall we try and get together?'

This time there was a babble of sound from all around her. 'We're lost too.' The voice was on a level with her waist. 'Miss Smith went to get help, but it got dark and we started to walk. We're holding hands.'

'Who are you, and how many?' asked Deborah. Someone small brushed against her and a cold little hand found her arm. 'Oh, there you are,' it said tearfully. 'We're so glad to find someone—it's so dark. We're a school botany class from St Julian's, only Miss Smith lost the way and when the mist came she thought it would be quicker if she went for help. She told us to stay where we were, but she didn't come back and we got frightened.' The voice ended on a sob and Deborah caught the hand in her own and said hearteningly: 'Well, how lucky we've met—now we're together we've nothing to be afraid of. How many are there of you?'

'Eight—we're still holding hands.'

'How very sensible of you. May I hold hands too, then we can tell each other our names.'

There was a readjustment in the ranks of the little girls; the circle closed in on her. Deborah guessed that they were scared stiff and badly needed her company. 'Who's the eldest of you?' she enquired.

'Doreen—she's eleven.'

'Splendid!' What was so splendid about being eleven? she thought, stifling a giggle. 'I expect the mist will lift presently and we shall be able to walk to the road. It's not far.'

'It's miles,' said a plaintive voice so that Deborah went on cheerfully, 'Not really, and I can find it easily.

My name's Deborah, by the way. How about stamping our feet to keep warm?'

They stamped until they were tired out. Deborah, getting a little desperate, suggested: 'Let's sit down. I know it's a bit damp, but if we keep very close to each other we shall keep warm enough. Let's sing.'

The singing was successful, if a little out of tune. They worked their way through 'This old man, he played one', the School Song, 'Rule Britannia' and a selection of the latest pop tunes. It was while they were getting their breath after these musical efforts that Deborah heard a shout. It was a nice, cheerful sound, a loud hullo in a man's voice, answered immediately by a ragged and very loud chorus of mixed screams and shouts from the little girls.

'Oh, that won't do at all,' said Deborah quickly. 'He'll get confused. We must all shout together at the same time. Everyone call "Here" when I've counted three.'

The voice answered them after a few moments, sometimes tantalisingly close, sometimes at a distance. After what seemed a long time, Deborah saw a faint glow ahead of them. A torch. 'Walk straight ahead,' she yelled, 'you're quite close.'

The glow got brighter, wavering from side to side and going far too slowly. 'Come on,' she shouted, 'you're almost here!'

The faint glow from the torch was deceptive in the mist, for the next thing she knew Gerard was saying from the gloom above her head, 'A fine healthy pair of lungs, dear girl—I've never been so glad to hear your voice, though I'm glad you don't always bellow like that.'

Surprise almost choked her. 'Gerard! Gerard, is it

really you? How marvellous—how could you possibly know...'

'Your Aunt Mary told me that you had gone for a walk and it seemed a good idea to drive along the road to meet you. When the mist got too thick I parked the car, and then it was I heard these brats squealing'—there were muffled giggles to interrupt him here—'and I collected them as I came.'

'You haven't got the botany class from St Julian's too?' she gasped. 'You can't have—I've got them here.'

'Indeed I have—or a part of it. A Miss Smith went for help and left them bunched together, but being the little horrors they are, they wandered off.'

'There aren't any missing?'

'No—we counted heads, as it were. Seven young ladies—very young ladies.'

Deborah had found his arm and was clutching it as though he might disappear at any moment. 'I've got eight of them here. What must we do, Gerard?'

'Why, my dear, stay here until the mist goes again. The car is up on the road, once we can reach it I can get you all back to Twice Brewed in no time at all.' He sounded so matter-of-fact about it that she didn't feel frightened any more. 'Your aunt has got everything organised by now, I imagine. She seemed to be a remarkably resourceful woman.' His hand sought and found hers and gave it a reassuring squeeze. 'In the meantime, I suggest that we all keep together, and don't let any of you young ladies dare to let go of hands. Supposing we sit?'

There was a good deal of giggling and a tremendous amount of shuffling and shoving and pushing before everyone was settled, sitting in a tight circle. Deborah, with Gerard's great bulk beside her, felt quite light-hearted, and the children, although there was a good deal of whining for something to eat, cheered up too, so that for a time at least, there was a buzz of talk, but gradually the shrill voices died down until there was silence and, incredibly, she dozed too, to wake shivering a little with the cold despite the arm around her shoulders. She whispered at once in a meek voice: 'I didn't mean to go to sleep, I'm sorry,' and felt the reassuring pressure of Gerard's hand.

'Not to worry. I think they have all nodded off, but we had better have a roll-call when they wake to be on the safe side.'

'Yes. I wonder what the time is, it's so very dark.'

'Look up,' he urged her, quietly. 'Above our heads.'

By some freak of nature the mist had parted itself, revealing a patch of inky sky, spangled with stars. 'Oh, lovely!' breathed Deborah. 'Only they don't seem real.'

'Of course they're real,' his whisper was bracing. 'It's the mist which isn't real. The stars have been there all the time, and always will be, only sometimes we don't see them—rather like life.' He sighed and she wondered what he meant. 'You see that bright one, the second star from the right?'

She said that yes, she could see it very well.

'That's our star,' he told her surprisingly, and when she repeated uncertainly 'Ours?' he went on: 'Do you not know that for every star in the heavens there is a man and a woman whose destinies are ruled by it? Perhaps they never meet, perhaps they meet too late or too soon, but just once in a while they meet at exactly the right moment and their destinies and their lives become one.'

In the awful, silent dark, anything would sound true; Deborah allowed herself a brief dream in which she indeed shared her destiny with Gerard, dispelled it by telling herself that the mist was making her fanciful, and whispered back: 'How do you know it's our star— it's ridiculous.'

'Of course it's ridiculous,' he agreed affably, and so readily that she actually felt tears of disappointment well into her eyes. 'But it's a thought that helps to pass the time, isn't it? Go to sleep again.'

And such was the calm confidence in his voice that she did as she was told, to waken in the bitter cold of the autumn dawn to an unhappy chorus of little girls wanting their mothers, their breakfasts, and to go home. Deborah was engulfed in them with no ears for anything else until she heard watery giggles coming from Gerard's other side, and his voice, loud and cheerful, declaring that they were all going to jump up and down and every few minutes bellow like mad. 'It's getting light; there will be people about soon.' He sounded quite positive about that. So they jumped and shouted, and although the mist was as thick as it ever was, at least they got warm, and surely any minute now the mist would roll away.

It did no such thing, however. They shouted themselves hoarse, but there was no reply from the grey blanket around them. First one child and then another began to cry, and Deborah, desperately trying to instil a false cheer into her small unhappy companions, could hear Gerard doing the same, with considerably more success so that she found herself wondering where she had got the erroneous idea that he wasn't particularly keen on children. She remembered all at once what he had said about Sasja who hadn't wanted babies—the hurt must have gone deep. It seemed to her vital to talk about it even at so unsuitable a time and she was on the point of doing so when the mist folded itself up and disappeared. It was hard not to laugh; the little girls were still gathered in a tight circle, clutching each other's hands. They were white-faced and puffy-eyed, each dressed in the school uniform of St Julian's—grey topcoats and round grey hats with brims, anchored to their small heads by elastic under their chins. Some of them even had satchels over their shoulders and most of the hats were a little too large and highly unbecoming.

There was an excited shout as they all stood revealed once more and a tendency to break away until Gerard shouted to them to keep together still. 'A fine lot we would look,' he pointed out good-naturedly, 'if the mist comes back and we all get lost again.' He looked round at Deborah and smiled. 'We'll hold hands again, don't you think, and make for the road.'

They were half way there when they saw the search party—the local police, several farmers and the quite distraught Miss Smith who, when they met, burst into tears, while her botany class, with a complete lack of feeling for her distress and puffed up with a great sense of importance, told everyone severally and in chorus just how brave and resourceful they had been. It took a few minutes to sort them into the various cars and start the short journey to St Julian's.

Deborah found herself sitting beside Gerard, with four of the smallest children crammed in the back. She was weary and untidy, but when he suggested he should drop her off at Aunt Mary's as they went past, she refused.

On their way back from the school she began, 'How did...?' and was stopped by a quiet: 'Not now, dear girl, a hot bath and breakfast first.'

So it was only when they had breakfasted and she was sitting drowsily before a roaring fire in Aunt Mary's comfortable sitting room that she tried again. 'How did you know that I was here?'

'I telephoned your mother.'

'Oh—did she ask—that is, did she wonder...'

'If she did, she said nothing. Your mother is a wise woman, Deborah.'

'Why did you come?'

He was lying back, very much at his ease, in a high-backed chair, his eyes half shut. 'I felt I needed a break from work, it seemed a good idea to bring the car over and see if you were ready to come back.' He added: 'Smith is breaking his heart—think about it. Why not go to bed now, and get a few hours' sleep?'

Deborah got up silently. Smith might be breaking his doggy heart, but what about Gerard? There was no sign of even a crack; he was his usual calm, friendly self again, and no more. She went up to her little room and slept for hours, and when she came downstairs Aunt Mary was waiting for her.

'I told you to have patience, Debby,' she remarked with satisfaction. 'Everything will come right without you lifting a finger, mark my words.'

So when Gerard came in from the garden presently, she told him that she was ready to go back with him when he wished. She woke several times in the night and wondered, despite Aunt Mary's certainty, if she had made the right decision.

CHAPTER NINE

IT WAS TWO days before they returned to Amsterdam, two days during which Gerard, who had become firm friends with Aunt Mary, dug the garden, chopped wood and did odd jobs around the house, as well as driving the two ladies into Carlisle to do some shopping.

They left after lunch, to catch the Hull ferry that evening, and Deborah, who had been alternately dreading and longing for an hour or so of Gerard's company, with the vague idea of offering to part with him and the even vaguer hope that he would tell her how much he had missed her, was forced to sit beside him in the car while he sustained a conversation about Aunt Mary, the beauties of the moors, the charm of the small girls they had met and the excellence of his hostess's cooking. Each time Deborah tried to bring the conversation round to themselves he somehow baulked her efforts; in the end, she gave up, and when they reached Hull, what with getting the car on board, arranging to have dinner and their cabins, there wasn't much need to talk. Quite frustrated, she pleaded a headache directly they had finished dinner and retired to her cabin. She joined him for an early breakfast, though, because he had asked her to; he had, he told her, an appointment quite early in the morning at the hospital and didn't wish to waste any time.

He talked pleasantly as they took the road to Amsterdam and Deborah did her best to match his mood, but at the house he didn't come in with her, only unloaded her case and waited until Wim had opened the door before he drove away. She followed Wim inside. Gerard hadn't said when he would be home, nor had he spoken of themselves. She spent a restless day until he came home soon after tea and, as usual, went to his study. But before he could reach the door she was in the hall, a dozen things she wanted to say buzzing in her head. In the end she asked foolishly: 'What about Trudi? Did you get someone to take her place?'

He had halted and stood looking at her with raised eyebrows. 'Oh, yes—a middle-aged married woman, very sober and conscientious. You must go and see her for yourself some day.'

Deborah was left standing in the hall, her mouth open in surprise. Did he suppose her to be jealous of something absurd like that? She mooned back into the sitting room, Smith at her heels. Of course she was jealous; he filled her with rage, he was exasperating and indifferent, but she was still jealous. She would have to cure that, she told herself sternly, if she was to have any peace of mind in the future—the uncertain future, she had to allow, and wondered why Gerard had wanted her back. But if she had hoped to see a change in his manner towards her, she was doomed to disappointment. He was a quiet man by nature, he seemed to her to be even quieter now, and sometimes she caught him staring at her in a thoughtful manner; it was a pity that his habit of drooping the lids over his eyes prevented her from seeing their expression. There was no hint of a return of those few strange moments on the moor; they had been make-believe, she told herself, and took pains to take up the smooth, neat pattern of their life together as though it had never been ruffled out of its perfection.

She visited his family, arranged a dinner party for a medical colleague who was coming from Vienna and bought yet another new dress to wear at it. It was a very pretty dress, fine wool in soft greens and pinks, with a wide skirt. It would go very well with Tante Emmiline's garnets and perhaps, she hoped wistfully, Gerard might notice it. She hung it carefully in her clothes cupboard and went to get ready for the orphans' hour and for a number of muddled but sincere reasons, took almost every penny of her remaining allowance and when she reached the orphanage gate, stuffed the money into the alms box hung upon it, accompanying the action with a hotch-potch of wordless prayers—and later, when one of them was answered, took fresh heart. For Gerard noticed the new dress; indeed, he stood looking at her for so long that she became a little shy under his steady gaze and asked in a brittle little voice: 'Is there something wrong? Don't you like my dress?' She achieved a brittle laugh too. 'A pity, because it's too late to change it now.'

His eyes narrowed and a little smile just touched the corners of his mouth. 'Far too late, Deborah,' he said quietly, 'and I wouldn't change a single...' his voice altered subtly. 'The dress is delightful and you look charming.' He turned away as he spoke and the old-fashioned door bell tinkled through the house. 'Our guests, my dear. Shall we go and meet them?'

The other prayers must have become mislaid on the way, thought Deborah miserably as she got ready for bed later that evening, for when their guests had gone

Gerard had told her that he would be going to Vienna
for a five-day seminar in a day's time. When he had
asked her if she would like him to bring back anything
for her she had replied woodenly that no, there was
nothing, thank you, and made some gratuitous remark
about a few days of peace and quiet and now was her
chance to take the new Fiat and go and see Abigail, who
was still in Friesland.

Gerard had paused before he spoke. 'Why not?' he
agreed affably, and looked up from the letters he was
scanning. 'When is the baby due—several months,
surely.'

'Almost six. I've knitted a few things, I'll take them
with me.'

He nodded and went to open the door for her. 'Good
idea.' He patted her kindly on the shoulder as she passed
him. 'Sleep well, my dear,' and as an afterthought: 'I
had no idea that you could knit.'

The pansy eyes smouldered. 'It's something I do
while you're away or working in your study. I get
through quite an amount.' Her voice was very even
and she added a pleasant: 'Good night, Gerard.'

She didn't see him at breakfast, although he had left
a scribbled note by her plate saying that he would be
home for lunch—not later than one o'clock.

But it was later than that, it was six in the evening.
She had eaten her lunch alone, telling herself that was
what being a surgeon's wife meant; something she had
known about and expected; it happened to all doctors'
wives—the young houseman's bride, the GP's lady, the
consultant's wife, they all had to put up with it and so
would she, only in their cases, a shared love made it
easier. Deborah sighed, and loving him so much, hoped

with all her heart that he, at least, was satisfied with
their marriage. Apparently no more was to be said about
Claude or any of the events connected with him, and
in any case it was too late for recriminations now—besides, she wasn't sure if she had any; living with him,
in the house he loved and which she had come to love
too, was infinitely better than never seeing him again.

She was in the garden playing with Smith when he
joined her. He looked weary and a little grim and she
said at once: 'I've a drink ready for you—come inside,' and then because she couldn't bear to see him
looking like that: 'Must you go tomorrow, Gerard? Is
it important?'

He took the glass from her and smiled in a way which
somehow disturbed her. 'Yes, Deborah, I think it's very
important—I have to be sure of something, you see. It
involves someone else besides myself.'

An icy finger touched her heart and she turned away
from him. 'Oh, well, I'll telephone Abigail.'

'I thought you had already arranged to visit her.'

'No—it had quite slipped my mind,' she improvised
hastily, because the reason she hadn't telephoned was
because she had hoped, right until this last moment, that
he might suggest her going with him, but he wouldn't do
that now. Hadn't he said that there was someone else?
She wondered if he had meant a patient and very much
doubted it. She telephoned Abigail there and then, being
very gay about it.

She wished Gerard a cheerful goodbye after breakfast the next morning and after a fine storm of weeping
in her room afterwards, dressed herself and drove the
car to Friesland where she received a delighted welcome
from Abigail and Dominic. They had come out to meet

her, walking together, not touching, but so wrapped together in happiness so secure and deep that she could almost see it. For a moment she wished she hadn't come, but later, laughing and talking in their comfortable sitting room, it wasn't so bad. Indeed the day went too quickly. Driving back Deborah contemplated the four days left before Gerard should come back. There was, of course, the orphans' hour, but that wasn't until Thursday. She would have to fill the days somehow. She spent the rest of the journey devising a series of jobs which would keep her occupied for the next day or two.

She was a little early when she got to the orphanage on Thursday evening, but although it still wanted five minutes to the hour, the children were already assembled in the long, bare room. At least, thought Deborah, as she took off her coat and prepared for the next hour's boisterous games, the evening would pass quickly, and the next day Gerard would be back. She longed to see him, just as she dreaded his return, wondering what he would have to tell her, or perhaps he would have nothing to say, and that would be even harder to bear.

She turned to the task in hand, greeting the children by name as they milled around her, separating the more belligerent bent on the inevitable fight, picking up and soothing those who, just as inevitably, had fallen down and were now howling their eyes out. Within five minutes, however, she had a rousing game of 'Hunt the Slipper' going—a hot favourite with the orphans because it allowed a good deal of legitimate screaming and running about. This was followed by 'Twos and Threes'. A good deal of discreet cheating went on here; the very small ones, bent on getting there first, were prone to fall on their stomachs and bawl until Deborah raced to pick them up and carry them in triumph to the coveted place in the circle.

There was a pause next, during which she did her best to tidy her hair which had escaped most of its pins and hung most untidily around her shoulders. But it took too long, besides, there was no one to see—the children didn't care and she certainly didn't. 'Grandmother's Steps' was to be the final game of the evening, and Deborah, her face to the wall, listened to the stampede of what the orphans imagined were their creeping little feet and thanked heaven that there was no one below them or close by. She looked over her shoulder, pretending not to see the hasty scramble of the slower children to achieve immobility, and turned to the wall again. Once more, she decided, and then she would declare them all out and bring the game to a satisfactory conclusion.

She counted ten silently and turned round. 'All of you,' she began in her fragmental Dutch which the children understood so well. 'You're out...I saw you move...' Her voice died in her throat and her breath left her; behind the children, half way down the room, stood Gerard.

He came towards her slowly, pausing to pat a small tow-coloured head of hair or lift the more persistent hangers-on out of his way. When he reached her he said with a kind of desperate quietness: 'I thought I should never find you—such a conspiracy of silence...'

Her hand went to cover her open mouth. 'Wim and Marijke, they knew—they discovered. They were sweet about it—don't be angry with them.' She searched his calm face for some sign; his eyes were hooded, there was the faintest smile on his mouth; she had no idea what his true feelings were. She went on earnestly: 'You see, it's a Catholic convent and you—your family are Calvinists.' Her look besought him to understand. 'You—you don't mix very well, do you? Separate schools and hospitals and...'

'Orphanages?' he offered blandly.

She nodded wordlessly and lapsed into thought, to say presently:

'Besides, you're home a day early.'

'Ah.' The lids flew open revealing blue eyes whose gleam made her blink. 'Am I to take it that that is a disappointment to you?'

'Disappointment?' Her voice rose alarmingly. There were small hands tugging at her skirt, hoarse little voices chanting an endless 'Debby' at her, but she hardly noticed them; she had reached the end of her emotional tether.

'Disappointment? Disappointment? This week's been endless—they always are when you go away. I'm sick and tired—I won't go on like this, being a kind of genteel housekeeper and wondering all the time—every minute of every day—where you are and what you're doing and pretending that I don't care...'

She was in full spate, but the rest of it never got said; she was gripped in an embrace which bade fair to crack her ribs, and kissed with a fierceness to put an end to all her doubts.

'How can a man be so blind?' Gerard spoke into her ear and the children's voices faded quite away from her senses. 'The star was there, only I didn't want to see it. I wanted to stay in the mist I had made—the nice safe mist which wouldn't allow anything to interfere with my work, because that was all I thought I had left. And yet I suppose I knew all the time…' He loosed his hold for the fraction of a minute and looked down into her face. 'I love you, my darling girl,' he said, and kissed her again; a pleasant state of affairs which might have gone on for some time if it hadn't been for the insistent pushes, tugs and yells from the orphans—it was story time and they knew their rights.

It was Deborah who broke the spell between them. 'My darling, I have to tell them a story—just until seven o'clock.' She smiled at him, her pansy eyes soft with love; he kissed her once more, a gentle kiss this time, and let her go. 'A fairy story,' she told him. '"Rose Red and Rose White"…'

His mouth twitched into a faint smile. 'In which language, dear heart?' he asked.

'Both, of course—I don't know half the words.' She smiled again. 'Heaven knows what they're thinking of us at this moment!'

'Nor I, though I'm very sure of what I'm thinking about you, but that can wait.'

He pulled up the tattered old music stool so that she could sit on it and the children jostled happily against each other, getting as close as they could.

'Rose Red and Rose White,' began Deborah in a voice lilting with not quite realised happiness, and the children fell silent as she plunged into the story, using a wild mixture of Dutch and English words and a wealth of gestures and mime and never doubting that the children understood every word, which, strangely enough, they did. They sat enrapt, their small mouths open, not fidgeting, and two of them had climbed on to Gerard's knees where he sat on one of the low window seats, listening to his wife's clear voice mangling the Dutch language. She had reached a dramatic point in her narrative when the room shook and trembled under the tones of the great bell from the church across the road.

'Seven o'clock,' said Deborah, very conscious of Gerard's look. 'We'll finish next week,' and added, 'Sweeties!' at the top of her voice, producing at the same time the bag of toffees which signalled the end of play hour.

She was marshalling her small companions into a more or less tidy line when the faint dry tinkle of the front door bell whispered its way along the passage and up the stairs. It was followed almost at once by the Mother Superior, who greeted Deborah warmly, the children with an all-embracing smile, and an extended hand for Gerard, admirably concealing any surprise she might have felt at finding him there.

'The little ones have been good?' she asked Deborah.

'They always are, Mother. Do you want me to come on Friday next week, or is it to be Thursday again?'

The nice elderly face broke into a smile. 'You will have the time?' The pale blue eyes studied Gerard, the hint of a question in their depths.

'I approve of anything my wife does,' he told her at once, 'even though you and I are in—er—opposite camps.'

She answered him gravely, although her eyes were twinkling. 'That is nice to know, Mijnheer van Doorninck. You like children?'

He was looking at Deborah. 'Yes, Mother, although I'm afraid I've not had much to do with them.'

'That will arrange itself,' the old lady assured him, 'when you have children of your own.' She glanced at Deborah, smiling faintly. 'Thank you for your kind help, my child. And now we must go.'

The line of orphans stirred its untidy ranks; they hadn't understood anything of what had been said, and they wanted their supper, but first of all they wanted to be kissed good night by Debby, who always did. A small sigh went through the children as she started at the top of the line, bending over each child and hugging it, until, the last one kissed, they clattered out of the room and down the stairs. Deborah stood in the middle of the room, listening to the sound of their feet getting fainter and fainter until she could hear it no longer. Only then did she turn round.

Gerard was still by the window. He smiled and opened his arms wide and she ran to him, to be swallowed up most comfortably in their gentle embrace.

'My adorable little wife,' he said, and his words were heaven in her ears; she was five foot ten in her stockings and no slim wand of a girl; no one had ever called her little before. Perhaps Gerard, from his vantage point of another four inches, really did find her small. She lifted a glowing face for his face, and presently asked:

'You're not angry about the orphans?'

'No, my love. Indeed, they are splendid practice for you.'

She leaned back in his arms so that she could see his face. 'You're not going to start an orphanage?'

'Hardly that, dear heart—I hope that our children will always have a home.'

'Oh.' She added idiotically: 'There are twenty-eight of them.'

He kissed the top of her head. 'Yes? It seemed like ten times that number. Even so, I would hardly expect…!' She felt his great chest shake with silent laughter. 'A fraction of that number would do very nicely, don't you agree?' And before she could answer: 'Don't you want to know why I have come back early?'

'Yes—though it's enough that you're here.' She leaned up to kiss him.

'Simple. I found myself unable to stay away from you a moment longer. At first, I wanted to keep everything cool and friendly and impersonal between us, and then, over the weeks, I found it harder and harder to leave you, even to let you out of my sight, and yet I wouldn't admit that I loved you, although I knew in my heart—I could have killed Claude.'

'But you let me go away—all the way to Aunt Mary's...'

'My darling, I thought that I had destroyed any chance of making you love me.'

'But I did love you—I've loved you for years...'

He held her very close. 'You gave no sign, Debby—but all the same I had to follow you, and then I found you in the mist with all those little girls in their strange round hats.'

Deborah laughed into his shoulder. 'You showed me our star,' she reminded him.

'It's still there,' he told her. 'We're going to share it for the rest of our lives.'

He turned her round to face the window. 'There—you see?'

The sky was dark, but not as dark as the variegated roofs pointing their gables into it, pointing, all of them, to the stars. The carillon close by played its little tune for the half hour and was echoed a dozen times from various parts of Amsterdam. It was all peaceful and beautiful, but Deborah was no longer looking at it. She had turned in her husband's arms to face him again, studying his face.

'Are we going home?' she asked, and when he had kissed her just once more, she said, 'Our home, darling Gerard.'

'Our home, my love, although for me, home will always be where you are.'

There was only one answer to that. She wreathed her arms round his neck and kissed him.

* * * * *

All Else Confusion

CHAPTER ONE

THE FOTHERGILLS WERE out in force; it wasn't often that
they were all home together at the same time. Annis was
always there, of course, being the eldest and such a help
in running the parish and helping her mother around the
house, and contrary to would-be sympathisers, perfectly
content with her lot. Mary who came next was in her
first year at college and Edward, at seventeen, was in
his last term at the public school whose fees had been
the cause of much sacrifice on his parents part. James
was at the grammar school in a neighbouring town and
Emma and Audrey were still at the local church school.
So they didn't see much of each other, because holidays weren't always exactly the same and they all possessed so many friends that one or other of them was
mostly away visiting one or other of them. But just for
once the half term holiday had fallen on the same days
for all of them, and since the February afternoon was
masquerading as spring, they had all elected to go for
a walk together.

Annis led the way, a tall, well built girl with glorious red hair and a lovely face. She looked a good deal
younger than her twenty-two years and although she
was moderately clever, she had an endearing dreaminess, a generous nature and a complete lack of sophis-
tication. She also, on occasion, made no bones about

speaking her mind if her feelings had been strongly stirred.

Mary, walking with Audrey a few paces behind her, was slighter and smaller in build and just as pretty in a dark way, while little Audrey, still plump and youthfully awkward, had her elder sister's red hair and cornflower blue eyes.

Emma and James were together, quarrelling cheerfully about something or other, and Edward brought up the rear, a dark, serious boy who intended to follow in his father's footsteps.

The church and the Rectory lay at one end of Millbury, the village to which their father had brought his young wife and where they still lived in the early Victorian house which had been considered suitable for the rector in those days, and was still suitable for the Reverend Mr Fothergill, considering the size of his family. Certainly it had a great many rooms, some of them far too large and lofty for comfort, but there was only one bathroom with an old-fashioned bath on clawed feet in its centre, and the hot water system needed a good deal of forbearance, while the kitchen, although cosy and plentifully supplied with cupboards, lacked the amenities considered by most people to be quite necessary nowadays. Mrs Fothergill, a gently placid woman, didn't complain, for the simple reason that it would have been of no use; with six children to bring up, clothe and feed, there had never been enough money to spare on the house. Her one consolation was that since she had married young, there was the strong possibility that all the children would be nicely settled in time for her to turn her attention to refurbishing it.

Reaching the top of the hill behind the village, Annis turned to look down at her home. From a distance its red brick walls, surrounded by the shrubbery no one had the time to do much about, looked pleasant in the watery sunshine, and beyond it the church's squat tower stood out against the Wiltshire Downs stretching away to more wooded country.

She turned her fine eyes on to her brothers and sisters gathered around her. 'There's plenty of wood in the park,' she suggested. 'Matthew told me that they'd cut down several elms along the back drive. Let's get as much as we can—a pity we didn't bring some sacks, but I forgot.'

'Well, with six of us carrying a load each, we ought to manage quite a lot,' offered James. 'I could go back for some sacks, Annis…?'

She shook her head. 'It'll be getting dark in another hour or so—it's not worth it.'

They followed the path running along the edge of the field at the top of the hill and climbed a gate at the end into a narrow lane, and it was another five minutes' walk before they reached the entrance to the back drive to Mellbury Park where Colonel Avery lived. The lodge beside the open gate had fallen into a near ruin and the drive had degenerated into a deeply rutted track, but they all knew their way around and with Annis still leading, started to walk along it. They came upon the cut down trees within a very short time, and just as Annis had said, there was an abundance of wood.

They worked methodically; almost everyone went wooding in the village, and the Fothergills had become experts at knowing what best to take and what best to leave and just how much they could carry. Presently, suitably burdened according to size, they turned for home. The bright afternoon was yielding to a grey dusk; by the time they reached it it would be almost dark. Annis marshalled her little band into a single line with Edward leading the way and herself bringing up the rear. Little Audrey, who was frightened of the dark, was directly in front of her, carrying the few light bits of wood considered sufficient for her strength.

They made a good deal of noise as they went, calling to each other, singing a bit from time to time, laughing a lot. They were almost at the lodge when Annis heard the thud of hooves behind her and stopped to turn the way they had come and shout at the top of her powerful lungs:

'Slow down, Matthew, we're just ahead of you!' And as a young man on a big black horse pulled up within yards: 'Honestly, Matt, you must be out of your mind! You could have bowled the lot of us over like ninepins!'

'No chance of that with you bawling your head off like that—you're in our park anyway!'

'So what? We come here almost every day.' She smiled dazzlingly at him. 'You use our barn for target practice.'

He laughed then, a pleasant-faced young man of about her own age, and shouted greetings to the rest of the Fothergills, scattered along the path ahead of her, then called over his shoulder, 'Jake, come and meet our neighbours!'

The second rider had been waiting quietly, screened by the overgrowth, and Annis hadn't seen him. He was astride a strawberry roan, a big man with powerful shoulders and a handsome arrogant face; it was dusk now and she couldn't be sure of the colour of his eyes or his hair, but of one thing she was instantly sure—she didn't like him, and she didn't like the smile on his face as Matthew introduced him, nor the unhurried study of her person and the still more leisurely survey of the rest of the Fothergills who, seeing that Matthew had someone with him, had come closer to see who it was. Jake Royle, Matthew had called him, a friend of the family who had been in New Zealand on business. 'You must come up and have a drink one evening,' said Matthew, and sidled his horse over to Mary. 'You too, Mary— and Edward, of course.'

'Well, it'll have to be soon,' said Annis briskly. 'Mary is going back at the end of the week, and so is Edward.'

'And you?' queried Jake Royle softly.

She gave him a quick glance. 'Me? I live at home.' He didn't answer, only smiled again, and her dislike deepened. How had Matt got to know him? she wondered; he was much older for a start, at least in his early thirties, and as unlike Matt's usual friends as chalk from cheese. She caught Edward's eye. 'We'd better be on our way; tea's early—it's the Mothers' Union whist drive this evening.'

'Good lord, you don't all play whist, do you?'

'Is there any reason why we shouldn't? Don't be an ass, Matt, you know quite well that only Edward and Mary and I go.' Annis turned to go and then stopped. 'Could you come over when you've got a minute and take a look at Nancy?'

'Yes, of course—we'll come now...'

She said hastily: 'Oh, there's no need for that—besides, you have Mr Royle with you. Tomorrow morning would be better.'

'Well, all right, if you say so.'

She said rather pointedly: 'I'll expect you about ten o'clock if that's OK for you?' She gave him a wide smile, nodded distantly to Jake Royle, and hurried to join the others, already on their way.

'Lifelong friends?' queried Jake Royle as the Fothergills disappeared round a bend in the track.

'Grew up with them,' said Matthew. 'Annis and I are the same age; knew each other in our prams.'

'A striking-looking girl,' observed Mr Royle, 'and interesting...'

An opinion not shared by Annis; on the way back they all discussed Matt's companion. 'He's very good-looking,' said Mary, 'didn't you think so, Annis?'

Annis had been brought up to be honest. 'Yes, if you like that kind of face,' she conceded, 'but I daresay he's the dullest creature, and conceited too.' She added rather unnecessarily: 'I didn't like him.'

'Do you suppose he's married?' asked Emma.

Annis gave the question her considered thought. 'Very likely, I should think. He's not a young man, not like Matt. Whose turn is it to see to Nancy?'

Nancy was an elderly donkey, rescued some years ago from a party of tinkers who were ill-using her. No one knew quite how old she was, but now she lived in retirement, a well fed, well cared for and dearly loved friend to all the family. It was Audrey's turn, and by common consent James went with her to the small paddock behind the house; she was only eight after all, and a small nervous child, and although no one mentioned this fact, her brothers and sisters took good care of her. The rest of them went into the house through the back door, kicking off boots and hanging up coats in the roomy lobby which gave on to the wide stone-flagged passage which ran from front to back of the Rectory. They piled the wood here too, ready for James or Edward to carry out to one of the numerous outbuildings which bordered the yard behind the house. They went next to a cold cupboard of a room used once, long ago, as a pantry, washed their hands at the old stone sink there and tidied their hair at the Woolworth's looking-glass on the wall, only then did they troop along to the front of the house to the sitting room.

Their parents were already there, their father sitting by the fire, his nose buried in a book, their mother at the round table under the window where tea had been laid out. She was still a pretty woman who had never lost her sense of humour or her optimistic belief that one day something wonderful would happen, by which she meant having enough money to do all the things she wanted to do for them all. She looked up as they went in and smiled at them impartially; she loved them all equally, although perhaps little Audrey had the edge of her brothers and sisters, but then she was still only a little girl.

She addressed herself to her eldest child: 'You enjoyed your walk, Annis?'

'Yes, Mother.'

Before she could say anything more Mary chimed in: 'We met Matt—he had someone with him, Jake

Royle, he's staying with the Averys. He's quite old but rather super...'

'Old?' queried her mother.

'About thirty-five,' observed Annis, slicing cake. 'I thought he looked a bit cocky, myself.'

Her father lowered his book. 'And he has every reason to be,' he told her with mild reproof. 'He's a very clever young man—well, I consider him young—he's chairman of several highly successful companies and commercial undertakings, owns a factory in New Zealand, and is much sought after as a financial adviser.'

Annis carried tea to her father. 'Do you know him, Father?'

'Oh, yes, I've met him on several occasions at Colonel Avery's.'

'You never told us,' said Mary.

'You said yourself that he was quite old, my dear.' His voice was dry. 'Far too old for you—perhaps he and Annis might have more in common.'

'Me?' Annis paused with her cup half way to her mouth. 'I don't know a thing about factories or finances—besides, I didn't like him.'

'Well, we're not likely to see him here, dear,' said Mrs Fothergill calmly, hoping that they would. 'Here's Audrey and James, perhaps you'd fill the teapot, dear...'

It was later that evening, after the younger ones had gone to bed and the rest of them were sitting round the comfortably shabby room, that Mrs Fothergill said apropos nothing at all: 'I wonder if Mr Royle is married?'

Neither Edward or James was interested enough to answer and Mary had gone to the kitchen for something. Annis said thoughtfully: 'I should think so; you say he's successful and clever and probably comfortably off. Besides, he's getting on for forty…'

'You said thirty-five, dear,' observed her mother. 'I should imagine that a man who has achieved so much has had little time to look for a suitable wife.' She didn't say any more, and Annis, glancing up from her embroidery, saw that her mother was day-dreaming—marrying off her daughters, or one daughter at least to Jake Royle. He would have given her loads of money, a huge house, several cars and a generous nature not above helping out with the younger children's education. Well, harmless enough, thought Annis fondly, just as long as Mary was to be the bride. Mr Royle, married or unmarried, held no attraction for her at all.

So it was a pity that he rode over with Matt the next morning, blandly ignoring her cold reception, contriving with all the ease in the world to get introduced to her mother, and her father as well, before going off with Matt to look at Nancy. What was more, she was quite unable to refuse Matt's cheerful: 'Come on, old girl— if it's Nancy's hooves we'll need your help.'

So the three of them crossed the cobbled yard to where Nancy lived in a boxed-off corner of the enormous barn. Once the days were longer and it was warmer she would go out in the small field behind this building, sharing it with a neighbouring farmer's two horses and a couple of goats, but today she was standing in her snug shelter very neat and tidy after little Audrey's grooming.

She knew Matt as well as her owners and obediently lifted first one hoof and then the other, munching the carrots Annis had thoughtfully brought with her and responding, much to Annis's surprise, with every sign of pleasure to Jake Royle's gentle scratching of her ears.

'Must like you,' observed Matt, looking up. 'She's a crotchety old lady with strangers. Still got some serviceable teeth, too.'

'Yes, you said she was off her feed.' He slid a large, well manicured hand from an ear to the little beast's lip and lifted it gently. 'Could there be an abscess, I wonder?' He uttered the question in such a friendly, almost meek voice, that Annis, prepared to snub him at every turn, found herself saying: 'I hadn't thought of that—she's always having trouble with her feet and I expected it to be that this time.' She tickled Nancy's other ear. 'Open your mouth, love.'

It took the remaining carrots and the three of them to persuade Nancy to allow them to take a look at her teeth. Annis, with her fiery head almost in Nancy's jaws and quite forgetting that she didn't like Jake Royle, exclaimed: 'You're quite right, how clever of you! It's at the back on the right.' She withdrew her hand. 'I'll get the vet.'

Matt said: 'Oh, hard luck—he's just put up his fees, too.'

'I've got some birthday money left,' said Annis matter-of-factly. She had forgotten that Jake Royle was still there; he had a stillness which made him invisible, a knack of melting into his surroundings. He didn't move now, only stared hard at her. She made a striking picture too, despite the old coat and wellingtons, and her hair in a wavy tangled mass. She tossed it impatiently out of her eyes and invited them into the Rectory for coffee. 'You'll have to have it in the kitchen,' she warned them, 'we're getting the sitting room ready for the Mothers' Union tea-party.'

She gave Nancy a final pat and led them back and through the kitchen door where they kicked off their boots and laid them neatly beside hers. Even in his socks Jake Royle was a very large man indeed.

The kitchen was large, stone-flagged and old-fashioned. There were no built-in cupboards, concealed ironing boards bread bins or vegetable racks and the sink was an enormous one of well scrubbed Victorian stone. But it was a pleasant room, much used by the whole family, its plain wooden table encircled by an assortment of chairs and two down-at-heel armchairs on either side of the elderly Aga, put in by the rector the winter before last in an effort to modernise the place. Both chairs were occupied, a sealpoint Siamese was sitting erect in one of them, the other was occupied by a rather tatty dog with quantities of long hair and a sweeping tail. Neither of them took any notice of the newcomers although Matt said: 'Hullo, Sapphro, hullo Hairy,' as he took his seat at the table.

'Sit down, Jake,' said Mrs Fothergill invitingly. 'You don't mind if I call you that?—Mr Royle's so stiff, isn't it? Coffee's just ready—everyone will be here in a minute.'

Annis had gone to phone the vet and came back with little Audrey, the rest of them following. Only the Rector didn't arrive. 'His sermon,' explained Mrs Fothergill. 'He likes to beat it into shape before lunch.'

She poured coffee into an assortment of mugs and Annis bore one away for her father. She would have liked to have taken hers too, but that might have looked rude and her mother was a great one for manners—besides, being the eldest she had to set a good example to the others.

Over coffee, Jake Royle maintained an easy flow of talk without pushing himself forward; he merely introduced topics of conversation from time to time and then left it to everyone else to talk. And the Fothergills were great talkers; being such a large family they held different opinions about almost everything—besides, it was a way of passing the evenings. There wasn't much to do in the village and Millbury was off the main road which ran between Shaftesbury and Yeovil; too far to walk to the bus, although Annis did a good deal of cycling round the village and the two smaller parishes her father served. There was a car, of course, an essential for her father with such a far-flung flock, but it had seen better days and it was heavy on petrol too. Only the Rector, Annis and Edward drove it, nursing it along the narrow lanes and up and down the steep hills. Mrs Fothergill, a born optimist, went in for every competition which offered a car as prize, but as yet she had had no luck. One day the car was going to conk out and would have to be replaced, but no one dwelt on that. When tackled the Rector was apt to intone 'Sufficient unto the day...' which put a stop to further speculation.

They were talking about cars now, at least the men and three boys were. Anyone would think, thought Annis gloomily, that there was nothing else upon this earth but cars. She listened to the more interesting bits, but in between she allowed her mind to wander. She still didn't like Jake Royle, but she had to admit that he had more than his share of good looks, and the very size of

him made him someone to look at twice. Not that she
had the least interest in him… She picked up the big
enamel coffee pot from its place on the Aga and offered second cups, caught his eye and blushed because
it was only too apparent that he had read her thoughts.

He and Matt went presently and Mrs Fothergill said
a little wistfully: 'What a very nice man. I suppose
he'll be going back to New Zealand soon—such a pity.'

'He doesn't live there,' Edward observed, 'only goes
there once in a while—he had intended going back in a
couple of weeks, but he said that something had come
up to make him change his mind.'

Mrs Fothergill couldn't help taking a quick peep at
her two elder daughters. Mary looked pleased and surprised, Annis's lovely face wore no expression upon it
at all. Nor did she show any elation when later that day
Mrs Avery telephoned to ask them, with the exception
of James, Emma and little Audrey, to go to dinner in
two days' time. Mrs Fothergill and Mary immediately
fell to discussing what they should wear, but when they
tried to draw Annis into the discussion, she proved sin-
gularly uninterested.

'It'll have to be the blue velvet,' she told them. 'I
know I've had it years, but this isn't London and fashion hasn't changed all that much.'

A statement with which Mr Royle couldn't agree.
He dated it unerringly as being five years old and on
the dowdy side, bought with an eye to its being useful rather than becoming. But the dark blue set off the
hair very well, he conceded that, and the dress, however badly cut, couldn't disguise her splendid figure.

She was a young woman who would look magnificent if she were properly dressed.

He greeted her with casual politeness and engaged her mother in conversation, while Matt made his way across the drawing-room to ask her how Nancy did. They became engrossed in the donkey's treatment and exactly what had been done, but presently they were joined by Mrs Avery, and with a hurried promise to come over on the following morning, Matt wandered off to talk to Mary.

The dinner party was small, the Fothergills being augmented by the doctor and his wife and daughter, and since they had all lived in the village for years, they were on the best of terms. Presently they all went across the gloomy raftered hall to the dining room, an equally gloomy room, its walls oak-panelled and the great table ringed by antique and uncomfortable chairs. Colonel Avery never ceased grumbling about them, but since the idea of replacing family heirlooms with something more modern wasn't to be entertained, everyone put up with them in silence.

But even though the room was gloomy, the people in it weren't: the talk became quite animated as they ate their way through chilled melon, roast beef, Yorkshire pudding, roast potatoes and sprouts and rounded off this very English meal with Charlotte Russe. There was Stilton after that, and since Mrs Avery was too old-fashioned to change her ways, the ladies, very animated after the excellent claret the Colonel had given them, left the men round the table and went back to the drawing-room.

Here Mrs Avery, a mouselike woman whose appearance belied her forceful personality, set about arranging her guests to her satisfaction. The doctor's wife and Mrs Fothergill were seated side by side on one of the sofas, Mary and the doctor's daughter were marshalled on to a smaller piece of furniture and Mrs Avery herself engaged Annis in conversation, sitting so that she could see the door when the men came in. For years now she had decided that Annis would make a very good wife for Matt. They had grown up together and liked each other, and Annis would do very nicely as mistress of the Manor House in which the Avery family had lived for a very long time. She lost no time, once she had decided upon this, in throwing them together on every possible occasion. It was a pity that neither Annis nor Matt had any inkling of this, and continued to see each other several times a week without feeling any desire to be more than good friends.

The men joined them quite soon and Mrs Avery signalled with her eyebrows to Matt that he should join them, only to be frustrated by Jake Royle, who somehow contrived to get there first and stayed inextricably with them until she was forced to circulate amongst her other guests.

Which left Annis on the sofa, rather apart from the others, and Jake Royle sitting beside her, half turned towards her so that he could watch her face.

'Was the vet able to do anything for Nancy?' he enquired in such a friendly voice that she found herself replying readily enough. They discussed the donkey at some length, and then, almost imperceptibly, he led the conversation round to her family and eventually to herself. He had discovered quite a lot about her before she realised what was happening and closed her pretty mouth with a suddenness which made him chuckle silently. She shot him a look as fiery as her hair and asked with something of a snap: 'And when do you return to New Zealand, Mr Royle?'

'I'm called Jake,' he reminded her gently, 'and I don't really know when I shall go there again. I live in England, you know.'

'No, I didn't. Do you like New Zealand?'

'Very much. Have you travelled at all, Annis?'

She had to admit that beyond a week in Brittany some years previously, and a long weekend in Brussels with a school friend, she hadn't.

'You would like to travel?' he persisted.

'Well, of course. I should think everyone would, some places more than others, of course.'

'And those places?'

She knitted her strong brows. There was no end to the tiresome man's questions, and why couldn't someone come and take him away? 'Oh, Canada and Norway and Sweden and Malta and the Greek Isles and Madeira.'

He said lightly: 'Let's hope you have the opportunity to visit some or all of them at some time or another.'

'Yes—well, I hope so too. And now, if you'll excuse me, I really must have a word with Colonel Avery about...' She had no idea what; he helped her out with a casual 'Yes, of course—time passes so quickly when one is enjoying a pleasant talk.'

She got up and he got up too, and she edged away, relieved to see that Miriam, Doctor Bennett's daughter, was poised to take her place. From the safety of the other end of the room, she saw the pair of them obviously enjoying each other's company. The sight quite annoyed her.

Half-term finished the next day and Annis was alone once more then with her mother and father and old Mrs Wells who did for them twice a week. She had come to the Rectory, year in, year out, for a long time and her work—doing the rough, she called it—had by tacit consent been honed down to jobs like polishing the brass, sitting comfortably at the kitchen table, or peeling the potatoes for lunch. But no one thought of telling her that she might retire if she wanted to. For one thing she didn't want to; she lived alone in the village and the Rectory supplied an interest in her life; besides, she would have been missed by all the family, who cheerfully cleared up after her, found her specs, gave her cups of tea and took the eyes out of the potatoes when she wasn't looking. She was devoted to all of them and went regularly to church, besides attending all the jumble sales, where she purchased her wardrobe, dirt cheap, three times a year.

She sat at the kitchen table now, mending a great rent in the sheet James had put his feet through, while Annis juggled with the washing machine. It was behaving temperamentally this morning, making a terrible din, oozing water from somewhere underneath, and having long bouts of doing nothing at all. Mrs Fothergill, coming into the kitchen to make the coffee, gave it a harassed look. 'Is it going to break down?' she shouted to Annis above the din.

'Shouldn't think so. I'll give it a rest before I put the next load in.'

Mrs Fothergill nodded. 'Yes, dear. Coffee will be ready in five minutes. We're in the drawing room.'

They almost never used the drawing room; it was a handsome apartment, so large and lofty that it was impossible to keep it really warm. Annis supposed her mother was turning out the sitting room. She made Mrs Wells the pot of strong tea she always fancied mid-morning, emptied the washing machine and went along to the drawing room.

She opened the door and went in, and only then re-alised that there were visitors—Matt, who didn't really count, Mr Royle and a small, elderly lady, almost completely round as to figure and with a pair of black eyes sparkling in a round face.

Matt and Jake Royle got up and Matt said cheerfully: 'Hullo, Annis. You look as though you're doing a hard day's work. We've brought one of my aunts over—it was Jake's idea. She arrived quite late yesterday evening and went to bed, too tired for the dinner party. Aunt Dora, this is Annis—a pity you've missed the others.'

Annis put a hand up to her hair, realised that it was in a hopeless mess anyway, and offered the hand instead to Matt's aunt.

'You could have told me,' she complained mildly to Matt. She smiled at the little lady. 'I would have tidied myself up.'

'You'll do very well as you are. Matt didn't tell you my name. It's Duvant—I'm the Colonel's sister and a widow.' She accepted a cup of coffee from Mrs Fother-gill and patted the sagging sofa she was sitting on. 'Come and sit by me. Your mother's an angel to re-ceive us so kindly, too. You must wish us all to kingdom come, but men never think about getting the housework done or cooking lunch, do they? And somehow I had the impression from Jake that you roamed out of doors a good deal...'

Annis gave Jake a look of dislike, which became thunderous when he smiled at her. How like him; never done a hand's turn in his life probably, and had no idea what it was like to run an unwieldy old house like the Rectory. She said politely: 'I like being out of doors. Do you know this part of the country well, Mrs Duvant?'

'I did in my youth, but things have changed even here. I've been living abroad for some years, but I fancied coming back here again. There is a house in Bath, which belonged to my husband's family. I think I shall go there for a while.' She paused to smile at Annis. 'This coffee's delicious—I think I'll have another cup if I may?' She beamed across at Mrs Fothergill. 'I expect you grind your own beans?' she asked.

The two ladies embarked on an animated discussion and Jake, refusing more coffee, suggested that they might take a look at Nancy. And since Matt agreed at once there was nothing for it but for Annis to get her coat and boots and go with them. 'Though I can't really spare the time,' she told them rather crossly.

'We'll hang out the washing for you,' offered Jake.

'Thank you,' said Annis haughtily, 'but I can manage very well for myself.'

They spent a little time with Nancy, pronounced her very much better and started back across the yard. At the back door Annis paused. 'I expect you'll want to join Mrs Duvant—I'm going back to the kitchen.'

They neither of them took any notice of her but went

along to the kitchen too, collected the old-fashioned basket loaded with damp sheets and towels and bore it off to the washing line at the back of the house. It hadn't been any use protesting; Matt had told her not to be so bossy and Jake Royle had merely smiled. She hadn't liked the smile much, there had been a hint of mockery about it.

She put another load into the machine, tidied herself perfunctorily and went back to the drawing room. Her father had gone, but the two ladies were having a nice gossip; from the way they both turned to look at her and their sudden silence, she suspected that they had been talking about her. Not that that worried her.

Mrs Duvant spoke first. 'I was just telling your mother that I want to go over to Bath and look round that house. She tells me that you drive; I wondered if you would take me one day soon, Annis? Matt says he can't be spared from the estate; they're doing the yearly inventory or some such thing, and Jake will be going to London tomorrow. We could have the Rover.'

Annis glanced at her mother and found that lady looking pleased. 'A nice change for you, darling,' said Mrs Fothergill. 'Just for a couple of days, and there's almost nothing to do now the others are away.'

'Well, yes—then I'd be glad to drive you,' said Annis. It was true she could be spared easily enough, and she liked Mrs Duvant.

The men came in then and Mrs Duvant told them, and Matt said: 'Oh, good, that's settled then,' while Jake Royle said nothing at all. It seemed to be a habit of his.

CHAPTER TWO

THE TRIP TO Bath was planned for two days ahead, mid-week, so that Annis would be back for the weekend to drive her father round the three parishes on Sunday and keep an eye on Emma, Audrey and James.

It was a pity that she hadn't anything really smart to wear, she decided as she packed an overnight bag; she could wear her tweed suit, a good one although no longer new, and there was a blouse she had had for Christmas which would do, as well as a sweater, and just in case Mrs Duvant changed in the evening, she could take the green wool jersey dress and wear her gold chain with it. She reflected uneasily upon Mrs Duvant's undoubtedly expensive clothes. She might be a dumpy little woman, but she had been wearing a beautifully cut outfit and doubtless the rest of her wardrobe was as elegant.

Matt drove the Rover, with his aunt in it, over to the Rectory soon after breakfast, declaring that he would walk back through the park. He added a careless: 'Jake went yesterday, gone to keep an eye on his millions—wish I had half his brains. Father's quite peevish this morning; no one to discuss the *Financial Times* with. I bet Jake enjoys himself in town!'

His aunt smiled at him. 'And why not? I should think he could have any girl he wanted with that handsome face of his. Are we ready to go, Annis my dear? I'm quite looking forward to this next day or two. I hope you are too.'

They drove via Frome and Radstock and Midsummer Norton, through a soft grey morning with a hint of frost in the air, and Bath, as they approached it, looked delightful, its grey stone houses clinging to the hills. Annis made her way through the town and then at Mrs Duvant's direction turned into a crescent of Regency houses facing a small park. Half way down she was told to stop and pulled up before a narrow tall house with elegant bow windows just like all its neighbours. She had expected to find an unlived-in house, but this one was freshly painted and bore all the signs of careful tenancy. As she opened the car door she saw the house door open and an elderly man cross the pavement to them.

'Ah, there's Bates,' declared Mrs Duvant happily. 'He and Mrs Bates caretake for me, you know.' She got out of the car and went to shake him by the hand. 'And this is Miss Annis Fothergill,' she told him, 'come to spend a day or two while I look round the place. I've a mind to come back here and live, Bates.'

The elderly man looked pleased. 'And I'm sure we hope that you do, madam. If you will go in, Mrs Bates will see to you. I'll bring the cases.'

The door was narrow with a handsome fanlight above it, and opened into a roomy hall with a pretty curved staircase at its back. Annis had time to see that before Mrs Bates bore down upon them; a large, stately woman with twinkling eyes and several chins. She received Mrs Duvant with every sign of delight, made Annis welcome, and ushered them into a small sitting-room, most comfortably furnished and with a bright fire blazing in the hearth.

'You'll like a cup of coffee, madam,' she said comfortably. 'When you've had a rest I'll take you up to your rooms.'

She sailed away and Mrs Duvant observed: 'Such a good creature, and a splendid cook.' She looked around her. 'Everything looks very nice after all this time. I'd quite forgotten...'

The coffee came and presently Mrs Bates to lead them upstairs and show first Mrs Duvant to a room at the front of the house and then Annis to hers; a charming apartment overlooking the surprisingly large garden at the back. Annis, used to the rather spartan simplicity at the Rectory, poked her head into the adjoining bathroom, smoothed the silken quilt and opened a drawer or two, lined with tissue paper and smelling of lavender. There was a built-in wardrobe too and a couple of small inviting easy chairs. Definitely a room to enjoy, she decided as she tidied herself at the little walnut dressing table, brushed her hair into a glossy curtain, and went downstairs.

Mrs Duvant was in the hall, talking to Bates. 'There's an hour or more before lunch, let's go over the house.' She was as excited as a small child with a new toy.

So with Mrs Bates sailing ahead of them, and Mrs Duvant trotting behind with Annis beside her, they set off. It was to be no lightning tour—that was obvious from the start. Mrs Duvant stopped every few steps to examine curtains, stooped to inspect carpets and insinuate her round person into cupboards. They started with the dining room, an elegantly furnished room with an oval mahogany table and six charming Adam chairs around it; there were half a dozen more chairs against the walls and a handsome sideboard, on which was displayed a selection of silver gilt. The walls were hung with sea green brocade and almost covered with what Annis took to be family portraits. A delightful room; she could find no fault with it, nor for that matter could its owner.

The drawing-room took a good deal longer; it was a large room with white panelling and a China blue ceiling, ornamented with a good deal of plasterwork, and the furniture was plentiful and elaborate; moreover there were innumerable ornaments scattered about its small tables. Annis found it a little too grand for her taste and uttered a sigh of pleasure at the morning room on the other side of the hall, a simple little room which Mrs Duvant dismissed quickly enough. The sitting room they had already seen and by then it was time for lunch, anyway.

Refreshed by oyster soup, omelette with a side salad and a rich creamy dessert, taken with a glass of white wine, Mrs Duvant declared herself ready to inspect the upper floors. And that took most of the afternoon, what with a long discussion about new curtains for one of the bedrooms, and a meticulous inspection of the linen closet on the top floor, but presently they were sitting by the fire having tea and with the prospect of the evening before them.

'I've got tickets for the concert in the Assembly Rooms, dear,' observed Mrs Duvant. 'If we have dinner a little early, we shall be in good time for it. It doesn't start before half past eight.'

Going to bed much later, Annis decided that there was a lot to be said for such a pleasant way of life—not that she would want to change it for her life at the Rectory, but like any other girl, she sometimes hankered after the fleshpots.

They spent almost all the next day shopping: Mrs Duvant, it seemed, was a great shopper and since money didn't seem to be any problem to her, she bought several things at prices which made Annis lift her eyebrows, but her companion's enjoyment was so genuine that she could find no objection, and after all, it was her money, and besides, Annis liked her.

They went to a cinema that evening and the following morning drove back with a firm promise to Bates that Mrs Duvant intended to take up residence in the near future.

They reached the Rectory at teatime and while Annis rang Matt to come over and collect the Rover and his aunt, Mrs Fothergill sat Mrs Duvant down before the fire and plied her with tea and hot buttered toast.

It was when Annis joined them that Mrs Duvant, between bites, announced that she would like Annis to accompany her to Bath. 'Just for a few weeks,' she said persuasively. 'I shall be a little lonely at first—if you could spare her? And if she would like to come?' She glanced a little anxiously at Annis. 'It would be a job, of course, I forget things and leave things lying around, and paying bills and so on, so you'd be quite busy, dear. Would forty pounds a week suit you? For about six weeks?'

Two hundred and forty pounds; Mrs Duvant had paid exactly that for a suit in Jaegar's the day before. A list, expanding every second in Annis's head, of things which that sum would buy for them all, slowly unrolled itself before Annis's inward eyes. A washing machine, a new coat for her mother, shoes for the boys, all the tobacco her father could smoke, the dancing slippers little Audrey had set her heart upon... She glanced at her mother and saw that she was doing exactly the same thing. She said promptly: 'Well, if Mother could manage, I'd love to come, if you think I'd be of any use.'

'Of course you will. That's settled, then. You've no idea how grateful I am, Annis.' She paused as the door opened and Matt came in. It wasn't until the hubbub of small talk had died down that she said: 'Shall we say on Saturday? That gives you four days. Is that time enough?'

Annis nodded. 'Plenty. Do I drive you again?'

'Yes, I think so. I can have the Rover for the time being. We must see about getting a car later on.' She bustled out on a tide of goodbyes, explaining to Matt as they went.

When the last sounds of the car had died away Mrs Fothergill said: 'You do want to go, darling? I shall miss you, and so will your father, but it will make a nice change and you'll have some money.'

'We'll have some money,' Annis corrected her. 'I've already made a list, have you?'

Her mother nodded happily. 'But it's your money, Annis. Now tell me, what sort of a house is it?'

Annis began to tell her, and it took quite a time; she hadn't quite finished when her father came in from a parish council meeting, and she went to get the supper and make sure that the younger ones were doing their homework properly.

Back at the Manor House, Mrs Duvant was writing a letter. She wrote as she did most things, with enthusiasm and a great many flourishes of the pen and she smiled a good deal as she wrote. It was a long letter. She read it through, put it in an envelope and addressed it to Jake Royle, whose godmother she was.

The house at Bath looked very welcoming as Annis drew up before it on Saturday afternoon. It had been a bright, cold day and now that the sun was almost gone there was already a sparkle of frost, but the house blazed with lights, and as they went in Annis noticed the great bowl of daffodils on the hall table and in the little sitting room where they at once went, the window held hyacinths of every colour. There was a vase of roses too, long-stemmed and perfect. Mrs Duvant picked up the card with them and chuckled as she read it, although she didn't say why.

'We'd like tea, Bates,' she said briskly, 'I know it's rather late, but perhaps Mrs Bates could put dinner back half an hour?'

So the two of them had tea together round the fire before going upstairs to unpack and get ready for dinner. 'I always like to change my dress,' observed Mrs Duvant. 'Nothing fancy, you know, unless I'm going out, but it somehow makes the evening more of an occasion, if you see what I mean?'

So Annis took the hint and put on the green jersey, wondering as she did so if she might get herself another dress when she was paid. She and her mother had pored over their lists, scratching out and adding until they had spent her wages, on paper at least, to the greatest advantage. Even after everyone had had something there was a little over for herself—enough for a dress—something plain and dateless to take the place of the outworn blue velvet. Doubtless she would have some time to herself in which to browse among the shops. Annis tugged her green jersey into shape with an impatient hand and went downstairs.

She discovered after the first few days that her duties were light in the extreme and consisted mainly in finding Mrs Duvant's spectacles, handbag, library book and knitting whenever she mislaid them, which was often, reminding her of the various things she wished to do each day, and unpicking her knitting when she got it in a muddle; that was pretty often too. The pair of them got on excellently together and since Annis got on equally well with the Bates, the household was a happy one.

She had been there a week when the even tenor of her days was unexpectedly shaken. Mrs Duvant had the habit of retiring for an afternoon nap after lunch each day, leaving Annis to do as she wished. Previously she had gone for a brisk walk, done some window shopping and taken herself round the Roman Baths, but this afternoon it was raining, not a soft rain to be ignored, but a steady, icy downpour. Annis decided on a book by the fire as she came downstairs after seeing Mrs Duvant safely tucked up. There were plenty of books in the sitting room and an hour or so with one of them would be very pleasant.

Bates met her on the stairs. 'Mr Royle has arrived, miss—he's in the drawing room.'

Annis stood staring at him, her mouth a little open.

'Mr Royle? What on earth…I didn't know Mrs Duvant was expecting him.' She suppressed the little spurt of excitement at the idea of meeting him again and reminded herself that she didn't like him, which made her voice sound reluctant.

'I suppose I'd better go…' her voice trailed off and Bates coughed gently. 'It would be a pity to disturb Mrs Duvant,' he reminded her.

Annis took a step down. 'Yes, of course, Bates.'

She went past him, crossed the hall, opened the drawing room door reluctantly and went unwillingly inside.

Jake Royle was standing, very much at home, before the fire. She said idiotically: 'Oh, hullo, Bates told me you were here. I'm afraid Mrs Duvant's having a nap, she always does after lunch.'

'Yes, I know that.' He smiled at her, and since it was obvious after a moment that he wasn't going to say anything else, she plunged into speech.

'Aren't you going back to New Zealand?' she asked.

His firm mouth twitched. 'Is that where you would consign me, Annis?'

'Of course not, Mr Royle. Why should I consign you anywhere?'

'My name is Jake.' He went on standing there, watching her and she sought feverishly for a topic of conversation. 'I'm staying with Mrs Duvant,' she said.

'Yes, I know that too.'

She frowned. At least he could give a hand with the conversation, the wretch! 'I expect you'll be staying for tea? I'm sure Mrs Duvant will want to see you.'

He grinned at her. 'I'm here for a few days—I visit

Aunt Dora from time to time—we've known each other since I was a small boy,' and at the look of surprise on her face: 'Oh, she's not a genuine aunt, just an adopted one.'

'Oh, yes, I see. Perhaps you'd like to see your room?'

He answered her gravely enough, although his eyes danced with amusement.

'I expect Bates has taken my things upstairs for me. I'd love some tea—we can always have it again when Aunt Dora comes down.'

Annis, intent on being coolly impersonal, only succeeded in looking delightfully flustered as she rang the bell and rather belatedly asked if he would sit down, rather pink now at her lack of manners and a little cross because Jake seemed to have the power to make her feel shy and awkward, something which she, a parson's daughter, had learned not to be at an early age. And when tea came she was furious to find that her hands shook as she poured it. Jake, observing this, smiled to himself and embarked on a steady flow of small talk which was only interrupted by the arrival of Mrs Duvant, who came trotting in, her round face wreathed in smiles.

'Now isn't this nice?' she asked them. 'Annis, ring for more tea, will you? And I've left my spectacles somewhere… Jake, I hope you can stay for a few days— you've got your car with you, I suppose? you can drive us… Ah, thank you, dear, I knew I'd put them down somewhere.' She paused to pour tea. 'There's a concert at the Assembly Rooms this evening, will you come with us?'

Jake agreed lazily. 'Anything you say, Aunt Dora. I hope it's not Bach?'

'Strauss and Schubert and someone singing, but I can't remember the name.'

'As long as she's nice to look at.'

Annis, drinking her unwanted tea, wondered what on earth she should wear; the green or the blue velvet? She had nothing else, and if only she'd known she would have bought that blue crêpe dress, the one she had seen in Milsom Street; after all, she had her first week's money in her purse. Now it was too late. She knitted her brows; there was no earthly reason why she should fuss over what she should wear. What was good enough for her and Mrs Duvant was good enough for Jake Royle, it couldn't matter in the least to him what she wore. There would be dozens of pretty girls there, wearing gorgeous outfits. She became aware that they were both looking at her, Mrs Duvant smiling, Jake with his brows lifted in amusement. They must have said something.

'I'm sorry, did you ask me something?'

'No, love—I was just telling Jake what a delightful week we've had together.'

So why was Jake looking amused? Annis gave him a frosty look and offered him more cake.

She wore the green with the gold chain, and when she went downstairs it was a relief to find that Mrs Duvant was wearing a plain wool dress, and although Jake had changed, the suit he had on was a conservative grey. She had to admit that it fitted him very well. So it should, considering what it had cost to have it made.

Dinner had a slightly festive air, partly due to the

champagne Jake had brought with him, and partly
owing to Mrs Duvant's high spirits. She was such a
happy person it was impossible to be ill-tempered or
miserable in her company.

They set off for the Assembly Rooms presently, in
the best of spirits, driving through the rain-swept streets
in Jake's Bentley, Mrs Duvant beside him wrapped in
mink, and Annis behind, in her elderly winter coat.
She was enjoying herself so much that she had quite
forgotten that.

They sat with Mrs Duvant in between them and
listened to the excellent orchestra, and later when the
singer appeared, and turned out to be not only a very
pretty woman but with a glorious voice, Annis couldn't
stop herself from turning a little and peeping at Jake. He
wasn't looking at the singer at all, but at her. He smiled
before he looked away, leaving her with the feeling that
although she didn't like him, she was becoming very
aware of his charm.

When the concert was over they had a drink before
going back to the house and she was nonplussed to find
his manner towards her casual to the point of coolness;
she must have imagined the warmth of that smile, and
anyway, she told herself peevishly, why was she getting all worked up about it? She couldn't care less what
he thought of her.

When they got back she waited merely to ask Mrs
Duvant if she needed her for anything before saying
goodnight and going to her room. It had been a lovely
evening, she told Mrs Duvant, and she had enjoyed herself very much. Her goodnight to Jake was brisk and

delivered to his chin, since she wanted to avoid looking at him.

It would be a pity, she thought as she undressed, if he were to upset the gentle pattern of their days, but since he was to stay only a short time, that didn't really matter. She dismissed him from her thoughts and went to sleep, to dream, most infuriatingly, of him all night.

Mrs Duvant wasn't at breakfast the next morning, but Jake was. He was at table, reading the paper and making great inroads into eggs and bacon when Annis went down at her usual time. He got to his feet, wished her a friendly good morning, hoped that she had slept well, passed her the coffee pot and resumed his breakfast. Only good manners, she felt, prevented him from picking up his newspaper again.

Instead he carried on a desultory conversation, just sufficient to put her at her ease. Indeed, by the time their meal was finished, she found herself talking to him with something which amounted to pleasure.

'Aunt Dora wants to visit the American Museum this morning,' he told her as they left the room together. 'There's some embroidery exhibited there she intends to study. You'll be coming?' His voice was nicely casual.

'I expect so, Mrs Duvant likes someone with her, but perhaps if you're going there...'

He gave her a glance full of amused mockery. 'My dear Annis, I know absolutely nothing about embroidery.'

She left him in the hall, wishing as she went upstairs that he was as nice as he had been at breakfast all the time, and not just when he felt like it. The way he looked at her with that horrid half-smile... She bounced into her room, dragged a comb ruthlessly through her hair, which didn't need it anyway, and went along to see how Mrs Duvant did. If it were possible, she would see if she could get out of going out that morning.

It wasn't possible. Mrs Duvant was so enthusiastic about the outing, pointing out how useful Annis was going to be, although Annis couldn't quite see why, that she didn't even suggest it. And as it turned out, Jake was charming, and once they got to the embroidery exhibition, wandered off on his own, leaving Mrs Duvant to exclaim over feather-stitching, smocking and the like while she made Annis write down a variety of notes which she thought might be useful to her later on.

It was during lunch that Jake observed that he would have to go back to London in two days' time. Annis was shocked at the keen disappointment she felt when he said it; she couldn't stand the sight of him—well, for most of the time anyway, but she would miss him. Which made it all the stranger that she hesitated about going downstairs again after she had tucked Mrs Duvant up for her post-prandial nap. But as she left Mrs Duvant's room she saw Jake disappearing out of the front door. She would be able to go downstairs and read by the fire in the small sitting room; she didn't want him to think that she was avoiding his company—that was if he thought about it at all, nor did she wish to bore him with her own company if he had a mind to be on his own. She found her book and curled up in one of the deep armchairs drawn up to the cheerful fire.

She had read two pages when the door opened and Jake came in. 'Ah,' he said blandly, 'I had an idea you might have gone into hiding for the afternoon.'

A remark which instantly set her on edge. 'And why should you think that?' she wanted to know tartly. 'I have no reason to hide.'

'Oh, good, I can't help feeling that if we see more of each other we may eventually become friends. How about coming to dinner tomorrow evening? We'll go to Popjoy's and then go on somewhere to dance.'

A distressing vision of the blue velvet and the green jersey floated before Annis's eyes. She'd heard of Popjoy's, it was smart and expensive, and nothing would induce her to go there in either of these garments. With real regret she knew she would have to refuse, and the awful thing was that she actually had the money in her purse to buy that pretty blue crêpe she'd seen, only there was no time in which to buy it.

'That's awfully kind of you,' she said carefully, 'but I—I'm afraid I can't accept.'

'Why not?'

She sought for a good reason in a frenzy and couldn't think of one. Being a parson's daughter and the eldest, with a good example to set the others, she had been taught to speak the truth; only if it was going to hurt the hearer was it permissible to prevaricate. Well, she couldn't see that Jake was going to be hurt. If anyone was, it would be herself, having to admit that she had nothing to wear. She gave him a very direct look and explained: 'I haven't got a dress.' She had pinkened slightly in anticipation of his amusement, but she didn't look away.

Jake didn't smile, he said in a calm voice: 'That's a problem, but surely we can get round it? Have you got enough money to buy one?'

Strangely she didn't feel offended at the question. 'Well, yes—Mrs Duvant paid me, but you see I wouldn't have time to get to the shops.'

'Any particular shop?'

'Jolly's in Milsom Street.'

'I take it that if you did have a dress you'd come to dinner with me?' He wanted to know.

'I'd like to, that's if we could...that is, if we wouldn't get on each other's nerves.'

He did smile then, but in such a friendly fashion that she smiled back. 'You never got on my nerves,' he assured her. 'Tell me, are you one of those women who take hours to buy something or could you find what you wanted in half an hour or so? Because if you could, we'll go now: I'll run you there in the car.'

Annis was out of her chair and making for the door. 'Give me five minutes!'

The dress was still there. She left Jake browsing in a bookshop and went to try it on. The colour was becoming, a shade darker than her eyes, and the dress, although inexpensive, was quite well cut, made of some thick silky material with a chiffon ruffle outlining the neck and the cuffs. Examining herself in the fitting room, Annis decided that it would do very well; it could take the place of the blue velvet and that garment she could consign to the jumble sale. She didn't think it was quite the sort of dress Jake's girl-friends would wear, but since she wasn't one of them that didn't matter. She paid for it and on the way out spent most of the change on a pair of bronze sandals going cheap but nonetheless elegant.

Jake was still in the bookshop, but he picked up the

armful of books he had bought when he saw her and took the dress box from her. 'Twenty minutes,' he remarked. 'Not bad. Did you find what you wanted?'

'Yes. I hope it'll do. We don't go out much at home and I don't often buy that kind of dress.'

Jake gave her a quick look. If the deplorable blue velvet had been anything to go by, he could not but agree with her. 'I'm sure it will be very charming,' he said comfortably. 'If you've got all you want, we'll go back. Aunt Dora will be wanting her tea.'

She was waiting for them, sitting in the small straightbacked chair she favoured, leafing through a pile of fashion magazines.

'Such a pity I'm all the wrong shape,' she greeted them. Her eyes fell on the dress box. 'You've been shopping—how delightful! Do let me see.'

'Since you're playing bridge tomorrow evening, Aunt Dora, I've asked Annis out to dinner.' Jake had strolled over to the fire with his back to Annis, busy undoing her purchase.

'Now that is a good idea,' enthused Mrs Duvant. 'Hold it up, dear.'

Annis did so, suddenly doubtful because in the splendidly furnished room with Mrs Duvant's wildly expensive outfit it looked what it was; a pretty inexpensive dress off the peg. But she was reassured at once by Mrs Duvant's warm admiration. 'Oh, very nice,' she declared, 'and such a lovely colour. Shoes?' She had glanced down at Annis's sensible low heels.

'Well, just as I was leaving the shop I saw these.' Annis produced the sandals and the two ladies examined them. 'They were going cheap and they'll be useful, because if I ever buy another dress, they'll go with almost anything.'

This ingenuous remark brought a smile to Jake's mouth; it was a very gentle smile and amused too. He had thought, when he first met Annis, that she was a bossy elder sister, prone to good works and with far too good an opinion of herself. That she was quite beautiful too, he had admitted without hesitation, but he hadn't quite believed her occasional dreaminess and her apparent contentment at the Rectory. Now he admitted that he had been quite wrong; she had made no effort to impress him—indeed, she had avoided him, she dealt with Mrs Duvant's endless small wants without as much as a frown, and he had been touched by her frank admission that she couldn't go out with him because she hadn't got a dress. He reflected ruefully that any of the girls he knew who had said that to him would have expected him to have taken them out and bought them one—and nothing off the peg either. He rather thought that if he had suggested to Annis that he would pay she would have thrown something at him. For all her sensible calmness he fancied that at times that red hair of hers might exert itself.

That evening after dinner they played poker, a game Annis had to be taught and which she picked up with ease, rather to Jake's surprise, until Mrs Duvant remarked that it was only to be expected from a girl who had five A-levels to her credit, and one of these pure Maths. He just stopped himself asking her why she hadn't gone on to university, because of course, even with a grant, that would have cost money, and there were Edward and James to educate.

They played for high stakes, using the haricot beans Bates brought from the kitchen, and although Jake made a fortune in no time at all, Annis wasn't far behind him. Mrs Duvant, her black eyes snapping with pleasure, lost over and over again and when they at last called a halt, thanked heaven that she had been playing with beans and not money. But it had been good fun. Annis carefully gathered up the beans and returned them to Bates before going upstairs to bed with Mrs Duvant, leaving Jake by the fire, a briefcase of papers on the floor beside him, and a glass of whisky on the table.

The next morning Mrs Duvant announced that she had a wedding present to buy for a friend's daughter, and since Jake said that he had some work to do, she and Annis went to the shops together. It took almost all the morning, trying to decide between table linen and silver tea knives. In the end Mrs Duvant, never one to cavil over money, bought both.

And after lunch Jake went back to his work and since Mrs Duvant had retired for her usual nap, Annis got into her outdoor things and went for a walk in the park. It was a chilly, blustery day and somehow it suited her mood; she was feeling vaguely restless, but she couldn't think why. Everything was all right at home; she had a letter that morning, in another day or two there would be forty pounds in her pocket and she had no worries. She came to the conclusion that Jake's visit had unsettled her. She had never met anyone like him before; Matt she had grown up with and treated much as she treated her brothers, but Jake made her feel self-conscious and shy, although she had to admit that she was beginning to enjoy his company. She marched briskly into the

teeth of the wind and went back presently, her face rosy
with fresh air and with a splendid appetite for her tea.

Seen under the soft lighting of her bedroom the blue
crêpe looked nice; so did the sandals. It was a pity that
she had to wear her winter coat, but she didn't suppose
that would matter overmuch; no one would see it. She
went downstairs with it over her arm, admiring the
sandals as she went.

'Very nice,' declared Jake from the hall. 'Stunning,
in fact. What's more, you're beautifully prompt.'

He was in the clerical grey again, looking older and
very assured. Looking at him, Annis felt sure that the
evening would go without a hitch; he would be a man
able to get the best table in the restaurant and instant
attention. She said thank you rather shyly and went to
say goodnight to Mrs Duvant.

She had been quite right, she told herself as she got
ready for bed in the early hours of the next morning; the
evening had been one to remember, for her at any rate—
although it seemed likely that Jake had spent so many
similar evenings with other, more interesting companions, that he would probably forget it at once.

Popjoys was the kind of place she had read about in
the *Harpers* Mrs Avery occasionally lent her. In a Beau
Nash house where its guests drank their aperitifs in the
elegant drawing-room before going to the equally elegant dining room, it was a world she had never expected
to enter. They had eaten mousseline of salmon, spiced
chicken with apricots and finished with chocolate soufflé, and just as she had guessed, they had a well placed
table for two and the proprietor had welcomed them
warmly, conjuring up wine waiter and waiter and rec-

ommending the best dishes. Her mouth watered at the
thought of the salmon. The wine had been nice too; she
had almost no knowledge of wines and beyond Jake's
careless: 'I think we'll drink hock, shall we?' he didn't
bother her about it. She drank what was in her glass and
found it delicious. By the time dinner was finished she
felt very happy about everything, and when Jake suggested that they might dance somewhere for an hour
or two she had agreed very readily. Her sleepy head on
the pillow, she couldn't quite remember where they had
gone; an hotel in the town, although she hadn't noticed
its name. They had had a table there too and Jake had
ordered some wine, but they had got up to dance before it was brought and since the floor wasn't crowded
and the band was good they went on dancing for quite
some time.

Back at the table they talked, but there again she
couldn't remember what they had said, only that it had
been pleasant and they had laughed a good deal. She sat
up in bed suddenly. Perhaps she had drunk too much
and made a fool of herself, but she couldn't have been
too bad, because they had gone on dancing for a long
time before getting into the car and coming back. The
combined pleasure of the evening lulled her to sleep;
she was on the very edge of it when she started awake.
With vivid clarity she remembered kissing Jake goodnight in the hall. True, he had kissed her first but she
need not have kissed him back with quite such fervour.
At the time it had seemed a perfectly natural thing to do,
but now she wasn't so sure; when she got back home to

the Rectory she was going to remember it with hideous embarrassment. And pleasure, a small voice at the back of her head persisted.

CHAPTER THREE

ANNIS TOOK AS long as she possibly could to dress in the morning. She would have to meet Jake sooner or later, but she wanted it to be later. Her cheeks grew red each time she thought of the previous evening, but awkward or not, she would have to go down to breakfast and there wasn't much use being cowardly about it. She marched downstairs and went into the dining-room, to find it empty, and when Bates came in with the coffee pot he informed her that Mr Royle had already left for London.

Quite unreasonably, she was instantly furious. Jake might at least have left a message, told her the evening before, given some hint that he wouldn't be seeing her again. She ate without appetite and was hard put to it to be cheerful when Mrs Duvant came down presently, wanting to know if she had enjoyed her evening with Jake, where they had been, what they had done, and what a pity it was that he had had to go back to London. 'Though I daresay we'll see something of him before you go back home, dear.'

Annis said: 'Oh, yes—how nice,' and hoped with her whole heart that she'd never see him again. At the same time she felt such a wave of regret at the very idea that she was quite bewildered.

'Of course,' went on Mrs Duvant, at her most gossipy, 'he has so many friends that every moment of his leisure is filled, and he doesn't have much leisure, I can tell you. And all the girls are after him, and who can blame them? He's quite something to look at, isn't he? and with more money than he knows what to do with and not married.' She shot a quick glance at Annis, sitting quietly unravelling Mrs Duvant's endless knitting. 'I thought at first that you didn't hit it off together, but perhaps I was wrong.'

Annis answered guardedly: 'We haven't much in common, Mrs Duvant, and I rather think that Jake asked me out just by way of filling in an evening. I enjoyed it, though.' Especially being kissed at the end of it, she added silently. She would have to forget that, of course, but no doubt in a few weeks' time, when she was home again, it would all seem like a dream, and dreams had a habit of fading. She gave the knitting a vicious tug and sat up straight. Besides, she still didn't like him; he was far too sure of himself, and if he had thought for one single minute that she was going to be like all those other girls and make a play for him, then he was going to be sadly disappointed... She ripped out a row of stitches that had nothing wrong with them at all and had to knit the whole lot again.

It was a good thing that Mrs Duvant had an urge to go shopping, so that the morning and a good deal of the afternoon was taken up with this agreeable pastime, and in the evening there was a film which she particularly wanted to see.

She was a tireless little woman. One day succeeded another and on each of them she discovered something different to do, and when they weren't somewhere, guide book in hand, they were at the house, discussing new curtains and covers and whether it would be a good idea to have the hall close-carpeted over the polished wood blocks. All in all, the days were filled from morning until bedtime and Annis had little time to feel even faintly regretful of the few days of Jake's company.

It seemed to her that Mrs Duvant was doing too much, and rather hesitantly she said so.

'Nonsense, my dear,' said that lady cheerfully. 'I'm not one to sit around in a chair and wait to grow old.' She chuckled. 'Well, I'm that already, aren't I?'

'Of course you're not, only you look thinner, Mrs Duvant—do you suppose you should rest a little more? Perhaps an hour before dinner each evening?'

'Certainly not, Annis. What a waste of time that would be! There's that play we simply must see and the concerts at the Assembly Rooms, and I've promised to play bridge at least once a week. No, dear, I'm very happy as I am. Now let me see, where was it we saw that velvet I thought might do for the new curtains?'

So Annis said no more, although she still felt uneasy.

And two days later she knew she had been right. They had just sat down to their dinner when Mrs Duvant said in an urgent voice: 'Annis, I feel ill…'

Annis took one look at the grey face opposite her and got out of her chair. Mrs Duvant looked awful, but Annis wasn't the eldest of six, all prone to accident or illness from time to time, for nothing. She scooped up Mrs Duvant from her chair and carried her carefully across the hall, meeting an astonished Bates on the way.

'Open the sitting-room door, will you, Bates, and telephone the doctor to come at once. Mrs Duvant isn't well!'

She laid her burden down on one of the sofas in the room, put a cushion under her head and felt for her pulse.

'I'm not dead yet,' whispered Mrs Duvant, opening one eye.

'Of course you're not,' agreed Annis bracingly and wishing Mrs Duvant wasn't such a frightful colour. 'I've asked the doctor to come, though, just to take a look—you may have been doing too much, you know.'

'Impossible,' whispered Mrs Duvant, and smiled tiredly.

Mrs Bates had joined them silently and Annis asked her to get Mrs Duvant's bed ready. 'Because I'm sure the doctor will want her to rest for a day or two. Can you think of anything else we should do?'

Mrs Bates shook her head and went away, and after a moment Mrs Duvant said more strongly: 'Telephone Jake—tell him to come, he'll understand.'

'When the doctor's been,' suggested Annis gently.

'No, now.' She gave the ghost of a chuckle. 'It's all right, I shan't go away.'

So Annis went across to the telephone and looked up Jake's number in the elegant leather book on the table and dialled it. His voice, deep and decisive, answered almost at once.

'Mrs Duvant asked me to phone you; she isn't well, we're waiting for the doctor. She would like you to come.'

He didn't ask any questions, although she had expected him to, even to suggest that he should wait until the morning. 'Tell her I'm now on my way,' he said abruptly, and hung up.

The doctor, when he came, which was within minutes of Bates's phone call, wouldn't hear of Mrs Duvant being moved for the moment, and rather to Annis's surprise he didn't do much; he took his patient's pulse, her blood pressure, peered into her eyes and then said rallyingly: 'I warned you, Dora, you've been burning the candle at both ends and they're on the point of meeting.'

'Oh, pooh,' said Mrs Duvant in a voice which was a shadow of its usual strength. 'I told you I was going to do as I liked.'

'And now I'm going to do what I like,' observed the doctor firmly. 'You're going to have an injection, just enough to take away the pain and give us a chance to get you comfortable and into your bed.' He glanced at Annis. 'If you would be so good as to hold Mrs Duvant's arm steady.'

Mrs Duvant's eyes closed within minutes. 'I'll carry her upstairs, perhaps you and Mrs Bates can get her undressed?'

Annis nodded. 'Is Mrs Duvant very ill?' she asked.

He looked surprised for a moment. 'She's dying. She's had cancer for some months now; I've nursed her along, but we both knew that she wouldn't have long. You didn't know?'

Annis shook her head. 'No. Should anyone be told? She asked me to ring her godson, and he's on his way. She has a brother...'

'Colonel Avery—yes, let him know, will you. Are you a member of the family?'

'No, my parents are friends of the Averys'. I'm here as companion to Mrs Duvant for a few weeks while she

settles in here.' Her hands were shaking and she put
them behind herself longing for Jake to come.

Between them, she and Mrs Bates got Mrs Duvant
into bed, and although she roused a little as they did
so, she dozed off once more and didn't wake when the
doctor came to take another look at her.

'She should sleep for a while,' he told Annis. 'I have
another urgent visit to pay, but I'll be back. Can you
manage or shall I try and get a nurse?'

'I can manage, and Bates and Mrs Bates are very
good. Is there anything I should do? Will she be in
pain?'

'She won't rouse for another two hours at least, possibly longer, and I'll be back by then; if you're worried
about her let me know at once and I'll come.'

The house was very quiet after he had gone. Bates
crept in with a tray on which there was a bowl of soup
and had put it down on the table by Annis's chair. 'Just
take this, miss,' he urged. 'The night's going to be a
long one.'

She thanked him, urged him to see that both he and
Mrs Bates had something to eat too, and warned him
that Jake would be coming—a piece of information
which Bates received with relieved satisfaction.

'Me and Mrs Bates, we knew that the mistress had
had bad turns from time to time; Mr Jake warned us of
that, but we never expected anything like this, miss.'

He looked so shocked and upset that Annis got up
and went to put a hand on his shoulder. 'Perhaps it
won't be as bad as it looks,' she said, knowing how
empty her words were and that neither of them believed
them, anyway.

Bates came back presently to fetch the tray and ask anxiously if there was any change and when might Colonel Avery be expected. 'Because he'll need to stay the night, miss,' he reminded her.

'Yes, of course—I'm sorry, Bates, I forgot to tell you that Colonel and Mrs Avery were out, so was Matthew. I left a message and asked that they should get it at the first possible moment, but they'd gone to some friends for dinner, and unfortunately no one knew who they were. I expect it will take a little time to find them.' Annis glanced at the clock. 'It's only ten o'clock, though, they're bound to telephone as soon as they hear.'

'Yes, of course, miss. What a blessing that you're here, miss. Mrs Bates asks if she should sit here for a bit.'

'How kind of her! But I'm all right and the doctor's coming back round about midnight. I thought I'd stay here until he comes, perhaps he'll know more by then.'

There was no sound in the room when Bates had gone save the faint ticking of the clock and the even fainter sound of Mrs Duvant's breathing. Annis pulled her chair a little nearer the bed just in case its occupant should wake, and composed herself to wait.

Half an hour later the door was softly opened and Jake came in. Annis turned her head and looked at him, not speaking. He looked as calm and unruffled as he always did, immaculate in a dinner jacket, bringing with him the strong feeling that he would be able to cope with anything no matter how awkward the situation.

He said, 'Hullo, Annis,' in a quiet voice and went past her to the bed. 'The doctor's been?'

'Yes, at about half past eight. He's coming again before midnight. I'm to ring him if it's necessary.'

His eyes examined her pale face. 'I see.' He didn't say anything else until Bates, who had followed him in, had put down a tray of coffee on one of the tables and gone again, then he poured for them both, added brandy to both cups and brought one over to her. 'Drink that, and tell me what's happened.'

The brandy warmed her cold insides and the coffee cleared her head. She gave a succinct account of the evening without adding any comments of her own, and any doubts she had had about doing the right thing were dispelled by his quiet, 'You've been splendid.'

He refilled her cup and drew up another chair on the other side of the bed, and presently when Mrs Duvant opened her eyes and said in a quite strong voice: 'How long have you been here, Jake?' he answered her in a perfectly normal voice. 'Twenty minutes ago, my dear.'

'Had to leave a date, did you?' she chuckled, and it was like dry leaves rustling.

'I did; a delectable blonde who turned into a flaming virago when I stood her up.' He picked up a hand lying on the silk coverlet and kissed it. 'You're worth a roomful of blondes, but I've told you that before.'

Mrs Duvant smiled at him. 'We've had some good times together. I didn't have any children, but now it's like having a son and a daughter with me.' She turned her head and looked at Annis. 'You make a darling daughter, my dear—one day you'll make some lucky man a darling wife.'

'Why, thank you.' Annis managed a perfectly natural smile, taking her cue from Jake, although there was a lump in her throat fit to choke her. 'I think you'd make a lovely mum—' She paused as the door bell sounded faintly and Bates's elderly voice spoke to someone downstairs—the doctor.

The two men shook hands and the doctor said: 'You made good time, Jake, not much on the roads.'

'Hardly a thing. Do you want us out of the way while you talk to Aunt Dora?'

'No, that won't be necessary.' He bent over the bed, taking Mrs Duvant's pulse and then her blood pressure. 'I'm going to give you another injection,' he told her. 'The pain's starting up again, isn't it?'

She nodded. 'I should have loved to have talked to Jake, we've only had a few minutes.'

'I'll be here when you wake up, darling,' said Jake from the window, and turned to give her a grin. 'I'll stay here and nod off in a chair and we'll have a cup of tea together.'

'And Annis?'

'She'll be here too. I'll take a few days off next week and we'll play poker.'

Mrs Duvant smiled slowly and allowed Annis to lift her arm for the doctor to give the injection. 'I'll look forward to it,' she answered him in a voice hardly to be heard now.

She drifted off without speaking again, and presently the doctor went and Jake went with him. He was back again in a very few minutes, though, to sit down again opposite Annis. 'Bates is bringing up a pot of tea,' he told her, and at her look: 'That's what Aunt Dora would like.'

'I'm sorry,' she felt her cheeks grow warm, 'that

was silly of me.' And when the tea came she meekly accepted a cup. It had the effect of dissolving the lump in her throat so that, quite against her will, tears began to pour down her cheeks.

Jake crossed the room and took the cup from her and pulled her gently out of her chair. 'Now look, darling, you must stop crying. Aunt Dora wouldn't like it, for one thing, nor do I for another.' He put an arm round her shoulders and held her close; she could feel his immense vitality wrapped round her like a cloak and felt instantly better.

'So sorry,' she managed.

'No, don't be sorry for a warm heart, Annis—there are enough cold ones around.' He fished a handkerchief out of a pocket and started to mop her face. 'That's better. Do you think you can go on for a bit? It won't be for much longer.'

She stared up at him. 'Isn't Mrs Duvant... You said we'd all have a cup of tea...'

'So I did. You're not very grown up, are you, darling?' He kissed the top of her head, a small gesture which did much to comfort her, and went on: 'I think—I know that Aunt Dora would like it if we were to stay here with her, but if you feel you can't she'd understand.'

'I'll stay.' Annis leaned away from him and he dropped his arms at once.

'That's my girl! Sit down again and finish that tea and I'll tell you about Aunt Dora. She's had a most interesting life, you know.'

He rambled on quietly, sitting by the bed, a small limp hand in his, talking about Mrs Duvant's travels, which had been numerous, and all the things she had done without the approval of her relations. 'She had a splendid life, and she and her husband adored each other; when he died she disappeared for several months—trekked through darkest Africa, or was it America?'

His gentle musings, needing no reply, gave Annis time to pull herself together, and when after a little while he said: 'Well, it's over, my dear,' she said quite calmly: 'What do we do now? How can I help?'

And then she went to the bed and knelt down like a child for a few moments, then got to her feet and stood looking down on the quiet face. 'She lived until the last minute, didn't she? I mean, so many elderly people start dying slowly years before they need to.'

Jake had his back to her, looking out into the night. 'You've hit the nail on the head, bless her. I'll phone the doctor, and will you see if the Bateses are still up?'

The remainder of the night passed in a blur of happenings: the Colonel arriving, the doctor, Mrs Bates whisking her off to bed… Annis woke late, astonished that she had slept.

Everyone was at breakfast when she got down—Jake and the Colonel, Mrs Avery and Matt. They bade her a cheerful good morning and the Colonel asked at once if she would like to go back with them later in the morning.

Annis, without realising it, looked at Jake.

'I'd like you to stay, Annis, I'll need some help, and there are some things the Bateses can't do.'

Mrs Avery said crossly: 'It's a great pity that we can't stay, but we can't put off the Lord Lieutenant…' She shot a glance at Matt, stolidly working his way through a good breakfast. 'Matt, surely you could stay?'

'But why, Mother? Jake can cope with everything, you know that, and Annis can manage perfectly well.'

His mother said even more crossly, seeing her matrimonial plans sliding away before they'd even got going: 'You and Annis have always done everything together...'

'But, Mother, we're not children any more.'

Annis, playing around with a bit of toast, held her tongue, while Jake sat back at his ease, drinking his coffee, smiling just a little.

But he looked perfectly grave when Mrs Avery turned to him. 'Matt's right,' he told her soothingly, 'there's not much he could do, as long as Colonel Avery doesn't mind me getting on with things...'

Colonel Avery surfaced from toast and marmalade. 'Of course not, dear boy. After all, you're one of the executors, and I must get back...'

'Of course.' Jake was at his most bland. 'If anything comes up, I'll phone you.'

And so the Averys went away again presently, and Jake took Annis by the arm and marched her into the sitting-room. 'Sit down quietly,' he told her, 'and read the papers. I'll join you for coffee presently.'

'Yes, but isn't there something I should do?'

'Not for a little while,' he told her gently.

So she pretended to read the news while she listened to quiet feet going up and downstairs and the murmur of voices, and then Jake's firm footfall crossing the hall and going into the drawing-room.

Half an hour later he joined her. 'It's just occurred to

me—shouldn't you ring your family? Will your mother object to you staying here?'

'Of course not. Not if I can be of some use…but I'll ring her, if you don't mind.'

He nodded. 'The funeral is in four days' time. I'll stay until then, and I hope you will too. This afternoon, if you feel you can, I want you to sort through Aunt Dora's jewellery. I know about her will, of course, she's left a good deal of it to members of the family, and it would help a lot if you could check it.'

'Are there a lot of nephews and nieces?'

'Dozens. Matt will get quite a nice little legacy, she was fond of him.'

He looked at her as he spoke, but her face showed no interest at this news.

'It will come in handy when he marries,' persisted Jake.

'Yes, I expect it will; is there anything I can do?'

'Yes, come for a brisk walk with me.'

Which they did, through Royal Victoria Park, the Botanical Gardens and across High Common. It was a fine morning, still cold but right for walking, and they arrived back more than ready for their lunch.

The afternoon passed quickly. There was an astonishing amount of jewellery to sort through and they did it together in front of the sitting room fire, while Jake talked about Aunt Dora, so naturally that it seemed as though she wasn't dead at all, and when Annis remarked on this he said briskly: 'Well, in a way, she isn't, and I for one don't believe in hushed voices and drawn blinds and nor did she.'

They ate their dinner on the best of terms and afterwards Jake went away to do some more telephoning. When he joined her by the fire in the sitting-room presently, he observed: 'How pleasant, just like an old married couple.'

He didn't seem to expect a reply, which was just as well, as she couldn't think of one, but sat down opposite her and picked up a newspaper.

Five minutes passed. 'How dull,' observed Annis thoughtfully.

Jake lowered his newspaper. 'What's how dull?'

'Being an old married couple.' She glanced up at him and then went back to her knitting.

'Now let us go into this in some depth.' He put the paper down and stretched out in his chair. 'I should imagine that after the hurly-burly of years of married life, it must be very pleasant to share your fireside and your declining years with someone you've loved and still love.'

'That sounds too good to be true.'

'No, it's not. I for one intend to make it true.'

Annis dropped a stitch. 'Oh? Are you thinking of getting married?'

'I've got past the thinking stage. I now know I am.'

'How—how nice.' It was ridiculous to feel so forlorn about it. Annis knitted fiercely, making a botch of the pattern, reminding herself that she didn't like him, after all—arrogant, too self-assured, more money than was good for him, far too good-looking, and all these quite drowned out by a persistent little voice at the back of her head reminding her that he could, when he wished, be kind and thoughtful and amusing and always knew what had to be done without being bossy about it.

'And you?' went on Jake. 'Do you and Matt intend to marry?'

She dropped several stitches. 'Me and Matt? Get married? Whatever do you mean? We grew up together.'

'Some people would say that was an excellent basis for a successful marriage.'

'Pooh, what utter nonsense! I can't imagine anything more dull—besides, Matt's only a boy.'

Jake settled further into his chair. 'Do you mind if I smoke?' and when he had got his pipe going: 'So he's not your ideal husband?'

'You must be joking!' Annis let her work fall into her lap and went on dreamily: 'Someone who doesn't expect me to go out in all weathers and notices if I've got something new on.' She paused. 'Though I can't blame Matt for that, because I don't have many new clothes for him to notice.' She stared at the wall opposite her, quite forgetful of her companion. 'Always polite and never shouting me down, considerate of my every wish, noticing if I've got a headache, remembering anniversaries with red roses…' She stopped because Jake was laughing at her. She said huffily: 'You would laugh!'

'Darling, you're such a child and yet you're a practical young woman too—a delightful mixture.'

Annis frowned. 'Don't call me darling, that's the third time. It doesn't mean anything, not—when you say it like that.'

He said very softly: 'No? Well, you can make what you like of that, Annis.'

A remark which kept her silent for quite some time, trying to decide just what he meant; or perhaps he hadn't meant anything at all. That was why she didn't like him, she told herself, because she was never quite sure if he meant what he said.

But during the next few days she found herself forgetting more and more often that she didn't like him. He was a good companion, and what was more, he kept her busy helping him with the hundred and one small tasks which had to be done, and each afternoon, whatever the weather, he marched her off for a long walk so that she began to look like her old self again. He expected her to help with the arrangements for the funeral too, treating the whole thing with a matter-of-fact air which robbed it of too much solemnity, and made it easy for her to greet the host of relations and friends who arrived. Her mother and father came at the same time as Colonel and Mrs Avery and Matt, and Mrs Avery, hoping to take advantage of the circumstances, did her best to throw Matt and Annis together on every possible occasion. She had no success at all. Annis had too much to do and Matt, after a perfunctory 'Hullo, old girl,' had made a beeline for a cluster of pretty cousins he hadn't seen for some time.

It was when almost everyone had gone again and only a handful of family were left that Mrs Avery broached the subject of Annis going back with Matt. 'We came in his car,' she pointed out, 'and he'll be glad of your company—I expect you want to get home as soon as possible, Annis.'

Annis, poised at the door with a tray load of cups and saucers for the Bateses to wash up, stood very still, it had struck her forcibly and in utter surprise that she had no wish to go home. She loved her parents dearly and she had no objection to Matt but she wanted to stay where she was until the last possible moment. And the reason for that was standing across the room from her, talking to her father: Jake, looking even more self-assured than usual, very much in command of the occasion and to all intents and purposes unaware of her existence.

She took a firmer grip of the tray; now was not the time to discover that she was in love with him. How much more convenient if she could have made the discovery in the peace and quiet of her own room without Mrs Avery's keen eye boring holes in her back. And her mother, bless her, had turned round to hear her answer, too.

The first one to speak was Jake. 'Oh, I'm sure you won't mind if Annis stays for another day or two. Mrs Fothergill, will you be an angel and allow me to bring her back, say, the day after tomorrow? There's still quite a lot of tidying away and clearing up to do and she's been so useful.'

It would have been hard to have refused, and anyway, her mother liked him. She said now: 'Well, of course, Jake, if Annis doesn't mind. I'm glad she can be of help at such a difficult time. And you'll bring her back?'

'With pleasure, and many thanks.' He glanced at Annis. 'You won't mind, darling?' he asked deliberately.

Annis felt her cheeks glowing like hot coals. The wretch, with his beastly little mocking smile! She didn't love him at all, she hated him. She said coldly: 'If I can help, I'll stay,' and sailed through the door with her tray.

When she got back, her cheeks cool once more, everyone was getting ready to leave. She kissed Mrs Avery's cross face, dutifully hugged her mother and father, said goodbye to Matt and the Colonel, and waved them away from the doorstep, with Jake standing beside her for all the world as though he owned the place.

Which, she was to discover, he did. She hadn't been present at the reading of the will, nor was she particularly interested. From the remarks she had overheard from various members of the family, Mrs Duvant had been more than generous. It was only as they stood in the hall once more that she asked, anxious to fill the silence between them: 'Do you have to put the house up for sale? Do you want an inventory made?'

'Lord, no. I've no intention of selling it, I like it too much. I shall keep the Bateses on, of course, and come down whenever I can.'

Annis stopped her walk to the drawing-room and turned to look at him. 'You mean it's yours? This house?'

'Don't look so shocked! Don't you think I'll look nice living in it? Conjure up a picture in your romantic mind of me, surrounded by the wife of my choice and an assortment of kids.'

He leaned against a console table, his hands in his pockets, smiling at her, and because she had a vivid imagination anyway, she did just that to such good purpose that she felt tears filling her eyes and with a quite unintelligible mutter she turned and ran upstairs to her room.

She stayed there, pleading a severe headache, and although she was famished, made do with a tray of thin soup which Mrs Bates brought up during the evening. What with hunger and misery, she had a poor night.

CHAPTER FOUR

THERE HAD BEEN time, during the hours she had lain awake, for Annis to pull herself together. By the time she went downstairs to breakfast the following morning, she felt able to cope with any situation which might arise, so it was with a distinct feeling of being let down that she sat down to table, for Jake greeted her in a casual manner which put her strongly in mind of her brothers and beyond a few brief observations about the weather and the news, had nothing much to say to her.

She ate dreamily, imagining what it would be like to be married to Jake and eat breakfast with him every morning of her life, only he'd have to talk to her, not sit buried behind the *Financial Times*. But dreaming was a waste of time, especially about him. She said loudly: 'What would you like me to do? You said yesterday that there was still some clearing up to be done.'

He lowered the paper and studied her. 'Now I wonder what I've done—or not done. You look as though your hair is going to burst into flames at any minute. Did I really say that? I couldn't have been thinking. Half an hour's telephoning should see the finish of our day's chores. I thought we might take a run into the country.'

Annis was quite unable to stop the smile spreading across her pretty face. 'Oh, that would be super!' She didn't dare say any more or he might be put off by too much enthusiasm. 'Are you quite sure there's nothing more to do?' she wanted to know.

'Quite sure. I'll go and do my phoning now and you can tell Mrs Bates that we won't be back until the evening, ask her to arrange a dinner which won't spoil if we're a bit late.'

'Where on earth are we going?' She looked down at her tweed skirt and sweater. 'Will I do as I am?'

Jake said gravely, his eyes dancing, 'You'll do very nicely, Annis,' and went away, leaving her to drink her last cup of coffee and hurry along to the kitchen to see Mrs Bates.

It wasn't until they were leaving Bath behind that Annis asked: 'Where are we going?'

'Oxfordshire, on the edge of the Cotswolds—a village called Minster Lovell.' She waited for him to say more, but he didn't, so she asked: 'Why?'

'It's my home—I have a family, you know.' He shot her a sideways glance. 'Why do you look surprised?'

'Well, you—that is, you don't seem the kind of man to have a family.' She went a little pink. 'I don't mean to be rude, but it's hard to explain.'

'Ah, you mean a lone wolf with no one to cut him down to size and only himself to bother about.'

'No, I didn't mean that at all.' She didn't know what she meant. She longed to be able to put into words what she felt about him. 'I can't explain, I don't know how.'

He went on talking just as though she hadn't spoken. 'Minster Lovell is a charming place, I think you'll like it. Not quite Cotswolds but near enough, I've always thought. We'll stop in Cirencester for coffee.'

He stopped at the King's Head in Market Place and

kept up a casual flow of amusing small talk while they
had their coffee before going on again. The day was
fine and clear and the country around them delightful
in the thin sunshine; Annis began to enjoy herself. She
had expected to feel awkward in Jake's company now
that she knew that she loved him, but she felt no such
thing—indeed, she was dreading the moment when he
and she would part company.

He had taken the road through Burford and before
they got to Witney turned off to the north to where Minster Lovell lay, nicely hidden from the rest of the world
with the River Windrush woven into its heart.

Jake drove over the bridge at the beginning of the
village, along its street and up the slight incline at the
farther end. Here the houses were rather grand, their
walls of Burford stone, and stone-tiled too. He turned
in at the gates of one of these houses, standing solitary overlooking the village, and stopped the car in the
small semi-circular drive. In summer it would be pretty
with roses and Virginia creeper and clematis. Now it
was rather bare, with a few early daffodils poking up
reluctant heads. The house was of Burford stone, like
the others, with a steep pitched roof and a great many
gables and small casement windows. It had a sturdy
front door that was opened as they got out of the car.

The woman standing there was elderly, tall and
boney and fierce-looking, and when Jake called out:
'Hullo, Poppy, lovely to see you,' Annis thought what
a very inappropriate name she had.

The rather craggy face softened as Poppy opened
the door wider. 'Well, it's nice to see you, Mr Jake.'
Her eyes slid past him to Annis. 'And the young lady.'

'Miss Annis Fothergill—meet Poppy, family friend and general mainstay.' He kissed Poppy and then kissed Annis, and at her look and heightened colour, 'Just to even things up,' he explained.

There was a narrow hall that widened into a square room which had several doors in its walls as well as two passages leading from it and a carved wood staircase, it was furnished simply with wall tables, upon which were bowls laden with spring flowers, a pair of carved wooden chairs, and a Gothic oak chest, worn smooth with age. The floor was gleaming oak too, half covered by a faded but still beautiful needlework carpet.

One of the doors was partly open. Jake pushed it wider and propelled Annis gently through it, into a low-ceilinged room, light and airy and agreeably furnished with chintz-covered chairs, several small tables, a mahogany break-fronted bookcase with glazed doors, and a large velvet-covered sofa. The sash window was curtained with mushroom velvet, and the carpet was the same colour; a restful room as well as being very pretty.

The same adjectives could be applied to the lady who got out of one of the chairs and came towards them. She was small and plump, her grey hair elegantly dressed, her round, merry face nicely made up. Her eyes were blue and twinkly and she was smiling widely. Hard on her heels came an elderly man who could have been no one else but Jake's father. Annis thought with a little flair of temper, Jake could have told me... But the thought was swallowed up in the little lady's warm greeting. She was made to feel at home instantly, kissed heartily first by Jake's mother, then his father, and then finally and for no apparent reason by Jake. Twice in ten

minutes, she thought, and blushed, because she had
liked it.

'Well, isn't this nice?' Mrs Royle wanted to know of
no one in particular, and tucked an arm through Annis's. 'You come and sit with me, dear—there's time for
a drink before lunch and I want to hear all about you.'

'But there isn't anything to tell,' protested Annis,
and then found herself, a glass of sherry in one hand,
answering the questions her companion lost no time in
putting to her. By the time Poppy came to the door to
tell them that lunch was ready, she reckoned that Mrs
Royle had a very good idea of her family and background and, strangely, she didn't mind: the questions
had been put so kindly.

Jake had got to his feet and gone out of the room behind Poppy, to return within a minute or two, his arm
tucked into that of a very old, very small lady, dressed
with great elegance in black, her white hair waved in
the style of the thirties: she looked frail, but there was
nothing frail about her voice.

'Ah, there she is, and just as pretty as you said: quite
a beauty, in fact. I hope she likes children?' She had
come to a standstill and Annis realised that she was
waiting for her to go to her. She advanced willingly,
quite composed though a trifle bewildered by the old
lady's remarks. Was she being vetted for a governess's
post? she wondered. Jake might have thought she would
welcome a job after working for Mrs Duvant. She shook
the small bony hand carefully and smiled down at the
old lady.

'I'm Jake's grandmother. I seldom come down to
lunch, but I wanted to meet you. I like your name and I

like you, my dear—there's plenty of you and you look healthy.'

Annis pinkened slightly, aware of Jake's dark eyes on her face. She said a little breathlessly: 'Yes, I'm always very well, thank you.'

The old lady nodded to herself and then looked up at her grandson.

'Well, you took your time,' she told him, 'and a good thing too as far as I can see.' She added with a faintly peevish air: 'Where's lunch? I'm hungry.'

Her son and daughter-in-law had listened to her without comment, now they assured her soothingly that lunch was on the table and there was no reason to wait a minute longer. They all crossed the hall into a smaller room with a round table at its centre, a thick brown carpet and apricot-coloured curtains, adding a splash of colour to the cream walls. A restful room, thought Annis, and sat herself down where she was bidden—opposite Jake. She would have preferred another place, away from his frequent dark glance, but she was a sensible girl and she was hungry. She ate a delicious meal, taking care not to catch his eye. Not too difficult as it turned out, for the conversation was general with old Mrs Royle taking more than her share of it. But she made no more reference to Annis, only showing a lively interest in her grandson and his work.

'Made your million yet?' she wanted to know with a chuckle. 'How's that factory in New Zealand?'

'Coming along nicely, Grandmother.' Jake's saturnine face broke into a smile. 'How about coming with me next time I visit it?'

'Take care I don't,' she answered. 'You'll have other

company with you, I've no doubt, and I've no wish to play gooseberry.'

Did that mean, thought Annis bleakly, that he had a girl-friend, that he was going to marry? She turned a polite ear to Mrs Royle's gentle chat about the garden while she pondered the matter, and came to the conclusion that probably he had.

They went back to the drawing-room for their coffee and old Mrs Royle was led back again upstairs where she had her own rooms. Annis found herself sitting beside Mrs Royle while that lady rambled pleasantly from fashion to housekeeping and back again. But not for long. Jake came back, refused coffee and pulled her to her feet. 'Come and see the garden,' he suggested. 'Father's already asleep and Mother always has a nap after lunch.'

True, Mr Royle was sitting back in his chair, his mouth slightly open, his eyes shut. Any moment now he was going to snore. But Mrs Royle didn't look in the least sleepy, although she laughed and nodded at Jake. 'And get a wrap for Annis,' she begged. 'It's cold outside.'

They went out through a small side door, Annis swathed in an old Burberry from a miscellaneous collection of coats hanging in the passage; they reminded her of home, and made her feel a little homesick until Jake took her arm and walked briskly down a brick path towards a shrubbery at the far end.

He said unexpectedly: 'I'll take you home tomorrow.'

'Oh—yes, of course. Thank you very much.' The words sounded silly, but she had been taken by surprise.

He spoke again and now his voice was very smooth

and faintly amused. 'Grandmother approves of you, isn't
that nice? She longs to be a great-granny.'

Annis gave him a puzzled look and stopped walking. 'Whatever has that got to do with me?' she wanted
to know.

'I told her that I was going to marry you.' He sounded
so casual that she could only gape at him.

'You what?' she managed.

'Told her that I was going to marry you,' he repeated
patiently. 'I daresay,' he went on thoughtfully, 'I might
not have mentioned it for a few days, but she rather pre-
cipitated things.'

'But I don't…you don't…we don't know each other,
we're not even friends.'

'No? I thought we were. Granted, initially we may
not have taken to each other, but having got to know
you, I fancy that you're just the wife I'm looking for.'
He went on deliberately: 'Notice that I don't mention
the word love. I think I've become a little cynical about
that, Annis, I'm not even sure that I believe in it any
more.' Her ear caught the bitterness in his voice and
she wondered what had happened to put it there: a girl
who'd rejected him? Someone he couldn't have? Someone who'd died? She was sure that he would never tell
her, and she wanted to know…

'I need a wife, someone to make a home, someone to
come back to, someone to entertain my friends, someone I can talk to. You happen to fit the bill.'

Surely no girl had ever had such a cold-blooded proposal? She said roundly: 'I've never heard such nonsense! There's only one good reason for getting married
to someone, and that's because you love them.' She went

scarlet then because she had that reason, didn't she, but Jake apparently did not.

'I hope to prove you wrong, darling. Suppose we give it a try? Six months if you like. See how we get on, getting to know each other, becoming friends, nothing more if you don't want that.' He gave her a long austere look. 'That's a promise, Annis.' And when she didn't answer him: 'That's why I'm taking you home tomorrow, so that you can have time to think about it.' He tucked a hand under her arm and began to walk on. 'And don't say no without considering first. You're a sensible girl, and practical, and your head isn't cluttered up with romantic ideas.'

It was on the tip of her tongue to tell him how mistaken he was but that would never do. She said rather primly: 'Very well, I'll think about it.'

'Good. If we go down this path there's a nice little herb garden at its end. Mother started it when she was first married and it's her pride and joy.'

'Oh, is it?' answered Annis blankly: apparently they weren't to mention the subject of their future again.

And indeed, she was right. The rest of the day was spent in the company of Jake's parents. They had tea together and then she was taken upstairs to say goodbye to his grandmother, who lifted a cheek for her to kiss while at the same time observing that she hoped the wedding would be a quiet one, since she couldn't abide too much fuss at her age. Apparently here was the one person sure of their future. The thought was followed by another one: old Mrs Royle wasn't the only one, Annis herself was quite sure, even without pondering the matter too deeply, that she would marry Jake because she loved him, that he was arrogant and far too self-assured and wrapped up in a successful business were things she would have to live with. And she could see no reason why she couldn't make him love her, given time. He had mentioned six months to see how it all worked out, if she couldn't get him interested, to say the least, in that time, then she would have to think again. She bade his parents goodbye with composure and got into the car beside him, answering his small talk on their way to Bath with an equal composure.

They had dinner together later and over it Jake began to tell her something of his work. He was highly successful, but he didn't stress the fact, merely mentioning that he had to travel a good deal. 'You like flying?' he asked her casually.

'I've never been in a plane.' Probably, thought Annis, she was the only girl in the country who hadn't. She added by way of an explanation: 'There are too many of us, you see. The children have heaps of friends and go away in their school holidays, but we don't all go away together.'

She started to work out what a holiday—say, in Italy—would cost if the eight of them went for two weeks and her mind boggled.

'Just so,' observed Jake, watching her face with amusement. 'But you live in a beautiful part of the country, don't you?'

'Oh, yes, and there's always such a lot to do…' A look of unease came over her face. She had remembered that if she married Jake there would be no one to help her father. Mary wasn't home and it wasn't likely that she would be, and Emma was barely twelve and her mother had far too much to do around the house. She lifted a troubled face to his. 'I'd forgotten,' she said simply, and didn't have to go on because he had understood at once.

'Naturally if you were to—er—leave home, I would take steps to see that there was someone to fill your shoes. That's a small matter, Annis, easily dealt with.'

The way he said it, she actually believed him.

They left the next morning in pouring rain and were back at the Rectory in plenty of time for lunch. Annis hadn't telephoned her mother, and the look on that lady's face as they went indoors told her at once that lunch was to have been a scrappy affair with no one there but her parents. Annis left the men in her father's study and repaired to the kitchen. She had her final week's salary in her pocket, and though she hadn't earned nearly as much as she had hoped, there was enough to fill the larder at least. With their heads together, she and her mother concocted a decent meal and she left her parent peeling potatoes while she flew down to the village shop, coming back presently with a laden basket, and viewed with some interest by Jake from the study window.

The Rector, joining him at the window, observed gently: 'I see Annis has been down to the village.' He added hopefully: 'We ought to get a splendid lunch.'

Jake turned to look at him. 'I should like to marry your daughter, sir.'

The Rector took off his glasses, polished them and put them on again—the better, presumably, to look at Jake.

'She will make a splendid wife,' he observed. 'As

long as that's what she wishes to do, I've no objection
and I'm sure her mother won't have any.' He chuckled.
'We have four daughters, you know, and mothers like
daughters to get married.'

'Annis is concerned about the amount of work she'll
leave you with…'

'True, very true, but difficulties are made to be overcome.'

'And if you'll allow me, this is one difficulty which
can be overcome easily enough.'

'You're a clever young man, doubtless you know
the answer. I really feel that we might have a glass of
sherry…'

'Annis hasn't agreed to marry me yet.' Jake's voice
held amusement.

'No? She never was a girl to be hurried. Give her
time.'

'I intend to. I should like, if I may, to come and see
her in a few days' time.'

'Of course, we shall be delighted to put you up. You
intend to remain in England for the time being?'

'Yes—I may have to go abroad for a few days from
time to time, Annis would naturally go with me if she
wanted to.'

The Rector chuckled. 'She'll be a fool if she doesn't.
She's hardly ever been out of the country, you know.'

Annis, going along the short stone passage leading
to her father's study, heard them laughing together. She
looked rather less than her usual neat self; there had
been a lot to do in the kitchen, but now a nicely cooked
meal was ready and she thanked heaven that the men
had found each other's company pleasant and not no-

ticed the time. She opened the door. 'Sorry we weren't quite ready for you,' she told them, 'but everything's on the table now.'

No one mentioned getting married over their meal, although Mrs Fothergill, interpreting her husband's speaking look more or less accurately, was bursting to ask questions. The conversation was strictly general, and it wasn't until Annis was in the kitchen again with her mother that that lady was able to indulge her curiosity.

'Tell me about Jake,' she demanded. 'There is something, isn't there?'

'Not yet, Mother. He's asked me to marry him, but I haven't said I will.'

'You're going to? You love him?' And when Annis nodded, 'That's all that counts, my dear. I couldn't wish for anyone better for you—only do remember you've got red hair,' she added obscurely.

Annis stacked the dishes tidily and turned on the taps. 'I don't know anything much about this man,' she volunteered.

Her mother wasn't listening. 'A quiet wedding,' she murmured. 'We can have the reception here. Phyllis Avery will be as mad as fire, she always wanted you for Matt.'

Annis was washing up briskly. 'Matt's keen on Mary.'

Mrs Fothergill brightened. 'Oh, I wondered...that would do just as well, wouldn't it?'

'Much better,' Annis assured her. 'Do you suppose Jake will stay for tea?'

He stayed for tea and for supper too, eating macaroni

cheese and drinking cocoa as though they were his favourite diet, and when finally he went, his leavetaking was so friendly that Mrs Fothergill, watching the tail lights of his car disappearing down the lane, remarked: 'What a dear boy he is. I'm sorry to see him go.'

Annis silently agreed with her. Jake had bidden her a pleasant, rather casual goodbye with the half promise that he would be back in three or four days. It was only as he was leaving that he mentioned that he would be flying to Brussels in the morning. Mrs Fothergill, to whom a day trip to Bath was a major event, was impressed.

Annis, anxious not to be caught up in her mother's cross-questioning, saw Audrey off to bed, made sure that Emma would follow her and came down again to help James with his Maths. And by the time they had washed the supper things, she was able to go to bed herself.

'We could have a little talk,' said her mother hopefully.

Annis kissed her fondly. 'And so we will, darling— tomorrow. I'm a bit tired, and you must be too.'

The next morning, as they made the beds together, Mrs Fothergill asked anxiously: 'You're going to marry Jake, aren't you, dear?'

Annis said slowly: 'I think that perhaps I love him more than he does me.' She sighed. 'Does that matter?'

Mrs Fothergill frowned. 'Darling, I don't see how you can be sure—I mean that Jake doesn't love you as much as you love him, he's not the kind of man to wear his heart on his sleeves, is he? I think in your shoes I'd take the risk.' She added softly: 'Love is very strong, darling.'

Annis took herself off for a long walk that afternoon, the same walk she had taken with her brothers and sisters not so many weeks ago. There was spring in the air now and the going was easier. She paused when she reached the spot where she had first met Jake and tried to remember what she had thought then, but that was obscured by her love now. All she could think was that she loved him very much and life wouldn't be the same ever again if she were to let him go out of her life.

Jake came again three days later after telephoning from the airport, so that they had time to add soup to the supper menu and Mrs Fothergill was able to make one of her mouthwatering pies. And the Reverend Mr Fothergill, shaken from his habitual calm, fetched two bottles of claret from the cellar; the last two there, as it happened.

But if Annis had expected a romantic reunion, she was doomed to disappointment. Jake took her hand briefly, dropped a kiss on her cheek and turned to her mother and father. 'Not inconvenient, I hope?' he wanted to know. 'I have to go to Washington in a week's time.'

They had tea round the fire and James, Emma and little Audrey did most of the talking, but presently when the tea things had been cleared, Jake said: 'Does anyone mind if Annis and I go somewhere and talk for a while?' He glanced out of the window. 'It's nice enough to go for a walk.'

She got to her feet. 'I'll fetch a coat,' she said quietly, and when she got downstairs again, he was waiting in the hall for her.

They walked in almost complete silence until they reached the spot where they had first met. 'This seems an appropriate place,' observed Jake cheerfully. 'Are you going to marry me, Annis?'

She looked away from him to hide the disappointment in her face. He was being so matter-of-fact, so businesslike—but then wasn't their marriage going to be that too? At least for the first few months...

She said in a clear voice: 'Yes, Jake, I'll marry you—on—on the conditions you mentioned. I don't know much about you, I can't even begin to—well, I have to get used to you...'

'You'll have every opportunity. I'm going to be rather busy for a month or so, but whenever I have to travel you shall come with me, and if you're interested I shall tell you something of my work. I suggest that we get married quite soon. I have to go to Lisbon at the end of the month, we might get married in time to go there together. I hope you share Grandmother's views about big weddings.'

Annis had no doubt in her mind that his granny had had a wonderful and very grand wedding—white satin, orange blossom, bridesmaids, the lot. It seemed that she herself was going to have to make do with a two-piece and a hat...!

'You'll wear white, of course.' Jake's voice broke into her musings. 'Girls like wedding veils and so on, don't they, and I wouldn't want to deprive you, but could we keep the numbers down—family and close friends?'

'Yes. Father and Mother couldn't afford a big reception anyway, and I'd like it to be at home.'

'Good. Let me know as soon as you've laid your plans—about three weeks' time? Don't bother with clothes, you can get all you want later.' He added: 'I'm a rich man, Annis.'

'Yes, I thought you might be, that's why I'm not absolutely certain...'

'That's silly of you. Money makes no difference at all, not the way you're looking at it, at any rate—besides, as I said before, you've got too much good sense.' He bent and kissed her suddenly and she drew back quickly before she could fling her arms round his neck.

'That's by way of being a betrothal kiss,' he said, and his voice was dry. 'I won't make a habit of it.'

They began to walk on. 'I'd like you to come up to town tomorrow and see my flat—your people won't mind if we get back late?'

'No, of course not. I—we'd better tell them; Mother will want to invite people and plan the food...'

'I'll come over for you all one day next week, and your parents can meet mine. In the meantime they can send the invitations out and so on. Not more than fifty on each side, would you say?'

Annis nodded, outwardly as cool and casual as he, while her insides quivered with excitement and her mind raced. A Vogue pattern for her dress—she would have to make it herself with her mother's help—and they could manage food for the reception between them. Audrey and Emma would be bridesmaids—Laura Ashley print wasn't too expensive, and she could make their dresses too... She was quite absorbed, and Jake, looking down at her, smiled a little. She looked quite beautiful in her old coat, her vivid hair blowing in all directions. She would pay for dressing, he could see her in his mind's eye at the foot of his table, entertaining his guests, running his house without fuss, listening intelligently to what he had to say. He had had his fair share of girl-friends, but he had never until now felt the urge to marry, and he wasn't quite sure why he wanted to do so now. Perhaps he was tired of a bachelor existence, certainly he had wished during the last few months that there had been someone to welcome him at the end of a day's work. But he hadn't wanted a romantic attachment; it was a long while ago since he had come to grief there. He said thoughtfully: 'Grandmother will be delighted,' and Annis thought sadly that it would have been nice if he had said just once that he was delighted too, but he didn't add anything, and presently she said: 'She's a very nice old lady, and I like your parents.'

They walked a long way making a few vague plans, but she sensed that Jake wasn't really interested in those. She began to ask him questions about the work he did and for the rest of the walk he talked about that. A busy life, she gathered, but in between whiles, a social one too; she rather dreaded that part of it.

CHAPTER FIVE

THEY LEFT AFTER breakfast the next morning, and since Jake had little to say for himself, Annis contented herself with mulling over the previous evening. There had been no doubt at all that her parents were delighted at their news, and the children had been beside themselves with excitement. The wedding plans had been discussed until late, and although she had peeped at Jake once or twice to see if he were bored, he had shown no sign of that, but had joined in with everyone else, suggesting some scheme quietly, agreeing with almost everything. He had been firm about the date, though, when Mrs Fothergill wanted to postpone the wedding for another week, declaring that three weeks wasn't long enough. He had persuaded her with a silkiness which Annis could not but admire; no wonder he was chairman of so many boards! By the end of the evening he had everyone doing exactly as he suggested and nothing but admiring eyes turned in his direction, and that included Hairy and Sapphro. It occurred to her that she knew very little about him, in fact, the more she saw of him the more remote he seemed—about himself, that was. She would have to remedy that smartly.

'You said you lived near Grosvenor Square...'

Jake slid past a slow moving Austin using the crown

of the road. 'Between it and Green Street, you know where that is?'

She shook her head. 'We always go to Oxford Street and Regent Street if we go to London—shopping, you know.'

'It's quite near Oxford Street. The flat is in a converted house in a narrow side street, nearer the square than Oxford Street. It's remarkably quiet too. I hope you won't find it too different from Millbury. There's no garden, but there's a wide balcony at the back and Green Park and Hyde Park aren't far away.'

'Is it big, the flat?'

'Oh, there's ample room for the two of us. There's a daily housekeeper—Mrs Turner; she sleeps in whenever I want her and whenever I'm away.'

He slowed the car as they approached Egham. 'Shall we stop for coffee? There's quite a good place here.'

It seemed that he didn't want to talk any more about the flat, indeed he brushed aside the one or two tentative questions Annis put and instead told her a little of the places he had been to, and presently, as they neared London he lapsed into silence.

Annis didn't know London well; after a while she became hopelessly lost and she let out a small sigh of relief as Jake stopped the car halfway down a short, quiet street lined with terraces of Regency houses, their doors opening on to a short flight of steps to the pavement.

He opened the outside door with his key and ushered her into a small vestibule which in turn opened into a roomy hall. There was a lift there as well as a broad staircase and a porter sitting behind a small desk. Jake nodded to him and made for the stairs, his arm on Annis's.

'A little exercise won't hurt us after the car,' he commented, 'it's not far.' His own front door was the only one on the second floor and he unlocked it briskly. 'Your future home, Annis—our future home, and welcome.'

She strained her ears for a small hint of feeling in his voice, but it sounded disappointingly casual and matter-of-fact. As she was led into the sitting-room she wondered if she was making a dreadful mistake in marrying him, and then, seeing him standing there, large and assured and smiling gently, she knew that she hadn't. She might have bitten off something more than she could chew, but she had strong teeth!

'Why do you look like that?' Jake wanted to know, and looked amused. 'As though you were arming yourself for battle.'

She smiled at him then. 'I didn't imagine it would be like this,' she said the first thing that came into her head. 'It's lovely!'

As indeed it was. The room was a fair size, furnished in pale colours which made a perfect background for the pictures on its walls, landscapes mostly. Annis, who knew very little about such things, thought they were good. She went closer to inspect them. 'That looks like a Turner,' she said thoughtfully.

'It is. Come and see the dining-room.'

This was a smaller room, furnished with an oval Sheraton table and chairs and a delicate sideboard, no pictures on the walls here, but a charming silk wallpaper, a far cry from the faded greens and brown of the Rectory.

They went through another door to the kitchen and Jake said: 'Mrs Turner will be out shopping. I told her not to bother with lunch, we can go out for that, but she'll have tea for us before we go back.'

They went out of the kitchen into the hall again and he turned a corner into a short passage with several doors. 'Bedrooms,' he said briefly. 'I daresay you'll like to have the end one with the balcony. Mine's at this end and there are a couple of bathrooms. Have a look round if you like, there are one or two phone calls I must make.' He nodded over one shoulder. 'I've a small study.'

Left alone, Annis opened a door and looked in. This would be Jake's room—no flowers, dark masculine colours, an austere bedspread but more lovely pictures on the walls. The next door led to a bathroom and the next to a smaller room, very prettily furnished but having an air of not being used very much, there was a bathroom there too, and she admired its comfort before opening the last door. Her room, Jake had said.

It was larger than the others, and lighter, because the french windows opened on to a balcony, wrought iron and roofed with glass. The room was charming, its cream walls toning with the cream and rose brocade curtains and bedspread, its furniture a pale wood she thought might be apple, inlaid with yew. The bedhead was beautifully carved with flowers and wreaths as was the mirror standing on a long table serving as a dressing table. The pictures here were flower paintings and small delicate water-colours of little animals and beside the burnished steel fireplace were two comfortable chairs. A delightful room and one in which she knew she would feel instantly at home. She peered into the adjoining bathroom and wondered who had matched the towels and soaps and jars with such care. Jake hadn't struck her as being the kind of man to bother overmuch about such things, but perhaps it was a side of him she hadn't encountered yet.

She sat down at the dressing table and tidied her hair and powdered her nose, then went slowly out of the room. She could hear Jake's voice from behind a closed door as she went down the passage, back to the sitting-room, to sit quietly until he joined her presently.

'Had a good look round?' he wanted to know. 'If you don't like anything, say so and we'll have it altered.'

'It's all perfect,' she told him seriously. 'Did you plan it all yourself?'

The little mocking smile she hated curled his mouth. 'Fishing, darling? Am I to feel flattered, though I can hardly expect jealousy—that's for those in love, isn't it? Just female curiosity? I did most of it myself, but the odd feminine touch was added by whichever girl-friend happened to be here taking an interest.' He added in quite a different voice: 'You needn't mind, Annis, none of them mattered.'

'I wasn't meaning to pry—I'm not very interested in your past life.' And that was a lie if ever there was one, and she a parson's daughter! 'That doesn't mean to say that I'm not interested in you and I expect when we've been married for a while I might ask you things, but that doesn't mean that you have to tell me—but if

I do it will only be because I'm curious about something or other.'

Jake was leaning against the table looking at her and the nasty little smile had gone. 'You're a very nice girl,' he said deliberately. 'I count myself a lucky man to be going to marry you and once we get to know each other, who knows…?' And at her look: 'I loved a girl once, Annis, a long time ago now. I've forgotten my love, but not the promise I made myself that I'd never get deeply involved with a girl again. I'm not going to get deeply involved with you, you know that already, and that suits both of us, doesn't it? There's something very restful about you, darling, like an old friend who's ready to listen or laugh at will—and you've a good brain. If I want to talk business I'll be able to without boring you to tears.'

She supposed that this was the highest praise he could give her and with it she would have to be content, for the time being at least. But she would break down the wall he had built around himself, although it would take time. In the meantime she would be what he wanted, a friend ready to laugh or listen—and she would learn to be a good wife. Only she wished he wouldn't call her darling, a word which should mean so much and which meant nothing.

'Thank you for telling me,' she said quietly, 'about the girl, I mean. I'm sorry. That's why you work so hard, I expect, and I hope you will tell me about your business deals when you want to, it's all new to me, and fascinating.'

'It's certainly that; it's a challenge too!' Jake stood

up. 'How about lunch? I booked a table for half past one; we can just make it.'

He ushered her into the magnificence of Claridges with the air of a man who had been there before and took it all rather for granted, and she wasn't sure if she should be pleased or vexed that he also took it for granted that she shouldn't be overawed. Which she was. The thick carpeting, the buzz of conversation absorbed by the size of the place, the pink and blue and gold and ivory everywhere; the elegant women, the executive types escorting them, the eye-catching staircase, they all combined to make her aware of her last year's suit, her no longer new leather handbag and her shoes, brilliantly polished but as elderly as the handbag. All the same, she sat down composedly and drank the sherry Jake ordered for her, then followed the waiter to their table in the adjoining restaurant. She held her head high, pretending to herself that she was accustomed to strolling into Claridges for lunch any day of the week which suited her, and strongly under the impression that the eyes watching her were scorning her suit. As a matter of fact, they were on her fiery head and lovely face—appreciative or envious according to sex.

With discreet help from Jake she chose lobster patties, tournedos Rossini, pommes de terre Berny, and when the sweet trolley came, a delicious confection of ice cream, honey, pear and fudge, helped nicely on their way by champagne followed by a bottle of Château Talbot, which she recognised quite rightly as a claret while remaining unaware of its price. She took an appreciative sip and pronounced it very nice, and Jake agreed with her, his eyes snapping with amusement.

He was entertaining, telling her amusing little
stories of his travels, his work, the deals he had pulled
off, but he made no effort to resume their conversation
in the flat. That, Annis guessed, was to be decently forgotten, perhaps one day he would tell her about the girl
he had loved and why he hadn't married her—but that
would be a long way ahead, once they had got to know
each other and established a sound friendship. Unless of
course it didn't work out and they agreed to part. And if
ever that happened, she vowed silently, he would never
know her real feelings; she'd die first.

'Coffee?' asked Jake gently, and looked at her enquiringly. 'You were very far away just then, darling?'

Annis rushed into speech; a jumble of thanks for her
lunch, the heavenly food, and because she had had too
much claret, her near-panic at being there at all.

'You're doing very nicely,' he assured her. 'It's time
you realised that you're a beautiful young woman, quite
able to hold your own wherever you are. You'll be stunning when we've got you some new clothes.'

He had spoken deliberately, his dark eyes on her face.
'And don't get on your high horse, Annis, you know as
well as I do that you'll knock 'em cold in the latest fashion. If you can look beautiful in that blue velvet sack
you wore to the Averys' dinner party, you'll attract all
eyes in couture.'

She felt rage boiling up inside her, and then suddenly
giggled. 'But it was all I had, you know there's never
been much opportunity...'

'So I gather. I hope you gave it to the church bazaar
or sent it to the jumble.'

'As a matter of fact, I gave it to our Mrs Wells; she wanted some new cushion covers.'

Jake let out a bellow of laughter so that people around them turned to look at them, and Annis exclaimed: 'Oh, hush, do, everyone's looking!'

'My dear girl, they've been looking at you ever since we sat down.' He passed his cup for more coffee. 'Shall we go and buy you some dresses now?'

She said no quite firmly, although she couldn't quite keep the regret out of her voice or her face.

'We are engaged, you know,' he said with faint mockery. 'It would be quite proper.'

'Yes, I know…it's hard to explain…'

He said with a trace of impatience: 'Then don't. But I hope you're not going to shy away from a ring?' He looked at her capable, well kept hands clasped before her on the table. 'Have you any preference?'

Her eyes glowed. 'Sapphires—well, a sapphire,' she amended hastily. 'That's if you don't mind.'

He smiled. 'I like them myself. Shall we go and get it now? There's plenty of time before tea.'

They went to Asprey's where a velvet cushion was laid on a table and a selection of rings were laid upon it for her choice. She sat staring down at them; they all looked very expensive, but she had no idea of the price. She looked rather shyly at Jake and when the nice elderly man serving them had moved away for a moment, whispered: 'Jake, they all look very pricey.'

He only smiled at her. 'You'll only be engaged once, darling, so we might as well do the thing properly.'

Which somehow made it all seem very mundane— besides, she sensed that he wasn't very interested; she was to please herself and she had no doubt that he would pay what it cost with the utmost good humour.

She decided on three sapphires, set close together and ringed by diamonds set in gold. It was a beautiful ring, but she took care not to rhapsodise over it, slipping it on to her finger quickly because he was already getting out his cheque book and had shown no sign of wanting to put it on for her. It looked strange there and far too opulent for the rest of her, but it stood for something too, her love, she would be reminded of that each time she looked at it.

They went back to the flat for tea after that, and while Mrs Turner was getting it, Annis thanked Jake with careful warm friendliness. 'It's quite beautiful,' she told him, 'and thank you for being so generous.'

He glanced at her hand. 'It becomes you very well, you made a good choice. We should have bought a wedding ring at the same time. They'll have your size, of course. Have you any preference?'

She wanted to tell him that she wanted most strongly to choose her own wedding ring, but she managed not to. 'No,' she said quietly, 'gold—plain gold. Will you have one too?'

He looked surprised. 'I hadn't given it a thought. But if you want me to I'll get myself one at the same time.'

He sounded as if he was going to buy an extra packet of something on the grocery list, but at least he was willing to wear a ring. Somehow she felt it was a small triumph.

They ate their tea unhurriedly and left immediately after. 'We'll eat on the way,' Jake told her. 'I told your mother not to keep anything hot.' And in the car as they were roaring down the motorway: 'I'll have to leave tomorrow; I've got a board meeting I must attend and if we're going away after the wedding I'd better hurry things forward a bit.'

'When will you be back? There's the time of the wedding to settle and who's to be asked…'

'Oh, morning, don't you think? You decide that—and as few guests as possible, don't you agree? Could we whittle them down to about twenty-five on either side? I'll remember to phone Mother about it. I'll come down as soon as I can—at the moment I don't know when that will be.'

And with that Annis had to be content. They stopped in Shaftesbury for dinner and got to the Rectory about ten o'clock, to find her mother and father still up, obviously waiting for them.

The next hour was spent drinking tea, admiring the ring and discussing the wedding, and even if, as Annis suspected, Jake wasn't deeply interested in the conversation, he concealed it very well, agreeing to the plans her mother was making, agreeing too to her father's suggestion about the actual service, apologising with charm because he would have to leave early in the morning. And when they went up to bed, he kissed her lightly on her cheek in a fashion which won her mother's approval: Mrs Fothergill, while romantic at heart, deplored demonstrative affection before an audience. 'You'll see each other in the morning,' she observed comfortably as she followed Annis upstairs.

But only briefly. Annis, setting the breakfast she had cooked for him on the table, hoped in vain for a word or two of regret at his having to leave her. Beyond thanking her for her efforts, he ate the meal in silence, his mind, she had no doubt, already on his forthcoming board meeting.

Beyond a hasty peck on her cheek and a terse: 'I'll ring you,' he had nothing further to say. She stood at the door, watching the car out of sight, feeling lost.

Her mother came down presently. 'I waited until Jake had gone,' she said. 'I knew you'd want to be together.' She sighed and smiled. 'You aren't going to see much of each other before the wedding, are you?'

'No, but everything's decided, isn't it? We can go ahead with the invitations and we'd better go to Bath and get the material for my dress and the little girls.' Annis smiled brightly at her mother. 'We're going to be busy, darling.'

Which they were. Mrs Fothergill hadn't enjoyed herself so much in years, she confided to Annis, even though money was tight. And Annis, her mouth full of pins, cutting out her wedding dress on the drawing-room floor, had to agree with her; the house rang with excited voices and the kitchen table was littered with lists of food and drink, recipes for canapés and replies to invitations. Annis was to be forgiven if she rather lost sight of Jake for a week or two. True, he had phoned from time to time, but she knew that he didn't want to be bothered with details; as long as she was there, walking down the aisle on Colonel Avery's arm on the stroke of half past ten, nothing else mattered very much.

It was Matt who was her right hand—taking the dog for a walk if she hadn't the time, driving up to Bath to collect the material she had ordered, driving her to Salisbury to get her slippers, sitting at the kitchen table, laboriously stoning fruit for the cake, which Mrs Fothergill had decided to make herself. Annis and she were both clever cooks; they could ice it together and no one would know.

Mr and Mrs Royle came over one day, bringing with them a dozen bottles of champagne which they declared they had been saving for their son's wedding, and the two ladies, luckily taking to each other on sight, spent a delightful afternoon mulling over their own weddings and this one in particular. 'Such a beautiful girl,' sighed Mrs Royle, 'and so sweet, and a good housewife, I'm sure—not that she'll have to bother overmuch with that. Jake has an excellent housekeeper. The house we live in will be his one day, of course, but I believe he's thinking of buying one for himself. There's a delightful place going at Gilford St Charles, and of course Aunt Dora's house in Bath is his now.'

Mrs Fothergill's bosom swelled with pride; her dear Annis had done well for herself. Jake was a splendid man, good-looking, comfortably off, clever—and Annis loved him. He loved her, of course, otherwise he wouldn't have asked her to marry him. 'They'll make a splendid couple,' she observed proudly, and her companion agreed.

There was only a week to go when Jake arrived early one afternoon. Annis was grooming Nancy, escaping for an hour from white satin, bridesmaids' dresses and whether or not the potted plants Mrs Avery had sent over would be too large for the drawing-room. She was in slacks, wellingtons and an old shirt of Edward's and her hair was tied back in a no-nonsense fashion which on any other girl would have rendered her plain.

'I just hope,' said Annis to the donkey as she started on her shaggy coat, 'that they remember to look after you properly—there's your hoofs to be done in May, and the vet had better have another look at those teeth...'

'I see no reason why we shouldn't be able to pay a visit before then,' observed Jake from the door. He startled her so much that she dropped the brush and spun round to face him, her mouth open, her eyes surprised.

'My goodness, you gave me a fright!' and when he walked over and kissed the top of her tousled head: 'How nice to see you.' And then, fearful of not appearing sufficiently pleased at his arrival: 'Are you staying?'

'For the night, if I may. I must go home on the way back,' he added dryly. 'I'll be back in time for the wedding. Is everything fixed up?'

Annis had picked up the brush and was working away at Nancy's coat: it gave her something to do. She was feeling strangely shy. 'If I'd known I'd have tidied myself...'

Jake was lounging against the side of the stall. 'You look charming as you are. Have you nearly finished, or shall I give you a hand?'

She looked at the impeccable grey suit, the silk shirt and the Italian silk tie. 'I've nearly finished,' she told him, and suited the action to the word, rewarding Nancy with a carrot and bidding her to be a good girl.

'Have you been busy?' she asked as they walked towards the house.

'Very. I should warn you that I shall have to meet one or two people while we're away. I hope we shall be able to get away for a week or so during the summer.'

'We'll be at the flat?'

He shot her a quick glance. 'Yes—at least you will, I may be travelling from time to time. You can come here as often as you like. I've ordered a car for you so that you can get about—a small Talbot…'

Annis stopped in her tracks. 'Jake—oh, Jake, how absolutely super! Just for me?'

'Just for you. It will make you independent—you can go wherever you want, within reason.'

She was silent. She didn't want to be independent and if she went anywhere she wanted to be with him, but quite obviously he didn't feel the same way. 'Thank you very much, Jake, it's very kind of you, and thoughtful. I shall love driving it and I'll be able to come home if—if you're away.'

'That's what I thought; no need for you to moon around on your own at the flat.'

It sounded bleak put like that, but she refused to be daunted. She said cheerfully: 'No, of course not. Does Mother know you're here? We'll have supper early if you like.'

Jake was gone the next morning with a parting: 'Shan't be able to get down until the wedding, I'm afraid, so I'll see you at the church.'

Her face was serene as she waved him goodbye, but back in her room she allowed herself the luxury of a good cry, knowing that if her mother noticed her red eyes—and she would, of course—she would put it down to a quite natural reluctance to say goodbye to Jake.

The few days left went quickly with the house in a ferment of cleaning and polishing, china, stored for years on top shelves of deep Victorian cupboards, brought out to be washed and stacked neatly, cutlery to be polished, glasses to be burnished, the menu conned again and again and everything needed for it. There was the cake to admire too, looking positively professional after Annis and her mother had spent back-aching hours icing it. Now there was only the baking to do and the sandwiches to make, and that was last-minute work.

Annis, decorating the church with flowers sent over by Mrs Avery, heaved a sigh of relief that by this time tomorrow it would all be over. If this was a quiet country wedding, what must a big affair be like! But then, of course, there would be caterers and someone to do the flowers and a hairdresser. Which reminded her that she would have to wash her hair when she got home.

Matt came into the church just as she was gathering up the mess she had made. 'That looks nice,' he told her. 'Lord, Annis, I never thought when I introduced you to Jake that you'd be getting married within a month or two.'

'Nor did I,' said Annis soberly. 'I can't quite believe it, even now.'

'You'll come down and see us?'

'Of course. Jake's given me a car, so when he's away I can drive myself.'

'Won't you go with him?'

'I expect I shall sometimes, but perhaps it won't always be convenient.'

Something in her face stopped him from saying more. 'Everyone's home for the big event, I suppose?'

Annis nodded. 'Yes, Mary got here this morning, Edward came last night.' She frowned. 'I hope it isn't going to be too much for Mother—I mean, the children...'

'I don't see why it should be, they're all at school

and there's only little Audrey who needs an eye kept
on her, and I'll do that.'

'Oh, will you, Matt? Thanks awfully. She's still so
small.'

Matt scuffed his shoe on some ancient brass let into
the church floor. 'Well, I'm almost family, aren't I? Besides, I'm going to marry Mary.'

'I thought perhaps you might. I'm so glad. Does she
know?'

'Well, in a way. We'll wait until she's finished her
training. Mother always thought it would be you.' He
took the odds and ends of stalks and leaves from her
as they started to leave the church.

'Yes, I know—what a crazy idea!' They laughed together as they went back to the Rectory, where Matt
was instantly pressed into moving furniture out of the
drawing-room and Annis, much against her will, was
told to go upstairs and do something about her hands.

'There's some pale pink varnish on my dressing
table,' Mary told her. 'For heaven's sake use it, Annis,
and rub in lots of cream.'

By the time Annis came down again, her hands
nicely done and her hair washed and still damp, the relations had begun to arrive. Not many of them, and there
were rooms enough in the Rectory to house them all.
Supper was a noisy family party, and directly after it,
Emma and Audrey were sent to bed so that they would
be up early. Annis was sent to bed too, with strict instructions to stay in bed in the morning. 'Breakfast in
bed,' ordered her mother, 'and you'll have to be up and
getting dressed directly after.'

So she went obediently up the stairs and into her

room. Her case was packed with the new clothes they had somehow contrived to buy: not very many of them, but what there was was good. And her wedding dress hung in the wardrobe, white satin, very simply made, with the plain net veil folded neatly over the shabby chair by the window. The shoes were there too, narrow white satin with little heels because she was a tall girl already and didn't want to tower over Colonel Avery as they went down the aisle. She went and sat down at the mirror and stared at her face. It looked back at her, a little apprehensive as well as excited. She wished she could have seen Jake for just a little while that evening. She was suddenly afraid that perhaps she had bitten off more than she could chew.

'Have I been a fool?' she asked her reflection, and naturally got no answer. Not then, at any rate.

She had it the next morning, going down the aisle on the Colonel's stout arm, a vision of loveliness even if a little pale; her hair blazing above the white satin of her gown, only half hidden by her veil. She looked calm and serene, although her insides were churning with excitement, but her eyes sought Jake's large, reassuring figure the minute they entered the church. He was standing with his back to her, but he turned his head as Mrs Twigg at the organ broke into an enthusiastic rendering of, 'Oh, perfect love,' and smiled. The smile was for Annis alone and she smiled back at him. He might not love her, but she loved him enough for both of them—a dicey state of affairs, she thought dreamily as they paced through the little church, but a challenge. She lifted her chin; she liked a challenge and she had her answer—even if she was a fool, she was a loving fool. Was it John Donne who wrote, 'I am two fools for loving thee…?'

She was standing beside Jake now. His hand caught hers for a second and gave it a friendly squeeze and she looked up at him, searching, even at that last minute, for what she longed to see… It wasn't there, but in his face there was liking and even affection. They would do to go on with.

CHAPTER SIX

GOING DOWN THE aisle, her hand tucked in Jake's, Annis had the sensation that she was in a dream. The church was packed, for not only had the invited guests come, but the village had turned out, man, woman and child. Even old Mrs Crocker in her wheelchair had been parked by the font so that she could get a good view. She smiled and nodded, touched that they had all come to wish them happy. Mrs Phipps from the village pub had got a new hat—a large felt, wide-brimmed, quite unsuitable for anything but a wedding, but then there were still five of the Rector's children…and Phipps himself, with whom she had had many a wordy tussle about sending the children to Sunday School, was beaming at her with all the goodwill in the world. And Mrs Wells wearing one of Mrs Fothergill's old hats, sent to the jumble sale last year… Annis passed them all and then paused with Jake in the porch while the photographer took a picture, to the great delight of the Sunday School class posed to throw confetti.

'Who said it was to be a quiet wedding?' asked Jake as they drove the short distance to the Rectory.

'Well, I've lived here all my life,' Annis pointed out almost apologetically. 'Besides, it makes a bit of excitement…'

She was relieved to hear his laugh.

The reception was, from the villagers' point of view, a resounding success. The some seventy-odd guests Jake and Annis had finally agreed on inviting were swelled, not altogether legitimately, by those living in the village who had the nous to walk through the open Rectory door and join everyone else. Nobody minded, and if the Rector had qualms about the way the champagne was being got through by those who shouldn't be there, he was too good a man to say anything. The sandwiches and vol-au-vents and tiny sausage rolls Annis and her mother had slaved over were gobbled up as fast as they appeared, and it was only because Mrs Fothergill slipped away with some of the wedding cake, to hide it in a tin in the kitchen, that there was any of that saved, either.

What with the speeches and telegrams and everyone wanting to say a few words to the bride and groom, it was a good deal later than they had planned by the time Annis and Jake got into the car, to drive off in another hail of confetti and shouts of, 'Good luck!' from the mass of people on the Rectory lawn, swelled to vast proportions now by the rest of the village who had just popped up to have a quick look.

Out of the village, Jake pulled up, got out and removed the old boot, the coloured balloons and the chalked messages scrawled on the back of the car.

'I suspect the hand of brother James,' he observed as he got back in. 'Be sure to remind me to do the same on his wedding day.'

Which remark gave Annis a pleasant little glow because it sounded so permanent.

'Did you get anything to eat?' he asked her.

'Me? Oh, a sandwich or two and a piece of cake. Why?'

'We shan't have time to stop for dinner—not if we're to catch the plane I've got tickets for. We can have supper in Lisbon.' He made it sound as though Lisbon was just round the corner.

And after that they hardly spoke while the Bentley slid with silent power up the motorway towards Heathrow.

There was someone waiting to take the car when they reached the airport and a porter to take their luggage, and because they had cut it rather fine there was no queueing, just a brisk walk along endless corridors after they had gone through Customs. They were the last on board the plane and since they were travelling first class they had the compartment more or less to themselves. Annis, excited now, strove to look as though she'd done it all before—all the same Jake had to do up her seat belt for her and reassure her as the plane began to move forward. She wasn't exactly nervous, she hastened to assure him, but it was the first time...

'It's exactly like a bus without the stops,' he assured her kindly, 'and it's a very short flight.'

It seemed even shorter by reason of the coffee and sandwiches, the drinks, the magazines and papers, interlarded by Jake's casual talk. In no time at all the lights of Lisbon were pointed out to her and they were coming in to land.

There was a car waiting for them at the airport. Annis, accustomed to queue for a bus or wait for a taxi, wondered if this was the way in which Jake always travelled or whether it was because they were on their

honeymoon, although perhaps honeymoon wasn't quite
the right word; after all, Jake had some business to attend to while they were there. She refused to think about
that and looked out of the window at the brightly lighted
streets. Presently they crossed an enormous square with
a magnificent archway facing the sea, and opening out
on to a broad tree-lined avenue.

'The best shops are here,' said Jake, breaking into
her thoughts. 'You can get a taxi from the hotel easily enough.'

Annis said, 'Yes, of course,' in a bright voice, wondering if he would be free to spend any time with her at
all, and then went on, just as brightly: 'This is a beautiful avenue...'

'It stretches for miles; there is a wonderful tropical palm garden at its end. We'll find time to go there.
Here is the hotel.'

A magnificent building, streaming with bright lights,
exuding luxury from every window. They went inside
and someone—the manager, Annis supposed—came
to meet them, before handing them over to a porter,
who ushered them into a lift and sent them soaring up
to the third floor.

Their rooms were at the back—because of the noise,
Jake explained—and overlooked a large garden. There
was a small sitting-room dividing them and a bathroom
at each end, and Annis, never having seen anything like
it before in her life, gaped at the marble bath and piles
of thick towels.

She wandered back into her room presently, admiring the dark, heavy furniture, the bowl of flowers, the
fruit arranged so invitingly on a little table. This was

certainly something to tell everyone when she got home again. She pulled herself up short; she would have another home now, with Jake.

The sitting-room was charming and long windows opened on to a balcony. She went outside and looked around her. It was evening now, at home they would be thinking about going to bed, but from the subdued noise coming from the streets, everyone here was still very much awake. A pang of homesickness made her gulp and she turned away to find Jake standing just behind her, watching her.

'All rather different, isn't it?' he asked. 'And it's been an exciting day for you too. I've asked them to send a meal up here—I think you'll like that better than going down to the restaurant at this time of the evening.'

'Thank you, Jake—it's all rather strange. I expect you've seen it all before and you're used to travelling.'

'Yes, but it's lonely sometimes. I'm not doing anything tomorrow, we'll have a day sightseeing, if you like.' He crossed to a cabinet against a wall. 'We'll have a drink before dinner, shall we?'

And when she was sipping her sherry: 'You'll have plenty to write home about. Little Audrey wanted to come with us, didn't she? We must send her a postcard. You can ring your mother up in the morning, too—it's a bit late now, isn't it?'

Annis looked at him with gratitude. 'I'd love to, and I'm glad you don't have to work tomorrow. I don't know much about Lisbon...'

'I'll tell you something about it while we eat. Here's the waiter...'

The meal was delicious, although she wasn't sure

what she was eating. They drank *vinho verde* with it and then sat for a little while over dark, rich coffee, until Jake said briskly: 'You look like a tawny owl. Go to bed, Annis.'

She wished him goodnight, giving him a quick kiss on the cheek, because all her life she had kissed her parents goodnight and it was going to be a habit hard to break. As she undressed she must remember, she told herself sleepily, not to do it anymore. There was an awful lot to remember if their marriage was to be a success; Jake had suggested six months living together on nothing more than a friendly footing, but she thought they would know long before then if it was going to work out. Of course, she reminded herself, yawning hugely, she already knew her own mind. All she had to do was to make Jake fall in love with her.

She curled up in bed, her wits already woolly with sleep. Was it possible for a man to fall in love with someone he regarded as nothing more than a friend and partner? She wasn't sure, and she was far too tired to bother.

Breakfast was a disappointingly silent meal—not that Jake was ill-tempered, merely that he wasn't accustomed to talking at that meal; he had the *Telegraph* and the *Financial Times* folded by his plate, and after he had asked her if she had slept well, and what she would like to eat, he had nothing more to say. So Annis ate her rolls and ham and fruit and drank the three cups of coffee, not saying anything at all until he finally put the paper down, passing his cup for more coffee as he did so.

'I'm sorry,' he told her, half laughing, 'I'm so used

to breakfasting by myself and I do enjoy the peace and quiet.'

Annis's fine eyes flashed with instant rage. If that was how he felt why in heaven's name had he married her? She said with the utmost sweetness: 'I like peace and quiet too, perhaps you could order me a newspaper each morning?'

Jake put down his coffee cup. 'You sound just like a wife,' he observed blandly.

'Well, I am, aren't I?'

'Certainly you are. I'll mend my ways at once, otherwise your hair will catch fire.'

He was laughing at her and after a moment she burst out laughing too. 'I promise I won't nag,' she told him. 'Do you have to work at all today?' She gave him a direct look. 'Because if you want to, that's OK—you did say you had to come here on business, you don't have to take me out…'

He lounged back in his chair looking at her. 'I've a meeting tomorrow morning, but until then I'm free. I thought we'd take a look at the town: you'd like to see the shops, wouldn't you?' And when she nodded: 'As soon as we get back, I'll arrange for you to have an account at my bank, in the meantime we'll get some *escudos* for you.'

'I've got a little money,' began Annis, conscious of the few pounds in her purse.

'Now you're my wife, I prefer to give you an allowance.' Jake sounded austere, so she took the hint and said no more about it, only went to get the knitted jacket which went with the dress she had bought: a pretty knitted cotton in a pale coffee shade which brought out the best in her hair. It was a warm day and the sky was blue. Crossing the foyer with Jake, she felt suddenly elated. Things would turn out all right. They were already good friends; he liked her. She would have to present a different image in a little while, just enough to startle him out of his acceptance of her as a good friend and nothing else. She almost skipped out of the door, only remembering just in time that she was now a married lady and must mind her manners.

There was a car outside, with a man lounging in the driver's seat, but he got out when they reached him, said something to Jake and went away.

'I've rented a car,' Jake explained, holding the door open for her. 'It saves a great deal of time, and we can get around more.'

He drove down the long avenue, back towards the square she remembered, but just before they reached it, he parked the car and invited her to get out. The street was lined with elegant shops, but he walked her past the first two or three and opened the door of a jewellers.

'I haven't bought you a wedding present,' he explained, and she went red, remembering the leather wallet she had bought for him and then hidden away in her case because if she had given it to him, he might have felt compelled to get her something in return.

Jake eyed her with amusement. 'You should blush more often,' he told her. 'It suits you.'

'There's no need—' she began, but he wasn't listening, and already there was a small dark man advancing to meet them, bowing and smiling.

'Mr Royle,' he bowed again. 'I am delighted that you come again.'

So he'd been before—buying what for whom? Annis glanced up at Jake and encountered a look of such amusement that she felt her cheeks grow hot again. She heard him say airily: 'You see now why it is such an advantage to have no—er—sentimental feelings about each other.' His smile mocked her. 'Earrings, I think. Shall we see if there is something which will match your ring?'

She sat down obediently on a little velvet chair before a small table with a winged mirror, and presently, deep in the enthralling task of trying on one jewel after another, she quite forgot what she had been angry about. They settled on a charming pair; sapphire drops surrounded by diamonds hanging from a short diamond-studded chain. Annis, examining them in the mirror, thought them exquisite. 'I'd like to keep them on,' she decided.

'Why not?' agreed Jake idly, writing a cheque.

They were on their way out when she stopped to admire an antique brooch, a true lovers' knot from which was suspended a little diamond heart.

And when Jake asked: 'Do you like that?' she said quite unthinkingly: 'It's lovely!'

Jake nodded to the salesman. Before she could protest the brooch had been taken from the glass case, encased lovingly in velvet, and Jake was writing another cheque.

'But I didn't mean...that is, you had no need to buy it. I've got my present.'

'I've yet to hear a law stating that a man may not give his wife whatever he chooses.' He grinned wickedly at her. 'Let's go and look at some dresses.'

'But I've got three new...' She stopped at the look in his eye, and said meekly: 'All right, Jake.'

An hour later they were in the car again, the boot cluttered up by a number of dress boxes. They had stopped for coffee at a little pavement café and now they were on their way to the tropical garden. Four dresses, thought Annis happily, and almost choked at the memory of their price. But Jake hadn't turned a hair, indeed he had urged her to buy the ones she had deliberately discarded because they were very expensive. So she had. She sat now, going over their perfections in her mind, not noticing anything much until Jake slowed the car and turned into what appeared to be the beginnings of a park.

There was a small gate to one side, almost hidden by trees and shrubs, and someone was standing there selling tickets. They went through and Annis, for the moment at least, forgot her new clothes and jewellery. There were ferns and tropical plants all round them, the damp air fragrant with them, little riverlets running in and out amongst their roots and steps cut in rocks so that one could wander at will. They spent an hour there, getting vaguely lost from time to time, discovering a cave hidden away with a pool at its centre and benches against its walls so that one might, if one wished, sit and contemplate the water. And there were ducks and waterfowl and swans and fish. Annis peered and stared, nipped up and down steps and sniffed at the strangely exotic flowers and would have stayed for the rest of the day if Jake hadn't reminded her that it was well past noon.

She said at once: 'Oh, I'm sorry, Jake—I got carried

away, I've never seen anything like this before. I hope you've not been bored. Have you been before?'

She wished she hadn't asked that, for his face assumed a bland expression and he said shortly: 'Oh, yes, several times.'

And on one of those times something had happened to make him angry—or unhappy. She thought crossly that it was like reading a book and coming to a page which wasn't there.

But they lunched amicably enough and in the afternoon he drove her to Sintra, where they went round the palace with its strange shaped chimneypots, and then drove back to the coast to visit Caicais and Estoril. They had tea here, at the very English tea-shop, then drove back to Lisbon in time for Annis to change into one of her new dresses—a pale green crêpe-de-chine which transformed her into a quite breathtakingly lovely girl and made a splendid background for the sapphires. 'And I would have worn the brooch,' she explained to Jake, 'but I thought it might be too much of a good thing.'

He agreed, staring rather hard at her. Excitement had given her a colour and she had done her hair in a careless knot which accentuated her pretty neck. 'Is something the matter?' she asked, seeing his look.

'Do tell me. I'm not used to dressing up, you know.'

'There's nothing wrong,' he said slowly, 'and you—you look charming. Shall we go down?'

The evening was an unqualified success. Annis, rather heady by reason of the admiring glances cast at her and the knowledge that her dress was by far the most charming in the room, drank rather too much champagne, which made her even headier, so that when Jake suggested that they might dance, she was more than willing.

'Mind you,' she warned him, 'I'm not much good. There are dances in the village hall at home, of course, but I daresay they're a bit out of date. And when there's been a disco for the youth club I've gone to help with the food and that sort of thing.' She gave him a disarming smile, a bit hazy because of the champagne. 'I'll do my best, though.'

He didn't answer, only smiled a little and whirled her on to the floor. The band was playing an old-fashioned foxtrot and after a moment or two of fright that she might tread on his feet or use the wrong foot herself, she forgot all about it and enjoyed herself. Jake was a good dancer, and for once she had a partner who was taller than herself; it had always been her fate to be partnered by small men: instead of looking over a head she could only see a black tie.

They danced for a long while, only stopping for a drink from time to time, until Jake said: 'I'm sorry to break up a delightful evening, but I have to be at a meeting at half past eight tomorrow.'

Annis looked up at the ornate gilt clock on the wall by their table. 'But it's one o'clock!' she exclaimed in horror. 'My goodness, why didn't you say so before?'

He sounded surprised. 'I was enjoying myself.'

'Me too.' In their sitting room she wished him goodnight, keeping well away in case he might think that she was going to kiss him again. 'Will you be back for lunch?' she wanted to know brightly.

'I doubt it. Will you be all right? Take a taxi down to the shops and see if you can find something pretty for Audrey. You can have lunch up here if you like—it might be a good idea.'

At the door she paused. 'Thank you for a lovely evening,' she said dreamily. 'It really was super.'

She hadn't been looking forward to being on her own, but it wasn't as bad as she'd expected. A taxi was found for her at once and deposited her near the shops, and she blessed Jake's forethought in stuffing a roll of *escudos* in her handbag, because she hadn't given it a thought. She counted the notes quickly, rather taken aback at the amount; there would be more than enough to buy something for her little sister.

But there was plenty of time. She saw some exquisite handkerchiefs, just the thing for Mary, and a set of embroidered table mats which would do for her mother, by the time she had bought them she felt she deserved her coffee and sat down in the same café she and Jake had gone to. A mistake, as it turned out, because several men asked if they might join her. She dismissed them with an unselfconscious dignity which was far more effective than a display of indignation, drank her coffee at leisure, then went on her way.

She found what she wanted for little Audrey finally, a silver chain, as fine as a spider's thread, with a little cross studded with turquoise at its end. She put the little box in her handbag and waved to a passing taxi: it was almost one o'clock and she was hungry. Pleased too that the morning had passed so quickly without Jake. She had just got in and was giving the driver the name of the hotel when another taxi went past, going slowly. Jake was in it, and sitting beside him was a pretty woman, dark and vivacious and smiling. Smiling at Jake. Annis gave a snort of rage and looked out of the other window. She was sure that Jake hadn't seen her; he'd been staring too hard at his companion. At the hotel she bounced out of the cab, tipped the driver at least twice as much as she needed to, and went inside.

The manager came to meet her, looking fatherly. 'Madam will lunch in her sitting-room?' he asked.

Annis's eyes kindled. 'No, thanks. I'll come down to the restaurant.'

She sailed past him and hurried up the magnificent staircase, arriving a little out of breath on the third floor, but all the better for having worked off some of her temper.

It only took a few minutes to tidy herself, then she went back downstairs again in a more leisurely manner and went into the restaurant. She was given a table for two in the window, where the sunshine shone on her brilliant head and made a lovely picture of her, so that several people looked at her and then looked again. She had disposed of iced melon and was about to start on her lobster Cardinal when a dark, merry-faced youngish man crossed the room and stopped beside her.

'Mrs Royle? You will forgive me, but I am an acquaintance of your husband and I am desolated to see you lunching alone. Would you consider that I should join you? I also am alone. Jake does not come, perhaps?'

Annis put down her fork. 'You know Jake, I don't think he mentioned having friends here...'

'Roberto Gonzalez. I am in the wine trade, and our paths have frequently crossed.'

Annis held out a hand. 'Annis Royle. Do sit down, Mr Gonzalez, and have your lunch with me.'

'You are kind.' He took the chair the waiter had drawn from the table, and gave his order. 'You do not drink wine?' he asked. 'You will allow me to order a light white wine—our wines are excellent.'

He was a good talker, and Annis, still smarting from Jake's behaviour, was more than ready to be friendly. They were chatting like old friends over their coffee when she glanced up and saw Jake standing just inside the door.

He didn't smile as he walked towards her, indeed there was no expression on his face at all, which was she found a little intimidating, all the same she smiled up at him and said: 'Hullo, Jake. Have you had lunch? I think you know Mr Gonzalez...'

Her companion had got to his feet. 'Your wife was lunching alone and I ventured to suggest that we might share a table. How are you, Jake?'

'Very well, thank you. We must meet and have a chat some time, but now you must forgive us, we have an appointment.'

'Of course—and I also must work, alas. Mrs Royle, it has been a great pleasure meeting you, I hope that we may do so again, and very soon.'

Annis held out a hand and gave him a wide smile, then pinkened when he kissed it instead of shaking it as she had expected. All the same, it was rather nice and perhaps Jake would benefit by a little competition.

Alone with him, she asked cheerfully: 'What appointment?' and when he said briefly: 'We will go to our sitting-room, Annis,' she walked ahead of him out of the restaurant and into the lift, looking, she hoped, cool and composed.

The room was pleasantly cool because the shutters had been closed for an hour or more, but she crossed to the window and opened them to let in the bright sunshine before she turned to face Jake.

'I asked you to have lunch here.' He spoke casually.

'Yes, I know you did, but I felt like being with people. Do you mind?'

'I mind very much. I didn't take you for such a fool, Annis. A pretty—a very pretty girl lunching on her own in a restaurant and picking up any Tom, Dick or Harry who chooses to speak to her.'

'Are you jealous?' asked Annis with interest.

He looked surprised. 'Jealous? I? Heavens, no, but I am annoyed that you deliberately went against my wishes.'

Annis sat down, crossed one long leg over the other and studied her elegant high-heeled shoes. 'I didn't pick anyone up, you know—that was a very nasty thing to say, and quite unjustified. Roberto said he was a friend of yours and he was very pleasant. I like him.' She added dreamily: 'I liked having my hand kissed too.'

She had the satisfaction of seeing Jake wince. 'Well, don't expect me to do anything so silly,' he begged her coldly.

'Of course I don't. It wouldn't be nice if you didn't both like it, would it?' She gave him a limpid glance. 'You said we had an appointment?'

'Only to get rid of Gonzalez. I have to go back almost at once.' He left the door where he had been standing and sat down opposite to her. 'I wanted to make sure that you were all right.' He added nastily: 'Obviously you were. What do you intend doing this afternoon?'

'There's a museum I'd like to see, I've forgotten its name, but the girl at the desk told me that it was wonderful.'

'You'll take a taxi, Annis?'

'Yes, Jake.' She looked so meek that he studied her quiet face for a moment frowning.

'I hope to be back about four o'clock, perhaps a little later.'

'Yes, Jake, I'll be back by then.'

He got up and started for the door and she got up too. She was a little shocked at herself, a parson's daughter, feeling so strongly that she must get even with him. 'Just a minute,' she told him, and went up close and picked something off his shoulder. 'A hair,' she said serenely, 'a long black hair. Shall I get a clothes brush? It would never do to go to a board meeting looking—well, untidy.'

He caught her hand in his and burst out laughing. 'So that's it? You vixen! Shall I tell you who she was?' He caught sight of the time. 'No, I can't—I haven't a minute left.' He kissed her suddenly and very hard and slammed through the door, leaving her a prey to mixed feelings. The worst of which was that if she took exception to anything he did when she wasn't there, he could easily guess that her feelings were rather more than friendly. She had been very silly and childish. She went and sat by the open window, all desire to visit museums gone; she was still there when Jake came quietly in two hours later.

'I finished early,' he told her. 'Did you enjoy the museum?'

She had been so deep in thought that she had a faintly bemused look.

'I didn't go.'

'You've had tea?'

She shook her head and he crossed the room and stood looking down at her. 'You're feeling all right? I'll ring for tea, shall I?'

'Yes, please,' and then: 'Jake, before you do, I'm sorry for all the silly things I said. I didn't mean them—I mean, I don't really like having my hand kissed, you know, and—there wasn't anything on your shoulder, I made it up.' She added, lying with sincerity: 'I really don't want to know about your friends—or what you do when I'm not there. It's entirely your own business and I'm sorry, I really am.'

Jake pulled her to her feet and stood with his arms lightly around her.

'Did I ever tell you what a nice girl you were?' he asked. 'And I shall mind very much if you don't take some interest in me, you know. And I'm sorry too, behaving like a tyrant because you were lunching with someone. You see, I thought that you might be lonely and I came back prepared to…well, never mind that now.' He tapped her nose very gently with a finger. 'And the dark-haired lady—she's the wife of an old friend of mine, he couldn't attend the board meeting because he was under the weather, so she brought down some important papers to be signed; he had to sign them too, so I went back with her to get it done.'

His arms felt very comforting around her. Everything was going to be all right; she had been stupid, but she wouldn't make the same mistake again.

'Thank you for telling me,' she smiled up at him. 'Father always says I jump to conclusions—it must be my red hair.'

He let her go and dropped a careless kiss on her bright head as he did so. 'Then I must take care to remember that, mustn't I? Shall we have tea?—I had *bifes de atum*—that's tunny fish—for lunch, nice but highly flavoured.'

He crossed the room to ring for a waiter. 'Like to go dancing this evening?' he asked, he sounded casually indulgent, like an old friend.

CHAPTER SEVEN

THEY SPENT ALL the next day together. There was nothing that couldn't wait until the following morning, Jake told Annis over breakfast, and how would she like to go to Caicais again; they could lunch at one of the delightful fish restaurants close to the beach and go for a brisk walk along the shore.

And it was a lovely day, even better than she had hoped for. They had spent the morning poking round the shops, buying anything that took their fancy, and drunk their coffee at a small cheerfully canopied café. Lunch had been a success too. Annis had eaten *bacalihau pudim*, which sounded very glamorous even though it was dried cod soufflé, and then *bolo de mei*, a rich cake of honey, cinnamon, spices and nuts. She had drunk the white wine Jake had chosen for her and then, at his suggestion, topped off the lot with a glass of Malmsey. Thus sustained, she was quite prepared for the long walk along the beach, although they didn't hurry; it was delightfully warm, so Annis had left her jacket in the car, and presently she had sat down on a convenient rock, taken off her shoes and done the rest of their walk with bare feet, occasionally going down to the water's edge to dabble in the still rather chilly sea.

They had gone back to the car later and driven to Estoril where they had tea at one of the fashionable hotels along the boulevard and then taken the road through Sintra and so back to Lisbon, tired from their wanderings, but not too tired to dance that evening.

Annis had been careful not to ask Jake if he were free on the following day, too, so she was prepared, more or less, when he told her that he would be away for most of the day. 'But I thought we might have Rosa and Emmanuel to dinner in the evening. I'll arrange a table for four and we can dance afterwards.'

She had agreed quickly, wondering if he found her a dull companion. She had no witty conversation and she tended to talk too much about her family. She made a mental resolve not to mention them for several days.

She sat up in bed, long after they had said goodnight, writing home. There was a great deal to write about and without actually saying so, she implied that Jake was with her all the time; she skimmed over that part rather, but writing a lot about her earrings and brooch and the new dresses and then, because her father would be interested, enlarging at length about Sintra and its history. It was after two o'clock when she finally put down her pen and turned out the light. She made herself dwell on the highlights of the day and went to sleep finally, happy because she had spent all of it with Jake.

She was determined not to be lonely the next day. They had breakfasted early because Jake had to be in the city by half past eight, which left a great deal of the day to get through. Annis took a taxi to the museum and did it very thoroughly before going back to the hotel to have lunch; this time in their sitting-room. The shops would be closed until three o'clock, so she read the English newspapers and then took another taxi to the shops in the Chiado. She still had a lot of money in her purse. It was nice to buy presents without bothering too much about the price—cufflinks for Edward, a camera for James, a filigree silver bangle for Emma and, since little Audrey already had a present, a beautifully dressed doll in national costume. Which made it unfair for Emma; Annis settled for a hand-knitted sweater, hoping that she would be able to squeeze it into her luggage; she already had all those extra dresses, and while she was about it, she might as well make room for a delightful pair of kid sandals which caught her eye. They were wildly expensive, but they would go with all her new dresses.

A glance at the time sent her hurrying for a taxi. Jake might already be back at the hotel and they had guests for dinner.

He was sitting with his feet up on another chair when she reached their sitting-room, sleeping peacefully. She stood looking at him for a long minute; he was tired. She looked at him with love and then almost jumped out of her skin when he spoke without opening his eyes.

'Have you had a good day?' One eye surveyed her and her parcels. 'Ah, I see you have.'

'Yes, thank you. I'm sorry I'm late, the shops are terrific…have you had tea?'

'I waited for you.' Jake got to his feet, not looking in the least tired now and rang for a waiter. 'Rose and Emmanuel won't be here until half past eight, we have plenty of time.' He pulled a chair forward for her and sat down himself. 'What have you bought?'

Annis opened her parcels, quite forgetting that she wasn't going to mention her family again; she chatted

happily while they looked at the things she had bought
and then had tea until she remembered. She stopped in
mid-sentence and sat staring at him.

'Well, go on,' Jake begged her, and looked surprised
when she muttered:

'Oh, it was nothing, I've forgotten what it was I was
going to say.' She got up slowly. 'I'd better go and dress.'

'Wear that blue thing with the pleats.'

She was pleased because he remembered that she
had some new dresses. She nodded happily and wandered off, her head already full of a daydream wherein
she appeared in that same dress and Jake was so overcome at the sight of her in it that he fell in love instantly.

It wasn't quite like that. He was standing at the window, looking out at the evening sky when she joined
him. He barely glanced at her, but moved away to get
her a drink, glancing at his watch as he did so with the
remark that they still had half an hour in which she
could enjoy it.

It was a superb sherry, but it could just as well have
been tap water as far as Annis was concerned. She was
aware that she looked very nice: she had done her hair
so that the earrings might show to the best advantage.
The diamond brooch looked just right pinned on the
bodice of the new dress and the sandals were a pure
delight, so why couldn't he look at her just once? After
all, he had asked her to wear that particular dress.

She did her best, strolling about the room, sitting
with one leg swinging over the other so that he couldn't
fail to see the sandals, putting up a hand to touch an
earring. He noticed none of these, so that presently she
sat primly, her feet tucked beneath her chair, well away

from the lamps. She had a childish desire to burst into tears, even scream a little so that she might relieve her feelings. As it was, she answered his random remarks in a polite small voice and longed for them to go down to the restaurant.

They had only to wait a few minutes for their guests. Annis, shaking hands with Rosa, discovered that she was as pretty as she had thought, but a good deal older, and as for Emmanuel, he was rather short and dark with bright dark eyes and a charming manner. Annis had been rather dreading the evening, but after a while she began to enjoy herself. Their guests were amusing and witty and spoke excellent English and there was a seemingly endless stream of small talk. And Emmanuel was a good dancer; she was too tall for him, of course, but she forgot that. It was late when they said goodbye and it was Rosa who said, 'You must both come and dine with us before you leave. When will that be, Annis?'

Annis blinked; she had no idea. Jake said smoothly: 'Five days' time, Rosa, and we'd love to, wouldn't we, darling?'

'Good. I'll telephone you.' She kissed Annis's cheek, offered her own for Jake to salute, and waited while Emmanuel kissed Annis. Social kisses—Annis wasn't sure if she would get used to them, but she supposed she'd have to.

Over breakfast the next morning Jake told her that he had no more meetings for three days and suggested that they might go farther afield, perhaps stay the night somewhere. 'We could drive down to the Algarve,' he suggested. 'There is a good hotel at Praia da Rocha, or we could go to the *pousada* at Sagres, visit Cape St Vincent, see Prince Henry's Fort and watch the fishermen.'

'Oh, please, Jake, that sounds absolutely great. When can we go?'

'Now.'

'Now?' she almost squeaked. 'But I haven't packed...'

'You'll only need stuff for the night.' He was laughing at her. 'You can have ten minutes.'

'What about you? Shall I...'

He interrupted her. 'It will take me less than five minutes. I'll ring the desk.'

'Are we coming back here?'

'Yes, of course—now run along.'

She flung night things into her overnight bag, added make-up haphazardly, poked a gossamer-fine dress into a corner, added the new sandals, snatched up her shoulder bag and declared herself ready. If she looked faintly dishevelled she wasn't aware of it, and Jake, glancing at her, only smiled; she was such a lovely girl it didn't matter at all.

It was a clear sunny morning and the Salazar bridge across the Tagus, high and slender above the water, looked almost fairylike, but once on it they met the incoming traffic from the south and they were soon surrounded by cars and lorries and unending noise, but halfway across Annis forgot that, staring at the statue of Christ, high on the hills on the farther side and then down to the busy river and the sprawling city below.

'Is this the only road to the south?' she wanted to know.

'No, but it's one of the busiest. It goes as far as Alfambra before it splits. We'll take the road to Vila

Dobispo and then on to Cape St Vincent and to Sagres.
We can go back through Monchique, over the mountains and get to Lisbon from the south-east.'

They stopped for coffee presently at a small wayside
café and then went on through ever changing country,
sometimes orange and lemon groves, vines and olive
trees, sometimes forests of cork trees, winding up steep
slopes and then through a dry and arid countryside. As
the morning passed, it became warmer, and with Vila
Dobispo behind them, they stopped for lunch, eating it
out of doors in front of the inn; sardines grilled over a
charcoal fire and a salad, crusty rolls and a local wine
to wash them down. The country around them was
wooded and hilly, with the mountains behind them and
the sea not so very far away. 'We'll park the car at the
pousada,' said Jake, 'and explore if you're not too tired.'

Annis looked at him in astonishment. 'Me, tired?
But I've not done a thing for days!'

The sea when they reached it looked delightful with
the sun sparkling on it, lapping the distant rocky coast-
line and the beaches of Sagres. There were small fishing
boats being unloaded and people shopping in the main
street as they went through the little town to where the
pousada stood on a hill overlooking the beach. It looked
big and a little bare from the outside, but its interior was
charming with a large airy set of rooms sparsely but
very comfortably furnished with big chairs grouped
invitingly round coffee tables and upstairs their rooms
overlooked the sea with wide doors leading on to a balcony. Annis unpacked in no time at all, gave her hair
and face a very perfunctory going over, and pronounced
herself ready to go out. This wasn't like the hotel at Lis-

bon at all; for the first time she felt as though she were really on holiday. She would have liked to have told Jake, but it might sound ungrateful.

They spent the rest of the day strolling round the town, having tea in a café by the beach and buying postcards. And after dinner that evening they strolled along the beach and since the evening was chilly, Annis swathed herself in the shawl Jake had brought for her that afternoon. She was happy, at least as happy as she could be, she reminded herself, and Jake seemed quite content to potter around with her, although she wasn't sure he wouldn't get bored after a day or two. But it was only going to be a day or two, anyway.

'Where do we go tomorrow?' she asked.

'Along the coast road to Portimao, up into the Monchique Mountains and on back to Lisbon, but first we'll go to Cape St Vincent and take a quick look at Prince Henry's fort.'

'It sounds wonderful.' She took a deep breath. 'I suppose we couldn't stay another day here, Jake?'

They were almost at the hotel again and in the lamplight she saw his quick frown. 'Afraid not, Annis, I've several more people to meet. Besides, we're dining with Rosa and Emmanuel.' She didn't speak, but perhaps he sensed her disappointment, for he added kindly: 'We'll go back on an evening plane and spend the day wherever you like.'

'Oh, Jake, I'd love that! Someone was telling me about the museum of coaches, I'd like to see them, and I wondered could we possibly hear a *fado* singer? Colonel Avery was talking about them and told me that they were quite extraordinary.'

They were standing in one of the airy reception rooms, almost empty because most of the residents were still at dinner. 'Why not? I'll see what can be arranged.' He gave her a gentle nod. 'I daresay you're tired. I'll go along to the desk and settle up, it'll save time in the morning. Sleep well.'

The smile he gave her was placidly friendly: she could have been a well-liked aunt or cousin. She found it difficult to smile back.

They breakfasted early and drove the short distance to Cape St Vincent, where they walked round the lighthouse, bought a hand-embroidered tablecloth from one of the stalls in the shadows and then drove back along the towering clifftop to inspect Prince Henry's Fort, but they didn't stop long here. Annis sensed that Jake was impatient under his impassive good humour and declared herself ready to go on again, sitting quietly beside him as they took the coast road to Portimao.

They stopped for coffee at Praia da Rocha and travelled on, to pause and watch the fishing boats leaving the harbour at Portimao, and then, because the morning was almost gone, turning north to the mountains and Montchique. They lunched there at an *estalagem*, the furniture and the rooms so elegant that Annis didn't quite believe Jake when he told her that it was an inn. They ate seafood and drank Lagos wine, and Annis finished her meal with some little tartlets of figs and almonds and honey, very rich and delicious.

It was nine o'clock before they reached the hotel and Jake suggested that Annis might like to have dinner in their sitting-room, but she had already decided that he had had enough of her sole company for the time being;

she opted for the restaurant and spent half an hour bathing and changing into one of her new dresses. Rather a waste as it turned out, for Jake was immersed in a sheaf of papers and although he got to his feet when she joined him, he barely glanced at her before going quickly down to dinner—a meal they ate with discreet speed because, he told her, he had a good deal of homework to do before his meeting in the morning.

'Thank you for my two lovely days,' she said as they said goodnight. 'I hope they didn't mean you'll have to work extra hard tomorrow.'

He shrugged enormous shoulders. 'They made a nice break, but I won't see much of you tomorrow, nor the following day. I expect you've got some more shopping to do.'

She answered that she had—a lie told brightly and with no sign of the disappointment she felt.

She filled in the days somehow; she had money to spend, time in which to spend it, and the weather was glorious. She told herself these facts repeatedly and presented a bright face to Jake when he returned in the evening, declaring that she was only too glad to sit with a book while he worked at his endless papers. Not that it would always be like that, he assured her; he had a competent secretary at his London office who coped with a good deal of the spade-work.

By the end of the second day she found herself looking forward to their dinner party with Rosa and Emmanuel; it would be fun to chat over drinks and idle over the meal. Besides, Jake was going to take her out the following day; she had hugged the thought to her during the lonely two days.

She had changed and was sitting on the balcony when he came back in the evening. He greeted her briefly, asked her to pour him a drink and went away to shower and change. There was still time to sit quietly before they needed to leave and she didn't bother him with questions; it was obvious that he was tired and, for some reason, ill-tempered.

The reason came to light quickly enough. 'Something's come up,' he told her. 'I'm afraid I'll have to go to Setúbal—there's a canning industry there—the management have asked me if I'm interested in taking up some shares, and it would be foolish to go back home without looking into it. It'll mean I'll go early in the morning and probably be away all day. Perhaps you'd pack for me? We can have dinner before we leave.' He added irritably: 'I'm sorry, we shan't be able to spend the day together.'

So that was why he was ill-tempered, building up a bad humour against her expected tantrums and disappointment. She had no intention of giving him the satisfaction, though. She kept her voice pleasantly quiet, although it was a bit of an effort.

'Well, of course it would be quite stupid to go all the way home without going to see these people, and to tell you the truth, I don't mind a bit: I found a small shop in the Baixa where they sell gold and silver filigree work, only I didn't have time to look properly. Now I'll go there tomorrow and choose something for Mother. I'll have lunch out and come back in plenty of time to pack for both of us.' She returned his hard gaze with a placid smile. 'Did you have a successful day?'

His terse, 'Yes', didn't encourage her to pursue the

subject, and presently they went down to the car and drove through the city to its outskirts where Rosa and Emmanuel lived in an old house halfway up the hills overlooking the river.

Later that night, lying awake in her bed, Annis went over their evening. It had been a pleasant one; Rosa and Emmanuel were a delightful couple and they had a beautiful home. Annis had looked at photos of their four children, all in their teens. And agreed with Rosa that families were fun. She hadn't looked at Jake as she had spoken, although she was very well aware that he was listening, and because she had wanted to hurt him, she had added clearly: 'Besides, in a family a child learns to give and take. An only child so often just takes, and will stay that way all his life, poor dear.'

Rosa had patted her hand. 'You and Jake will have lovely children, I am sure,' she had said kindly.

It didn't bear thinking about. Annis gave a great sniff, buried her head in her pillows and had a good cry.

She cried for a long time, so that when finally she went to sleep she was tired and overslept. She didn't wake until Jake's voice from the door roused her. 'I'm just off—sorry if I woke you. You'll be all right?'

He was looking at her intently, although there wasn't much to see beyond a great deal of fiery hair. Annis, aware that very likely her eyes were red-rimmed and her nose the same colour, prudently kept her face tucked well into the pillows.

'Never better,' she told him cheerfully. 'I hope you have a successful day.' She wished he would go away before she burst into tears again. Instead he came right into the room and stood looking down at her.

'I really am sorry about our day together—you're not too disappointed?'

Her voice was nicely muffled by a pillow. 'Heavens, no. I've never enjoyed myself so much, pottering around on my own—it's luxury after five brothers and sisters, you know.'

His voice was dry. 'I wouldn't know, being an only child. Annis, I'll see you about five o'clock.'

He turned on his heel and went out of the room, closing the door quietly behind him. So he had minded about her remark to Rosa. Annis felt suddenly mean; he had been kind and generous to her and she was ungrateful. She promised herself then and there that she would tell him how sorry she was the moment he came back.

She got up presently and, being a practical girl, planned her day over her breakfast. The shop in the Baixa, since she had told Jake she would be going there, and then the coach museum, so that she could tell Emma and little Audrey and James about it, and she must remember to buy some small present for Mrs Turner. If she didn't hurry, she would be able to fill her day nicely.

All the same, the hours dragged. Long before five o'clock she had packed and changed into travelling clothes, and now she was sitting on the balcony for the last time, warm in the sunshine and a little sleepy. But not too sleepy to remember what she had promised herself that morning; when Jake came into the room she got up at once and went to him.

'Hullo, Jake. Did you have a successful day?' and without waiting for him to speak: 'Jake, I'm sorry about what I said to Rosa yesterday evening, about an only child not giving—I don't know what made me say it. It's not true anyway...'

He had put down his case and lounged over to the window. 'My dear girl, what makes you think I would worry about a rather silly remark like that?' His voice was smooth and without expression. 'We solitary ones are blessed with a strong sense of our ability to get ahead of everyone else, didn't you know that? I daresay you would call it arrogance.'

He smiled at her, the nasty little smile she had so disliked when they first met. 'I'm going to shower before dinner—and don't waste your pity on me, darling.' He paused at the door to look at her. 'I wonder why you're making such a thing about it?'

He had gone before she could think of an answer to that.

They had an early dinner in the restaurant and Jake carried on a bland conversation which made it impossible for her to do more than answer him in like vein, and after that there was the quick drive to the airport and the flight back. It was late by the time they reached Heathrow, but the car was there, waiting for them, and the roads fairly empty, so they reached the flat without any delays and Annis, going through the door Jake opened, could hardly believe that a few short hours ago she had been sitting in a hotel in Lisbon.

Mrs Turner had left a note. There was a light supper in the fridge, coffee in the percolator, and she would be round the next morning at her usual time. Annis brought in the tray and put it on a small table while Jake opened the pile of letters waiting for him. There were two for her too—one from her mother and one in

Matt's handwriting—but she didn't open them at once. She poured Jake's coffee, drank half a cup herself and then told him she would go to bed. It hurt a little that he made no demur, only told her to sleep well, and not to bother to get up in the morning. 'Mrs Turner brings tea when she gets here and she'll get the breakfast. I'll just run through these, there may be something important.'

She stayed awake a long time, too tired to think much about things but too unhappy to sleep, so that when she did at last it was to wake to Mrs Turner's voice.

'Good morning, madam dear. Mr Royle said as how to leave you to have yer sleep out, which I've done, and there's a nice little breakfast waiting for later, so just you drink this and get up when you fancy.'

Annis sat up, very wide awake. 'Mrs Turner—good morning. Heavens, it must be late…'

'Nine o'clock just gorn, mum, and Mr Royle been out of the 'ouse this hour or more.'

Annis said hastily: 'Oh, yes of course—he had to be at the office. Did he leave any message?'

Mrs Turner looked surprised. 'No, mum, he'll 'ave told you when 'e'll be 'ome.'

Annis poured her tea and fussed with the milk and sugar. 'Oh, yes, of course—I'm not properly awake.' She smiled at Mrs Turner, who smiled back widely. She had been a little nervous of the housekeeper, but she saw she need not be; Mrs Turner was a younger edition of their own Mrs Wells. She said now: 'Mrs Turner, could you spare the time to show me round this morning, and perhaps there are some jobs I can do to help you? It's a big flat for one and Jake told me that you're a very good cook as well.'

Mrs Turner looked pleased. 'Well, though I says it as shouldn't, I've got a light 'and with pastry. I'll be pleased to take you round, madam, and as for the odd jobs—well, there are always the flowers and such, and bits of shopping…'

So the morning passed in a thorough going over of the flat and its contents, and Annis managed to convey in the nicest possible way that she had no intention of encroaching upon Mrs Turner's preserves, although they settled between them that she should do the shopping, the flowers and polish the silver if she felt inclined. 'And there's no earthly reason why I shouldn't switch on the washing machine from time to time,' suggested Annis, 'and I do like ironing.'

'Now that would be an 'elp, mum. Mr Royle, as you well know, wears silk shirts and the finest cotton, and the time it takes to get them just so you'd never believe.'

Annis lunched off a tray in the sitting-room while she made a shopping list of the things Mrs Turner would need, then took herself off with her basket. There were shops quite close by, Mrs Turner had assured her, and she had told her how to get to them, elegant shops lining a small street five minutes' walk away, a far cry from the village stores at home, she thought, choosing back bacon with an experienced eye.

Mrs Turner went soon after four o'clock, bringing in the tea tray with her hat on, ready to go. 'And there's a nice steak and kidney pie in the fridge,' she told Annis. 'Just needs a good warm through, the veg are ready to cook, I've done them little peas and baby carrots, and there's a nice sherry trifle—Mr Royle's partial to sherry trifle. I'll say good afternoon, madam.'

'Goodbye, Mrs Turner, and thank you very much. You don't have to get tea for me, you know, I'm sure you've enough to do.'

'Time on me 'ands, mum, with you doing the shopping.'

Annis, pouring her tea, reflected that she was going to have time on her hands too.

Mrs Turner had set the table for dinner, with Spode china and shining silver and glass. There was nothing to do, so she wandered through the flat and presently found a small pile of ironing waiting to be done. She was making an excellent job of the last of Jake's shirts when he came home.

'I'm in the kitchen!' she called as she heard his key in the lock, and looked up and smiled as his head appeared round the door.

He came right in and dropped a casual kiss on her head, then observed in surprise, 'I thought Mrs Turner did the ironing.'

'She did. We've had a nice cosy talk and I said I'd do the ironing and the shopping—it's a big flat to keep clean, you know.'

'Do what you like, Annis. Have you enjoyed your day?'

'Very much. It's all so labour-saving, and the shops are very good…' She folded the shirt expertly. 'Not at all like the village stores.'

'Which reminds me, I thought we might go home on Saturday, leave early in the morning and spend an hour there and then go on to your place. We can drive back the same evening and have a quiet Sunday here. Would you like that?'

'Very much—I'll take the presents with me.'

'Your car will be delivered tomorrow. I'll try and get home early and you can try her out.'

Her eyes shone. 'Oh, Jake, thank you!'

'You'll be able to drive down to Millbury when you feel like it.' He went to the door. 'I'm going to have a shower—is dinner at the usual time?'

'Yes, Mrs Turner's put it all ready.'

'Good. By the way, we shall be dining out quite a bit—I've got a number of friends and they want to meet you.'

Annis eyed him uncertainly. 'I'm not awfully good at dinner parties...I haven't much conversation.'

He said deliberately: 'I shouldn't worry about that, darling, you're pretty enough to get away without making any effort at anything.'

'Oh, do you think I'm pretty?' She stared at him over the pile of beautifully ironed shirts.

'Why else should I have married you?' he asked carelessly, and went whistling to the bathroom.

On Saturday they left at eight o'clock after breakfast eaten at the kitchen table because Mrs Turner didn't come at the weekends. Annis was surprised when Jake offered to wash up while she tidied the flat. There was a great deal she didn't know about him, she reflected as she collected her bag and a jacket and her shopping basket crammed with presents. She had something for everyone, for Jake's family too. His mother had sounded a little surprised that they weren't staying to lunch, only hoping mildly that they would find time to go to stay for the weekend soon, and as for her own mother, she had been delighted at the idea of seeing them, merely observing that there was always a room for them when they could manage to stay overnight.

But neither mother mentioned the brevity of their visit. They were received warmly at Jake's home, the presents were exclaimed over, Jake's grandmother, brought down to the sitting-room to meet them, was unusually quiet, only as they were leaving did she pull Annis down to kiss her. 'A tricky business, marriage, Annis, but you're a good girl. I've no doubt you'll make a success of it.' And she added: 'Only don't take too long about it.'

It was delightful to see her own family again. They came pouring out of the house, Mary and Edward home for the weekend, the three younger ones enveloping her in hugs. The time went too quickly. By the time the presents had been admired, lunch eaten, Nancy inspected and a quick visit to the Averys made, it was time to return to London. And as they began a round of goodbyes, Mrs Fothergill said gently: 'I do hope you'll be able to stay for a night or two soon. I know how busy Jake is—your father has been explaining his work to me. I had no idea that he was quite as important as that.'

It was on the tip of Annis's tongue to say that she had no idea either, but she nodded and smiled and said: 'Oh, yes,' vaguely, and when her mother added: 'You're happy, darling?' she made haste to say that she was—very.

It was her father who declared loudly that they all missed her. 'You really must come for a week or so. Sapphro and Hairy miss you too, not to mention Nancy.'

'And us,' shrilled little Audrey. 'Why don't you come every weekend?'

'Well, we have to go and see Jake's mother and father too,' said Annis reasonably.

Audrey was disposed to argue. 'I don't see...' she began with a hint of tears.

Jake swung her high into the air so that she shrieked with delight. 'Tell you what, young Audrey, suppose I bring Annis down and let her stay for a week, would you like that?'

She threw small skinny arms round his neck. 'Oh, Jake, yes, please! But can't you stay too?'

'Me? I have to work.' He gave her a hug. 'But that's a promise.'

They stopped for a meal on their way back to London. Jake hadn't said much as they drove, only as they neared Wootton Bassett he said: 'How about stopping here for dinner? There's a place in the High Street— the Magnolia Room.'

And when they were seated, he looked up from his menu to say 'I enjoyed today, didn't you? You have a delightful family, Annis.'

She smiled at him widely. 'Yes, I know, but your family is nice too—I love your granny.'

'I meant what I said. I'll drive you down and you can stay for a week—better still, you can drive yourself down.'

'I'm a bit scared of the traffic in London.'

'You did well enough the other evening. We'll drive round a bit more if you like—you'll soon get used to it.' He smiled a little and bent his head over the menu again.

Annis studied her own menu, remembering his casual good nature when she had taken her little car round the squares and quiet streets near his flat. He hadn't been impatient at her nervousness, but he had been aloof too; rather like a polite driving instructor. She wondered if he was regretting marrying her—after all, so far she hadn't been much of a companion, as she hadn't had the chance, and she hadn't been a hostess to his friends, either, something she rather dreaded now that they were actually married.

His voice asking her what she would like to eat roused her from her thoughts, and she cast an eye down hastily. 'Oh, the courgettes and mushrooms, I think, and then the sole.' She looked round her. 'This is rather nice, isn't it?'

'Yes, we haven't been out much, have we, Annis?' He smiled at her with such charm that she found herself murmuring that it didn't matter, that he was busy...

'I can take it easy for a while. We'll have an evening out soon, and have a few friends to dinner. You'll like that?'

She stared down at the courgettes and mushrooms. 'Oh, yes, I should like to meet your friends.' And that was a fib; she was scared stiff at the very idea.

'They're your friends too,' he observed blandly, and smiled again.

She made coffee when they got in later and they sat drinking it in the sitting-room, and she almost dropped her cup when Jake asked abruptly: 'Are you happy, Annis?' and before she could answer: 'Shall we go to the house in Bath and spend a few days? We could visit our families from there...I can spare a week.'

'That would be lovely. Oh, Jake, could we really— you wouldn't feel bored?'

He gave her a long considered look. He was on the

point of saying something, but he stopped and said
lightly: 'Darling, you never bore me.' He got up and
poured more coffee for them both and she said quickly:

'Jake, please don't call me darling—I know everyone does but, but—well…' She hesitated and he interrupted her silkily:

'You're an old-fashioned girl who thinks that only
people who love each other should use the word. Is
that it?'

'Yes, Jake. Do you mind?'

'Not in the least, but don't expect me to stop calling my women friends darling, will you? They might
think it odd.'

It was impossible to tell if he was angry or amused.
Annis waited a minute and when he didn't say any more
she asked: 'When shall we go?'

'To Bath? Oh, we might travel down next Sunday. I
believe we're to be asked to a party on Saturday, a welcome to the newly married pair.'

'You didn't tell me…'

'I thought you might take fright—all my friends will
be there.'

She gave him a worried look. 'Whatever shall I
wear?'

'I gather it's to be quite an affair—a long dress, I
should imagine. Why not get yourself something? Pale
green, I think, with that hair. I've opened an account
for you at Harrods.'

'You're very kind to me Jake—thank you. I'll find
something.'

He got up as she did. 'Not dark blue velvet,' he said,
and they both laughed. It seemed a long time ago, an-

other world—a lonely world without Jake, she reminded herself, and wished him goodnight, offering a cheek for his light kiss. It would be nice to give way to impulse and throw her arms round his neck. While she got ready for bed she speculated as to what he would do. Nothing, she concluded, but that was her own fault, she wasn't making any efforts to attract him. To tell the truth, she was afraid of being blandly and coolly snubbed. She wished she had a little more experience of men. Matt was the only man she had known, and one couldn't count him.

CHAPTER EIGHT

IT WAS JAKE who wakened her in the morning, sitting on the side of her bed with a tea tray on his knees. Annis shot upright, still only half awake.

'I've overslept…whatever is the time?'

'Eight o'clock, and it's Sunday. Church this morning, don't you think? It's pouring with rain, so we can spend the afternoon reading the papers with easy consciences.' He poured tea and when he had had he strolled to the door. 'I never bother with breakfast, but that's because I'm too lazy to cook for myself.'

Annis took the hint. 'Bacon and eggs,' she promised, 'in about half an hour.'

It was the kind of day she had dreamed of—just the two of them, with Jake sprawled in his chair and the Sunday papers spread all round them. They had sandwiches and a drink after church and then a long-drawn-out tea with Mrs Turner's fruit cake and a great pile of buttered toast, and in the evening, Annis went into the kitchen and cooked steak and chips and made a salad, then anxious to let Jake know that she could cook, made a rhubarb pie, lavishly topped with clotted cream. And while she was laying the table Jake fetched a bottle of claret: 'Something worthy of that delicious smell coming from the kitchen,' he told her.

They had never been so close, Annis thought as she

got into bed and allowed daydreams to take over until
she slept.

And as the week passed she began to think that they
were getting back to the warm friendship they had had
before they married. Perhaps it was being in Lisbon
that had made them so uncertain; for Jake had been
that, she was sure, perhaps not avoiding her, but certainly not over-eager to be with her, and she herself had
felt awkward and stiff. But now that they were back at
the flat they were settling into a pleasantly easy way
of life together. He came home each evening content,
it seemed, to relax over a drink and tell her about his
day. Half of it she didn't understand, of course, but she
was learning fast. In her turn she told him of her day,
glossing over the dull bits, telling him news from her
home and his and then after dinner, sitting opposite
him working painstakingly over the tapestry work she
had bought herself or knitting the complicated sweater
Emma wanted for her birthday.

But she didn't tell him about the dress she had bought
for the party they were to go to—organza patterned
in green, with a pie-frill neck, long tight sleeves and a
long full skirt. And since she no longer needed to be
so careful over spending, she bought satin slippers to
match. They were wildly expensive and no one would
see them, but the pleasure she would have in wearing
them was worth it.

She was very nervous about the party by the time
Saturday came round. She packed for their few days
in Bath in the morning and then with Jake drove down
to an inn on the Thames outside Maidenhead, where
they had lunch, taking their time over it while they

made a few plans for their stay in Bath. And since it was a pleasant afternoon and they had time to spare, Jake took a road through Windsor Great Park before joining the A30 and going back to the flat. They had stopped for tea on the way, so that by the time they got in, it was time to dress.

Annis hadn't told Jake that she was scared of meeting his friends. She dressed in a flurry of nerves and presently joined him in the sitting-room with a heightened colour and an outward calm which threatened to turn to hysterics at a moment's notice.

He stood looking at her for a long moment. 'Very beautiful indeed, you'll knock them cold. You'd better have a stiff drink, though, you're wound up like a top.'

'I don't know anyone.' She tried to speak casually and her voice came out in a squeak.

'You know me,' he said, half laughing. 'Come, come, Annis, you've been facing Mothers' Unions and Sunday School and choir practice for years and I think you'll like my friends—I hope they'll be your friends too.'

She swallowed the drink he gave her and followed him meekly out to the car, and just to let him see that she was perfectly at ease, chatted animatedly all the way to Hampstead where the party was being held. And as for Jake, he hardly spoke, only when he stopped the car before an important-looking house in a quiet road, he bent and kissed her cheek. 'I'm very proud of you,' he told her, and got out to open her door.

Contrary to all her worst forebodings, the evening was a great success. They were welcomed at the door and swept into a vast room crowded with people, all smiling and shaking hands and in the case of several elderly gentlemen, kissing her with relish. Just at first she was scared that Jake might leave her, but he stayed by her, an arm through hers. He knew everyone there and there was a good deal of joking and laughter, and after the second glass of champagne, Annis began to relax and enjoy herself. By her own home standards these people were very grand, but they were friendly too and talked about the same things as the people she knew in Millbury—babies and children at school and how difficult it was to get daily help and what did she think of her new home…

She was with a small group of people when she found that Jake had gone, and she spent the next few minutes looking for him. Although the room was crowded she was sure he wasn't in it. It was a few minutes later when the music started up and they began to dance that she saw him coming into the room with a slim dark girl in a scarlet dress. She turned her back at once and smilingly accepted a young man's invitation to dance. She didn't like him overmuch, he was extravagantly dressed for one thing, and he stared at her in a way that made her uncomfortable, but any port in a storm.

She wasn't sure what happened next, but there was Jake dancing her off as cool as you please and all she could do was mutter: 'Well, how rude!'

'I suppose it's that red hair that makes you so impetuous,' said Jake softly. 'I could see your dire thoughts from where I was at the door—I thought we'd agreed that jealousy is only for those in love?'

More and more couples were taking to the floor and it was getting crowded. He guided her expertly through the crush and she followed his steps just as expertly.

Millbury Village Saturday evening hop had been a splendid breeding ground for all the latest dances. 'I don't know what you mean,' she said airily. 'I just happened to glance in that direction and you...' And when he only chuckled, she added: 'She's a very pretty girl. What's her name?'

'I've no idea. She just happened to be in the hall as I was coming out of Howard's study—he wanted my advice about some shares.' He laughed a little. 'This is a splendid party, isn't it?'

'Yes,' said Annis, she knew her voice was peevish, but that was how she felt.

She danced with a great many other men after that and every now and again she found herself with Jake who, while they were dancing together, gave her the impression that he enjoyed it very much and then confused her by handing her over with cheerful willingness to her next partner.

It was towards the end of the evening when they were dancing together again that the music stopped suddenly and their host made his way towards them carrying a silver tray upon which was a small silver coffee pot, a sugar bowl and cream jug. He halted in front of them and everyone closed in to hear what he had to say. He made a neat little speech, handed Jake the tray, wished them both a long and happy married life from all their friends there and kissed Annis heartily. Which was the signal for everyone else to crowd even closer and to shake hands and offer congratulations.

Someone took the tray from Jake and he put an arm round Annis's waist, and when someone cried 'Speech,

speech!' he thanked them with a dry humour which had them all laughing.

They drank champagne after that and presently the party broke up. Back in the flat Annis arranged the coffee tray on a sofa table in the sitting-room. 'A lovely party,' she observed, and yawned mightily. 'What time do you want to leave in the morning, Jake?'

'No hurry—eleven o'clock will do. Go to bed, Annis, you're tired. I'm glad you like my friends.'

'Oh, I do, I do. Shall we have them all to dinner in turn? I was scared of meeting them, you know, but not any more.'

'We'll certainly have them round, half a dozen at a time.' He was sitting on the arm of a chair swinging an enormous leg. 'You're a remarkably beautiful woman, my dear. I'm very proud of you.'

She had had a little too much champagne, which could have been the reason why she crossed the room and kissed him. 'Thank you, Jake. Goodnight.'

It was raining when they left London the next morning, but by the time they reached Bath the sky had cleared, and a thin sunshine washed over the grey stone of the city, peaceful in its Sunday calm. They had come in from the London Road and Jake turned and twisted down one-way streets until he stopped finally outside the house.

The Bateses welcomed them with decorous pleasure and the prospect of one of Mrs Bates's splendid teas, and presently when they had unpacked, gone round the garden and Jake had dealt with the bills tidily laid out for him by Bates, they sat down in the drawing-room and Mrs Bates, who had a poor opinion of anyone else's cooking but her own, trotted in and out with scones and fruit cake, cucumber sandwiches, cut paper-thin, and little chocolate and walnut cakes, all of which she begged them to sample.

'No weight problems, I hope?' asked Jake as Annis poured the tea.

She eyed him with some coldness. 'I'm already on the big side,' she pointed out.

'Ah, yes, but your—er—vital statistics seem to me to be very nicely proportioned.' He wasn't looking at her, so she was able to blush in comfort. 'Mrs Bates will be hurt if we don't try everything at least once.'

So they made a very good tea between them and since Bates had hinted that dinner was to be a very special affair, seeing that it was their first day in their new home, Jake took Annis for a good brisk walk, through the park and past the reference library and across Queen Square into Milsom Street, where they slowed their steps to peer in the shop windows.

To Annis it was heaven. They chose enormous diamond rings, fabulous necklaces and bracelets, shoes with three-inch heels so flimsy that a good brisk walk would have ruined them. There was nothing flimsy about their price, though, as Annis pointed out—they wouldn't be a sensible buy; half a dozen wearings and they would be shabby...

Jake turned to look at her. 'Don't you ever buy anything just because you like it and it's pretty?' he asked with a hint of impatience. And then: 'That was a stupid thing to say, wasn't it? I'm sorry.'

'That's all right. I daresay I'll get used to being able

to buy what I want when I want it.' She smiled at him. 'I'll need some practice, that's all.'

He grunted, a friendly rumble which could have meant anything, and stopped before Jolly's shop window. 'Now that's a pretty dress,' he observed, pointing to a gleaming satin gown draped in a tawny chiffon scarf.

Annis pressed her pretty nose up against the window and studied it carefully. 'Yes, it is. But how does one keep the scarf just so for hours on end?'

'Pins, will-power? I wouldn't know. It would go very nicely with your hair. Have you any allowance left?'

She turned to him in astonishment. 'Good gracious, Jake, I've hardly used any of it.'

'In that case we must come shopping tomorrow.'

They walked back briskly through the park, which was a good thing, for Mrs Bates had a magnificent meal for them that evening. 'Their first meal in their new home,' she pointed out, as she supervised Bates's serving with an anxious eye—lobster patties, medallions of beef garnished with a rich cream sauce, with tiny new potatoes and baby green peas, and then a soufflé Harlequin. Annis declared that she had never eaten anything so delicious in her life, and Jake told Bates to open another bottle of champagne and bring Mrs Bates to the dining-room so that they could drink her health. But first Bates requested the honour of drinking the new owners' healths, and made a little speech wishing them happiness and long life, so that dinner took quite a time, and Annis grew heavy eyed over their coffee afterwards. Jake, sitting opposite her, had glanced up from the paper he was reading, and suggested that she should go to bed, and she had gone obediently and was asleep before she thought two coherent thoughts.

She hadn't really believed Jake when he had said that they would go shopping, which, she had to admit to herself, had been silly of her, as he seldom said anything he didn't mean. They spent the morning in a delightful if expensive fashion and returned for lunch laden with parcels. Not only had he bought her the black dress, but there were elegant satin slippers to match, a quilted silk coat to go over the dress, and an evening bag which, he had decided with careless interest, was just right to go with the slippers. And when she had paused to look into a jeweller's window and admired a rose diamond and pearl brooch, he had bought that too.

She thanked him rather shyly before they sat down to lunch and had her happy excitement considerably doused by his casual: 'Glad you like them—there's no reason why you shouldn't buy these things for yourself, you know. I can afford them.'

Annis made polite conversation over the meal while she pondered that remark—so he'd bought the things because she was his wife and as such had to be suitably dressed, not because he had wanted to give her a present. Disappointment tasted bitter in her mouth; just for a little while she had been hopeful… She looked up and saw him looking at her thoughtfully, and for lack of anything to say, asked when he wanted to visit his parents.

They went two days later; two days quite nicely filled with shopping for the house, taking long walks and driving out into the country round Bath; it was her mother's birthday in a week or so and Annis had set her heart on finding a silver photograph frame simi-

lar to the only one her parent possessed and treasured.
Jake had driven her to Stow-on-the-Wold where they
had roamed in and out of the antique shops lining the
wide old-fashioned street of the pretty little town, and
she had found what she was looking for. It had been a
good deal more money than she had expected, but Jake,
taking one look at her doubtful face, had said: 'That's
the one, isn't it? Buy it.' So she had.

She had bought a charming little vase for her mother-
in-law too, and a trinket box for Jake's grandmother,
and when she had hesitated over some trifle for her
father-in-law, Jake had undertaken to get a bottle of
whisky for him.

Annis dressed with care for their visit; a Jaegar
three-piece of cotton jersey in cream and lime green
and the sandals she had bought in Lisbon. She looked
incredibly beautiful as she got into the car beside Jake
after breakfast, and he told her so; but he uttered the
words with the coolness of a polite host wanting to
please a guest and she took no pleasure from them. But
nothing of her feelings showed; she turned a serene face
to him and thanked him nicely.

The day was an unqualified success. Jake's parents
greeted her as if she were indeed a daughter and his
grandmother, after one or two outspoken remarks about
the possibility of a great-grandchild, settled down to
cross-examine Annis about her day-to-day activities.
Annis obliged willingly enough; there was plenty to tell
the old lady, and when she observed again, rather sourly,
that she hoped that she wasn't going to be kept waiting too long before she could be a great-grandmother,

Annis remarked calmly enough that they hadn't been married very long, had they?

'Long enough,' grumbled their irascible companion, 'but you're a nice healthy young woman, and pretty, too. I hope Jake looks after you properly.'

Annis had said promptly that indeed he did and described the pearl and diamond brooch, aware that Jake was listening to every word and enjoying it.

They spent the whole day there, lunching and then strolling in the garden and presently sitting on the wide verandah at the back of the house. The two men talking in a desultory fashion while Mrs Royle sat beside Annis, gossiping gently about the house in Bath. 'And do you like it better than the London flat?' she had wanted to know.

'Oh, yes, though the flat's pretty super, too, but I've got to get used to it, you see—I've always lived at the Rectory and there's a big garden there and sheds and things, I rather miss that…'

They had tea presently and Jake and Annis had gone for a walk afterwards, through the village and up into the wooded hills beyond, and Jake had been a delightful companion, although he hadn't talked about them at all.

Two days later they went to her home, and somehow or other everyone had contrived to be there so that they all talked at once and Annis was dragged here and there to see Nancy, a stray kitten which had been adopted, the bantam chicks which had hatched out, the painting Emma had done of the house…there was no end to the things she had to see and admire. She hardly spoke to Jake until they were sitting at lunch, when during a lull in the talk he observed: 'How would you like to come down for a week or two darling? I'm going to be very busy and it might be lonely for you in London.'

She had hesitated, taken by surprise. 'But there are three dinner parties—the Mottrams and the Dawes, and we're having some people at the end of next week, and you suggested we should go to that aunt of yours...'

'All dealt with during the next two weeks; after that you'll be free as air.' Jake spoke pleasantly, but she could see that he had no intention of allowing her to argue.

'I'd love to, if Mother will have me.'

The entire family, it seemed, were only too delighted. 'And you'll be able to come down as often as you can, won't you, Jake?' asked Mrs Fothergill comfortably without waiting for him to answer.

On the way home later, Annis asked a question she had made up her mind to ask anyway. 'Why do you want me to come home while you're away? Why couldn't I go with you? You said, before we married, that when you went somewhere I could go too.'

'That was before we married!'

She stared out at the countryside, trying to think of an answer to that, and gave up, but it didn't stop her next question. 'Don't I fit in with your life in London? Don't your friends like me? Don't you want me to be there?'

His voice was cool. 'Are you trying to pick a quarrel, Annis?'

'No, I just want to know, that's all. I—I suppose I feel inadequate.'

'No need—you're being fanciful, that's all. Women don't use their heads.' He gave a little laugh. '"Man with the head and woman with the heart: Man to command

and woman to obey; All else confusion". Tennyson—
sounds a bit old-fashioned, but he had the right idea.'

'But I'm a person!' began Annis fierily. 'Why should
I obey blindly just because you want me to?'

'We're quarrelling again. What shall we do tomorrow?'

And that was the end of that; he'd retreated behind
that bland, casual good humour that told her nothing.

But tomorrow was another day. She cheered herself
with that thought before she slept that night, and got up
the next morning determined to present a pleasant front
at all costs. She succeeded very well, exchanging an
undemanding talk with Jake, agreeing willingly to his
suggestion that they might explore the Roman Baths,
and accompanying him with every sign of enjoyment
to a concert in the Pump Room in the evening. And she
kept it up for the rest of their stay, never once referring
to the future and asking no questions at all, although
the desire to do so was almost past bearing at times.

They went back to London in the evening and found
the flat at its most welcoming, with flowers in the vases,
a meal ready in the fridge and a pile of letters for Jake.
He picked them up with a muttered excuse and went
into his study and shut the door, and Annis, left to herself, unpacked slowly and then got their supper. It was
a cold meal and she didn't disturb him, but sat quietly
pretending to read until he joined her. She wanted to
ask about his mail, if there had been good news or bad,
if he was going away, but she merely remarked mildly
about the pleasant evening while she wondered what he
would do if she threw something at him and demanded
to be allowed to share his life.

Over supper he told her briefly that he would be away all day and reminded her that they had two dinner parties that week, and their own the following week. 'Mrs Turner is a tower of strength on these occasions,' he told her carelessly. 'I should leave the arrangements to her.'

Something Annis had no intention of doing. With great difficulty she bit back the hasty remark on the tip of her tongue, and nodded meekly. Her, 'Yes, of course, Jake,' was equally meek, so that he looked at her sharply—a look she met with a charming smile.

The week ran its course and she found plenty to do. She didn't know London well. She formed the habit of going out each day on a voyage of discovery, although she didn't bother Jake with these jaunts when he came home in the evenings. Beyond hoping that she had had a good day, he asked very few questions and so she held her tongue and listened carefully to how his own day had gone. She was a good listener and he seemed to enjoy explaining the intricacies of big business to her. Once or twice, at the end of an evening, when he had relaxed, he would ask her if she wasn't bored with her days, and she answered quite simply that she found plenty to keep her occupied, which was true enough. She had explored the parks, walked miles with a guide book in her hand, watched the changing of the guard at Buckingham Palace and stood, along with a great many other people, outside St Margaret's, Westminster, in order to see a society bride emerge after the wedding. She hadn't planned to do it, but she happened to be passing and it seemed too good an opportunity to miss. But all this she kept to herself. Jake wouldn't want to know—indeed, he might laugh at her naïveté.

The dinner parties weren't the frightening affairs she had expected. The first one was given by an older couple with a large family of grown-up and teenage children and they had invited friends of all ages. Dinner was a cheerful noisy affair and Annis, sitting between the two older sons of the family, enjoyed herself hugely. And the second dinner party, although a quite different cup of tea, was just as much fun. The Dawes were young, not long married and extremely sociable as well as very smart. Annis was glad she had worn the black satin dress, for the women guests were all incredibly fashionable. But they were nice to her, too: admiring her dress, envying her hair, wanting to know what she thought of London and being married to Jake. Going home afterwards she discovered that she was no longer nervous about their own dinner party.

That was a roaring success too. She and Mrs Turner had concocted a splendid menu between them and Annis had done some of the cooking; she had arranged the table too—a white damask table-cloth and napkins, the silver polished to an incredible brightness, the very best of the glasses and as a centrepiece, an old-fashioned épergne dripping the flowers she had chosen so carefully from the florists in the next street.

She dressed early in a silvery grey crêpe dress and then donned an apron and went into the kitchen where Mrs Turner was busy at the Aga. Everything was all right, they told each other, smiling like conspirators.

And it was. The chilled watercress soup was delicious, so was the fish; sole grilled simply and served with creamed spinach, and the beef *en croûte* melted in the mouth. Mrs Mottram voiced the opinion that the vegetables tasted as though they had just been picked from the garden, and everyone agreed, and Annis beamed with pleasure like a happy child. And the syllabub to finish this repast and which she had made herself was eaten with such relish that she wished that she had made twice as much of it.

It was when the last guest had gone that Jake, sitting at ease reading the evening paper, observed: 'That was a splendid meal, Annis. Mrs Turner certainly did us proud.'

And when Annis didn't answer he put the paper down and looked enquiringly at her.

She said coldly: 'Don't you credit me with any skills at all? Why should you suppose Mrs Turner did it all?' She gave up being cool and added with a snap: 'I made the soup, and I cooked the vegetables, and I made the syllabub too—and I did the table and baked those little biscuits with the drinks.'

Jake folded his paper and got up. 'My dear girl! I'm sorry if I hurt your feelings—I had no idea that you were so good a housewife. I think you're fantastic.'

She eyed him with mounting rage. 'No, you don't!' she declared in a voice throbbing with temper. 'I can't think why you married me, and I can't think why I married you either!'

She shot off to bed without waiting to hear his answer.

She had it the next morning in an oblique sort of way. Jake had wished her good morning exactly as usual without a word about her show of temper the previous evening and she had done her best to behave just as she always did at breakfast, not saying much, letting him skim through the post, seeing that his coffee cup was replenished. She had been unable to disguise her red-rimmed eyes completely, but she had counted on him not noticing, he so seldom looked at her—really looked. So she was quite taken by surprise when he said, as he gathered up his letters preparatory to going: 'I'll drive you down on Saturday, Annis, I'm sure you'd love a week or two with your family. I'm going to be away a good deal.'

She put down the piece of toast very carefully, just as though it would break otherwise. Her insides had gone very cold. 'Could I not come with you, on some of the trips? I wouldn't get in the way.' She had meant to sound casual, but her voice came out in a gruff mumble.

'Oh, I don't think so. You'll be far happier down at Millbury,' and when she opened her mouth to argue: 'No, Annis, I should like you to go.' He half smiled. 'Remember Tennyson?'

She tried again. 'I'm sorry about last night…' She was breaking the toast into tiny pieces on her plate. 'I didn't mean it.'

Jake ignored that. 'We'll leave directly after breakfast,' he told her blandly. 'Will you telephone your mother and let her know we're coming?'

'Yes.' She tried very hard not to sound eager. 'Will you stay too? Just for the weekend?'

'No—I can't spare the time.'

'Then why did you marry me?' Her voice was a whisper that he didn't hear, because he'd gone.

Then she spent the day packing and making arrangements with Mrs Turner about the running of the flat, and when Jake came home that evening she did her best to behave as though everything was all right between them; not very successfully, but all the same, she tried.

Everyone was home again by the time they reached the Rectory, so that it wasn't noticeable that she and Jake hadn't much to say to each other. They had a leisurely lunch, all talking at once, and after a stroll to visit Nancy and an early tea, Jake declared that he had to go back to London, pleading pressure of work. 'Then you must try to come back next weekend,' declared Mrs Fothergill. 'You work too hard, Jake.' She added: 'And you've been married for such a short time too!'

He had made some laughing reply, said goodbye to everyone and asked Annis to go out to the car with him. Annis strolled down the path with him, conscious that her family were peering from the windows. At the car she asked: 'Will you come next weekend, Jake?'

He gave her a quick mocking look. 'I don't know—perhaps.' He bent and kissed her, his hands on her shoulders. Probably, thought Annis miserably, he knew about the eyes watching too.

'Enjoy yourself, Annis.' He got into the car and drove away with a casual wave as he went. She stood and watched the empty lane, listening to the purr of the engine getting fainter and fainter, so near to tears that instead of going back to the drawing-room she went straight upstairs.

She felt better when she had had a good cry, and when she went downstairs again no one remarked upon her red eyes; it was natural enough for a bride to weep if her husband had to go away, even for a few days.

The week slid away, one placid day succeeding the last. Annis busied herself around the house, although the splendid young woman Jake had found in the village and who came twice a week to do the hard work left her little enough to do. But there was old Mrs Wells to gossip with, Hairy to take for a walk, and little Audrey to amuse when she came out of school, as well as Emma and James home each evening. And when she was at a loose end there was always Nancy to groom and lead into the field at the back of the Rectory now that the weather was warmer.

She had wanted to telephone Jake, write to him, perhaps, but she doubted if he would want it. It was all the more surprising that he should ring her each evening. The calls were brief and totally lacking in any kind of endearment, but they were a comfort to her. The second time he phoned she asked: 'Are you home, Jake?' and was taken aback when he told her carelessly that he was in Copenhagen. And the next evening, he told her without being asked that he was in Oslo. He also told her casually enough, as though it was an afterthought, that he wouldn't be down that weekend.

Saturday and Sunday had never been so long. Annis took Hairy and Audrey for a long walk each day, attended the village whist drive and went to church twice on Sunday, but time dragged. She longed for Monday, so that it would be another week and Jake might come at the weekend.

It was on the Wednesday, when Annis had carried in the lunch and gone to call little Audrey from the garden, that she couldn't find her. Not particularly worried, she went into the fields around and called, then went round the house, but there was no sign of the small girl. So she went once more into the garden, in and out of the barns and sheds and through the wicket gate, then she went indoors, told her mother briefly that she would go down to the village and take a look there. 'Audrey often goes to play with the Banner children, doesn't she? I'll fetch her back—she's gone and forgotten the time.'

But the Banners hadn't seen her, nor had several other children Annis encountered. She was on the point of going back to the Rectory to see if her small sister had turned up when Mrs Thomas, who kept the poky little shop which sold everything from cheap sweets to odds and ends of household requirements, poked her head round her half open door.

'If it's your little Audrey who you're wanting, I seen her not 'alf an hour gone, along with they tinkers.'

'Tinkers? Which way did they go, Mrs Thomas?'

Mrs Thomas was in the mood for a nice chat. 'Nasty thieving folk, and your little Audrey marching along between two of them—ever so friendly like, arm-in-arm they were.'

Annis frowned; somehow it didn't sound much like Audrey, who was on the timid side, especially with strangers. 'Which way did they go?' she asked.

'Up the 'ill to the downs, love. Got an 'orse and cart and a couple of sorry-looking dogs.'

She would have gone on for a good deal longer but Annis, well used to her ways, cut in briskly: 'Thanks very much, Mrs Thomas. I'll pop back home and tell them to keep lunch hot. I'd better go and fetch her.'

Her mother frowned and looked puzzled when she was told. 'But Audrey never goes off on her own—she knows she mustn't…' And her father said thoughtfully

'Tinkers, did you say, my dear? I think perhaps I'd best go after her.'

'I'll go, Father, but will you ring Colonel Avery and make sure she's not there, and if she's not, phone anyone else you can think of who might know where she is—she's only been gone a couple of hours, she can't be far.'

'Probably having a whale of a time and forgotten all about lunch.'

Annis changing into a pair of low heeled shoes as she spoke, said: 'Shan't be long, dears,' and set off through the village, following the road until it turned into a lane and then a rough track winding its way between tall hedges towards the woods at the top.

Annis walked fast. She was a little scared but keeping her head. There was no use in calling Audrey; it was ridiculous to imagine that the tinkers were keeping her small sister against her will, but there was always that remote chance.

She reached the trees at last and took a well-worn track to the left, wide enough to take a cart, which would bring her out eventually on the farther side of the trees and on to the wide sweep of downs beyond. She went slowly now, stopping often to listen. But there was no sound, and no smell of wood smoke. It began to rain and she came out on to the high ground clear of the trees, but there was nothing to be seen on the downs beyond; she turned back, retracing her steps, searching each small path as she came to it, until she was back where the track started. There was a similar track on the other side of the wood and she started off once more, making herself go slowly, stopping to listen again. She was halfway down the track when she heard the faintest of sounds behind her—footsteps, coming steadily nearer, not hurrying. Her heart thumped with fright, but she made herself turn and face the track behind her. There was a sharp bend a few yards from her, half hidden by undergrowth, and whoever it was wasn't making great efforts to keep silent, although there was no unnecessary noise.

She drew a calming breath and let it out, then gasped as Jake came round the bend. He didn't speak until he reached her. 'Your mother told me where she thought you might be—is there any sign of little Audrey?'

He hadn't greeted her, hadn't even said hullo. Annis swallowed her fright and disappointment and found her voice. 'No, none at all. I've been to the farther edge of the wood and there's no sign.' She added: 'It's getting misty.'

'Every minute,' he agreed cheerfully. 'We'd better keep together and be as quiet as we can. If anyone's here they'll give themselves away sooner or later. I asked your mother to give us an hour. Your father's scouring the other side of the village; the Colonel's with him.' He slid past her and took the lead. 'Is there a hollow anywhere here, where a horse and cart could be sheltered?'

Annis thought. 'Yes, there's a hollow between the tracks and there's a way down, but I don't think I remember exactly where it is.'

'Then we'll look.' He sounded patient and calm and not in the least worried. 'Probably they've pulled the undergrowth into a screen as they left the track.'

It took them less than ten minutes to find it, searching to and fro in the undergrowth; quite a well-worn track, still slippery with last autumn's leaves, edging its way between the trees and going steadily downhill. They were nearly at the bottom when Jake stopped and caught Annis's hand. Just ahead of them a horse whinnied.

A moment later, a few cautious steps further, and they were almost in the clearing. The cart was there, so were the horse and dogs, wet and bedraggled, and three people, a woman and two men, were leaning against the cart, and standing in front of them was little Audrey.

Annis had her mouth open ready to call to her when Jake's hand, cool and firm, closed over it.

Audrey's voice was a shrill indignant treble. 'If you don't let me go, and the dogs and the pony, I'll tell my father of you!' She aimed a childish kick at the nearest tinker's leg and caught him off balance, and while he was hopping around on one leg Jake pounced.

'Here, to Annis!' he called to little Audrey, and as she scuttled away, made short work of the two tinkers. He stood over them rubbing his knuckles and bade the woman just stay where she was while the tinkers pulled themselves together.

But they were in no hurry, sitting on the ground, nursing their jaws, and Jake looked over his shoulder at Audrey, standing, in tears now, with Annis's arm round her. 'What happened, love?' he asked gently. The story came out slowly between sniffs and sobs; she'd seen the tinkers going through the village while she was leaning over the Rectory gate, and they had been belabouring the pony and kicking the dogs. She had told the tinkers what she thought of them and then, with rather more imagination than truth, told them that her father was a very important man and would see that they were punished. Not unnaturally this disturbed the tinkers, and since by now she was outside the gate, they had walked her off with them, threatening the number of horrible things they would do to the pony and dogs if she so much as squeaked. Later, they promised her, they would let her father know and he could slip them a couple of hundred pounds and she should go free. So she had gone with them, anxious for the animals and a little worried as to whether her father had so much money. 'And I'm hungry,' she finished tearfully.

Annis mopped the small face and hugged her, and Jake said: 'That's my brave girl! We'll go straight home to lunch this very minute—at least, you and Annis go. I'll catch you up.'

His eyes rested on Annis's white face for a long moment. 'I daresay Nancy would like company, and I'm sure we can find homes for the dogs.' He turned away. 'Run along now.'

He had spoken mildly, but Annis knew better than to argue. She waited just long enough to see him pull the men to their feet and put a hand in his pocket for his wallet. He was going to buy the animals, of course; the tinkers, half dead with fright, would be punished enough; they would have to find another pony, for a start.

They were almost home when Jake caught them up, leading the pony and with the two dogs at his heels. It took some time to explain it all to the Rector and his wife, but they were so relieved to see little Audrey again that they accepted the animals without a murmur. So lunch was postponed for yet another half hour while the three beasts were fed and housed and generally tidied up, and by the time they were seated Mrs Fothergill's steak and kidney pie was barely worth the eating. Not that Annis noticed; if she had been served a slice of cardboard she would have eaten it without being aware of it. Jake had come, that was all that mattered. After lunch she would talk to him, ask if they might start again and get back into their former friendly footing.

Only it wasn't as easy as that. Jake went away to talk to her father the moment they got up from the table and he had said that he was driving back to London that evening. Annis washed up in a hurry, fearful of missing him, only to learn, when she at last escaped from the kitchen, that he had left her father in the study not ten minutes earlier and had gone over to see Matt. She set the tea tray ready and wandered out into the garden; she would catch him as he came back. Only he didn't come. She listened to the church clock chiming four, remembering that he had said that he must leave by five o'clock. There would be no time to talk, and she supposed unhappily that he didn't want to. She turned away from the house and her mother's faintly worried gaze and crossed the yard to Nancy's stall. James had just brought her in for the night and was out in the field again, bringing in the pony. The little donkey lifted a lip for the carrot she always got and stood munching it, while Annis leaned against her woolly side.

'I don't know what to do,' said Annis, and flung an arm round Nancy's neck. 'You see, I can't tell him—at least I do want to, but I'm scared to. He said six months, but it isn't working out, is it? And he bought me all those lovely things. I'll have to tell him some time...'

'But not now, I think.' Jake's voice from the door

behind her made her grab Nancy's neck so tightly that the little donkey tossed her head. 'I was going to suggest that you might like to come back with me, Annis, but I think it might be better if you stayed another week or two.'

Annis's eyes glinted. 'Don't you frighten me like that again!' she warned him, and then, in a quite different voice: 'But I'd like to go back with you, Jake.' She took her arm from Nancy's neck and stood up, facing him. 'Why don't you want me to come? There must be some reason…'

'I think it might be better if we don't see each other for a while.' He looked at her unsmilingly. 'I'm going now, I'll tell your mother that you've decided to stay a little longer.'

Before she had an answer to that, he had gone. Annis very nearly flew after him, but pride forbade that, so she buried her face in Nancy's soft coat and burst into tears instead.

CHAPTER NINE

NOBODY SAID ANYTHING when she went back into the
house. Her father had gone to his study, Emma and
James were already busy with their homework and little Audrey was in the kitchen, brushing the dogs. She
had quite recovered from her adventure with the tinkers, largely because Jake had made light of the whole
episode. When Annis went into the kitchen, Audrey
looked up from her task with the information that Jake
had given her ever such a lot of money so that she could
buy food for the dogs and hay for the pony and have
the vet as well. 'He says Hairy and Sapphro won't mind
having them here a bit, he says animals understand such
things, he says I'm a brave girl, he's going to send me
the biggest box of chocolates he can find!' Little Audrey
paused for breath. 'I like Jake, I wish he didn't always
go away again as soon as he gets here.'

'So do I,' agreed Annis so fervently that her small
sister took a good look at her.

'You've been crying,' she pronounced. 'You never
cry—is it because Jake's gone away?'

Annis bent to stroke one of the dogs; he was elderly
and uncertain of his luck still, but after a few moments
stroking he closed his eyes and grinned as she tickled
his ears. 'Yes,' she said at last, 'I miss him very much,
darling.'

'Well, you've got him for ever, anyway, haven't you?' observed Audrey, 'and you can always go after him— think how nice it would be for him to go home and find you there.'

'Yes, I'd thought of that too, but you see he won't be there—he has to travel quite a bit to other countries.'

'Well, next time he'll have to take you with him. He was super today, wasn't he? I didn't mind a bit once I saw him though, did you? He looked so furious, didn't he?' Audrey sighed happily. 'What an adventure!'

'Yes, love, but I don't think we want another like that—we were all a bit worried about you, you know.'

'Me? I thought it was you—I heard Mummy tell Daddy that she was ever so worried about you…'

'Oh, well, I daresay you didn't hear properly—it was you frightening the lives out of us.' Annis stood up. 'Shall we take Hairy for a walk and leave these two to have a snooze? We'll feed them again when we come in and take them out after tea in the field and let them meet Hairy there, they're more likely to be friends that way.'

The rest of the day seemed endless, and Sunday was even worse, although she filled it from end to end with walking the dogs, going to church, cooking Sunday dinner, grooming Nancy and the dogs, and the pony and helping James with his Maths. And even with all this activity, she didn't sleep a wink, and got up heavy-eyed and utterly miserable.

The moment breakfast had been cleared away she went into the study and picked up the phone. She was past caring what Jake thought. She would have to tell him that she loved him even if it meant never seeing him again, because that was what it would be, she had decided during the long night. He only wanted a pleasant companionship, someone to come home to and entertain his guests. What a fool she had been to have imagined anything else! She dialled the flat and got no reply, but she hadn't really expected it, so she dialled Jake's office. Miss Butt, his personal assistant, answered; an efficient lady, who appeared to work all hours effortlessly and without ever getting in the least bit flustered or untidy. No, she said briskly, Mr Royle was away from the office, she wasn't sure when he would be back, would Mrs Royle like to leave a message in case he phoned in later on?

'No,' said Annis, 'thank you, Miss Butt. Where is my husband?'

'Naples, Mrs Royle.' There was a faint note of surprise in Miss Butt's voice because Annis didn't know that.

Annis didn't hesitate. 'Will you book me on a flight there first thing tomorrow morning, please? I'm driving up today and I'll call in the office and pick up the ticket.'

Miss Butt's efficiency was slightly dented by surprise. 'Mr Royle may have already left…'

'I'll chance that. Will you let me know where he's staying—and thanks.'

She rang off before Miss Butt could spoil her plans with sensible suggestions.

Her mother was surprisingly matter-of-fact about it when Annis went to tell her. 'What a nice idea,' she observed. 'I'm sure Jake will be thrilled to see you.' She didn't seem to notice Annis's silence. 'How will you go, dear?'

'If Father could drive me into Yeovil I'll get the afternoon train, that will give me time to pack a few things and collect my ticket from Jake's office.'

'Yes, dear. Why bother to take everything with you? You can fetch the rest of your things when you come next time—so much easier with the car.'

If there'll be a next time, thought Annis dolefully, and the next moment told herself not to be so faint-hearted.

The flat, thanks to the redoubtable Mrs Turner, looked welcoming, and now that she had added a few bits and pieces around the place, almost like home. She left a note for Mrs Turner who would be back to sleep later, and took a taxi to Jake's office, on the third floor of a palatial building in the City, where she found Miss Butt sitting neatly behind the desk in her office, using a typewriter as though it were a grand piano.

She lifted her hands gracefully as she saw Annis and laid them in her lap, for all the world like a concert pianist, and Annis, a trifle lightheaded by now, suppressed a giggle.

'Good afternoon, Mrs Royle. I have your ticket—your flight is at nine o'clock from Heathrow, you should be in Naples in time for a late lunch. I've also obtained some money, both English and Italian, from the bank—I wasn't sure you would have the time…'

Annis could have hugged her. She had forgotten about money; she had some with her, of course, but possibly not enough. 'Oh, how very thoughtful of you, Miss Butt,' she said thankfully. 'I'd forgotten that.'

Miss Butt gave her a kindly smile and said in a superior voice: 'Mr Royle relies upon me to remember these things, Mrs Royle.'

'Oh, I'm sure he does, he thinks the world of you,' said Annis. She took the ticket and the money and started for the door, accompanied by Miss Butt.

'If I may say so, Mrs Royle, you don't look too well. I hope you won't find the flight too much for you.'

It wasn't the flight Annis was dreading, but what would happen when she got to Naples and Jake discovered that she had followed him. 'I expect I'll be OK.' Even in her own ears her voice sounded very uncertain.

Money did make a difference, thought Annis, sitting in comfort in the plane, watching England grow smaller beneath her. It solved so many small problems—a taxi to the airport, never mind the fare, porters and coffee, an armful of magazines to keep her from thinking too much about meeting Jake—if he was there. That was something she would have to face, but not until it became necessary. She drank the coffee which was offered her and opened one of the magazines, to stare at one page and go on thinking. Her family had been sweet. Her mother had undertaken to let Jake's mother know that they were both abroad. She would let Matt know too—Annis remembered that she had said that she would go over to the Manor that afternoon and go for a walk with him. Little Audrey hadn't said much, only hugged her and begged her to come back soon and bring Jake with her, and she was to be sure and tell him that the pony and the dogs were settling in very nicely and could he help her to think of names for them.

Annis shut the magazine and leaned back and closed her eyes; she hadn't slept much during the night, but now she had, so to speak, reached the point of no return and there was nothing else to do. For no reason at all she remembered what Jake had said: 'Man with the head and woman with the heart...' Perhaps that was where the trouble lay, he cool and detached and deliberate, and she rushing into something just because her heart told her to. He had been so calm, almost casual, when they had found little Audrey, if he had had any feeling for her at all surely he would have acted differently... She drifted off into sleep and didn't wake until the air hostess asked her to fasten her seat-belt.

She reached the hotel soon after two o'clock, paid the taxi driver and went inside. Mr Royle was indeed staying there, the clerk at the desk told her, but was out at the moment. Would madam care to wait?

The clerk looked at her admiringly. She stood, her hair glowing above her pale face and her eyes enormous from too little sleep. A light meal, he suggested or a cool drink and perhaps a tray of tea in half an hour or so? The foyer was very comfortable and madam could rest. And her luggage?

Annis pointed to the Gucci overnight bag which was all she had brought with her. 'If I could just wait here?' She smiled at the clerk, who came round from behind the desk and led her to a cushioned cane chair, put her case down beside her and snapped his fingers at a passing waiter.

The long cool drink revived her and presently she found her way to a palatial powder room, where, surrounded by marble and blue velvet, she re-did her face and her hair. She was very pale, the result of fright at what she was doing, the flight and quite forgetting to have any lunch, otherwise she didn't look too bad. Her knitted cotton three-piece was the height of fashion and suited her, her sandals and handbag were exactly right: she studied herself in the long mirror very carefully, anxious to give a good impression—cool, poised and assured—when Jake saw her.

She went back to her chair and sat down, doing nothing, not noticing the people coming and going all around her, her eyes on the door. And an hour went and another half hour. Not long now, she promised herself, and because she was tired and lightheaded from hunger, closed her eyes.

When she opened them, Jake was sitting in the chair opposite her. She wasn't cool or poised or assured, she looked like a small girl who had been naughty and expected to be punished.

'Hullo,' said Jake gently. 'Shall we have tea? You look as though you could do with it.'

'I didn't mean to go to sleep.' Annis put a hand up to her hair and he said:

'No, leave it, it looks nice.' He beckoned to a hovering waiter and ordered tea, then he sat back in his chair. 'Is there something wrong at home?' he asked, still gently.

Annis shook her head. She was on the verge of tears: everything had gone wrong; what in heaven's name had possessed her to go to sleep, probably she had been snoring too. She pleated the skirt of her dress with hands that shook and didn't look at him. She was still searching desperately for something to say when the tea arrived and Jake poured her a cup and put it into her hands.

'Lunch?' he queried, and held out a plate of tiny sandwiches.

She sipped her tea and found her voice. 'I forgot.' She drew a deep breath. 'Jake, I must talk to you…' She broke off and looked around her. The foyer had filled up with little groups of people, the women very smart, the men prosperous looking. 'Not here,' she added urgently.

He put down his cup and crossed his legs, the picture of a man who was comfortable and didn't want to move. 'I hardly think you would have come all this way for a little teatime chat,' he remarked mildly, 'but do have some more tea—we'll go for a run in the car presently. I'll go and have a shower and be with you in ten minutes or so.'

He picked up his dispatch case and added casually: 'I'm booked on the seven o'clock flight home, by the way.'

Annis gazed up at him in utter panic. Her head was filled with terror strongly mixed with rage, there was only one urgent thought in her mind: to get away fast. While he was having his shower, she'd go…she had no idea, but she'd go.

Jake was watching her telltale face. 'I shouldn't if I were you,' he advised her softly. 'You can't run away for ever, Annis, and it's a long way to have come, just to chicken out at the last moment.'

The rage was uppermost. 'Chicken out? What a simply beastly thing to say, and what do you know about it anyway?' Her pale face was flushed now and her eyes flashed.

'Perhaps more than you think,' he told her, and walked away, not hurrying.

She fumed for thirty seconds or so, aware that he was quite right; of course, it would be silly to go back

tamely without having said what she intended to say
and got it over with. She went back to the blue velvet
and marble and did her face and hair once more, then
went back to sit, very dignified, until Jake reappeared.

He looked pleased with himself, which was annoying. He also looked very tired, which made her loving
heart ache with sympathy, so that she got to her feet
meekly enough and went out to where a Porsche Car-
rera was waiting.

In answer to her enquiring look Jake said: 'Rented—
I have to get around, and it's time-saving.' He opened
the door for her and then went round to the driving
seat, switched on and joined the tangle of traffic going
out of the city.

After a minute or two Annis asked: 'Are we going
to the airport? How will I get back?'

He glanced at his watch. 'There's plenty of time for
that. We're going to Pompeii; it'll be nice and empty of
tourists by now, and you can improve your mind while
you're saying your piece.'

She had always wanted to see Pompeii, but not in
such circumstances. Besides, she had to concentrate
on what she wanted to say, and it would be impossible
there. 'There's no need,' she began. 'Couldn't we just
stop for a few minutes?'

'Impossible, my dear girl. Just look at the traffic—no
one stops. It would be almost impossible to get going
again.' They paused briefly to pay the toll as they joined
the motorway. 'Tell me,' he said blandly, 'what are your
plans?'

Annis hesitated. She really hadn't made any: she
hadn't looked farther than seeing him and talking to

him. 'I haven't any,' she told him baldly. 'At least, I hadn't, but I'll get a room at the hotel if you wouldn't mind taking me back before you drive to the airport.'

'You plan to stay in Naples?' his voice was silky. 'Did you leave your luggage at the airport?'

Her face was very pale again. Her anger had left her; she felt miserable and hopeless and wondered for the hundredth time what had possessed her to embark on such a harebrained scheme. Jake couldn't care less if she loved him; he would be charmingly polite and unfeeling and briskly businesslike. 'Man with the head,' she muttered, not knowing that she had said it out loud, and Jake, who had heard her, didn't choose to say so.

'I haven't any luggage,' she said into the silence between them, 'just my night case.'

And since Jake had nothing to say to this, she looked out of the window at the mountains looming a mile or two away.

'Vesuvius is the one on the right,' said Jake, and she stared at it without speaking. It wasn't a bit as she had imagined it to be, but then neither was Naples—the little bit of it that she had seen. Someone had said: 'See Naples and die.' She felt like that too, but not for the same reasons.

Pompeii was some thirteen miles from Naples and they were there in ten minutes. Jake parked the car under the trees opposite the entrance and they went through the gate where he bought their tickets, and up the sloping path, over the cobbled road and under the low archway into the city. There were few people about, mostly couples and solitary students with guide books, and a happily noisy family with a great many children on their way out. They called out as Jake went past and he answered them with a laugh. He sounded positively happy, thought Annis crossly, and stood obediently while he explained that the stones under their feet were two thousand years old, that the dust between them was volcanic dust, just as old, and did she know that there were some splendid Doric pillars in the Forum?

She wasn't quite sure what a Doric pillar was, and at that moment she really didn't care. She mumbled a reply and tried to recall the words of her carefully rehearsed speech, only to find that she couldn't. There was only one thought in her head; that she loved Jake and never wanted to leave him again, and that it was quite pointless because in a very short time now he would be gone—back to England. Of course she could go with him if she asked, but pride forbade that—besides, by the time she had said her piece, she would be too embarrassed to stay with him. Her mind boggled at the thought of getting herself home. She had been a fool to come in the first place, but now she was here, she'd jolly well do what she had come to do. She would also make it quite clear that Jake didn't have to do anything about it.

They had reached the Forum by now and she stood still again while he pointed out with tiresome exactitude the courthouse, the magnificent arches, the still standing walls of two-thousand-year-old bricks, and when she had turned her head this way and that he had twice twirled her round and pointed ahead of her. 'And that's Vesuvius…' Seen like that, through the ruins, it looked decidedly more menacing and rather grand.

There was no one near them, now was the moment…

but Jake caught her arm and said: 'There's something you have to see, the House of the Vettii—it's a perfect example of a well-to-do merchant's house, and the friezes are wonderful.'

He hurried her along narrow streets lined with the shells of houses and finally into one of them, and just for a brief spell Annis forgot her own worries. It could have been any house, allowed to fall into disrepair. Most of the rooms were without damage, their walls were painted with colours chosen by some housewife all those years ago, there were murals on the dining-room wall, painted by some long-dead artist, an almost perfect frieze in another room, a charming little garden on to which the rooms opened, a miniature centre courtyard. Annis ran a careful finger over the stone carving of a small boy's head. 'Oh, I wish Father could see this,' she said.

'We'll certainly arrange that,' commented Jake. 'Your mother, too.'

And when Annis stared at him, on the point of explaining at last why that wouldn't be possible, he took her arm and led her out of the house back into the sunlit street again.

'That house belongs to the dead,' he said firmly. 'Our problems have nothing to do with them.'

He took her hand and led her back the way they had come, back to the Forum. It was quite empty now, the tourists had long since gone, even the students and the couples had left in search of coffee or drinks in one of the cafés outside the gates. It was now or never. Annis came to a halt by the temple of Jove, staring at the magnificent ruin with unseeing eyes, determined to stay that way and not look at Jake.

'I'll be quick,' she began, 'because it must be almost time for you to go—you have to be there an hour before the plane leaves...' She broke off and started again. 'I expect you think I'm quite mad coming here like this, but you see I didn't know you were here—I mean, I had to ask Miss Butt. I couldn't wait until you came home. Anyway, I wasn't sure if you wanted to see me again...'

'Go on,' prompted Jake in a voice which gave nothing away.

'Jake, it's not going to work, is it? Us being married. You've been so kind and generous and patient, but it's quite hopeless. I'm not—that is, I don't think I'm right for you—you keep sending me home...' She choked on a sob, but she had the bit between her teeth now and wasn't going to give up. 'I said some horrid things to you and I'm sorry; I didn't mean them, you know, but I was frightened. I thought everything would be all right again the other day when little Audrey disappeared, but all you did was tell me to stay at home—and you didn't look a bit upset...'

Jake said very gravely: 'If I'd wasted time being upset, the tinkers would have had the advantage.' He was standing behind her and now he flung a casual arm over her shoulder. 'But go on, Annis.'

'Well, that's all really. There is just one more thing— why I came. I thought I'd better tell you before you... that is, before we saw each other again. You did say, before we married, that perhaps we'd get to like each other, even have an affection...' She was beginning to gabble, anxious to get it over with. 'Well, I've fallen in love with you, Jake, and I can't go on living with you, just pretending to be a good comrade. I've thought about it a lot and I don't think it would work.'

'I'm damned sure it wouldn't work.' Jake swung her round and put the other arm round her too. 'Tell me, who were you talking to in the barn?'

She said stupidly: 'What barn? Oh, the barn at home. I was talking to Nancy, if you must know. I had to tell someone.'

'Then why didn't you tell me?' he asked softly.

'I did try, only you were always going somewhere: I thought you were avoiding me.'

'Well, I was, my darling.' And when she made an indignant effort to get free: 'No, love, stay where you are, that's where you belong—and listen to me. I fell in love with you the moment I set eyes on you, but I didn't know it at once, and you didn't think much of me, did you? I had to play it very cool, and once we were married it seemed logical to give you time to learn to love me too. And once or twice I thought I'd failed.'

He lifted her chin with one hand and she looked up and saw the love in his face. 'Then you don't mind my coming all this way? Just to tell you?'

Jake bent his head and kissed her slowly. 'My dearest darling, it's the most wonderful thing in the world that you came.'

Annis kissed him back; it was very satisfying, to say the least. 'Yes, but you're going back this evening. Can I come with you?'

'No, because we're not going. I phoned from the hotel before we left and cancelled my flight. I phoned Miss Butt too, she can cope for another few days. Our honeymoon is long overdue, my darling, and this is a very good place in which to have one.'

Annis leaned back in his arms to look at him. 'There are several things,' she began, 'to talk about...'

'Not now, dear heart. I can't help thinking that talking for the moment would be a great waste of time.'

He was holding her so tightly that she could hardly breathe, but there was really no need for her to say anything, and in any case, she agreed wholeheartedly.

* * * * *

Enjoy this sneak preview of
THE RETURNING HERO,
the first in Soraya Lane's
THE SOLDIERS' HOMECOMING *duet!*

"LET ME STAY for a few days, let you catch up on some sleep while I'm here."

His voice was lower than usual, an octave deeper. She shook her head. "You don't have to do that. I'll be fine."

She might have been telling him no, but inside she was screaming out for him to stay. Having Brett here would make her feel safe, let her relax and just sleep solidly for a few nights at least, but she didn't expect him to do that.

And her intentions weren't pure, either. Because ever since she'd starting thinking about Brett in a certain way last night, remembering how soft his lips had been, how sensual it had been pressed against his body, she'd thought of nothing other than having him here. Keeping him close. Wondering if something could happen between them, and whether he wanted it as much as she did, even if she did know it was wrong.

"If I'm honest, Brett, having you here for a few days sounds idyllic." She wanted to stay strong, but she also wanted a man in her house again. Wanted the company of someone she could actually talk to, who wasn't afraid of the truth. Of what had happened to her husband. Because she had no one else to talk to, and no one else to turn to. She'd

HREXP0214

lost her dad and then her husband to war, and she was tired of being alone. "But only if you're sure."

She listened to Brett's big intake of breath, watched the way his body stiffened, then softened back to normal again.

"Then I'll stay. As long as you need me here, I'll stay."

She dropped her head to his shoulder. "He would have liked you being here. You know that, right?"

Brett shrugged, but she could tell he was finding this as awkward as she was. "You know, he made me promise to look out for you if anything ever happened to him. I just never figured that we'd actually be in that position."

Jamie smiled. "I'll never forget what you've done for me, Brett."

Brett was her friend. Nothing more. She just had to keep reminding herself of that, because falling in love with her husband's best buddy? Not something that could happen. Not now, not ever.

Brett could have been the man of her dreams—*once.* But now wasn't the time to look back. Now was about the future. The one she had to build without her husband by her side. No matter how much she was thinking about *that* kiss.

Don't miss THE RETURNING HERO by Soraya Lane, available March 2014. And look out for the second in this heartwarming duet, HER SOLDIER PROTECTOR, available April 2014.

HARLEQUIN®

Romance

Road Trip With The Eligible Bachelor
Michelle Douglas

The beginning of a very long journey…together?

Quinn Laverty and her young sons are planning to start a new life on the other side of the country! With her family abandoning her, and her ex choosing wealth and privilege over fatherhood, her boys are all she's got.

But when an airline strike interferes with her plans, Quinn finds herself taking the car and up-and-coming politician (who is seriously gorgeous!) Aidan Fairhall to Sydney. Quinn and Aidan are trapped together on a weeklong road trip and sparks soon fly as they begin the most unexpected journey of their lives….

Available next month from Harlequin Romance, wherever books and ebooks are sold.

HARLEQUIN®

Romance

Safe In The Tycoon's Arms
Jennifer Faye

The man behind the headlines...

When billionaire Lucas Carrington returns
to his neglected New York mansion, he never
expects to find beautiful stranger Kate Whitley.
Invited by his aunt to stay, he discovers she's
a woman in need. She's trying to raise funds
for her sick daughter, so he agrees to let her
stay—temporarily!

Kate may not belong in Lucas's world, but
behind closed doors, she sees there is more to
this tycoon than the headlines realize. Yet with
so much at stake, Kate must decide whether
to trust herself and her heart with New York's
most eligible bachelor!

Available next month from Harlequin Romance,
wherever books and ebooks are sold.

HR74282

HARLEQUIN®

Romance

Rescued by the Millionaire
by Cara Colter

Wanted: A second pair of hands!

Daniel Riverton is handsome, eligible…and a
confirmed bachelor. The only thing he finds more
frightening than commitment? Children!

So when his neighbor Trixie Marsh appeals for
his help with her twin nieces, his instinct is to
steer clear. But there's something about Trixie
that makes her hard to say no to….

Only problem is, the more time Daniel spends
with this little family, the less he likes the idea
of his empty apartment. There is one way to
solve his dilemma…but is he up to
the challenge?

Available February 4, 2014 from
Harlequin Romance wherever
books and ebooks are sold.

www.Harlequin.com

HR74277

Turbot Mogador Glac
Vacherin